Lipstick and Lies

Lipstick and Lies

Margit Liesche

Poisoned Pen Press

First Edition 2007

10 9 8 7 6 5 4 3 2 1

Library of Congress Catalog Card Number: 2006902900

ISBN10: 1-59058-320-5/ISBN 13: 978-1-59058-320-3 Hardcover

Poisoned Pen Press
6962 E. First Ave., Ste. 103
Scottsdale, AZ 85251
www.poisonedpenpress.com
info@poisonedpenpress.com

Printed in the United States of America

For my mother, Natalia,
and her sister, Margit, my heroes...

Acknowledgments

I cannot imagine having written this book without Amy Beauchamp, Claudia Bluhm, Caiti Collins, Mary Cone, and Terri Tate, wonderful writers and friends who read the manuscript in its various lives and provided invaluable feedback and steadfast support.

Many, many thanks to my talented writing buddy, Dan Flora, for enduring the roller coaster ride and for not allowing me to lose my sense of humor.

I am deeply grateful to Judy Greber, brilliant writer and teacher, and generous soul, who saw something worthwhile in my earliest efforts and nodded encouragingly, then continued to believe.

I take pleasure in acknowledging Katherine Forrest for her insightful critiques along the way and Barbara Peters for bringing another new writer along.

I also thank the WWII experts, Betty McIntosh and Peggy Slaymaker, for sharing their personal experiences and historical perspectives, covered more fully in the Afterward. And, for his invaluable assistance in helping me uncover the wonderful historical nuggets at the National Archives, a very special thanks to my now dear friend, senior archivist John Taylor.

My deepest gratitude goes to Peter Lillevand, my rock, and to my family, for their unwavering love and belief in me.

Chapter One

The first rule I broke upon landing at Willow Run in Detroit was forgetting to dab on lipstick.

"We must exit the cockpit looking like a lady," my boss, Jackie Cochran, head of the Women Airforce Service Pilots, always said.

It was 0830, 26 September 1943, and I was co-pilot for Clayton Gumble bringing in a B-24 Liberator, one of our military's least reliable four-engine heavy bombers. The runway where we landed was at one end of the sprawling L-shaped factory. At the other, a pair of water towers probed a pale autumn sky. Judging by what I'd seen from above, the administration building where I was to meet Miss C was adjacent to the towers, nearly a mile away.

On long flights, or in combat, Libs fly with a crew of up to ten. Today's duty, returning a craft to its manufacturer for repairs, required a pilot and co-pilot only. But we'd had a passenger on board as well, Wilbur Twombley. Twombley, a Ford efficiency expert, had been on official business in Newark. In a rush to return to Willow Run, he'd begged a ride. Captain Gumble had seated him in the separate compartment usually reserved for the radioman. But Twombley, a restless chatterbox, had spent the bulk of the trip in the cockpit, consuming much of our two-hour flight dishing up facts and lore about the government-owned Ford-operated Lib manufacturing plant. He was still in the cockpit bending Gumble's ear when I'd made my exit, following shut down. Between his patter and my eagerness to get away, I had neglected my grooming.

At the tarmac's edge, I paused. Twombley had bragged about the interplant transportation system. Directly ahead a main thoroughfare ran along the edge of the airfield. The passenger shelter was vacant and I didn't see any sign of the buses he claimed serviced the artery regularly.

A ground crew clad in dark coveralls sporting the Ford logo approached. I cut the end man from the pack. "Where do I catch the next bus heading for administration?"

The crewman removed his cap. Sparse hair combed in wet strands swept a bumpy scalp. He wiped his brow, checked his wrist. "0830 musta just left. Next one's in twenty-eight minutes." He pointed his cap at the shelter. "You catch it there."

A string of detached buildings stood between the roadway and the plant, partially blocking my view of it. A few factory workers and executives in suits hurried among the structures on foot. "Ahh," I said, spying a power-scooter with a sidecar. It zipped past the windowless brick exteriors and darted into a passageway.

The crewman looked me up and down and grinned. "It's a plant delivery vehicle. You gotta be quick, but you won't have trouble flagging one down. Take the alley where he was heading. It's the messengers' main route."

Just beyond the alleyway entrance, an unoccupied scooter waited near a doorway. Its driver was my obvious bet. I slipped through the unlocked entrance, following a short corridor emptying into a dimly lit cavernous garage. Off to my right a door, marked MEN, closed with a click. I assumed the messenger had ducked inside. I panned the shadowy room and waited.

Company transportation and delivery vehicles in various stages of repair littered one side of the vast section to my left. Perpendicular rows of tall metal shelving crammed with spare parts stretched before me. I ventured a few more feet inside. A string of overhead lights illuminated a small table with a pair of folding chairs in the repair area. One seat had fallen over. On the floor in front of the tipped chair I could make out the raised outline of something. Or was it a *someone*?

I edged closer. A young man about my age lay face-up on the floor. A dark crimson puddle framed his head and shoulders. I forced myself to look at his face. A ceiling lamp accentuated the pasty-blue tinge of his skin. I thought his eyes were open, but couldn't be sure. Mine clamped shut as my stomach lurched, sending my last meal to my throat in a terrible burn. My heart pumped wildly, but I took a deep breath and looked again, this time focusing on the smear of blood along his neck, tracking it to a blood-soaked collar. The shirt was gray, and for the first time I realized the victim was a plant protection officer.

"*Trouble*," warned a voice inside my head. "*Mind your own business. Leave now.*"

An intelligence operative who minds her own business would be a contradiction in terms. I leaned closer, scrutinizing the bloodied area while at the same time mentally scrolling through the textbook "Death By—" illustrations I'd studied at spy school a month earlier. There. A dark spot marked the point of entry just below his ear. Stiletto thrust, I guessed.

The dead guard's uniform cap had landed upside down at the far edge of the puddle of blood. Nearby, an apple, a separated sandwich, and a few cookies spilled away from a tipped-over lunch pail.

The guard wore a Sam Browne belt. My eyes traced the belt's strap across his chest, noting his name tag, *Walter Blount*, before pausing at the .45 stowed in the belt's holster at his hip. I kneeled at his left shoulder. My eyes strayed back across the man's waist. His left hand was bent at an impossible angle. I shifted to see how it had happened. The dead man wore a prosthesis. Its hook jutted out from the cuff of his sleeve.

I started to get up. An envelope peering out from his jacket pocket called me back. If I had excelled in anything at intelligence school it was Flaps and Seals, the art of opening and resealing documents so deftly that no one would ever be the wiser. I plucked the envelope out. A pocket in the lower leg of my flight suit contained a slim leather case of miniature tools. The envelope's exterior was blank. I selected a razor-thin blade and, flipping it over, slid the blade beneath the flap. The seal gave way and I unfolded the paper inside. My neck prickled. It was a technical drawing, stamped TOP SECRET. In the lower margin, someone had printed: "Night Bombing Gyro." My hands trembled but I replaced the drawing and resealed the flap. *Was the dead guard a spy?*

I was inserting my razor through the proper slit in the leather case when the sudden press of a hard cold object at my temple interrupted.

"Freeze," a man's voice said. The word echoed loudly off the concrete surroundings. Someone tripped another bank of lights. "Get up."

"Okay, sure." I blinked, trying to get a fix on who had barked the orders. I saw a tall man wearing a dark suit over a bearish physique. He held his gun straight out in front of him, the barrel trained on my chest. My heart was in my throat, but my gaze met a pair of thick-lashed dark eyes and held.

"Sir…Agent Dante," a man said from somewhere off to my left. "I got your back."

An agent? White shirt, dark suit…*FBI?*

The new voice belonged to a second armed man in a dark suit standing beneath the glow of the newly triggered bank of lights. He was in front of a metal door about twenty feet away. It was how they had entered. Why hadn't I heard them?

Agent Dante wore a felt hat with a pinched crown. He shoved the hat higher up on his forehead and glared. "What's the idea? Who asked you to snoop around?"

"Snoop? But I was just—"

"Just what?" Dante asked between his teeth. "Breaching a crime scene. Tampering with evidence?"

"Well, uh…" I stammered.

Everyone at Willow Run was required to wear a badge at all times. A panoply of color-coded options matched bearer with department. Mine, tagged for administration, had been issued in Newark. Agent Dante assessed the badge, I assessed his face. Dante had a sweet mouth, the kind Michelangelo liked to paint on cherubic angels. Finally, he looked up. He was restraining a smile and something in his expression suggested he recognized me. Impossible, I thought, my nerves unwinding a bit as he lowered his gun.

Two men in plant protection uniforms barreled through the door. One of them raced over. "What's she doing here?" He made a grab for me.

Dante grasped his arm. "Don't bother. Miss Lewis has a meeting to make. How 'bout finding her a ride?"

The G-man *had* recognized me.

"Yeah, sure, you're the boss." The guard ambled toward the hallway. His associate and the dark-suited man I assumed was a plain clothes inspector circled in close.

"How do you know—"

Dante cut in. "Your questions will have to keep, Miss Lewis. We need to get to the bottom of what happened here. Now step back or I'll have to ask you to wait outside with one of these gentlemen."

My chin shot up, but I put it in reverse.

"Poor Walt," the protection man said, looking at the corpse. "Been walkin' on clouds last coupla days. Wife's gonna have a baby." He nodded to a photo I had missed alongside the lunch pail. The image, a woman's face, was crossed with a red tongue of blood.

Dante loosened his tie and unbuttoned the stiff collar of his shirt. "Anyone check his pockets?"

The guard gave a low grunt. "Not hardly. We got our orders. Anything suspicious, we ring up the Bureau, direct."

Dante nodded. "Right. And Headquarters notified me straight away. Lucky break I was on my way here already." He kneeled beside the body. Using a handkerchief, he pulled the envelope out of the dead guard's pocket. He slid the evidence inside a folder handed to him by his associate. "A set of Miss Lewis' prints is included in her OSS, Office of Strategic Services, record. Make a note. Lab needs to compare those with what they find here."

I shifted uncomfortably.

Dante reached into the dead man's pockets. "Keys, some money…"

"Is that something in his fist?" I said.

The plain clothes investigator spoke. "Looks like—" He hesitated.

Dante lifted the man's stiff right arm. "Looks like what?"

"Uhm, well, it's something frilly."

Dante lowered the rigid arm to the ground. "Care to guess?"

The investigator's expression suggested he would, but he declined. "Medical examiner is on his way. We'll know soon enough."

◇◇◇

The protection man had found the scooter's driver. Folded into the sidecar beside him, I wedged my B-4 bag between my feet. I was about to see my boss. Dipping inside, I found my lipstick tube and swiped some on. It was warm for my leather flight helmet but an open car ride might get windy. I tugged it on.

Normally, I ferry super-fast pursuit fighters from my home base in Long Beach to designated points in the east, usually New Jersey, catch a flight back, start the routine over. Last night, I had been passing through the Ready Room in Newark when the call from Miss C came through, turning routine on its head.

"You're needed at Willow Run," she announced. "I've wangled you the co-pilot's seat in a Lib taking off at 0600. Be there."

"Okay, sure. Except, well, what's—"

Miss C wasn't listening. She was muttering something about "those OSS boys playing right into your independent streak." *This* from a pilot who refused to set her sights lower than a man's? A woman who, early in the war, had resolved to prove to U.S. and British officials that women could handle heavy warplanes; and who became, in June 1941, the first woman to ferry a bomber across the Atlantic to embattled Britain? It was on the tip of my tongue to say, "Look who's talking—" but a distinct tension in her voice as she hurriedly completed her instructions had stopped me cold.

Ten hours later I was in the sidecar of a scooter with a surprisingly capable engine. The messenger got every ounce of speed out of it, careening along the interplant passageways, before shrieking to a halt near a sidewalk leading to the administration building's entrance.

A black Ford Deluxe was parked near the curb. I walked wobbly-legged to the passenger door, opened it and peered in. The well-coifed blonde on the driver's side giving me the frosty look was my boss, Jackie Cochran.

I tossed my grip in back, climbed in. "Hi, Miss C. Sorry if I kept you waiting. You won't believe—" I peeled off my helmet.

She laughed. "Good God, Lewis, what's that? Dye and repair job gone haywire?"

A month ago, on the road and bored, I'd decided to jazz up my looks. The purchase of peroxide along with a *Silver Screen* magazine featuring a Hollywood hairdresser to the stars resulted in my new color: pumpkin orange. A self-trim to lop off the fried ends—a cut aimed to resemble Amelia Earhart's—bore a closer likeness to the pelt of Sarah Bernhardt, my orange tabby. In the weeks since, I'd managed to convince myself that the cropped cut suited my face and hectic schedule.

My mind returned to the real crisis, the horror in the garage. "It was eerie, I tell you. First, I couldn't find a ride. Then—" I stopped. Every WASP knew the drill: Miss C liked having the floor first. She zapped me with a piercing gaze, then turned to observe a dark, sturdy-looking man with thick eyebrows, thick lips, and thin brown hair strolling past her side of the car.

The windows were open against an Indian summer heat. The muted step-slide sound of shoe leather scraping rough concrete penetrated the hush of the car's interior. My boss remained absorbed in the man's passing, or maybe in his slight limp, and I watched along with her. He looked hardy enough, but his suit was baggy, its collar gaping at the back of his neck. Something about his cheery expression didn't fit quite right either. He turned and started up the main sidewalk to the entrance.

At last, pulling her gaze from the receding executive, Miss C adjusted the rearview mirror, checked her reflection. She appeared to be sorting through something troubling her. I tapped my nails on the leather arm rest, waiting.

My boss' interest in appearance bordered on the obsessive, her 1938 victory at the prestigious Bendix Race from Los Angeles to Cleveland a classic example. The grueling annual event, open to both male and female pilots, always drew a big crowd. That year, the competition fell on my eighteenth birthday and my dad, feeding my passion for flying, took me there as his gift. The throng on the tarmac was thick but we were near the front, cheering as she landed. Eager to catch my first glimpse of a female ace, I wormed in closer. She did not disappoint. After flying eight hours, ten minutes, and thirty-one seconds under rigorous conditions, she kept us all waiting, including Mr. Bendix, while she touched up her face before exiting the plane to accept her trophy. Gutsy woman, I thought, knowing in that moment that I would one day follow in her slipstream.

Her shoulder dipped and the large rosette diamond at the center of her trademark propeller-shaped pin winked at me from the lapel of her plum-colored suit. The chic getup and glitzy adornment made me think of another runway incident.

Uniforms, like so many other things, were in short supply. Miss C, presented with cast-off WAC suits to outfit her new unit, pronounced them "hideous," and promptly headed off to Bergdorf Goodman's in Manhattan. With her own funds, she authorized the design of a WASP uniform. She'd run the prototype, a Santiago blue suit with a cute beret, by me, but I wasn't enrolled to help sell it. For this, she recruited a Pentagon employee who might otherwise pass for a fashion model, and had someone less alluring don a WAC hand-me-down. The trio marched, Miss C in the lead, directly into General Marshall's office, demanding he choose.

"Well, I like the one you're wearing, Miss Cochran," he said.

"You can't have this one," she replied, explaining the simple but expensive suit had been purchased in Paris before the war.

"The blue one is best," Marshall then admitted. "You'll get your uniforms."

Now, inside the Ford, Miss C jutted out her prominent jaw, examining its reflection in the rearview mirror as if searching for a flaw. "You said you couldn't find a ride when you got here?" she asked archly. "What's that about? Part of a cover you're practicing?"

"*What?*"

"Sure had me buffaloed. Never would have expected someone so dedicated to country and to flying would"—she fluttered a hand—"run off, take an extended break from her duties like that."

I bit my lip. She hadn't yet bothered to explain why I'd been summoned, but surely she had not dragged me here to slap my wrists for the OSS training stint?

Another angle hit me like a severe blow. Was she jealous that I'd been singled out for the specially tailored course? That our government had in mind giving me the occasional home front undercover girl assignment? I looked over at her. All the while I'd been thinking she'd summoned me here to discuss a mission. Was the opposite true? Did she hope to toss a monkey wrench into the government's plans?

"I wasn't away for long," I said, a little too sharply. "It was a condensed course. I was out of action for just three weeks."

With the lift of an eyebrow, she returned to the mirror.

Diplomacy was not my strong suit. I'd learned to live with the effect my directness had on some, but Miss C had never been among those unstrung by it. Not hardly. She respected standing up for your rights and was bothered by women who were "blahs." So what had her so peeved? What was my sin?

Life as a PK, Pastor's Kid, can be tricky. There's a pressure, especially in public, to maintain an image. But I was always more chaff than seed. And trying to be what I wasn't wore on me. In my teens, I started imagining scenarios from my future life as a commercial pilot. We lived in Chilton, a one-horse suburb of Cleveland, and dreaming big in a small town was not that easy. At least until Civilian Pilot Training came to our community college. Eventually I earned my pilot's license, but while I'd always pictured myself one day ferrying passengers to Africa or Alaska, too soon I discovered that, as a woman, my dream to fly professionally was just that: a dream. A degree in journalism was my hole card. With it, I planned to make a living the way other lady pilots did, by writing for magazines about flying.

A position knocking out spec sheets at an aircraft factory followed. I had begun to accept that I would be eternally chained to a desk, when along came the WASP. I owed my luck to Miss C, the program's founder. In hindsight, how could I have been so thick-headed as to miss why she was so upset?

"Miss C," I began softly. "I hope you don't think I applied for intelligence school behind your back. I would never do that. There was an oversight, wasn't there? My orders came through OSS channels, direct. They ought to have come through you. I'm sorry. I should have realized sooner."

Her dark eyes bored into mine. She didn't speak, but I knew I'd hit home.

She smoothed a wave in her perfectly permed hairdo. "Forget it, Lewis. Not your fault. There was no clear line for you to follow. But you're right. I *should* have been involved." She leaned back with a shrug. "Well, boys will be boys. Guess one of them wanted to be sure I remembered it's still the men who run the show."

A company bus pulled up at the sidewalk in front of us. The doors parted and our attention momentarily shifted to watch the passengers, all of them factory workers, spill out. The flow stopped while a small man, around four feet tall, making a slow descent, hopped off the bottom step.

This must be one of the dwarfs Twombley had told us about while describing an early production problem involving the Lib's main wing. The interior space was so cramped, he'd said, that an average-sized person could not get in there to buck the rivets needed to fasten the outer wing to the center section near the end of the assembly process. He had solved the problem by creating a highly specialized team made up of a mix of women and dwarfs, recruited mainly from the entertainment business.

The small man yawned and stretched out his arms before starting down the sidewalk. Fair-skinned, his blond hair trimmed in a bowl cut, he was clad in dungarees and a short-sleeved chambray shirt. He vectored toward a side entrance to the factory and I stared after him, wondering if I might recognize him from a movie.

Two men, one with a pug nose and small protruding ears, the other with prominent nostrils and a scouring-pad mustache, got off the bus last. "Hey, Chaplin, wait for us," one of them called, racing to catch up with the small man.

Miss C had been eyeing the dwarf, too. "Where were we?" she asked, turning to me. "Oh yeah, the cloak-and-dagger stuff. Did you enjoy it, then?"

Did Tuesday follow Monday? Microfilm, invisible ink, ultraviolet light, secret weaponry, disguises, codes—what could be more exciting?

"It was swell," I said delicately. "I liked it fine, thanks."

Modesty had its rewards. "Let's cut to why you're here," she said. "Day before yesterday, I was in Washington planning my trip back to the ranch. Decided to break up the flight, surprise my girls at Romulus Field. Got in yesterday. Had barely touched down when a call came in, asking me to route you here."

"Really? Who called?"

Miss C had raised her voice to counter the noise of an approaching Lib. I was nearly shouting, too, but it was hopeless. We cranked up our windows. The sound was still deafening. While we waited, Miss C began twisting the cord of a two-way radio mounted on the dash between us. The radio's presence startled me. That I hadn't noticed it before seemed to underscore just how on edge I had been since entering the Ford.

A St. Christopher medal and a horseshoe charm hung from a chain looped over the rearview mirror. Odd enough to be meeting in a car in the first place, but *whose* car was it? For sure not Miss Cochran's.

Quiet again, we rolled down our windows. My queries about the caller went ignored. "You won't regret not going overseas with the others?" she asked.

OSS was responsible for intelligence work behind enemy lines. It was why candidates accepted into the program had to meet a foreign language requirement. It was also why I had been surprised when OSS approached me. I'd never mastered a second language.

"Who wouldn't want to go to the front?" I replied honestly. "But going in, I knew it wasn't an option."

My walk on the shadow side had opened up an entirely new approach to life in which suddenly everything that had once been forbidden now became a way of thinking in wartime. Heady preparation, but I had never been tested under fire. For that, I needed an assignment. A *home front* assignment. The dead spy with a knife wound in his neck lying on the floor of the garage at the opposite end of the factory was a ready-made prospect. "Miss C," I blurted, exasperated. "I'm happy staying stateside. I feel lucky and proud to be a WASP, *but—*"

Miss C appeared to reach some kind of resolution. "Good. You're an excellent pilot. I need you. But for the moment, the FBI needs you more."

My heart pounded. "Oh?"

"They handle domestic intelligence."

I knew that.

"They've got trouble here. Something to do with German spies operating from inside this plant." A movement outside the car drew her attention. "Ahh, here's Agent Dante. We drove over together. He'll do the explaining."

Chapter Two

The Ford Deluxe was Agent Dante's, courtesy of the FBI. Miss C had ignored my attempt to tell her about the body in the alleyway. We stepped out to greet the G-man and I was about to disclose that the agent and I had already met when a second car pulled up. It was Miss C's ride back to Romulus. The driver and Miss C shoved off, and I waited on the sidewalk while Dante, begging privacy, contacted his office using the car radio. Finished, he explained that he had expected to take me back to headquarters for my briefing. But now as things had become complicated by "an unexpected turn of events," before he could divulge certain aspects of my assignment, additional clearances were required. He'd made a hurry-up request and it was churning its way through channels.

"No sense driving into town until we have the go-ahead. How about we sit over there, get acquainted, maybe cover some basics?" He gestured to a bench under a pair of shady maples, standing watch like Queen's guards, beside the administration building's front staircase. "It'll be cooler than waiting in the car."

My curiosity over why the FBI had singled me out was piqued so high I would have sat just about anywhere. "Great."

The bench was positioned far enough from the building so that passersby, funneling in and out of the entrance, would not be able to hear our conversation. Dried leaves and bark scraps littered the bench. Dante brushed them off. Removing his suit coat, he flung it in the air, gracefully lowering it over the slats.

"Madame?" he said, inviting me to sit.

General Marshall had promised, but our official WASP suits had not yet been delivered. In the meantime, we wore the men's Army uniforms, choosing between olive drab and officer's pinks. This trip, I'd worn the pinks, actually a light khaki, a regrettable choice for the neutral-colored fabric picked up dirt like a vacuum cleaner. I looked down. Rorschach-patterned black marks, collected in the Lib, stained my pant legs.

"Thanks, but no need. And why wrinkle it?" I lifted the jacket, the weight of the badge in its breast pocket a sobering reminder that the man I was about to "get acquainted with" was FBI.

Dante had been turning up a sleeve of his once-crisp white shirt. He paused, mid-roll. "Suit yourself." His voice strained with what sounded like phony approval. "It's how you like doing things anyway, isn't it?"

I smiled. "Yes, I like doing things my way, Agent Dante. But these days I'm part of a unit serving the Army Air Forces. It's not about what I want, it's about what our government wants from me."

Dante seemed to ponder that. Then he smiled. "Name's not actually Agent Dante. It's Dante Cavaradossi." My jaw dropped. He laughed. It was a good laugh. From the soul. "Cavaradossi is too long," he added, "and too hard to pronounce. People never seem to get it right. So Dante is easier."

Elocution had nothing to do with why my mouth was flapped open. It was kismet. In my favorite opera, *Tosca*, the heroine bargains with the villainous Scarpia trying to convince him to spare the life of her artist-lover, Mario *Cavaradossi*.

I drew a wobbly breath. "Great. Then Agent Dante it is."

"Just call me Dante, why don't you."

He dug into his jacket pocket. A crumpled pack of Lucky Strikes emerged. He offered me one. I refused, then watched him press one of the smokes to his lips, letting it dangle as he patted pockets in search of a light. He flipped the cover of a matchbook and froze. My mind ricocheted back to enemy agents and the purpose of our meeting. Had someone left a secret message there? Leaning back, I strained to see.

The cover shut with a snap. "Shame on me. I quit two weeks ago." He wedged the smoke behind his ear but kept the matchbook in his hands, twisting it with his fingers. "Pu-ucci," he said, drawing out the syllables as if relishing the sound. "Where'd you get a name like that?"

He had read the FBI dossier. Surely it contained my full name, even the history behind my nickname, Pucci. I stifled a sigh. The only names we ought to be discussing were those of the spies skulking around the factory. Why were we lingering on me?

The "why" did not matter. He wanted to hear me tell it. I began by explaining that my uncle, Chauncy "Chance" Lewis, was a globetrotter and curio shop owner. His store in Chilton, Trinkets and Treasures, was chock-full of exotic items he'd collected on his adventures. I was a born listener, Uncle Chance was a natural storyteller, and the treasures in his shop were tickets to countless tales. One day, a *Tosca* poster taped to the front window stopped me in my tracks. A striking woman, draped in an elegant evening gown, was bent over a male corpse, also in formal wear, lying in a pool of blood. A knife protruded from the dead man's chest and candles circled his head. The candles' flickering flames highlighted the eerie calm in the woman's expression as she placed a crucifix over the man's heart. I was only ten at the time and was smitten by the high drama, glamour, and mystery of the scene. All the more mysterious because of the boldface foreign words printed along the poster's lower border.

My uncle was inside the shop. I dragged him outdoors. "Ahh, my latest. A Puccini direct from Venice. Performance at *La Fenice*. Magnificent opera house!" He clapped his hands and beamed. *"Bene."* I couldn't seem to peel my gaze from the poster. He noticed. He spoke in a grating whisper. "The dead man is Scarpia, the opera's villain. He deceived Tosca so she killed him." I continued to stare, the image etching into my brain what a woman with her back to the wall was capable of. *Could I kill someone under certain circumstances?* I imagined I could, and felt both empowered and ashamed at the thought.

Later, Uncle Chance recounted the entire storyline of the opera and the hook set. I wanted to know about the dramas underscoring *all* of Puccini's operas.

"But it will take weeks," he protested, struggling to contain his delight.

At some point in the process he began calling me his "little Miss Puccini." Later we agreed Pucci was better. Pucci Lewis.

"And no more Ruth Esther," Dante said, smiling.

As always, at hearing my real name I cringed. "Right."

Dante's gaze had drifted to my saddle shoes. Something about the way he was staring made me wonder if he knew they had once belonged to Amelia Earhart. Uncle Chance had come across the shoes at a charity auction, later giving them to me as a present. Was that tippy-top secret in my FBI dossier? Did they know about Miss C's obsession with them as well?

Antsy, I crossed one ankle over the other. Blood rushed to my cheeks. My ankle holster. I'd left it on. Inside was a non-regulation double action derringer. Quickly, I recrossed my feet.

Dante had removed the cigarette he'd tucked behind his ear and was rolling it between his thumb and fingers, studying it. "OSS issue?" He didn't bother looking up.

"No, gift from my grandmother." His eyebrows lifted inquiringly. "WASP graduation," I said crisply.

Whenever I'm assigned a plane with specialized equipment, radar, for example, a .45 is issued, along with my orders. But a .45 is heavy, cumbersome, and difficult to store in a P38's tight quarters. So I'd developed the habit of carrying Gran's derringer on my flights. Compact, lightweight, stowed at my ankle, it was handy for any emergency. Normally, though, I would have removed the holster, squirreling it away inside my B-4 bag before exiting my plane. This morning, my mind awhirl over Miss C's summons, I'd forgotten.

Dante chortled. "When I first heard about you, I thought you might be too skittish for our job. Now I'm sold. You can hold your own." His acceptance of me was evidently deep enough to warrant a security briefing.

"We began monitoring espionage suspects long before Pearl Harbor, even while the majority sentiment was to keep out," he said, "the task evolving, step by step with the inevitable—that we'd join the war."

Investigations were at an average of forty cases a year in '37, he told me, but leaped to over 250 in '38 when discreet checks on subversive groups, like fascists and communists, were sanctioned. The burgeoning workload resulted in a shoring up of the Bureau's staff. In '39, there were roughly 800 Special Agents on the government's payroll. Last year, in 1942, nearly 5,000 agents had been assigned to over 200,000 national security matters.

I whistled softly. "A lot of manpower."

"Necessary if we expect our home front to remain safe. We've also beefed up our record-keeping. Besides maintaining a Watch List of naturalized citizens from Axis countries, we've begun keeping files on all die-hard anti-Americans, monitoring those likely to be dangerous in time of war."

"Likely to be dangerous?"

"Those with family remaining in the old country, people who might have mixed loyalties, anyone affiliated with known fascist organizations or clubs."

"Ahh." I knew that without the appropriate approvals, Dante was weighing what he could and couldn't tell me, but I was doing some juggling of my own. What about an individual's right to privacy? The principle was part of the bedrock of our nation's foundation. Or was it okay, in wartime, to simply dismantle such civil liberties, toss them out the window temporarily? But then who decided where and when to draw the line? The FBI?

Provocative issues. But this was not the time—or the person—to try to engage in a debate. "Organized fascist groups are openly meeting, here, on U.S. soil? That surprises me."

Dante had left his hat inside the car. Without it, his hair was an unruly mop. He raked the thick mass with his fingers. "What do you know about the German-American Bund?"

"Nothing much." The name was familiar. I couldn't recall any particulars.

"It's a club for German immigrants. Detroit had a very active chapter."

He went on to explain that, pre-war, there were Bund chapters all across the country. The clubs had come under the FBI's scrutiny after it was learned that the organization was being run from Berlin. "Our field office hit pay dirt when a membership roster fell into the hands of one of our agents. A real eye-popper. Member names had been divided into four groups: Youth, Storm Troopers, Women's Auxiliary, League of Businessmen. Later, evidence of secret paramilitary training sessions, including drill and rifle practice, surfaced from another source."

"Past tense, right? These Bunds don't exist today."

Dante gave a thin-lipped smile. "Our discussions with the Pastorius boys alerted us to several underground factions."

"Operation Pastorius—" I whispered.

About a year ago, eight German saboteurs had been put ashore by U-boats off the Atlantic coast. Armed with an elaborate plan to cripple America's industrial might, the agents also toted a stockpile of high explosives and thousands of dollars in cash. In a break for us, two of them decided to betray the mission, code-named Operation Pastorius, and the entire team was captured within days of its arrival. A speedy trial before a military commission followed. The turncoat-duo drew life plus thirty years; the remaining six were executed.

"One of the Pastorius agents had a handkerchief with the name and address of Mama Leonhardt on it, written in invisible ink."

I was lost again. "Mama Leonhardt?"

"A German alien, part of the band of spies we rounded up a month ago. Press dubbed this one the Motor City Spy Ring. Heard of it?"

"You bet."

A month ago, FBI agents had charged eight Detroiters with conspiring to sell U.S. war secrets to Germany. In addition to two German aliens and five naturalized citizens, a prominent American-born Detroit gynecologist, Dr. Fred W. Thomas, was arrested. The treasonous act made the headlines in papers everywhere. Much as it had bothered me to learn that an American was part of the ring, I was equally astonished at discovering that four women, including a countess, had been incarcerated.

I remembered the juicy disclosures about the Countess, the gang's leader, disparagingly referred to as the Motor City Mata Hari.

Fresh out of Ast X, Berlin's Harvard of spy schools, the Countess had arrived in the States with Detroit and its burgeoning defense plants her target. Her plans unraveled when a letter to her from Berlin, containing a secret ink message, was discovered by Allied censors. Confronted by the FBI, she'd agreed to act as their counteragent, assisting them in weeding out Nazi spies.

"I read an article about it a few weeks ago. Wasn't the woman who ran the ring a countess?"

Dante sneered. "It's *Miss* Grace Buchanan-Dineen. The bogus title was part of the allure meant to distract her victims from her real goal—organizing other sympathizers and learning about our war production by cozying up to industrialist socialites."

"And Buchanan-Dineen—" my heart raced, just saying the spy's name—"is she the focus of my assignment?"

Something over my shoulder had diverted Dante's attention. I turned and saw the dark, sturdy-looking man with the thick lips and thin brown hair who'd captivated Miss C when I'd been with her in the Ford. Had Dante deliberately positioned us so that he might covertly observe the man's exit? He was descending the staircase. *Who was he?* Miss C had spoken in the plural when she'd said German spies were operating out of this plant. Was he, like Blount, a secret agent?

The man followed the main sidewalk, cutting left at the end of the path and passing the Ford without so much as a glance. I turned back. Dante's mouth formed a grim line. "Who was that?" I whispered. "Someone involved in your—*our*—case?"

A few beats passed. A barely perceptible nod followed.

He glanced at his wrist. "Let's go."

I waited on the sidewalk while Dante used the radio. I heard raspy static, then the faint sounds of a garbled voice on the other end of the mike. His broad back and shoulders shielded me from what was being said.

I paced the sidewalk, mulling over the situation ahead. The Countess, a trained spy, would be wily and cagey while I, a secret service novice, would be trying to trip her up. My stride quickened. And what about the factory spy? An enemy operative buried inside a government-owned plant would have nerves of steel. How would I deal with him? And the dead guard...Was his killer on the lam nearby?

My arms pumped with my pace, the beads dangling from the bangle I wore hidden beneath my sleeve fluttering. Miss C insisted we play up our femininity with makeup, but Army Air Forces regs had put the kibosh on adorning ourselves with jewelry. This bracelet, though, had special meaning, for it belonged to Liberty Leach, my roommate at intelligence school. On my last day of training, saying our goodbyes, we vowed to meet again soon. To seal the deal, I'd traded my Confirmation cross for the expandable silver bangle, a keepsake from Liberty's days in China. She'd explained that over there mothers slipped them on their children's ankles, letting the beads' musical tones inform them of their offspring's whereabouts. Wouldn't Liberty love to know where her bracelet was now?

"Finished," Dante called from the car.

I swiped damp palms on my pants legs and pinched the bangle for luck.

We followed a winding interior byway to the main gate, pausing long enough for the guard to check us off his register. Dante eased into the flow of traffic on Michigan Avenue, the main road from Ypsilanti to Detroit. A neatly folded *Detroit Free Press* rested on the seat between us. He patted it.

"Here, check the front page. Story's a few days old, but the background will help."

I plucked the paper from the seat. It had been weeks since I'd read about the case. Two of the four men accused had already pled guilty, but six others, including the Countess, had not yet entered pleas. It was expected they would be arraigned on an espionage conspiracy charge sometime in the following week. Meanwhile, the entire group was being held in county jail under the jurisdiction of the FBI.

Countess Buchanan-Dineen's picture, a glamour shot, appeared to have been lifted directly from the Society Page. She looked into the camera, smiling brightly, her chin resting on the heel of her palm, a cigarette clasped loosely between fingers loaded down with rings. An upswept hairdo and more posh jewelry, dangling at her neck and earlobes, completed the oh-so-sophisticated look. The stylized photo contrasted sharply with the others, mostly grim head shots, in the composite. It seemed especially odd alongside the photo of Mama Leonhardt's husband, Carl Leonhardt, staring fiercely into the camera, the sleeve of his Nazi uniform ringed with a swastika-emblazoned armband.

I returned the paper to the seat. "You've got a lot riding on this one. First case under the new Espionage Act, right?" The landmark statute had been cited in the article. "Two have pled guilty. Think the rest will follow suit?"

"That's our hope. And we need bullet-proof convictions. It's been a long ordeal, nearly two years. Guilty pleas would save the government additional expense. Arraignment's in a few days. We'll know more then."

"Two years?"

Dante shifted his weight, pulled a handkerchief from his pocket and blotted his forehead, damp from the heat. "Hoover's adamant we build a solid case prior to arrest."

I nodded. Before the war, the FBI had engaged in guerrilla warfare against underworld gangsters, the unsavory tactics earning the agency a reputation for being overzealous and unsophisticated in its information-gathering techniques. Now the Bureau's mission had shifted to domestic intelligence and Hoover had changed the FBI's approach. Brute force and psychological intimidation were out; legal investigative methods and by-the-book conduct were in.

Dante stuffed the handkerchief back in his pocket. "An informant came forward after we arrested Buchanan-Dineen and her gang. Identified a sleeper spy we missed."

"Who?" I felt an icy chill. "The corpse in the garage, Walter Blount?"

Dante lifted an eyebrow. "Guess again."

Didn't have to. I'd already uncovered the technical drawing in Blount's pocket. Why would a guard have something like that on him unless he was a spy? Still, it was Dante's game. I rolled again. "The man with the limp back at the factory?"

"Bingo. Name's Otto Renner."

Renner started as a draftsman at Consolidated Aircraft, the original manufacturer of the Lib. By the time Willow Run got underway he'd been in the field long enough to be considered an industry expert. Constructing a Lib involved more than the application of high-volume production principles, and the Ford team began drafting a pool of professionals from Consolidated, Renner among them. His current position, Supervisor of Tool Design, gave him access to top-secret blueprints. The FBI's source claimed he took them home at night, copied them onto tracing paper, then returned them the next day. He'd been engaged in the subterfuge for several months.

I stared, stunned. "But security is airtight these days. To get plans out of the factory, he'd have to bypass Plant protection. How?" I thought of Walter Blount. One way would be if you were quick with a knife.

Dante offered more alternatives. "Trusting colleagues. Greedy guards. Payoffs..."

Was he aware that Blount had been carrying a Top Secret document? Asking would mean admitting that I'd pried open the envelope. Why advertise? If he didn't already know about the drawing, he would soon enough. Besides, at the moment, Renner was up to bat.

"B-but still," I protested. "You don't just march out of a war plant with secret drawings. There are lots of checkpoints, lots of inspectors..."

"Renner has a bum leg. Wears a brace. This part is working theory only, but we suspect he rolls up the drawings and carries them out wrapped around his leg under the brace. Or maybe inside the lining of his suit." Dante rubbed a hand over his suddenly weary expression. "The inventory of what Renner's taken out shows nothing critical yet. He's under surveillance."

"Why not arrest him?"

"Blount's testimony was key. Without it, to make a conviction stick, we'll need to catch Renner with the goods. We want the big boys, besides."

"Blount? The dead guard? He was your stoolie?"

"Uh-huh. And early on, Renner's accomplice."

I shook my head. "So what happened? Renner realized Blount was squealing on him? Killed him?"

"We've had a tail on Renner, remember? He was home with his wife. He couldn't know Blount tipped us off, either. It's been so hush-hush we've let only one senior Ford executive in on the operation."

"But his associate's been murdered. Won't he get nervous, try to bolt?"

Dante felt for the cigarette behind his ear, but he had already returned it to its pack. His hand drifted to the pocket containing the smokes and rested there. "We're going to lay low, wait him out, long as possible. Plant Security will handle the initial soft inquiry. They know to steer clear of his department as long as possible, but they can't stay away forever. Once the heat moves in, sure, he may try to skip. Won't get anywhere though. We'll nab him."

I posed the big question. "And my role in all this?"

"We need someone to befriend the Countess, find out if she's been holding out about Renner or any additional spies who might be helping him. We'd especially like leads to Renner's handler."

I was excited, but I was also puzzled. "But she's your agent. Why not just ask her yourself?"

"Buchanan-Dineen *was* our agent."

He went on, disclosing that after the FBI had turned the Countess they wired her apartment and tailed her everywhere.

Numerous trysts had been recorded, including her meetings with Dr. Thomas, the U.S.-born gynecologist. Thomas had purportedly furnished her with reports on manufacturing facilities as well as provided the hard-to-get chemicals needed for secret ink. Renner, however, had not been seen with her. Nor was he listed in the book of contacts they'd confiscated from the Countess.

"But you've got her in custody. Why not just ask what she knows about Renner direct?"

"We're in…Well, let's just say, we're in a delicate position. At the arraignment, if Thomas pleads not guilty, there'll be a trial. We'll need her as a witness. Our key witness. So we've been doing all we can to keep her happy." Dante ran a finger under his collar, loosening it. "Trouble is she's slightly annoyed with us at the moment."

"Annoyed?"

"She didn't expect to be serving time."

"Why? Was she promised a deal?"

"In her dreams."

Surprised by Dante's biting tone, I glanced over. But we had reached the Federal Building. A broad marble staircase climbing to an expansive columned portico defined its entrance. Dante slowed and turned into a driveway. The Ford's nose dipped as it dove into an underground garage.

At a small guard house, a security man examined his credentials then released a metal arm. We traversed the gaping concrete space beyond, the Ford's tires squealing with each new turn. At a fleet of identical vehicles, occupying a series of numbered slots, we parked.

"Where were we?" Dante asked, looking over at me.

I recapped. "Otto Renner, who works at Willow Run, also steals bomber designs and plans for the Nazis. Walter Blount, a Plant protection man and Renner's helpmate, was the corpse in the factory repair garage. You don't know who killed Blount or who's running Renner, but you suspect the spy-turned-counter-spy, Countess Grace Buchanan-Dineen, has insider knowledge. If she has re-crossed the line and is, in fact, a triple agent, you want me to somehow get her to disclose whatever she might be holding back."

Dante smiled. "Bravo, Lewis. We've arranged for you to meet her, later today."

I smiled back. "A jail visit? Sure. What's my disguise? Social worker? Parole officer?"

"We need you inside."

"An inmate?"

"Don't worry. We'll be close by."

I swallowed. "Ahh…and where exactly will I be doing time?"

"The Hole." He pulled the key from the ignition and glanced at me. "Oh, sorry. Wayne County Jail. Women's Unit."

If the reference to a women's unit was supposed to make me feel better, it didn't. "Now?"

"Soon as we nail down your cover."

Chapter Three

My eyes flew open as I tried to piece together where I was.

It was the morning after a long, restless night and I was lying on a bunk in a cell of the Women's Division of the Wayne County Jail on Clinton Street between St. Antoine and Beaubien in downtown Detroit. Last evening, following my briefing, Special Agent Dante delivered me to the jail's property clerk, who had traded my street clothes for a dark blue jumpsuit. A stocky matron was summoned and I was escorted to a cell, cheek to jowl with the accused spy's.

The cells were part of a cellblock located in a remote wing of the sixth floor. The Countess had been isolated as part of a plan to protect her from her former sister agents. She had spent five months with the German loyalists, getting to know them and pumping them for information before switching sides. Now, instead of keeping house in the cozy bungalows where they had once conspired with her, the ex-cohorts were housed in the not-so-cozy confines of a separate cellblock at the opposite end of our wing. Stripped of their freedom and dignity, they pined for revenge.

Segregating the Countess might keep her safe from physical harm, but it could not protect her from verbal abuse. Last night, following lock-down, I'd been initiated into the means the ex-ring members had discovered for delivering their taunts.

First, there had been the ratcheting clamor of cell doors rolling then clanging shut in unison, a sound I shall never forget. A sort of shell-shocked silence followed, then lights-out. Later, under the cloak of night, when few matrons stood guard and inmates' voices could not be singled out, the hushed sound of men cooing and calling from their cells below began filtering up through the inch-wide ventilation space between the cell floors and the back wall. From our floor above the men's, the women, in turn, taunted and teased. The off-color repartee, hesitant at first, soon grew heated and coarse. Barren cement-block walls and concrete floors served as the ideal conductor, enhancing the pitch and volume. My skin crawled as I recalled the bombardment of ugly jabs meant for the Countess contributed by her sister spies. "Snitch," "skunk," "rat," were among the milder terms. A few guttural German expressions, none sounding too nice, made it into the mix as well.

In the darkest hours of the night, as the bursts of laughter became frenetic and the cries of desperation and anger turned haunting, my nerves had grown so frayed that I bolted upright in bed. Eventually I had settled into a semi-seated position, remaining that way until the first light of dawn, when the lights had been thrown on.

I was rearranging myself, trying to get comfortable, maybe catch another wink or two of sleep, when a matron barked, "Up and at 'em," and someone tripped the doors.

I shot from my bunk.

The County Jail did a brisk business. Ordinarily, the four cells comprising our cellblock would have contained two prisoners each. Security for the FBI's star witness meant that only two hand-picked inmates had been assigned to her section. I scurried into line-up. This was my first encounter with the women. I noted that one of the Countess' cellmates was mulatto, the other was Caucasian.

A barrel-chested guard doled out dishcloth-sized towels, ordering us to disrobe, while a second matron stood eagle-eyed slightly apart from our pitiful formation. "All right, listen up," the puffed-chested guard bellowed. "I'm gonna escort you, one by one, to the open stall at the end of the cellblock for a shower. Who's gonna be first?"

The Countess volunteered. She marched past; shoving reserve aside, I gaped.

A German agent, I had thought, would appear hardened, imposing, and intimidating. Yet her bird-like frame, carrying probably less than a hundred pounds, looked as though it would collapse under the weight. And her shoulders, well, they drooped pathetically, as though the weight of where she was and what she had done were more than she could bear.

We each had private cells. We made our beds, scrubbed our floors and toilets. At a signal from the matron, we lined up to turn in our cleaning gear.

"I am harboring a book beneath my jail costume," my mark said, falling in behind me. "Would you, perhaps, care to borrow it during our break?"

Jail costume? Talking in line was a punishable offense; a belly laugh surely would have been worse. I swallowed and turned slightly. "Of course," I whispered out of the corner of my mouth. "How kind of you to offer. Thank you."

I might be a fledgling operative, but I was not so naïve as to believe she was being kind simply to be kind. Dante had warned me. I was the new kid on the block, and she would want to test me. The offer of the book, I suspected, was step one.

The matron collected the scrub tools from the inmate in front of me. She dropped them into a receptacle. The tools hit home with a crash and I moved with the distraction. My hands slipped behind me and the Countess pressed a thin leather-bound volume into my waiting grip. The cover held her body heat. I slid the slim book through a gap in the front of my jumpsuit. Her warmth transferred to my skin, giving me goose bumps.

"It's my bible," she said softly.

Inwardly I groaned. The thought of reading religious materials—in jail or otherwise—repulsed me, for I had spent my youth treading in a sea of them.

Back in my cell, I discovered she had not been speaking literally. The "bible," actually a self-improvement guide, was titled *Personality Unlimited.* Leafing through the contents, I found chapter headings such as *Make-up, Dress, Manners, and Character Improvement*. Below, paragraphs of fine print covered the proper use of lotions, potions, necklines, hemlines, "may I's," "shall we's," and even "how to tell white lies." I shook my head. Even with nothing else to read, the book held about as much appeal to me as pickled pigs' feet.

"*Never say whoa in the mud.*" Now there was a tip I could relate to. My Uncle Chance said it all the time. And of course he was right. Surely I could learn something about my quarry from studying her guide. I flipped to the chapter on make-up and began reading about skin care, my eyelids growing heavier and heavier.

◇◇◇

The muffled sounds of two women engaged in conversation next door nudged me from my nap. After first checking to be sure the giant cockroach I'd glimpsed earlier hadn't returned, I arranged my pillow against the wall, leaned against it, and tuned in to the exchange.

"If I may be permitted to say once more, it is not your derriere, Bill-lay, that you must emphasize."

"Say again?" The puzzled, sassy voice was that of Billie Workaday, one of the spy's two select cellmates. Dante had said that Billie operated under an alias inspired by the Queen of the Blues, having decided that in reinventing herself she could also change her destiny. I could relate. For I had taken a name prompted in part by someone famous, too.

"You have more to offer," the Countess continued, "than your Rubenesque—how shall I say—uh, posterior."

"Countess, honey, no need to be uppity here. If you're talkin' about my tub'a lard ass just say so. In real English, *please*, so's I can understand, okay?"

Zeroing in on what the Countess had to say had been easy work so far. Canadian by birth, she spoke with a broad "A" accent impossible to confuse with the others. I smiled as several seconds of silence passed. The effusive Countess, fluent in

French, German, Hungarian, and who knew how many other languages, appeared to be having a devil of a time finding the plain English demanded by Billie.

"All of us possess at least one outstanding characteristic," she said, at last. "The idea is to drah-matize that one gift, and the others will take care of themselves."

Billie sounded lost. "Un-huh…"

"Yes? Do you mean, *yes?*"

Billie released an audible sigh.

The Countess and Billie made an interesting pair: a prostitute and whiz on the ins and outs of life behind bars contrasted with a woman born into privilege and convent-school educated in France who considered herself an intellectual and a gifted orator. So much so that she had arrived in Detroit posing as a professional lecturer. At ease with position and wealth, she directed her first assault on the city's social set. Easy prey for her arsenal of fine clothing, jewelry, and charm, awed by her knowledge of European centers and culture, the ranks parted. Hostesses vied for her presence; society pages blazed with all the news about her every movement.

At the same time the Countess was busy conquering the social front, she also began appearing before women's groups. The Birmingham League of Catholic Women, the Colony Club, and the Charm School at the YWCA were some of the organizations she dazzled. Initial presentations covered the life of women in war-torn Europe and the use of ersatz products. Her reputation grew and she began giving chatty talks on foreign affairs. "The Oppression of War," "Into the Light of Freedom," and, prophetically, "I Saw the Nazis in Central Europe," were a few of the titles Dante had mentioned. When she expanded her programs into advising the city's smart-set on how to increase their personal allure, almost overnight she became known as Detroit's most popular "charm consultant."

This ability to mix it up with the elite, get them to let down their guard, was part of a bigger scheme for collecting confidential personnel and production information for Hitler. Luckily, before she could exploit her strategically developed contacts, the FBI had interceded. She went from enlightening nabobs to bestowing tutorials on sister inmates.

Billie spoke again. This time her voice, still earthy, had airs. "That is *co*-rrect, ma'am. It is 'yes' that I mean. But distinguish myself? What for?"

The former consultant cleared her throat. "You have many competitors in your, uhm, chosen profession, correct?"

"Un-huh, I mean, *yes*. At times the streets, especially the stop-and-go corners, get elbow to elbow."

There was a pause, during which I envisioned the Countess scrutinizing Billie's face.

"You should ac-centuate your eyes, for example. The upward tilt at the outer corners makes them divinely exotic. Hmm, yes. We must reshape the brows to emphasize their slant, perhaps smooth a little dark rouge near the sockets, finish up with mascara on the tips of the lashes—and voila! Your eyes will appear larger, more dramatic."

"And..." Billie's voice held both a note of hope and uncertainty.

"*And*, you will stand out from the others. You will be remembered for your remarkable eyes. You will excel, attract more business than all your other sisters combined."

"A-men! Billie, you must to try what she say. Big success mean you not be living under thumb of pimp no more."

This forward-thinking suggestion came from a new voice, Irina Popov. Irina was from Russia and, like Billie, the path she had followed to Detroit and eventually to jail had been paved with hardship. A band of Holy Rollers had saved her, so her arrest statement claimed.

There was a pause, followed by the rustling of cellophane, then the striking of a match. A sensitive snout was one of my outstanding features. I detected the smoke of their cigarettes almost before they lit them.

Up to this point, the Countess' tone had reverberated with enthusiasm. Now it turned petulant. "Of course, as we have no make-up, an application lesson will have to wait until we are out of here." She sighed. "Meanwhile, we will request some tweezers from the matron."

I chuckled. I couldn't help it. The way she put it, requesting an item from a matron was no more complicated than ringing up room service. But while I liked her verve, the time had come to unmask the Countess and delve into the part of her core that I could never like. Nudged by the metallic sounds of breakfast trays being handed through a food slot in the cellblock's steel door, I rolled from my bunk.

Three metal picnic tables were bolted to the cement floor of the common area as if someone might actually try to walk away with them. The Countess, Billie, and Irina went directly for what I assumed was their favorite table while I, unsure of myself, placed my tray on another. The Countess, without hesitating, said, "Please, won't you join us, Miss Lewis."

With little time to rehearse a cover story, it was decided I would use my own name to avoid getting tripped up using a false one. The Countess, with a grand sweep of her arm, directed me to sit on the bench directly across from her. Billie and Irina, appearing to resent the intrusion, ignored me while I slid between the bench and the table.

"Girls—" The Countess' voice strained with patience and good manners. "Being kind in one's relations with others is the simplest definition of charm. This is our chance to practice." Friendly, albeit strained "hellos" followed.

Breakfast consisted of oatmeal, tepid milk, a slice of dark bread, sugar, and coffee. Silence prevailed as we nibbled at the food and I slyly observed the others. I had been briefed about them, too.

Billie of the exotic eyes and Rubenesque rump had full lips, a head of wiry auburn-dyed curls, and flawless, milky-coffee skin. Tall and thin, Irina had fuzzy dark blond hair, worn medium-length, and a putty-colored complexion marred by small pink acne scars.

I looked over the edge of my mug at the Countess. The image was a far cry from the glamour shot I'd seen in the newspaper clip. This morning, absent the jewelry and make-up, her face reflecting the strain of a month-long stint in jail, with the unhealthy pallor of her skin and her scraggly hair, she was downright disappointing.

She sensed my stare. Lifting her chin, she angled her head slightly to one side, drawing her swan-like neck taut. The pose was practiced, I thought, intended to show her best side to the house lights, the effort wasted in jail where even the aura flooding from ceiling lamps was cast with gray.

Her regal bearing in place, she latched cool blue eyes onto mine. "And what are you in for, Miss Lewis," she added as though suddenly recalling her manners, "if I may be so bold as to ask?"

"Stealing jewelry."

Billie was impressed. "You a jewel thief?"

"No," I answered primly. "A personal secretary. The woman who accused me, my employer—er, former employer—Mrs. Snodgrass, is elderly. Gets easily confused. *Thinks* I took a couple of necklaces and bracelets…" I knew next to nothing about robbery or fine jewelry and had been warned to avoid discussing the topics at any length. "Why would I take anything?" I countered hastily. "I'm a skilled secretary. I know the Gregg method of stenography. Studied it at—"

Billie let loose an earthy laugh; Irina gavc a knowing giggle.

"Un-huh," Billie said, nearly choking on another guffaw. "We *all* in here by mistake."

Their levity rattled my already shaky confidence. I focused on my spoon, watching it stir figure-eights in the watery remains in my bowl. Moments passed like this, until it dawned on me: the Countess had not joined the other women in mocking me. Why not?

I looked up. A private cellblock housed with select inmates was not the only privilege she'd been granted. Jewelry of any sort was taboo in jail—the Hole's property clerk had collected Liberty's bracelet from me—yet she was twisting a divine diamond and ruby ring. In a flight of fancy, I imagined she was uneasy because she'd fallen for my cover and thought the fiery band vulnerable.

The ring-turning stopped. "The name of your boss, Mrs. Snodgrass, seems familiar. By chance, might she be a member of a women's club? The Cosmos Club, perhaps?"

The porridge I had managed to get down sat like a brick. I didn't know a Mrs. Snodgrass; the name was a random pick. "Hmm…no, Countess. Far as I know, my Mrs. Snodgrass is not a club member anywhere. May I call you Countess, by the way?"

Her eyes brightened and her lips curled in pleasure. "Yes, certainly please. The news reporters have made a mockery out of my using the title. But it is mine to use. It goes back to my great-grandfather, you see…" As quickly as it had appeared the spark left. "Ahh, but that is another story. One not for now, I think."

A melancholy silence followed. I moved to fill it. "I've never met a charm consultant before. What exactly do you cover in your lectures?"

The topic turned out to be far broader than I expected and the morning's urn of coffee had been drained before she at last concluded her musings.

"How do you get invited to speak at clubs?" *And why would anyone want to sit through one of your lectures?* I nearly added, instead observing, "For example, to the place you mentioned earlier. The Cosmos Club, wasn't it?"

"The club's Enrichment Program committee chair, Kiki, ehm, Miss Barclay-Bly, is a dear friend. It was she, Miss Barclay-Bly, who invited me in to speak. The audiences were *fah*-bulously appreciative. I was asked to return several times." She sent me a significant glance meant to remind me of her illustrious past, adding, "It was Kiki's sister, Miss Deirdre Barclay-Bly, who introduced me to my fiancé." She began twisting her bejeweled ring again and her mind seemed to drift away.

Leaving the Countess to her thoughts, I coaxed a few additional facts about their professions from Irina and Billie.

Irina was a maid, employed by a custodial agency. The placements varied but she preferred steady work, like the position she had once held in a grand home with lovely people. She had lost the job, she explained, after too many no-shows, the absences due to injuries inflicted by her former boyfriend. Acne was not responsible for the scars on her face; they were cigarette burns. The bump on her nose was the result of one of the ex-beau's beatings. Ex because he was dead. Irina had killed him. Shot him straight through the heart in the midst of his drunken rage. "It was either him or me," was how she put it.

For Billie's part, life in jail was better than facing her pimp, who by now would have heard about her plan to change careers. Billie wanted to be a performer. Fed up with hooking, she wanted to sing or dance or act. It didn't matter which, she liked to do it all. And thanks to a loyal customer, a jazz club owner who offered her a start as an attendant in his joint's powder room, she had nearly snagged a break. Bad luck rarely comes at a good time. In need of funds to buy the uniform required for the job, Billie had solicited a john who turned out to be a cop, the turn of events chucking her off the path to performing and, once again, landing her in jail.

The Countess, having belabored the topic of life as a lecturer, skirted discussion of her secondary career as a spy after confirming that I, like everyone else, had already read the newspaper accounts of "the misunderstanding." Instead, she launched into her complaints about how the FBI had thwarted her and her "girls," attempts to obtain legal representation. "The situation is unjust," she declared.

My view wasn't solicited, and I didn't give it, but I thought she might as well quit her whining. Her treatment was governed by wartime rules and, according to what Dante had said, the government's position was not likely to change anytime soon.

Our breakfast hour over, we shoved our trays back through the food slot. Irina and Billie strolled to the opposite end of the cellblock, where Billie had left her cigarettes; I accepted the Countess' invitation to resume our places at the table.

Immediately, she leaned toward me. "Like you, I am wrongly accused," she whispered. "I am an FBI pawn, in jail due to a breach of trust. People are working to obtain my release, but the process is slow. We are stymied at every turn. My fiancé, Mr.

Butler, he was there when I was promised immunity. He will act as a witness, corroborate what they said. *Immunity!*"

I bent closer. "Oh?"

The Countess flicked her cellmates a stern look. "Those girls don't understand the nuances of my case. They think everyone thrown in jail, even those who are guilty, claim they are innocent."

"Yeah, I noticed."

"I am not guilty," she said staunchly, "and the government's treatment of me goes beyond unreasonable. They have cut me off from the outside world. They censor what I read, delivering only news reports meant to let me know how badly the war goes for the Axis, how I am despised by the press, and also by the public. They allow no visitors, not a lawyer, not my fiancé, it is only their agents who come."

Her gaze flitted to Billie and Irina again. "While I have been grateful for their company, I have been without an equal with whom I might discuss more sophisticated and urgent matters." Tears welled in her eyes before she could turn away.

While I had no sympathy for a fascist spy, particularly one who also came across as a bigoted snob, I saw my break. Reaching across the table, I patted her hand lightly. "It's none of my business, but if it would make you feel better to discuss things…"

She pulled her hand from under mine and dabbed her eyes. "You are the only one who thinks it is none of your business. The press, the public, everyone would like to crucify me. Even the other prisoners would like to see me strung up. They call me names, Judas, skunk, *verrater*, *hure*, traitor of traitors, names you have not heard before." Ah, but I had. Last night. "But what do they know?"

The Countess foraged in her jumpsuit pockets, extracting a pack of Camels and a mother-of-pearl holder, promptly stuffing it with one of the cigarettes. She took a drag and, scrunching her mouth sideways, let a long stream of smoke escape. "What I would like them to know is that it is the proud and pure all-American FBI who are the traitors. It is they who have deceived me."

"What do you mean?"

"I have done the citizens of America a wonderful service. I helped the FBI to entrap a bona fide ring of spies. I should be honored, not punished!"

She should be committed to a loony bin was what I was beginning to think.

"But what did they do?" she went on. "After promising that I would receive special consideration they lock me behind bars like a common criminal."

I glanced at the ruby and diamond ring, then nodded in the general direction of her cell. "But your special needs and comforts *are* being met."

"The privacy? The little luxuries?" she whispered in a shaky voice. "Not enough. Not nearly enough."

The four cells in our cellblock spilled into the common area, a caged open space shared by the inmates. It was where we took our meals and where, before I retired for my nap, the Countess and I had huddled in private. Unfortunately, before I was able to bring up the industrial spy, Otto Renner, Irina and Billie returned to our table, bringing the intimate exchange to an end. Afterwards, I had moseyed back to my bunk under the guise of wanting to read. What I really wanted was some quiet time to digest what I had learned in our initial session, and to plan my next move.

The doors to our cells had been opened in the morning and, barring any trouble, would remain that way until lock-down this evening. *Personality Unlimited* in hand, I stepped out of my cell and lingered at the threshold. Across the common area, outside the bars, a matron in a white shirt and dark skirt was on routine inspection. She scrutinized our activities from the catwalk, a narrow walkway encircling the common area's perimeter. Our monitor had beady eyes and a sour, pursed mouth.

"All okay in there?" The matron threw me a severe look. I answered with a cooperative nod.

Irina was lying on her back on the floor. She did not reply. The matron asked more directly, "Irina, you all right?"

Irina's eyes were closed. They flew open. "Uh-huh, yes, Matron. How nice you ask. I work on my posture. Must to lie here ten minutes. I do this and Countess she says I will soon stand straight and tall, like…" She hesitated, an image forming, and smiled broadly. "Like man who wear tall hat and lead band, marching in parade."

To my surprise, the matron returned Irina's smile, exposing an unfortunate top gum line with more open spaces than teeth. The smile vanished. "Hmm, improvin' yourself is a good thing, but watch out. Don't go letting Hitler's handmaiden in there boss you 'round too much or else you'll be marchin' straight-backed, imitating those goose-steppers in jackboots we been seein' parading through the newsreels lately."

Irina rolled her eyes, and the guard swept her gaze next door to where the Countess and Billie were talking. I stepped into the common area, eager to take a look myself.

The top bunk of the Countess' iron-framed bed had been removed, giving her quarters an added sense of spaciousness. She sat, primly perched, near one end of the mattress. Behind her, Billie was brushing her hair into a scraggly ponytail, holding it this way and that as if trying to find just the right style for doing time. While Billie fussed, the Countess chattered incessantly, her voice muffled by the bowed position of her head.

No wonder they had isolated her from the others, I thought, taking stock of her booty of special privileges, noting that besides providing docile cellmates and allowing her to wear jewelry, the Bureau had supplied her with a small stack of books. And while we all wore our own footwear, in my case, cotton socks and saddle shoes, the Countess wore leather pumps in a snappy red. The portion of her leg visible beneath the hem of her navy jumpsuit shimmered. My jaw dropped. Was she also wearing silk stockings?

At a question from Billie, she raised her head. Her pretentious voice suddenly carried and we were treated to an ersatz hair-care tip, currently all the vogue in Europe. "Chamomile tea and lemon juice for color. Beer or raw eggs for body," she recommended.

With a snort, the matron lumbered off. Irina remained on the floor. She had closed her eyes again.

"Heard you talking with the matron, Irina," I said. "I hadn't noticed a problem. Something wrong with your posture?"

Her lids fluttered. She smiled broadly. "Miss Pucci. How nice you up. No, it is not problem. Countess she say, way we walk and pose it tell much about us. I got habit always to stand one-legged, like stork, one foot wrapped round other. Look insecure, Countess say, like I going to topple over. I try instead stand proud, hands at sides, feet flat on ground. Make better impression."

I'd been favoring slumped shoulders, myself. I straightened up.

Billie tucked a final tendril of hair into the curve of the upsweep she had created. "There you go, Countess honey."

The former spy patted her hair. "How verr-y clever of you, Billie." She crossed the seven-by-twelve-foot cell and paused before a metal plate bolted to the wall above the sink. She tilted her head, straining to see her reflection. "Exquisite! Billie, this time you have ahb-solutely outdone yourself."

She stooped and casually dragged out a fur coat from beneath her bed. I stifled a gasp. Mink, I guessed, observing its glossy sheen, watching as the Countess, with the aplomb of a bull-fighter, swept the coat like a cape around her.

"A little cah-old in here, don't you know." She sashayed into the common area, the fur's hem swinging heavily at her sides. Her practiced eye swooped over me. "Now, whatever shall we do for you, Miss Lewis?"

I wanted to say, "Lend me the fur. Anyone would look like a million bucks in it!" But before I could react she zeroed in on my hair.

"Ahh, so interesting," she said, lifting a small section. "The orange coloring shows flair and is lovely contrasted with the porcelain complexion and green eyes. The jagged cut…" Her hand cupped her chin while, squinting, she eyed me top to bottom. "Well, it is unusual and the short length is good atop your trim figure. The Untamed Look I would call it. Perhaps, when you are out of here you will consider a henna rinse to deepen this flamboyant shade into a rich auburn. More sophisticated, don't you know?" She reached for my hands. "Your nails, hmm..." She scrutinized my self-manicure, then flipped my hands palms-up. Her eyebrows arched. "These are not the hands of a thief."

If she was fishing for a reaction, she got one. Blood rushed to my face; I felt suddenly hot. "I tried telling you this morning. I didn't do it. I was set up."

Her eyes narrowed and something in her look said, I don't believe you.

Billie hooted with delight. "Like I said before, honey, we all been set up."

The clanking of keys and the slamming of metal signaled the return of the vinegar-faced guard. "Preacher's here to see you, Irina. C'mon out of there." She jimmied a key into the lock of the cellblock door. "You, too, Billie, c'mon. Your lawyer says he's got news."

The surprised expressions on the faces of Billie and Irina as they filed out will stay with me forever. They were out on the catwalk before the Countess could fully grasp the situation. Yanking the remains of her cigarette from its ivory holder, she flicked the butt to the floor. "This is unfair," she said, stomping it out. "No one is permitted to visit me."

The matron was poised at the outer door. She turned and spoke over her shoulder. "Can't understand why you're so upset. You requested *private accommodations*."

The solid metal door opened and the trio tramped out.

Whatever falsehoods the Countess claimed she had seen in my palms were forgotten. She clasped her arms across her chest and began to pace. She tramped to the far end of the common area and returned, the hem of her heavy coat swaying.

"Separate housing is a necessity. I was threatened. I was fearful!" She shook a fist at the outer door. "It is not fair, I tell you! You are using my fears as a means to isolate me. You keep me from advisors, from my fiancé, and I am left with nothing. Nothing but broken promises."

She stalked the painted gray floor like a captured lioness, crossing from one barred wall to the next. I retired to one of the tables. At last, pausing, she grasped a pair of metal bars, her body convulsing with her attempts to shake them. A dreadful sob escaped. Slumped against the grated wall, she slithered to the floor, crumpling into a furry heap.

Agent Dante had cautioned me about the Countess. Desperate, crafty, without any loyalty, she would take advantage of anyone to further her own interests. She was emotional, too, he had warned, cautioning me not to give in to her high dramatics. Yet, listening to her sobs, I could not escape a twinge of pity. Not for her impassioned performance as a wronged counterspy, but for the woman in her who believed that she'd been used and betrayed. I'd experienced my own share of heartache over broken trust. Moreover, I tended to believe there was some truth to her claim that the FBI had led her down a primrose path. To win her cooperation and with "the greater good" in mind, the Bureau might have implied, without the handshake, that they would cut her a deal. But even so, Dante had been emphatic: there had been no firm deal, no promises.

The Countess was ripe for a shoulder to cry on, and I was here to listen. I slipped from my seat and went to her. "You're not alone," I said, patting her shoulder, savoring the downy plush of mink engulfing my fingers.

She cried harder and I continued patting until, as quickly as it had started, the weeping stopped. She looked up, nose running, eyes red. Snuffling loudly, she dipped into the folds of fur and removed a lacy handkerchief, the kind you would never expect to actually use. She blew into it noisily.

"What will you do?" I asked, dropping to the floor to sit next to her. "About the FBI, I mean. They're a powerful organization. Don't you have to do what they want?"

"I did. For a year and a half."

"But—"

"No buts. It was hard labor, mentally exhausting. Think of it. In the entire time I did their bidding, I had no privacy. I was followed, they tapped my conversations, watched me through a peephole in my apartment, even when I was with my fiancé. Imagine!" She shuddered. "I did what they asked. I helped them capture seven spies. Now they must keep their end of the bargain. They must free me. Now!"

Her lower lip quivered. I thought she might start crying again, but she continued. "On their last visit, three days ago, they had the nerve to suggest—no, threaten—I must cooperate. Plead guilty. Ha. I will not! Such a plea would result in a long prison term. There, someone would surely kill me…" She sighed. "If I do not die of depression first."

I tried again. "But—"

"I have already said no buts. I will tell the world they have threatened me. That I have been mistreated. Yes, even tortured." She made a dramatic sweeping gesture. "This place is torture. I have nothing left to lose."

I cleared my throat. "Maybe you should reconsider. Play along with the feds. It's possible they only want to keep you in custody until all of the pleadings are in. I read in the paper that two of your gang members have already pled guilty. If there's a trial, they'll need your testimony. But if the rest plead guilty too, there won't be one. If you cooperate, maybe they'll set you free then." I was lying through my teeth, trying to outgun an enemy spy, one who had fired more than her share of double-dealing ammo already. How sweet the offense.

She eyed me warily. "You know a lot about my case, about the feds and their ways."

"Rumors about home front spies are a hot topic of conversation at work. I read the papers," I emphasized firmly. My lips felt dry. I licked them and lowered my voice. "It's said that a couple of *Abwehr* agents connected to your case eluded the FBI's net. Do you know? Is it true?"

Her eyes were mere slits. "You talk about spies at work? With Mrs. Snodgrass?"

"Well, yes…"

The Countess, with her squinty eyes, resembled a cat about to pounce on a rat. "Tell me more, please, about how you came to be accused of stealing from her."

"Like I told Billie, Mrs. Snodgrass has so much jewelry she must have misplaced a few pieces."

"And they arrested you, brought you here, put you in a cell next to mine because they *thought* you stole her jewelry?" Entangled in the fur coat, she fought to free herself. Eyes blazing, she scrambled to her feet. "You're a liar! Someone pulled strings to get you in here. Why? Who?"

"Hear me out," I pleaded. "My situation is your situation, remember? It's all a big mistake…"

The Countess paced again. "Who are you? Why have they left me alone with you?" She pressed her back against the cell bars and looked around, a desperate animal trapped inside a cage. "Have you been sent to harm me? Matron! Help!"

With the clanging of keys and groan of a door, the matron appeared. But not because the Countess had beckoned. "Lewis, your lawyer's here to see you."

My lawyer?

"How'd you manage it?" the jailer asked, nudging me out the door and projecting her voice toward the Countess. "A lawyer from the *Detroit Free Press*—" The guard pressed her lips together, making one of those hmm-hmmm sounds people use to make you think they're impressed. "Best damn counsel in town."

Chapter Four

Special Agent Dante swung the Ford Deluxe around a garbage truck blocking the entrance to an alleyway. The Countess had seen through my false identity and I was staring out my side window, brooding. Dante nosed back into the traffic along Gratiot Avenue and I peered into the alley, catching a glimpse of a large-boned Negro woman wearing dark coveralls and a bright red bandanna, wheeling a trash can toward us. Struck by the woman's serene expression and her tall, purposeful walk, I was reminded of how the manpower shortage had changed women's lives. In my case, I was beginning to understand that sometimes the opportunities would come back to bite us. The FBI had given me an out-of-the-ordinary chance to strut my stuff and I'd muffed it. Now what?

Out of the corner of my eye I saw Dante concentrating on the congestion ahead. Minutes ago, purporting to be an attorney from the newspaper, he had arranged my release from jail. We were en route to the FBI field office, a short drive away. An awkward silence had fallen between us and I could only imagine the worst: he was quiet because he was sorting through the mechanics of returning me to my WASP unit. Pronto.

I was not sure how much Dante knew about what had transpired between the Countess and me, or what had inspired him to show up at precisely the right time. Or even why he had used the ruse involving the *Free Press*. But at the moment, if gaining understanding meant rehashing my botched assignment, I was not interested.

The queen WASP would be tickled, I mused glumly. Her stray would be buzzing back to the nest. We continued along Gratiot, Dante absorbed in his stony silence, me picturing my boss, aloft, doing somersaults in her private souped-up Staggerwing biplane. Abruptly, the hedge of low-rise granite buildings along my side of the car gave way; Woodward Avenue was just ahead. An elegant streetcar, its glass and brass aglow in the glare of the sun, glided along the track at the boulevard's center, bearing down on the passenger island just short of the intersection we had slowed to cross. The streetcar braked. Sparks flying from the connector rod rained down from the overhead wires as the Ford bumped, crossing the tracks. The reel of Miss C's aerobatics show, playing in my mind, fluttered and snapped.

"Your timing at the cellblock," I said. "What made you show up when you did?"

Dante looked over like I must be joking. "Our prisoner was spinning out of control."

"You warned me she was dramatic," I countered. "She'd begun seeing me as her ally. Another minute, I might have calmed her down."

"*Dramatic?* She's delusional. Only a psychiatrist would know the proper thing to do." Dante had been scowling. His expression softened. He glanced at me. "Our bogus Countess is a smart cookie. We knew winning her trust would be tough, but we had to start somewhere. And you urged her to cooperate. We appreciate that." Turning back to the road, he spoke in an exaggerated tone. "They are being unreasonable. I helped them catch spies. I made them look good. Now they must carry out their end of the bargain. They must release me. Now!" He laughed. "She's too much."

My breath caught. Dante had said they would be nearby in case I needed help. He hadn't said they would be eavesdropping. "The cellblock was wired?" My voice squeaked.

Dante's forehead creased. "Yes, of course."

"Why? Were you afraid I'd mess up? That I would miss something?"

"It had nothing to do with you or your abilities. It's standard procedure. Besides, listening through a wire is nothing like being there in the flesh. Nuances of speech, body language, those things are as important to understanding what a person might be saying as the actual words coming out of their mouth. And the equipment has its own set of limitations. Interference from noises, a voice slipping out of range, the person talking turns her back to the receivers. But you—" Dante looked at me with genuine appreciation and I felt a rush of warmth meeting his gaze, "you were there with our royal prisoner. You had the advantage of observing her expressions and body language."

"But if you knew you'd be listening in beforehand, why not tell me?"

"Didn't want you feeling self-conscious or nervous. Turned out, you were brilliant."

I smiled tenuously. "What about Billie and Irina? Yanking them out, was that part of the plan?"

He nodded. "A little private time to give our genteel spy a chance to spill her guts."

In truth, I hadn't given much thought to what the Countess had actually said. "Hear anything useful?"

"The Buchanan-Dineen, Barclay-Bly relationship is a new twist."

"Really? And it's important?"

Dante shrugged. "Barclay-Bly has a record."

"A record?"

"Uh-huh. We have a file on her."

"A file? The FBI is keeping dossiers on members of a hoity-toity women's club? Why?"

"Not all members. Kiki Barclay-Bly." Dante's cherubic lips tightened. He hesitated. "I've been thinking about the next part of your assignment. I need another round of approvals, but Agent Connelly's already working the cogs. Once we get the nod," he looked over, "and we will, I'll bring you up to speed on how

Barclay-Bly might play into our case. Meantime, we're going to need more dirt on Renner."

I straightened up. I wasn't being routed back to my WASP duties after all.

"Probably best to start at the beginning," he continued, "with Blount and what brought him over to our side. Blount was a night shift, eleven-to-seven regular. In his capacity as a protection guard, he simply looked the other way whenever Renner wanted to sneak out a blueprint. His privileges also gave him access to executive offices. If Renner wanted some bit of information, say from production or personnel, Blount simply let himself in after hours, found the desired notation in the proper manual or document, and photographed it.

"A week ago, Blount arrived at work a little early and bumped into Renner, who was leaving a little late. Renner invited him for a drink at the Orange Lantern, a tavern near the plant. They started drinking and Blount quickly realized they weren't there merely to hoist a few. Renner was lonely. He wanted to talk."

I frowned. "Why? What about?"

"A spy can't go home and celebrate with his wife about his accomplishments or gripe about his problems. So, two bottled-up operatives get together and start downing a few, they start comparing war stories. In this case, it's Renner, who's not much of a drinker, doing all the blabbing. He seemed depressed, according to Blount, but he should have been jolly. He had two secret projects in the works, both coming to a head. One involving a truckload of faulty engine castings en route from a subcontractor, being delivered to Willow Run the next day."

"Faulty castings?"

"Yup. Castings welded in a way that would weaken and give way, causing a plane crash. Renner doctored the designs."

I winced. "But there are systems to detect such flaws. X-ray machines, inspectors…"

Dante slowed for an elderly pedestrian, supported by a cane, as she entered the crosswalk. "According to Blount, Renner was confident the delivery and subsequent installations would take place without a hitch."

"Cripes." I sank back into my seat. "Meaning Renner has somebody on the inside in production helping him."

"Uh-huh. And Blount, who thought he knew everything Renner was up to, nearly toppled off his barstool."

"That why Blount came to you then? He felt betrayed? Figured the more people involved, the more likely they'd get caught?"

Dante's shoulder lifted in a half-shrug. "Could be. But Blount also claimed he wasn't particularly proud of what he'd gotten into. Blamed it on his disability."

"His left arm…He wears a prosthesis. What happened? Injured on the front?"

Dante shook his head. "No. Boot camp incident. Happened on a night compass run during maneuvers. Chief Instructor that night, a Lieutenant Mitchell, ordered them into an area he'd neglected to thoroughly check. A stream that was supposed to be only a foot deep ended up being six-foot-deep whitewater. Blount got swept downstream. Luckily, he got caught up on a limb and was rescued. Later, a wound got infected. Gangrene set in. Amputation was the only option. A tragic mishap."

"I'd say. Blount must have been bitter afterwards. I would be."

Dante nodded. "Especially as every able-bodied man he knew, including the other men in his unit, went off to fight for their country. His girl—now his wife—stuck by him, though. Which helped, he said. But also made him wonder if she truly loved him, or just felt sorry. Later, when Renner made him the offer, he thought the extra dough might help make things up to her."

"So why'd he give it up?"

"His wife seemed genuinely content. There was a baby on the way, remember? Plus, he had standards, he called them. Stealing information to help the enemy build its war arsenal was one thing, sending American pilots up in defective planes was another. The act seemed too personal, too cowardly. Said he had to step away."

It was easy to feel sorry for Blount, but he'd crossed a line. "A spy with principles. That's nice. So he waltzed over to you—" *And paid the ultimate price.* "What about the defective engine castings? The delivery was scheduled for the next day. That was a week ago. What happened?"

"There was a delay."

I looked over. "Delay?" Dante didn't reply and I knew from his wooden expression our discussion of the matter had ended.

He swung onto Fort Street. Flat-faced institutional buildings made of pre-cast concrete hemmed us in on either side. Swarms of men and women in business attire crowded the sidewalks, out for their lunch breaks, I presumed, consulting my watch.

I jockeyed around in my seat to face Dante. "Renner had something else up his sleeve. What was it?"

"He wouldn't give Blount any specifics, only that the project was top secret and it had to do with a bombing mission. Blount kept after it, though, until Renner also admitted he'd just completed copying the plans."

"That's it?" I asked. Dante nodded. "But surely you've covered the angles. Found out what the project was?"

"Yeah, we followed up. Blount knew about a secret gizmo in the works that makes night bombing or blind bombing possible. Figured it had to be that. We did some discreet checking, confirmed the project exists."

Icy fingers climbed my spine. "Uhm, the envelope in Blount's pocket…it contains a drawing of the device." A muscle along Dante's jaw line, in front of his ear, pulsed. "Sorry," I raced to add. "It's the training. Couldn't resist."

His mouth twitched. He let it go. "Blount insisted on getting us the sketch," he explained. "Thought the tangible proof might be useful to our case."

"And Renner also has a copy in his safe. How do you know he hasn't already passed it off?"

"His method for communicating with his handler," Dante said. His gaze shifting back and forth from the road to me, he laid out what he knew. That it was a complicated, pre-arranged system which became more complex and time intensive when Renner had something significant to pass off. In this instance, Renner had expected it would be several days before he heard when and where to make the drop. Until then, the plans would remain securely stored inside his safe.

"What about Blount's wife?" I asked. "Did you question her? Find out if she has an inkling into who might be behind her husband's death?"

"The wife is missing."

"Missing? You mean as in skipped town? Was she involved?"

"At this point in the investigation, everyone who knew him is suspect. It's also possible she was murdered as well."

Chapter Five

We entered the lobby of the Federal building through a door at the far end of the underground garage. To our left, two windows with shiny brass bars fronted a Postal Department service counter. From behind the grilled windows, female clerks wearing visors and blue uniforms helped a queue of women clutching letters and packages. At seeing the barred-in clerks, I was reminded of how good it felt to be free and back in my officer's pinks.

On the sixth floor, Dante and I traversed a bullpen of desks and chaos, eventually arriving at the office he shared with Agent Connelly. I had been there the day before for my briefing and knew the layout. The men's desks faced one another, their sides abutting a wall with two casement windows. The blue plastic wastebaskets at the ends of their desks, nearest the door, were official depositories for FBI "confidential trash": items that must be burned or otherwise disposed of in a secure manner. Dante was carrying a phone message someone had thrust into his hand on our way through the outer maze. Wadding it, he flicked the paper ball at his basket as we entered. It rimmed out. Special Agent Patrick Connelly was seated at his desk. "Nice shot," he said wryly.

Tall and fit, with square shoulders and a square jaw, Connelly resembled the comic book crime buster Dick Tracy. Even his hairstyle, precisely parted, rigid with pomade, was similar. Except that Connelly was blond. As Dante's partner on the Renner case, he had been in on our strategy session the day before. He'd barely kept a lid on his resentment over a woman joining the team and when asked for ideas in developing my now torn-to-shreds cover, he'd contributed just one, the trumped-up jewel thief charge.

Dante went to get a chair from the other side of the room. He placed it near the corner of his desk. "Hear anything on our request to expand Lewis' duties?"

Connelly had rolled his chair out from behind his desk and was circumventing me. He paused. "It's a go." The prospect clearly did not please him.

He positioned his chair between my seat and Dante's, completing the triangular conversational arrangement. We dropped into our respective seats. I was giddy over what might be coming next. Seeming to sense my mood, Connelly moved to wring out the starch.

"Well, well, well. So you uncovered the Buchanan-Dineen, Barclay-Bly connection. Lucky little break now, wasn't it?"

An American flag on a stand occupied the corner behind Dante to my right. On the wall to my left, above Connelly, were life-size photographs of a stern-faced J. Edgar Hoover and President Roosevelt in pince-nez. A brass FBI seal hung below the portraits. I stared at the motto *Fidelity-Bravery-Integrity* spanning the banner at the plaque's center, willing myself not to blurt something to Connelly I might instantly regret.

Dante was fishing in his desk's center drawer, his arm buried above the elbow. "It wasn't a 'little break,' Patrick," he said, pulling out a pack of Luckies. "She asked the right question at the right time."

In true FBI loyal-brave-honest fashion he had taken up for me. I smiled his way. "I presume the connection between the Countess Buchanan-Dineen and Barclay-Bly is more complicated than the coincidence of both women having hyphenated names," I observed blithely. Silence. Froth gone flat, I tried logic. "Barclay-Bly invited the Countess to lecture at her club. You said you have a file on Mrs. Barclay-Bly. There's a connection?"

Making a steeple with his hands, Connelly placed his chin on the point, staring at me with narrowed eyes. "It's *Miss* Barclay-

Bly. She reverted to her maiden name after several failed marriages. She comes from a privileged background. Big house in Grosse Pointe, tony neighbors, private schools…"

He seemed to be implying that a privileged background was a detriment. The reasoning escaped me, but I was dying to hear more. "Uh-huh. And?"

"Barclay-Bly attended college in the Twenties, during Prohibition. Duped her folks into leasing an apartment for her on the Detroit River. Then the good times rolled. Word got around she was hosting parties with bootleg booze. Purple Gang members began dropping in—"

"Purple Gang?"

"Local gangsters, active here in the Twenties. Built a reputation around armed robbery, hijacking, extortion, strong arm stuff. Big money, though, was in controlling the local wire service, providing racing stats to all the horse betting parlors and bookies."

"Is this Purple Gang connected to our investigation?"

"The link's not exactly direct." Connelly's tone held a hint of something intriguing.

"Patrick…" Dante waited to be sure his partner got his message. He looked at me. "Let's just say it's a sidebar to the investigation. Leave it at that for now, shall we?"

I didn't see that I had any choice. "You mentioned a new assignment?"

Dante had removed a smoke from the pack. He began twisting it with his fingers. "Two, actually. First, we're going to re-arm you, give you another shot at the Countess."

"Go back to jail? You can't be serious. I just got out."

The cigarette twisting stopped. "We are serious. Buchanan-Dineen claims she's performed a wonderful service for our country. She wants to be honored, not punished. She complains of the mental torture she's suffered at our hands. She wants people on the outside to know all this. So ask yourself, how could she do it?" Dante lifted inquiring eyebrows. "By talking to a reporter."

The Countess, we all knew, was thinking more along the lines of talking to a lawyer. Or her fiancé. "Hmmm…" I muttered.

Dante plunged on. "This time, posing as a journalist assigned to record her story, you'll play to her ego, convince her you're the ideal conduit for bringing her side of the story public. Once she gets what's in it for her, you'll be home free. Free to delve into what she knows about spying, free to slip in a query or two about the contacts the *Abwehr* expected her to make once she arrived, even work in a question about Renner while you're at it."

I looked at him admiringly. "So that's why you posed as an attorney for the *Free Press*. You were planting a seed to help convince her that I was actually a journalist, all along."

"Ha!" Connelly scoffed. "What we should do is throw a real reporter at her. Let her tell her poor-me tale to one of the boys from the *News* or *Free Press*. Let them write it up. Our besieged little spy might be surprised at the reaction from Detroiters. They'd want to lynch her, not cry for her."

I cocked an eyebrow at Connelly, then turned to address Dante. "You want me to tell her I'll get her story published. But, in truth, whatever she says will never get beyond our ears?"

"Right. And depending on how things go, with your background in journalism, maybe you could actually write something up and we could print it. In a faux edition, of course."

"*Background* in journalism is stretching it. I majored in journalism in college, yes, but that's the extent of—"

"You were a writer in your job at Midland Aircraft," Connelly butted in.

"But I wasn't a reporter. I cranked out instruction manuals and informational blurbs to help sell airplanes. There's a difference."

"Lewis," Dante snapped. "There are men out there right now who've never captained a battleship before, never holed up in a muddy trench with mortars exploding all around, never seen their buddies blasted to smithereens…" He paused to draw a breath. A quiet breeze entered the open window, rippling the flag at his back. When he spoke his voice was calm again. "We need someone capable and trustworthy. You're our man for the job."

I was duly humbled. And flattered. "Okay, I'll do it. But even with the proper credentials, what makes you think she'll believe me? Or trust me?"

"You'll figure something out. And don't worry. She'll be ready to talk. The isolation is getting to her. You heard her, she said so herself. Now, minus her cellmates, she's bound to feel more desperate yet."

"Where are Irina and Billie? Did someone put up bail?"

"Bail?" Connelly repeated. "No, no bail. We had a chat with the prosecutor. He may want to charge them later, but for now there was no point in holding the two any longer."

"Oh, I see..." The situation was undoubtedly more involved than Connelly was letting on. But I liked the women. They weren't hardened criminals and I was happy they'd gotten a break, however it had happened. I also knew there was no point in pressing for more information. If they wanted me to understand the nuances, they would have dished them up. Either way, their aim was clear. Billie's and Irina's release had been orchestrated to help cinch the noose around the Countess' neck.

"Say, what about Leo?" Dante asked. "Get a chance to talk with him?"

Connelly checked his wrist. "Left a message. Promised we'd try again right about now."

I'd missed something. Before I could figure out what, Dante begged me to excuse them and the two men stepped outside. I stood to stretch my legs. A bookcase occupied part of the wall on Dante's half of the office and I wandered over to inspect the array of books and manuals. The titles all related to crime-solving or FBI procedures. The technical material looked boring, but a framed snapshot of Dante shaking hands with a uniformed police officer held promise. I picked it up. The officer was presenting Dante with a flat rectangular object I assumed was an award.

I heard the door open. Dante and Connelly reentered the room.

"My dad," Dante said, seeing the photo in my hand. "Our bureau chief got a special dispensation allowing him to award me my badge."

I reshelved the memento. "Nice."

Dante went to his desk. Opening the manila folder he'd been carrying, he removed two 8x10 glossy photographs, arranging them next to one another on top of the file. I went to take a look. Connelly followed at my elbow.

One of the glossies was actually a composition of three mug shots of a woman, including right and left profiles. A full-length shot of her filled the other sheet. The subject had classic features, including an oval face, a fine nose, and wide-set eyes. Her straight dark hair was worn in a chin-length bob.

"Kiki Bly?" I asked, already sure I knew the answer.

"*Barclay*-Bly," Dante said, jabbing the full-length shot with his finger.

I leaned in for a closer look. Kiki wore a flapper dress with a drop waist and a mid-calf hem. For accessories, she'd added a long string of pearls and a feathered headband. In one hand she held a champagne glass, in the other, an elegant cigarette holder nearly identical to the one used by the Countess. Two swarthy men with slicked-down hair, wearing bowties and dark formal suits, flanked her.

"Why exactly was she arrested?" I asked, trying unsuccessfully to glimpse the accompanying paperwork.

"Like Patrick said, her apartment had become Prohibition party time headquarters. One of our agents assigned to covering Purples observed some gang members enter her residence, called in for backup, and she was arrested for possessing and serving bootlegged booze."

Which was probably being consumed by half of Detroit.

"Parents hired a bright lawyer," Connelly scoffed. "Never saw the inside of a cell."

Wish I hadn't.

Dante continued. "That chapter closed, she began running with a liberal circle, young swells with plenty of means and plenty of free time for throwing it around. The sort of group that, shall we say, was blasé about abiding by rules."

My gaze returned to the two toughs flanking Kiki. Purples, I assumed, grimacing. It was one thing to be rebellious, but as the saying went, You are the company you keep.

"The young Miss Barclay-Bly played nonconformist to the hilt," Dante continued. "Cigarettes, outlandish clothing, loose talk about free love and fascism…stirring things up wherever she went."

"Two oddball marriages, all the dirt that fell out from the subsequent divorces—she kept the local gossip rags in print," Connelly contributed. "As if she hadn't taken enough punches, she's remarried again."

Dante dropped the photos onto the thin ream of paperwork, lifting the stack and rapping it against the table, leveling the edges. A few yellowed news clippings had been fastened to the file cover. "The tattle-tale accounts?"

"Yup." Dante closed the file. "Our office has maintained periodic reports on her activities since the arrest."

I frowned. The folder was very lean. "Okay, so Barclay-Bly was once a free-spirit who hosted parties for gangsters. Now she's organizing guest speakers at a woman's social club. What are you getting at? What's the connection?"

"It's what we want you to find out." Dante removed the Lucky propped behind his ear and tapped it against the folder. "In the mid-Thirties, some of Kiki's friends were observed attending Bund meetings."

"And Kiki went, too? How many times?"

Connelly shifted his stance. "None that we know of."

"What about recent activities or affiliations? Anything suspicious?"

"Nothing obvious." Dante wedged the cigarette back on his ear. "But it's possible, older and wiser, she's more cautious, knows to keep a low profile."

"So you need someone to delve into Barclay-Bly's current activities. Find their true nature. My second assignment?"

Dante nodded. "Uh-huh. We've arranged for you to stay at the Cosmos Club. We'd like you to talk to the Barclay-Bly ladies, see what you can uncover about their relationship with Buchanan-Dineen, or whether they're using traditional trappings to hide something else sinister."

Jail cell to social club. I was moving up in the world. "Great." I looked at him. "Did you say Barclay-Bly *ladies?*"

Connelly smoothed the flat of his hand over his hair. It looked so brittle I half-expected to hear the sound of a crack. "Your tête-à-tête with our thorny spy raised two other correlations. Kiki Barclay-Bly's sister, Dierdre, introduced Buchanan-Dineen to her fiancé, Nelson Butler."

I nodded, recalling the Countess had admitted as much.

"In buttoning down arrangements for your stay at the Club," Connelly added, "we learned that Renner's wife, Clara, has been a hairdresser there for three years."

I gave a toneless whistle. "You're kidding! The Countess, the Barclay-Bly sisters, Mrs. Renner, they're all affiliated with the Cosmos Club. And you just pieced this together?"

Dante's response was measured. "The investigation has been in place for less than a week. Up until we thought of placing you in jail our focus was on maintaining plant security and surveilling Renner. Now, about *Mrs.* Renner—"

From the quick profile of Clara Renner that followed, I learned that the Detroit-born hairdresser was an only child, both parents deceased. She and Renner had married about a year ago and, at twenty-three, she was half his age. Recently, she'd been promoted to manager of the club's salon.

"The age difference could be the reason he turned to spying," Connelly observed. "You know, similar to what was driving Blount. The need to earn something extra, keep the little woman happy, be the big man about town..."

"What are you saying?" I interjected sharply. "That a younger woman would only love an older man for his money? Clara Renner is a beautician. She *works.* That means the so-called little woman has her own income, right?" I recalled the ordinary-looking man in the ill-fitting suit I'd seen walk past while Dante and I had been sitting outdoors at Willow Run. He hadn't looked like someone leading the high life. Maybe she did take it all. And what did she see in him, anyhow? What was the attraction? It would be interesting to find out.

Dante's dark eyes were shiny with amusement. He cleared his throat. "Patrick's theory is just that. A theory. And it's only one possibility. There are others. Ideological reasons get my vote."

"What about protecting family in Europe?" I wondered out loud.

"Nah, Renner is U.S. born," Connelly said. "From Texas."

We were all still standing at Dante's desk. "Okay, so I'm going to the club to explore the sisters' link to the Countess. What makes you think they're going to give me the time of day?" My gaze shifted from one man to the other.

"Your cover as a reporter will be ideal there, too. Tell them you'd like to do a story on the club's facility or its members..." Dante's hand waved dismissively. "It's a private women's club. There ought to be plenty to write about." He extracted a brochure from the file, holding it out to me. "Society types use the place to entertain and to debut their daughters. There are also private rooms. Members use them when they want to stay overnight or if they need to put up a guest."

Randomly opening the pamphlet to a lush photo of a guest room, I squirmed reading the testimonial beneath.

> *"We Bloomfield folks especially appreciate the convenience of the Cubicles. Many a time, after a day in town, I slip in for a tub and a rest before putting on a fresh frock and going out again for the evening."*
>
> *Miss Susan Louis Pembrook*

Maybe I'd been too hasty in thinking that a stay at an exclusive club beat going to jail.

"What exactly would you like me to get from Mrs. Renner?" I turned the page to an interior shot of the beauty salon.

"We don't know if she's involved in espionage, but you should be looking for suspicious signs. Also, her version of Renner's alibi for the time of the murder is critical. We need to know her story inside out so we can use any discrepancies in his version to trip him up when we question him. Anything related to her husband's spy dealings would be important, of course. Finally, we want to know about any contact she's had with the Countess."

There was a soft tapping on the door. A tall, shapely woman with thick spectacles and cascading chocolate-brown hair entered. "Phone call, Agent Connelly."

I watched him stroll to the door. The secretary did not budge. Interestingly, her sights were not set on Connelly's approaching figure, but on Dante. The thick lenses magnified the size of her eyes as well as the accusing look in them. I turned to Dante. Seated at his desk, shuffling the skimpy contents of the Barclay-Bly file, he had choir boy written all over him. Had an odd fissure or some sort of refraction in the secretary's lenses distorted my impression of her glance? I swung her way again but the door was closing behind her.

Dante launched into the particulars of my stay at the Club, beginning with the credentials I would need for pulling off my stint as a journalist. The forms would be processed overnight, he promised, and to avoid being tripped up by any subtleties involving local customs or personalities we agreed I should represent an out-of-town paper. I suggested my hometown rag, the *Cleveland Plain Dealer*. To build in flexibility, we made my assignment a Tri-City series encompassing metropolitan Chicago, Cleveland, and Detroit. By the time Connelly reappeared we had covered a good deal of ground, including the substance of the stories I would claim to be writing.

"That was the medical examiner," he said. "Nothing new in the autopsy. Killer knew what he was doing, death was instantaneous. Around six a.m., like we suspected."

Dante read his partner's expression. "*But?*"

Connelly gaze flicked to me.

"Go ahead," Dante said.

Connelly shifted uncomfortably. "Turns out the frilly thing in Blount's hand was a pair of women's underpants. Initials S.B. embroidered on them suggest they're Mrs. Blount's. Her name's Shirley. Taylor's over at the house now, checking for similar garments."

"*Underpants?*" I said, blushing at my immodest blurt. "Bizarre... But why is your man searching the house? Hasn't Mrs. Blount showed up yet?"

Dante rubbed his face. "No." He eyed Connelly again. "Something else?"

"Something was written on the garment. In blood." Dante and I stared. "Can't say whose it is yet—lab's doing more tests—but the message was 'Bye baby.'"

Chapter Six

I read about the Teatime Enrichment Program in an events calendar I found in my room and decided to pop in, hoping that I might bump into Kiki Barclay-Bly, the Enrichment Program committee chair.

Today's presentation, "Birds: Their Beauty and Their Song," was billed as an afternoon with Mrs. Miles Worcester singing bird songs illustrative of readings by Mrs. Peter Karp. The performance was already underway when I arrived. I ducked into the last row, delighted to find a seat near the entrance. About forty club members had turned out for the affair, held in the Fourth Floor Lounge. We sat in folding chairs facing one of the room's two fireplaces. Around us, tall, wainscoted walls were hung with brass sconces and huge oil paintings of misty landscapes and oriental vases filled with brightly colored flowers.

This new segment of my assignment, while a drain on my social skills, had a positive side. Before leaving FBI headquarters I was asked to relinquish my B-4 bag in favor of a larger piece of luggage filled with ensembles suitable for my mission. Whoever had orchestrated the wardrobe had stellar taste. While I had always preferred wearing slacks, who could knock being swathed in a dress made of lush silk?

My view of the act was partially blocked by the backs of well-coifed hair colored in various hues of gray. I shifted and panned the audience, looking for a match to the mug shots I'd seen in Dante's office. The photos were twenty years old and Barclay-Bly would have aged, but I didn't see anyone even remotely resembling her.

Worcester and Karp completed their number. A moment of silence was followed by a delicate fluttering noise as the audience members, most of them wearing gloves, applauded.

"Ladies, ladies, may I have your attention, please," a syrupy voice pleaded from the dais. The buzz of whispered conversations quieted. "It has been a delight to share our interpretations with you. We thank you for coming. By request, Jungle Birds will be our final number."

The performers took a moment to arrange their new material, giving me the chance to observe the women knitting Christmas stockings in the rows around me. The faint click-clicking of their metal needles had been going nonstop since I'd settled in my chair. A notice in the events calendar had urged members of the Stocking Drive Committee to bring their finished products, stockings which would be sent to our troops overseas, to the group's next meeting. I presumed these women were the designated knitters, clicking to meet their deadline.

My gaze shifted back to Mrs. Karp, a tall, gaunt woman with wire-rimmed glasses, who had begun reading a poem describing bird sightings on a jungle walk. Next to her, Mrs. Worcester, a full-figured woman of sixty or so, whistled and peeped through puckered lips. Having just recited the line, "in awe of the macaw," Karp paused. Worcester took off on a riff, croaking "cawww-cawww-ca-ca-cawww," borrowed from, I would have sworn, the Beer Barrel Polka.

I choked back a laugh. Desperate for a distraction, my glance slid to the woman seated at the far end of my otherwise empty row. A low chuckle had escaped her lips, and besides a kindred sense of humor, I was intrigued by her sense of style. Her ink-black hair was pulled back and wrapped into a twisted knot at the nape of her neck. The dark color, striking against the creamy tone of her skin, seemed all the more distinct because of a lone circle of white near her temple. Her eyebrows, though, were her signature feature.

Thick and dark, they grew with such abandon they nearly met in the center.

I recalled seeing another pair of eyebrows, exaggerated and painted to resemble a flying bat, on the surrealist artist Frida Kahlo, in the self-portrait Uncle Chance had on display in his shop. Flaunting such fanciful, prominent eyebrows suggested a rare breed, I thought. Most women would pluck them, especially since pencil-thin, carefully arched eyebrows were all the rage these days. But Miss Kahlo, and now this woman down the aisle, had decided not to conform. It showed an acceptance of self that I admired.

The bird singer hit a sour note. Another memory catapulted free. A family photo, capturing the Barclay-Bly sisters at a young age, had accompanied one of the yellowed clippings in Dante's file. The girls' features were fuzzy, but Kiki's sister definitely had thick eyebrows. Could it be?

Blessedly, my enrichment lesson ended. A round of restrained clapping followed. Spectators left their chairs and began mingling, their varied conversations filling the air with pockets of bubbly sounds. I rose and quickly side-stepped down the aisle. "Hi, Pucci Lewis," I said extending my hand.

The woman's handshake was relaxed. Her eyes sparkled with merriment. "You seemed to enjoy the program," she said, smiling and adding in a kind of slurred aside, "For the birds if you as-shk me."

My fellow critic patted the chair next to hers. Dropping to the seat I passed through a cloud of sherry. I had noticed a decanter, surrounded by tiny glasses, on the sideboard near the entrance when I arrived. Tempted, I'd resisted, whisking a cup and saucer from a silver tea service instead. This woman apparently had not shown such restraint. Besides the nearly drained glass she twirled in her hand, a matching one, now empty, stood on the floor near her foot.

"The program says Worcester and Karp were brought back by popular demand," she whispered, leaning close, the aperitif's essence floating toward me on her breath. "But it's not true.

Events having to do with flowers or our feathered friends are always held in the spring, not the fall."

There was a rule about wearing white after Labor Day, too. Who cared? I was at the club to learn about the person charged with selecting the speakers. "But that's the Enrichment Program chair's responsibility, isn't it? What was she thinking?"

The thick eyebrows merged into a singular dark line. "It had nothing to do with her. The chair is also running for club president. Certain members want her out of the race. A first step was overriding her at the committee level by insisting that the bird program go on as this month's event." My new cohort paused to smile through clenched teeth. Coolish nods were exchanged as a trio of women, their fur stoles dangling over their arms, sauntered past.

"Mrs. Preston Rice, Mrs. Colburn Standish, Mrs. Charles Horton Metcalf," she confided once the threesome had passed. "The enemy." I must have looked puzzled. "They're part of the group trying to sabotage my sister's bid for club president," she said.

"Ahh, club politics. Not my bailiwick."

"Mine neither," she laughed. "Wouldn't have expected Kiki to get so involved, but growing up she'd always loved being in the eye of the hurricane." She shrugged. "Maybe this is a manis-fi-fi-sta-shion."

While the woman struggled to unslur the word, I basked in my victory. I was swapping tittle-tattle with Dierdre Barclay-Bly, the sister of my mark, who was a mark as well.

"The committee chair, Miss Kiki Barclay-Bly, is your sister?" I asked, testing to be sure.

"Yes, that's right. Well, now she's a *Mrs.* Mrs. Anastase Andreyevich Volodymyr Vivikovsky." She stumbled over the name, but laughed cheerily. "Quite a mouthful, isn't it? It's why we call him V-V. And why Kiki prefers keeping our family name. Simpler, don't you know."

I managed to keep my composure while she belatedly introduced herself, imploring, "Please just call me Dee."

I scanned the small conversational cliques again. "I came to the program hoping to meet your sister. Maybe talk to her about the Book Faire. Is she here?"

"Sorry, no. Kiki didn't sanction this event, remember? I only came myself to get a sense of the movement swelling against her." Dee paused. "I'm sorry, why did you say you wanted to meet her?"

"I didn't." I smiled. "I'm a reporter from the *Cleveland Plain Dealer*. Here on assignment."

Dee swirled the last drop of sherry in her glass and drank it down. Her eyes, wary now, met mine over the rim of her glass. "Oh?"

"Don't worry," I added hurriedly. "My assignment has nothing to do with club politics. I'm the paper's Women in War Work columnist. I write vignettes on the jobs women are doing on the home front, filling in for the men."

Dee sighed. "Ah, you're a career woman. How fortunate for you to have found something fulfilling. Something other than a man…"

I frowned, straining to understand her final comment. And why did she sound so bleak? "Well, yes. But I still might only be an office girl if it weren't for these times," I said truthfully. "And being a reporter has been quite the boon. I've been able to learn firsthand what women are capable of doing, given the chance."

I ran through the short list of working stiffs I'd interviewed, including riveters, welders, and assembly line inspectors, adding, "An All-American Girls' Professional Baseball League player and the country's first woman air traffic controller were centerpieces of recent columns."

Dee looked impressed. "An air traffic controller? Ha-cha-cha."

I smiled. "I enjoy covering the unusual. It's what grabs me, and what I like to think draws my readers."

Dee's voice brimmed with curiosity now. "So why are you in Detroit? And why do you want to speak with my sister?"

I shrugged. "My editor's idea. A segment of the paper's readership, according to him a very large, very vocal segment, is wed to the traditional. They've let him know they're fed up with reading about the women workforce."

"And he wants you to cover the pursuits of non-working, upper-crust women instead?"

I smiled. I liked Dee. "You got it. He wants to include items with a volunteer angle for a while. In keeping with my column's theme, we're looking for projects related to the war effort. Since Cleveland has only two women's clubs we thought of interspersing a few stories from clubs in surrounding metropolitan areas. I've been to Chicago already."

"And?" Dee's thick eyebrows arched expectantly.

I had done my homework. I smiled smugly. "I've only just submitted the piece, so I'm not sure I should tell, but the Chicago club is asking its members for their costume jewelry. When the collection drive is completed there'll be a luncheon for members and guests, showcasing the display. The luncheon fee will be donated to a war cause. The jewelry"—I paused, heightening the drama—"the jewelry will be sent overseas to servicemen in the Pacific. They'll use it for bartering with island natives."

Dee looked stunned. Then she clapped her hands together. "Marvelous! Brilliant! What a hoot!"

I had not made up the project, nor did the scheme's originators consider their efforts frivolous or a hoot. Still, I had to smile. I held up my hands in mock surrender. "They claim there's a need."

"Okay," she said, serious again. "So what's hot about this club?"

"My aunt is a member, for one thing. And, well, there's the upcoming Book Faire. It's what I wanted to see your sister about."

Dee's eyes narrowed. "Lots of clubs have book events. Nothing out of the ordinary there."

"But your Book Faire raises money. For the war effort, right?"

Dee's eyes rolled heavenward. "Hard-ly. The funds are used to purchase decorations for the annual Christmas Ball." She paused, momentarily slack-jawed. "Say, what a swell idea. Why not contribute the proceeds to the cause? We'd be doing something worthwhile. Kiki would love that."

Just what I'd hoped. "Can you tell me where to find her?"

Dee reached for the drained glass on the floor. She stood, tottering slightly. "I can do better than that. She's in the library. I was going there to see her. You can tag along."

We paused at the sideboard near the doorway, giving Dee a chance to deposit her empty glasses. "They only hold a thimbleful," she said, raising the petite stemmed glass she'd grabbed as a replacement, gauging its amber contents.

"After your sister's Book Faire is over maybe she can organize an event to raise funds for more substantial glassware," I suggested lightly.

Instead of laughing, like I expected, Dee knitted her eyebrows. "When this phase is finally over, I'm going to see that Kiki takes a vacation. The strain has been awful."

I nodded sympathetically while declining her invitation to join her in a sherry. Belatedly, I noticed the remnants of dull colored stains embedded beneath her nails and around the cuticles of her hands. She took a sip from her glass—"so it wouldn't spill over"—and noticed me staring.

"They look terrible, I know," she said, correctly guessing the reason for my ogling. "I've taken up painting again. Good therapy, I'm told."

We left the lounge and followed a corridor straddled by carved cabinets displaying bric-a-brac in porcelain and alabaster. High above us, crystal chandeliers dangled from the ceiling. The library was on the second floor. We arrived at a corner staircase where a broad deep-toned runner descended stairs of polished mahogany. The banister and the paneled wall opposite it gleamed with a golden-red finish.

We paused on the landing. Brushing the railing's smooth finish, Dee chortled softly. "When Kiki and I were young, we lived in a house with a staircase exactly like this. One time we borrowed Mother's silver trays and used them as toboggans. Bumped and bounced our way down each and every step."

I regarded the steep downward pitch. "You're kidding. And you lived to talk about it?"

Dee laughed with delight. "Sure. Big trays, little girls. Our elbows, maybe a few other parts, were bruised, but no broken bones. The trays suffered the worst of the battering. Mother retired them afterwards, I think."

"She must have been furious."

Dee looked puzzled. "No, Mother was never upset. Thought it was amusing, probably." She smiled at the disbelief on my face. "It's true. Mother adored us. In her eyes, we could do no wrong." Her hand smoothed the banister again. The ritual, maybe the recollections, seemed to sober her. "Many times, as an adult, I've wondered if somehow things would have turned out better if we'd been taken to task now and then."

"What do you mean?"

Dee hesitated, seeming to consider what she should tell me. "Earlier you said that as a reporter you like to dig for the unusual. In her heyday Kiki liked going against the grain, too. By doing nothing to rein her in, our parents, I'm afraid, paid a dear price in the end."

We slowly descended the stairs. I withheld further questions, and simply listened. Through sherry-lubricated lips, Dee admitted to having been the quiet, obedient daughter, while Kiki, the wild child, had always pushed the boundaries. The ultimate test of their parents' love, she said, was Kiki's brush with the law over a party held in her riverside apartment during Prohibition.

"Something to do with bootlegged booze," she said, halting on the staircase and surveying the room below as if it drew memories from her.

Dee touched on other "phases," as she called them, of Kiki's early adulthood. In one phase, her sister was a rolling stone, constantly on the move, in search of adventure and excitement; another time, her behavior was the polar opposite. She rarely left the family home. When she did go out, Dee said, she liked to dress in long scarves and flowing gowns venturing no farther than to dance, nymph-like, about the grounds of the family estate.

There was no mention of the "phase" during the mid-thirties when Kiki fell in with an eccentric crowd and began espousing radical views, the period when, under the watchful eye of the FBI, her friends were observed entering German Bund meetings. Still, by the time we finally reached the second floor, I'd heard enough to convince me that the information contained in the government's report concerning Kiki's "glory days" was accurate.

On the second floor landing, a fine porcelain vase, laced with gold and resting on a trestle table, held sprigs of eucalyptus sprouting from among fall-toned mums. Their pungent scent followed us even as we rounded a corner and started down another richly appointed corridor.

"But your sister changed," I said, trying unsuccessfully to imagine someone who had once been so unconventional feeling at ease among the formal trappings. "What caused the shift?"

Dee stopped and set her glass down on a narrow table beneath a gilded mirror. "The usual, I guess. Maturity, death, trauma."

Dee wore a black dress, elegant in its simplicity, and all the more chic on her trim figure. I stood behind her, studying her reflection in the glass while she smoothed her thick eyebrows and adjusted the large pearl studs on her ears. Perfectly matched to the strand around her neck, the pearls glowed with a soft pink luster.

"And marriage?" I asked. "Was getting married part of the transformation?"

"Of course. Kiki and V-V have been together for nearly ten years. They were married in Paris. I'll remember the occasion always. We—Mother, Father, and I—received an Eiffel Tower postcard announcement. 'We're married! I'm hopelessly in love,' it said."

"Really? That's it? You weren't invited?"

Dee found a tube of lipstick in a pocket hidden in the seam of her dress. "No. We hadn't even heard of V-V until then. But we'd been through similar occasions before. It was Kiki's third wedding."

Agent Connelly had mentioned the multiple marriages. Still, I managed to look surprised. "Third?"

"Kiki's a big fan of marriage. Third time's the charm, though, it seems. She's settled. And very content, at last." She began applying a fresh layer of cherry-red to her lips.

"Anastase Andrey-yo-yo Viva...Vivi..." I paused and cleared my throat. "V-V has an interesting name. What nationality? Russian?"

Dee smiled at my attempt to parrot the name. "Oh no, Ukrainian. But they met in Paris. He comes from quite the lineage." The tube paused. "Friend of Kiki's introduced them."

"Oh?"

Dee blotted her mouth and smiled slyly. "If you have a chance to meet V-V, you'll understand why she fell for him. And it's not because of his background. He's a knockout. Impeccable manners and charm..." She hesitated. The smile remained, but the light in her eyes faded. "The type of man who once he's found you, never lets you go." She picked up her glass.

The heavy, double pocket-doors at the library's entrance had been left open. A woman was rolling a pushcart of books over the threshold as we arrived. She lifted the back of the cart, maneuvering the load to turn it. Several books tumbled off. While she bent to retrieve them, I peered inside.

The rectangular room had floor-to-ceiling shelves crammed with rows of books bound in dark leather. I counted four schoolhouse desks arranged in private nooks, and two Queen Anne desks positioned in opposing corners, all with occupants. The heavy drapes dressing the tall windows had been pulled against the ebbing afternoon light. Reading lamps with emerald shades cast warm spectrums of light, enhancing the ambience.

Having restacked her cart, the librarian began rolling forward again. Coming abreast of us, she glanced pointedly at the glass in Dee's hand before moving on.

Dee angled her head toward me. "Rules are rules," she chimed. "No food or drink inside." Down the hall, a carved table rested against the wall. She headed for it and I entered the library.

The crackling of wood burning in a fireplace drew my attention to a Wedgewood mantelpiece at the far end of the room. Near it, a man and a woman stood opposite one another on either side of an ornate antique desk. They were sideways to me, and I could only see their profiles, but I recognized the likeness to the mug shot in Dante's file immediately. The thick fringe of bangs was a recent change, but it was definitely Kiki.

The tall man with broad shoulders and strong features across from her was, I guessed V-V. A Continental-cut suit, draped softly over his muscular frame, made a refined contrast to his dark brown hair, worn on the longish side so that it brushed the collar of his shirt in back. He looked sophisticated but a bit rakish.

The couple was engaged in quiet conversation. Each had a hand on a book lying on the desk's polished surface. While they talked, the book moved back and forth as though it were a planchette on a Ouija board, guiding their hands not to letters of the alphabet, but to the dominant party's side of the desk.

Dee came up beside me. "Kiki?" I nodded to the couple.

"Uh-huh. And that's V-V across from her." She absorbed the scene more fully. "Oh dear, and they don't look too happy, do they?"

"There does seem to be some friction."

"I've been warning her."

"Warning her?"

"Well, warning might be too strong a word. But look—" Dee's tongue clicked in a tsk. "She's so pale and tired looking. It worries me."

I thought her observation reflected a maternal bent. Except for the dark circles under her eyes, in my view Kiki looked great. "Hmmm..."

Dee misheard me. "Yes. And him. I'm worried about him, too."

"Who, V-V? Why?"

"Kiki was a free-spirit at one time; these days she's anything but. She's so obsessed with getting this Book Faire off the ground it's all she does, day and night. She's neglecting her health, her husband—" Dee sighed, focusing on her sister. "They have a suite here. I'll bet she's been staying overnight again."

I observed the stubborn set of V-V's jaw. "He doesn't approve?"

Dee frowned. "Well, I guess you could say, like the library, he has his rules. And until now Kiki has been a saint in putting up with them…" Dee faltered as her thoughts took a slow turn. "Maybe it's time she held her ground. A woman should never submit to a man too completely." Her melancholy tone grew so soft I had to strain to hear her. "Not even a handsome, charming, adoring man."

◇◇◇

Dee and I wove past a handful of patrons occupying wing chairs upholstered in shiny brocades and dark velvets. The women, absorbed in their reading, barely looked up.

Kiki wore a filmy loden-green scarf draped loosely around her neck. One end had been tossed over her shoulder, the other flowed in a soft line down the front of a lavender blouse worn with loose trousers of pewter silk. Above the elegant clothing, her wide-set eyes were fixed on her husband. Sensing our approach, her gaze shifted, lighting up as she saw Dee.

Cued by the change in his wife's expression, V-V pivoted and faced us as well. Dee had not been exaggerating. A tall, well-built man in his early forties, V-V was ruggedly handsome with a strong chin, a long nose, faintly arched, and a precise mustache, like Clark Gable's. Relinquishing the battle over the book, he came toward us.

"Dee, my darr-ling," he said, drawing out the words, his rich accent resonating with warmth and charm. He spread his arms and drew Dee into his embrace.

Behind the desk, Kiki opened a side drawer. The small volume the twosome had been tussling over disappeared inside.

Dee introduced me to the couple, then began recapping the bird program. While the trio exchanged barbs about the women in attendance and assessed the event's political ramifications, I used the opportunity to observe the sisters. Physically, they were a close match: medium in height, with trim figures. They also shared the oval shape of their faces and the wide set of their eyes. Both women had black hair. But that was where the similarities ended. Kiki's dark tresses gleamed with the underlying blue sheen of a tint; Dee's dark color was natural. It was interesting. The hallmark patch of white I'd thought so flatteringly dramatic on Dee earlier, sent a different message when she stood next to her sister. It made her look like the elder of the two when the truth was just the opposite. Dee's tight chignon also added years while Kiki's contemporary bob, cut sharply at a diagonal across her cheeks, erased time.

Eventually, the conversation returned to me, and Dee acted as an unexpected advocate. First, she provided an excellent overview of the series I was writing, and then hinted I had an idea concerning the Book Faire, imploring Kiki to discuss it with me.

Kiki bristled visibly at hearing I was a reporter. She responded with a thoughtful, "Hmmm," seeming to consider the suggestion, but then did not bother pursuing it. A paper stack caught her eye. She dropped into her chair and began weeding it.

V-V bridged the awkward moment. "Ahh, you are a writer," he said, facing me. "Does this mean you are an avid reader as well?"

"Why, yes."

He displayed a second book he had been holding at his side. "Do you know E.T.A. Hoffmann?"

I tapped the index of my memory, spinning through authors' names, attempting to trace where I had heard of Hoffmann. I drew a blank.

"This one is *Tales of Hoffmann*," V-V said. "A rare edition and a memento from my past. Kiki brought it to the club thinking I had left it out as a donation for her Faire." He gave a deep-throated laugh. "A mistake. I would never willingly part with this."

I frowned. The volume had a foreign title.

"It is a German edition," he said.

"German?"

Kiki looked up. "We have a fine collection of works by international authors," she said, sounding somewhat defensive. She gestured to a section of shelving labeled *Foreign Works*. "Detroit is an industrial capital. Executives in our plants collaborate with business leaders from around the world. Our members often put them up here as guests. Also, many of our local leaders, or their wives, are direct descendants of immigrants. We have ladies who are fluent in German, French, Hungarian, Polish, Italian, Czechoslovakian…the list goes on and on. Some members, or individuals in their families, know several languages"—she smiled hesitantly at V-V—"like my husband."

The new point of discussion seemed to thaw Kiki's cool demeanor. "During our Book Faire, we hope to capitalize on this very same cross-section by offering foreign-language books in our sale." She shook her head and regarded V-V's keepsake. "Too bad you won't part with it, dear. Such a rare edition would spike up our profits."

"But that wasn't the book on the desk you two were fighting over," Dee interjected. "What was that all about?"

"Oh, that." V-V's gaze flitted to his wife. "I was only trying to save my darling a trip to the beauty shop."

"The beauty shop?" Dee looked confused.

"But I told you, dear," Kiki said, ignoring her sister and locking gazes with her husband. "I have to go there anyway, to make an appointment. I can take the book myself."

V-V reached to smooth the hair near her temple. "But your hair is lovely."

Kiki's smile was forced. "Now, dear, I said I'm going there to schedule a manicure, not a hair appointment, remember? And it's the manicurist who requested the book."

Her husband's hand lingered on her bangs. She gently removed it. The polish on her already perfectly groomed nails caught the emerald glow of the desk lamp, glimmering in the reflected light.

"Yes, yes, of course." V-V raised his hands in resignation. "I only wanted to help. You are so overworked."

"My sentiments, exactly," Dee said.

A smile beginning in V-V's eyes moved to his mouth. "To please us all, I will tell you what I shall do instead. First, I shall take Dee for an aperitif and leave you two lovely ladies to have your discussion. Then upon my return in say…" He raised his arm, exposing a gold watch beneath a monogrammed cuff. "In one half-hour, I shall chauffeur you home, personally. Meanwhile, I will call Cook and have her arrange a lovely dinner with fine wine. You will see, tonight we shall have a very relaxed, comfortable evening."

V-V's eyes danced with delight. Kiki sounded suddenly overwrought. "Oh no, not tonight, darling. I simply must stay over. This will be the last night for a while, I promise."

I sympathized with Kiki. She had workhorse tendencies. And while V-V's proposal might be exactly what a doctor would order to soothe her nerves, his domineering delivery had been irksome. More importantly, she had work to do and needed his support. Yet he acted as though he hadn't heard, bull-headedly insisting on whisking her away.

Dee took V-V's side. "Kiki, your husband is right. Tonight you should relax. You look peaked. Take a break, *please*."

Kiki turned to her sister. Her look suggested she would tell her where she could stick her nose. But she didn't. Her eyes softened. "Okay, you win."

"Good then." V-V beamed. "And since the weather is so grand perhaps soon you will even consider remaining at home for an entire day." He glanced from Kiki to Dee and back again. "Yes, this is a marvelous idea. Dee could pay us a visit and the two of you could take the electric boat out for a cruise on the river. It would be like old times. Remember?"

V-V's face was like that of a child getting his first glimpse of the family Christmas tree. Bells went off in my memory. "*Nutcracker and the King of Mice*," I blurted, startling everyone, including myself. All eyes turned on me. I blushed. "My Gran had an E.T.A. Hoffmann book. *Nutcracker and the King of Mice*. When I was small she liked to read from it at Christmas."

"Ahh, beautiful dolls, glittering jewels, marzipan castles in a sparkling woods." V-V smiled, the lines around his eyes fanning out from the corners.

I had always liked the tale, especially the part when the Nutcracker, who is about to be killed in a duel with the Mouse King, is saved by Clara, the unexpected heroine. V-V's succinct summary made the story sound queerly sappy.

"It's a festive romp," I insisted.

"But Hoffmann enjoyed the irrational and mysterious as well. In fact, many think that Hoffmann's darker tales enabled him to exercise his imagination to its fullest potential." V-V smoothed the book in his hand. "This volume of short stories, for example, contains 'Mademoiselle de Scudéri,' a personal favorite."

Kiki shuddered. He laughed. "My wife finds the tale too gruesome. Still, many consider it one of his greatest works. Some experts claim it is the first known murder mystery. But I do not treasure it merely for this." His expression softened. "The story is set in Paris, where I first met my lovely wife." He looked at her.

I smiled. When it came to spooky books I secretly sided with Kiki. But I was also a sucker for romance. "I love a good mystery. I'll look for it."

"At one time we had an English translation in our home. I shall try to find it." He leaned across the desk, gently brushing his wife's lips with his. He gallantly held out an arm. "Come then, Dee. A little refreshment now, shall we?" She smiled and latched on.

Kiki fingertips were at her lips. At first, I thought she might be savoring V-V's kiss, but her eyes suggested she was occupied with something not so romantic. Dee noticed. Her smile faded. "Cheer up, sweetie. A good night's rest will do you wonders. And wait until you hear what Miss Lewis has dreamed up. Could be just the thing to redeem your image. Win back votes!" With her last rah-rah comments, Dee pumped one arm in the air like a pep squad leader.

Kiki removed her fingers from her lips and sent her sister a slip of a smile.

"That's better," Dee said. "See you tomorrow."

They left and I looked over at Kiki. Her head was bowed and she held her forehead cupped between her hands. Sensing she needed a moment to herself, I quietly surveyed the tall piles of leather-bound volumes stacked on the floor behind her. Next, I let my gaze wander to a portrait of a servant girl with a porcelain jug sitting serenely at a well. A decent interval later, my gaze drifted back to Kiki.

At last, she massaged her eyelids and raised her head.

"Are you okay?" I asked.

"Sure. But they're right. I've been working too hard. Sit, why don't you?"

I took the armless chair across from her. The brocade fabric felt slippery and cool against the back of my thighs. "It was good of your sister to introduce us. Her passion for my project means a lot."

Kiki looked over my shoulder toward the door. "I'm worried about her. She's already had several drinks, am I right?"

I wasn't a snitch. I shrugged.

"Dee's had some personal difficulties. I hope you understand."

"Your parents' accident?"

The change in her eyes was barely perceptible. "You know about that?"

I didn't answer, stalling as I picked at a nub in my skirt, silently admonishing myself. Dumb slip! Now she probably assumed that I—the reporter—had been snooping into her past. But I hadn't. I'd heard about the senior Barclay-Blys' accident in my FBI briefing. They'd died in an automobile mishap three years ago. In their will, they'd left a two-hundred-acre plot along the Rouge River, near Dearborn, to Kiki. Subsequently, she and V-V had built a spectacular home they called LaVue Rouge, along the river's bank.

My paranoia over Kiki's jumping to conclusions about how I'd obtained the personal information turned out to be precisely that: paranoia. Better yet, in keeping mum I'd won some points.

"It's nice of you to protect her," she said with a sigh. "Dee tends to talk too much while under the influence. Especially about family. It's partly what concerns me."

"I understand," I said with empathy. "And sometimes, well, you can just read the grief in her face. They must have been very close."

Kiki nodded and surveyed the room. "There's another piece to the story. It's common knowledge around here anyway, and it may help to explain. Dee suffered another blow about a year ago. She was engaged to be married. But Philip, her fiancé, deserted her on the day of the wedding."

Connelly had been only too happy to broadcast Kiki's unfortunate break-ups. But there was no mention of this sad affair. "How awful."

"Worse than awful. She was at the church, dressed in her gown, when she found out second-hand. All the more tragic as Philip was her first and only love. I never understood how much he meant to her until she spiraled into this decline." There was a long sigh. "But then how could I? I was too busy chasing after what was around the next corner, never stopping long enough to think about anyone else but myself."

I shook my head. "You're being too hard on yourself. He was the cad. She's obviously better off without him."

She smiled ruefully. "True. But she was a near recluse after the jilting. Lately, though, this political rough spot I'm navigating has been a silver lining. By coming here, getting involved in trying to help, she's taken some baby steps toward rejoining the living. Hopefully, in time, she'll be able to do it without the crutch of alcohol."

"She's painting again. That's another positive, too, right?"

Kiki smiled. "Yes, and she must really like you to confide that. She's actually quite good. In the past, she'd get consumed in the process. A better choice of addictions—" She opened the side drawer of her desk. "We'd best get to why you're here. If you're set on reporting about our Faire there's a brochure in here somewhere I think will help."

She removed the spoils of her small skirmish with V-V, set it on the desk and reached back into the drawer. I squinted at the book's faded title. I blinked and looked again. *Personality Unlimited!* The book the Countess had lent me in jail. Incredible. The self-improvement guide's circulation was broader than I would have ever imagined.

"Say, that's the book Grace Buchanan-Dineen refers to as her bible, isn't it? I read about it in an account of her arrest. You mentioned you're going through a rough spot. Did you mean the flak you're taking because of your involvement with her?"

Kiki had found the desired brochure. Her hand shook slightly as with great deliberation she placed it on the desk before her. "The Club is sensitive to any discussion about the Countess. Certain members consider the publicity generated by her brief affiliation with us to be a blight on our reputation."

"Sorry, I didn't mean to step over any line, but her arrest, the arrest of her co-conspirators, what she did, what *they* did, the news has been in all the papers for weeks." I looked at her directly. "I'm not after a scoop. You can tell me off the record, if you'd like. You knew her. I'm curious, what was she like? Did you get along?"

Kiki looked poised to say something, then willfully held it back. I waited. A moment later, she waved a hand. "Oh, all right. Why not? It's just another one of those juicy bits everyone around here can't quit jawing on anyway. Truth is she was exactly what she billed herself to be. A talented, informed speaker. Worldly, very bright. And yes, I put her up for consideration. So, yes, I'm under fire. But the decision of who we bring in as a guest lecturer is not mine unilaterally. The invitations are by committee. However, once the decision is made it's my duty to make sure guests are able to find their way around the club. It's what I do with all of our speakers, so yes, I spent time with her, showing her around."

"But why are fingers pointing at you, then? You had no way of knowing she was a spy. She didn't exactly tip her hand, did she?"

I watched her face closely. It reflected nothing more than her exhaustion. She leaned back in her chair with a sigh.

"It's politics. My competition carries a lot of influence. As to whether the Countess gave any inkling into her true motives, she did not. It's ironic, though. The same women who a couple of months ago hung onto her every word, did a one hundred and eighty degree turn once she was arrested." Her mouth formed a sardonic smile. "Bunny Metcalf for example. She was a big fan. Yet I just read an article in the *Free Press*, quoting her." Kiki stuck her nose in the air, affecting a self-important voice. "*I didn't care much for her. She was typically continental and effervescently superficial. Right away, I thought she didn't ring true.*"

Just like her sister, Kiki had a good sense of humor when she let go. She laughed and I laughed with her.

"Did you become friends with the Countess?" I asked.

"We *all* liked the Countess. Quite honestly, the way she's being persecuted strikes me as odd. People seem to have lost sight of what she did for our government."

I whisked to the edge of the slick brocade cushion. "*Our* government? You mean what she tried to do for Hitler, don't you?"

Kiki gave me a disgusted look. "The Countess acted on behalf of our government as a counterspy. Her efforts may have…no, probably *did* save some lives."

"But she—"

"What I'm trying to say," Kiki interjected, "is that this country was built on the principle that a person is innocent until proven guilty. The accused spies, the Countess, they haven't had their day in court yet. I think 'we the people' should withhold judgment until we hear them out and until the court comes through with its verdict. Don't you agree?"

"I-I do." Had I not been aware of the FBI's suspicions concerning Kiki's loyalties, I would have endorsed her summation of the rights of the Countess and the others even more wholeheartedly.

Kiki shoved the brochure across the desk and checked her diamanté platinum bracelet-watch. "My husband will be back shortly and I still need to run down to the beauty shop. Maybe you'd like to look this over while I gather up my things."

She began packing papers into a needlepoint tote near her feet and I skimmed the bulletin. The week-long schedule of events was extensive, with author presentations and corresponding book signings interspersed between luncheons, teas, and other miscellaneous readings. I glanced up and saw the center drawer was partially open. I watched as Kiki removed a bottle of clear nail polish, staring at it as if considering whether to take it. In the end, she returned it and locked the drawer. Surveying her desk a final time, she absently brushed aside her bangs. A crescent-shaped strawberry birthmark on her forehead appeared, then disappeared as the curtain of hair fell back into place.

She lifted the tote and came around the desk, momentarily resting against its edge. "Say, what about the new twist Dee said you have for the Book Faire?"

I pitched my brainstorm for funneling the Faire's earnings into the war effort as we strolled toward the library's exit.

"It's a terrific idea. We'll simply use last year's decorations." Kiki's eyes twinkled. "Better yet, we'll do nothing. Put up no decorations whatsoever. Use the theme, *Don't you know there's a war going on?* Believe it or not, some people around here act as though they hadn't noticed."

Call me a cynic, but I believed her.

"I'm glad you like the concept," I said. "Dee's suggestion for using this publicity to help turn around the Club's negative association with the Countess has great potential. And I can provide the coverage to help. That is, if you'll agree to an interview. Will you?"

"Of course," she said. "Say tomorrow after lunch?" I nodded. She continued, "The Faire's inventory is stored in the Solarium. It's on the way to the beauty shop. If you like, I'll take you there. You can poke around, get a sense of what our collection holds."

Clara Renner, wife of the Willow Run spy, was a hairdresser in the Club's salon. I could hardly skip the chance to meet her. "Actually I could use a trim. Mind if I tag along?"

She assessed my hair. She looked puzzled, then shrugged. "Not at all."

We were descending the grand staircase leading to the lobby when V-V found us. Giving his wife a peck on the cheek, he glanced at the bag in her hand. "Ah, darling," he said, reaching to relieve her of it. "You are ready to go."

A corner of *Personality Unlimited* protruded from the tote's mouth. Kiki snagged the contentious book as her husband took the bag. "I still need to deliver this."

I hated controversy. Especially as I was now involved. It was my fault Kiki had been delayed. "I'm going there. I'll take it," I offered.

"I'd be ever so grateful," Kiki said, obviously relieved.

For the second time in less than a day, the Countess' bible had landed in my hands. I strolled, flipping pages, but could find nothing out of the ordinary in its contents. If anything, I was left with the same impression of the volume's vacuity I'd experienced while thumbing through it in jail.

The salon was tucked into a remote corner of the first floor. A sign on the plate-glass door read *Shear Heaven*. I found myself in a small waiting area with wicker furnishings and fern print wallpaper.

"Mrs. Renner is unavailable," said a squeaky-voiced blonde at the receptionist's counter. She motioned over her shoulder to the main part of the salon where three client chairs, anchored to a linoleum floor, lined a wall hung with corresponding oval mirrors. From the receptionist's glance, I gathered that the small woman with tousled auburn locks standing at the station closest to us was Clara Renner. She was spinning curlers into the hair of a client.

The telephone rang. "Excuse me," the receptionist said. She crooked the receiver between her shoulder and ear and began paging through her appointment book.

A hearty laugh from Clara Renner was followed by giggles from her client. I looked over, observing them while the receptionist finished her call.

Mrs. Renner was short, about five feet tall, with a zaftig, hourglass figure. A clingy pink smock accentuated her curves. Maybe it was her name, maybe it was her figure, but together with her heart-shaped face and the heavily made-up eyes, I pegged her as a ringer for the actress Clara Bow.

More bursts of laughter escaped as the beautician continued curling her client's hair. I tried picturing the sexy, good-natured, seemingly unaffected Mrs. Renner with the solemn middle-aged factory manager who had hurried past us at Willow Run. The image refused to gel.

The receptionist got off the phone. She looked surprised that I was still there. "I'd like to schedule a haircut with Mrs. Renner," I said.

"Mrs. Renner is working on her last appointment of the day," she replied, then appeared to notice my hair for the first time. Her eyes shifted. She leaned forward and in a high-pitched whisper confided that while cuts by Mrs. Renner were in high demand, the call she had just taken was a cancellation. "If you'd like, I can let you have the slot," she added in a soft peep. "It's for tomorrow afternoon."

It was risky letting a stranger cut one's hair. It seemed especially foolhardy in a joint like the Cosmos Club. But there was not much to cut or to spoil. And I would be doing it for my country.

No sooner was my time marked in the book, than the telephone rang again.

"Is the manicurist available?" I asked before the blonde could answer it.

There was an exasperated sigh. "She's with a client."

I waved *Personality Unlimited*, speaking swiftly as she snatched the ringing instrument. "I was asked to deliver this to her, personally."

The blonde nodded over her shoulder to a folding screen off to her left. She began speaking into the mouthpiece and I headed for the partition.

A fleshy, large-boned woman was seated with her back to me at the manicurist's table. Silhouetted in the bright light of a nearby gooseneck lamp, the woman was engaged in hushed conversation with the manicurist seated across from her. When it became apparent they hadn't noticed me round the screen, I cleared my throat. The manicurist leaned sideways to peer around her client. My heart lurched. Liberty Leach!

My friend and roommate from OSS training looked straight at me. Neither one of us so much as blinked. She didn't; I couldn't. I was paralyzed with surprise.

Liberty's normally wavy, golden-red locks had been dyed a mousy brown and styled to look stringy. Her goofy, horn-rimmed glasses were the same pair she'd used as part of her disguise when we had teamed up on a field test. What was she doing here?

The client had turned her head and was watching me, impatient to see what I wanted. Behind the woman, Liberty shook her head and mouthed, "You don't know me."

I took a shaky step forward. "Uh, library asked me to deliver this." Another step and I was at the table. I held the book out, uncertain where to place it.

Liberty took it and placed it on a shelf beneath the table. "Thanks."

The client's fingers were submerged in clear plastic dishes. She stared at us, wiggling her pinkies in the sudsy water as Liberty extended her hand. "Glossy Fingers," she said evenly. "I don't think we've met."

"No, can't say that we have."

Chapter Seven

The Cosmos Club was on Madison Avenue, a tree-lined street midway between the County Jail and the Federal Building a few blocks away. Built in the Georgian style, the stately four-story building had trails of ivy hugging its brick walls and curling around its tall, painted windows. A grand dame of the block, the venerable structure had a blue canvas canopy and a doorman at its entrance. An hour earlier when I'd called to report in, Dante had suggested we talk while grabbing a bite to eat. I waited under the awning until his Ford pulled up.

"How'd it go?" he asked, easing away from the curb.

"The early part of the afternoon was for the birds," I replied. "After that I did swell."

Dante's unbuttoned trench coat revealed the standard FBI dark suit, white shirt, dark tie. On his head was the narrow-brimmed felt hat he'd worn at the murder scene at Willow Run. His dark eyes volleyed from the road to me, crinkling with merriment while I launched into a critique of "the bird brain" reader and her "warbling" sidekick.

"Who do you suppose was sitting at the end of my row?" I added, waiting a beat to be sure I had his attention. "Dierdre Barclay-Bly."

"Ahh, Kiki's sister, the matchmaker who introduced Buchanan-Dineen to her fiancé, Mr. Butler. Excellent. Learn anything about her relationship with the Countess?"

"Not yet. We covered family matters, mostly."

I summarized what I had learned concerning Dee's love life, or lack thereof, and her current romance with alcohol. I shared my sense that Kiki, rebellious in her youth, in adulthood was the more resilient; Dee, historically the stable sister, grown-up was the more fragile. "They're devoted to one another," I said, editorializing on the women's relationship. "Dee frets over Kiki like a mother hen, and Kiki's equally obsessed with Dee's well-being."

"You met Kiki? What happened?"

"Not much. What struck me most was the shift from the free spirit she was twenty years ago. These days, she's ultra-conservative. Her main priorities are running for president of the Club and overseeing the annual Christmas Ball fund-raiser. I managed to get in a couple of questions about the Countess. But she was pretty guarded."

"Guarded? Think she's hiding something?"

"Dunno. I was with her for only a short time. She seemed protective of her. Thinks the news reports are overblown and that people might be putting too much faith in them. And something else—" I shifted and met his expectant glance. "They share the same interest in charm books."

"She's defending the Countess? You mean as in taking her side? Sympathizing with her politics?" He had bypassed my comment about the books.

I shrugged. "Not sure. The moment felt strained, that's all." My gaze had been resting on Dante's profile. From the set of his jaw, I sensed he had already pronounced Kiki guilty. "On the other hand," I added hurriedly, "her defense of the Countess' right to a fair trial is reasonable, perhaps even admirable. It's the American way, after all."

"Lewis, she was defending a known fascist and trained enemy spy."

"And counteragent who spied for us."

Dante's eyebrow shot up. "So you agree? You think she's right in supporting a criminal?"

I thought a moment. "I appreciate your position, believe me. I reacted the same way. But you can't expect me to crucify her, based on one brief encounter."

"Hmmm," he murmured.

Dante was showing a rigid side I hadn't expected. *Hadn't expected?* What was I thinking? He was FBI! I frowned, unable to think of what else to say.

He looked over and grinned. "Hey, relax. It's not worth etching lines into your pretty little puss over this. We have different views, so what?"

Instead of relaxing, the muscles in my forehead flexed harder.

"Sorry, that came out wrong," he said. "What I'm trying to say is, don't worry. If anyone can get a fix on whether Kiki is a party to our case, it's you."

I glared at the windshield. The patronizing comments were getting worse.

"Hey, don't shut me out. *Please.*"

Dante's soft, pleading tone was difficult—no, impossible—to ignore. I turned and met his gaze. "You've done an excellent job for us," he said. "This was your first afternoon at the Club and you've already met, and befriended, two of your marks. That's an outstanding effort. Better than we could have expected." There was a quiet pause. "Thank you."

He had that hangdog expression that made my heart melt. I smiled. "You're welcome."

A conciliatory silence followed. Dante turned back to negotiating the traffic and I stared out my window. I knew precisely where we were. The Cosmos Club was near the southeast arc of Grand Circus Park, a restful semi-circular preserve of greenery, statues, and fountains. Woodward Avenue bisected the preserve. We'd been motoring along East Adams. Now, swinging onto Woodward, Dante put us on a northerly course, heading deeper into the heart of downtown.

We began threading through heavier traffic and a call came in on the two-way radio. It was his office. He grabbed the mike. As he talked, I felt confirmed in my decision that, at least short-term, keeping mum about Liberty was for the best. She had been in disguise and I was in the dark about why. Dante continued talking on the radio and I tuned out, privately chewing on who or what might be behind her masquerade.

I felt confident that the FBI was not involved. Dante would not have positioned two operatives in the same place, on the same job, willy-nilly. The waste of womanpower, combined with the risk of botching the assignment, would be too great. Which could only mean that another intelligence arm, either Military or OSS, was directing her assignment and for reasons of security the FBI was being kept in the dark. Why? I hated to think so, but it was possible an interagency squabble was at the core of the mix- up. And it seemed most unwise to shake a hornet's nest that had Liberty and me in the middle of it.

After Pearl Harbor, the responsibilities of our three intelligence branches had been redefined to accommodate expansions in home front security. The FBI's Special Intelligence Service (SIS) was assigned domestic cases involving enemy infiltration, as well as espionage matters in Latin America; Army Intelligence (G-2) and the Office of Naval Intelligence (ONI) were given cases involving members of the armed services; the OSS' objective was to gather intelligence and carry out subversive missions overseas.

Although the duties of each group were differentiated, by mandate, representatives from each of the branches were expected to meet regularly to compare notes in the event certain cases might overlap. But I'd heard rumors that in instances involving high-profile or "pet" cases, the agencies often became territorial and select information was sometimes withheld. As the recent victim of a related bureaucratic battle involving Miss C, I did not care to become a casualty of rival American forces again, especially when fascism was the real enemy we should all be battling.

I sighed. There had to be a better explanation. And in twelve hours or less, I was counting on Liberty to give me one. In the Club's salon, after we'd recovered from our mutual shock, I'd scheduled a manicure appointment with her in the morning.

Rubbing a knot that had formed in my neck, I heard Dante ask whether Agent Connelly had reported in. A male voice crackled through the transmitter on the dash. "Negative, sir."

"When he checks in, tell him to call, immediately. Over." Dante snapped the mike back into its clamp.

"Everything all right?"

"Everything's fine." He shot his cuff and checked the time. "Things would be even better if this traffic would start moving."

Unlike V-V's, Dante's shirtsleeve was not monogrammed. Instead, fuzzy cotton balls clung to the threadbare edge of his cuff. A gold oval disk held the frayed fabric together. I squinted, intrigued by its raised design. I was expecting the FBI seal and was pleasantly surprised to see a musical instrument, carved in relief. A saxophone, to be precise.

"I have to make a stop at the Horseshoe. It's a night spot. There's a group performing tonight. Should be on just about now. They play the new jazz, be-bop. Have you heard it?"

I hadn't. I shook my head and Dante added, "Great. Then you can run in with me. We'll grab a bite after."

My stomach rumbled in protest and I coughed to cover the sound. "Sounds fun."

"What about Mrs. Renner?" Dante asked. "Get a chance to meet her?"

"She was busy with a client. It took some doing, but I got an appointment with her tomorrow afternoon. I'll talk to her then."

Dante looked perplexed. "A hair appointment? Why? What will she do with it?"

I smoothed my shorn locks. "Add some?"

He laughed. That good laugh that came from the heart.

The reflection of lights from an oncoming car illuminated his profile. Besides a good laugh, my FBI boss had a good face. A *great* face. Friendly. Open. Slightly full, not chiseled. And those dreamy dark eyes. Why were men always the ones blessed with such thick lashes? His right eyebrow had a minuscule bald line running through it at an angle, a scar from a cut that had healed, I guessed. My gaze settled on his mouth. That sweet mouth. Soft, perfectly shaped. Michelangelo and his cherubs popped to mind again.

Dante sensed me watching him. He sent me a warm smile. "It's good you'll be talking with Mrs. Renner, but don't let her change your looks. Your hair is already great the way it is."

I was grateful for the Ford's dark interior. My cheeks felt warm. I knew I was blushing.

Around us, the street was alive with cars and people out for a night on the town. Bold neon letters flickered from signs above the restaurants, bars, and supper clubs. I stared, awed by the profusion of lights. These days, homes and businesses were normally only half-lit at night to save energy and to act as a precaution against enemy air raids. These seemed so bright. *Too* bright.

I turned to watch the finely dressed people streaming into the Hotel Gotham, realizing for the first time we were in a Negro neighborhood. I checked the street sign. Maybe safety was a consideration in keeping the streets well-lit. We were in Paradise Valley, an area that had been under siege during the race riots that ripped apart New York, Los Angeles, and Detroit this past summer.

It was said that since Pearl Harbor, more than 300,000 southern whites and blacks had migrated north to find work in war plants. The sudden influx of transitory workers was blamed, in part, for the two-day melee that had engulfed downtown Detroit. Certain other accounts claimed that a fight between a white man and a Negro had touched off the widespread violence. Others blamed the trouble on the Nazis, saying the riots were instigated as part of a scheme to punch a hole in our nation's solidarity.

I looked over at Dante. He seemed relaxed enough. More at ease, in fact, than ever. So what was wrong with me? Why was I spinning my wheels, worrying about the city's use of electricity and fretting about our safety? My boss was taking me to a night spot. I worked hard. I had earned a good time. The occasional night on the town was important for morale, besides.

My wild side stirred. I fluffed my "perfect" hair. Kick up the lights. Why not?

Dante slowed to a crawl, stopping in front of Hattie's Chicken Shack, a half-block up from the Horseshoe Club's entrance. A thick-necked Negro bouncer leaned against the wall near the club's red lacquered door. He wore a mustard-colored sport coat, a shiny bronze tie, and wide-cut slacks breaking against alligator shoes. Dark glasses hid his eyes, and from his relaxed slouch, I thought he might be catching a snooze. The pose was an illusion. We arrived and he slid upright, spreading his feet, blocking our entry.

His chin tucked, he peered over the top of his glasses. "Well whatcha y'know. Special Agent Dante. How's things, my man?" His voice was easy enough, but his eyes were wary.

Dante smiled. "Drop the agent stuff, Prof. No business tonight. We're here for sounds, is all."

The bouncer had the torso of a wrestler. His broad shoulders drooped as the muscles supporting the weight of his arms relaxed. "That right? Okay, whatever you say, my man." The Prof sailed his gaze over me. Above the rim of his dark glasses, his eyes glimmered with guarded amusement.

Many restaurants and clubs had dress codes for women and it would have been safer to wear a dress. But after an afternoon of tea and guarded manners, the thought of donning another frock had seemed unbearable. By way of compromise, for my night on the town I'd selected a pair of loosely draped slacks so full they nearly passed for a long skirt. A satiny jacket and matching silk charmeuse shell in celadon, my favorite color, completed the outfit. In piecing together the ensemble, I'd yet again silently thanked the FBI secretary for her packing skills. Now I wondered if the choice had been so wise. Were we about to be turned away because of my slacks?

"Brought a friend, Prof," Dante said, interrupting his scrutiny. "Meet Pucci Lewis."

The Prof shoved his glasses up the bridge of his nose and grinned. "Ahl-right, Miss Pucci," he said, stepping aside. "Go on in. Have yourselves a time."

He opened the door, a blast of discordant music testing the strength of our eardrums as we ducked inside.

Chapter Eight

The Horseshoe's interior was cramped and dimly lit and thick with smoke. Round tables tightly packed with seated patrons formed a random pattern across a wood plank floor strewn with sawdust. Mixed in with the pungent smells of smoldering cigars and cigarettes were the yeasty smells of spilled whiskey and beer.

We pushed through the crowd, my trusty nostrils picking up a spritz or two of cheap perfume along the way. At last we arrived at a long bar with a brass railing. Across the room, an ensemble of musicians in rumpled, gangster-style, pin-striped suits performed on a small stage. The trumpet player, a short man with soft features and cheeks that ballooned when he played, began a serpentine performance of flaring solos. I gawked, mesmerized by the irregular stop-and-start flights of invention. Dante gestured to a vacant stool. Still absorbed in the irregular sounds, moving at a whirlwind pace, I hoisted myself up backwards onto the seat while my neighbor, an elderly Negro, hitched his stool sideways, creating a slot between us. Dante eased into the space and the two men greeted one another with mumbled, "Hey, how ya doins," and a few other pleasantries, suggesting they knew one another.

The older man had a wide nose, close-cropped, fuzzy salt-and-pepper hair, and a white stubble beard that stood out like spilled sugar against his dark, mahogany skin. He slipped his elbows onto the bar's railing, resting with his back propped against it and keeping his head half-turned, facing Dante, as they spoke.

Dante noticed my interest in his friend and introduced us over the driving sounds. "Leo meet Pucci. Pucci, Leo."

Connelly and Dante had discussed a "Leo" back at FBI headquarters. This must be him.

Leo's wiry hair glistened with pomade. He grinned, showing large white teeth, and pointed to his shiny coif. "Your 'do,' girl. It's go-ood, know what I mean? You got inventee goin' and that be go-ood."

He thought my haircut was original, I guessed. I took it as the compliment I thought it was meant to be and thanked him.

A bartender with a missing front tooth ambled over. Dante ordered a Vernor's ginger ale. On-duty FBI agents did not drink alcohol, but as an independent who had spent her afternoon sipping tea from a porcelain cup, I figured I deserved something with a kick. "Tanqueray martini, up, extra olive."

The olives were sustenance. I munched on them, then sipped my drink before turning to face the band again. On stage, the musicians were awash in the muted blue light projecting from colored spots on the ceiling. Three performers wailed on bass, alto sax, and trumpet while the fourth, hunched over a piano, raced his fingers over its keys. Dante had been right. Be-bop was like nothing I had heard before. The harmonies, melodies, and rhythms, all playing off one another, created an innovative, energizing resonance. Before I knew it, be-bop was inside me. My entire body swayed with the beat and my foot, resting on the base of my stool, tapped the metal rim.

Dante and I were wedged together. So closely that we moved from side to side, like a couple dancing. After a while, my partner added a subtle bouncing movement to our synchronized performance. I glanced down. Special Agent Dante was shuffling his feet, moving them in restrained, semi-tap steps. My gaze returned to his face. Lost in the moment, his eyes were closed, his thick lashes hovering dreamily over his slightly full cheeks.

Sensing my stare, he opened his eyelids lazily and smiled. Then, as if returning from wherever it was that he had been, he stiffened, suddenly self-conscious.

He had shown me an unexpected side. And I loved it. I smiled warmly, hoping to convey my unspoken approval.

"You're supposed to be watching the band," he whispered, his breath tickling my ear.

My hand was at my side. He reached for it, squeezing it in what I thought was a friendly gesture. But then he didn't let go. I felt his fingers thread through mine. Our palms touched and I sensed the heat of his flesh. I looked up and caught his questioning glance. Rather than object, I smiled, tightening my grip.

Our hands linked between us, we turned our attention back to the stage. Moments later, the musicians finished their set and Dante released my hand so we could join the rip-roaring round of applause that continued until the band left the stage to take a break.

The three of us, Dante, Leo, and I, swiveled to face the bar. I nibbled nuts from a dish, sipping the last of my martini, while the two men spoke to one another in low tones.

"What's goin' down here tonight, Pops?" Dante asked.

"Place is movin', you know, you know what I mean? Won't stop, gonna keep swingin' all night long. You know what that means, you know. We'll get a whole mix here, comin' and goin', all the dolls, all the gamblers and all the pimps. And that means likely we're gonna get trouble goin' here, too, you see. So I gotta watch the joint, watch the cats, watch what's goin' down. The gal you been wantin' to know about, havin' the bash few years back, she wasn't watchin' the comin's and goin's, is all. Look what happened. Bad rap."

I leaned in closer to Dante. Was Leo on drugs? Was he talking in code?

Dante's practiced eye had been scrutinizing the room while he was listening to Leo. He whispered something to which Leo replied, "Uh-huh, want me seein' red now is what you want. I'm seein' another bad rap comin', you know what I mean, you know?" Dante grunted and reached inside his suit. "Here you go, Pops. It's all set. Let's talk tomorrow."

Anyone else at the bar would have missed it, but alerted by their cryptic exchange, I caught the slight movement as Dante removed an envelope from his pocket. Leo palmed it.

The bar area was bathed in a red glow. Leo's unbuttoned sport coat hung loosely around him. The jacket was black but the fabric had a sheen. It shimmered, reflecting a glint of crimson as he pocketed what Dante had slipped him.

Dante gave Leo's shoulder a gentle squeeze, then cupped his hand lightly around my elbow. "Time to go," he whispered, his lips brushing my ear.

At the warmth of his breath, I felt a rush of tiny shivers. I slipped off my stool, conscious of feeling pleasantly weak, especially in the knees.

Prof the Bouncer was holding up the wall beside the door as we left. We exchanged nods and walked back to the car in silence. The night air was cool and with a light tug of my elbow, Dante pulled me close. I smiled up at him without objecting.

"Have the impression you would have liked to stay longer," I said. "For the music? For passing more envelopes?"

His eyebrows angled up and he grinned. "You don't miss much, do you?"

The windshield had fogged over. He flipped the defroster to full blast and we remained at the curb for a moment, waiting for it to clear.

"They seemed to know you pretty well in there," I prompted again. "Especially Leo. You called him Pops."

A small, nostalgic smile crossed his lips. "Leo and I go way back. He knew my dad. He also helps out sometimes in this part of town. We're not just rounding up enemy aliens these days, you know. Federal bank robberies, kidnappings, extortions, we handle all those investigations. We're also tracking down draft dodgers."

Was he playing the artful dodger himself? I tried a different tack. "So Leo's an informant?"

He shrugged. "Like I said, he helps us out. He's also part owner of the club."

Dante nosed out into the flow of traffic. "Enough about work. We were going to forget all that for a while, remember?" He glanced over. "What about the music? Did you like it?"

"Loved it. Thanks for taking me."

"I have some 78s I think you'd dig, too. Billie Holiday, know her?"

Billie Workaday, the other Billie I'd recently met in jail, flashed to mind. But I sensed where the G-man might be heading. My eyes met his. "Doesn't everyone? She's one of my favorites."

Dante's loosely noosed tie had slipped sideways. He centered it. "Say, I have an idea. How about having dinner at my apartment? Mrs. S brought me some manicotti last night, her specialty. What do you say?"

Dinner at his place was a bold move considering the brief time we'd known one another. If I agreed, would he think I was fast? And what about my professional status? Would it suffer? "Mrs. S?" I asked, buying time.

"Mrs. Sarvello. She's my landlady, a family friend. Don't worry," he chuckled. "Mrs. S lives below me and likes to amuse herself by monitoring what goes on upstairs. Besides, there's Connelly's call. It's important. You should be there, too. How about it?"

For a moment, I'd thought his reason for inviting me to his apartment involved seduction. Now he had flipped the work light back on. I smiled. Who cared? Work or romance, I was looking forward to some alone time with him. "Of course, let's do it. Sounds nice."

The traffic unsnarled. Dante gunned it. The chain, looped around the mirror, swayed madly. I reached for the medals and caught them.

"This horseshoe charm, is it special?" I asked, culling out the smaller one.

"My dad's. His legacy. Has to do with being a fan of the racetrack."

"Ah, I remember," I said, envisioning the framed photograph I'd seen on my recent visit to his office. "Your dad was in that picture of your graduation from the academy."

"No, that's my stepdad. My real father, owner of that medallion, died when I was twelve."

"I'm sorry."

He looked over, his eyes dark and soulful. "I'm sorry for you, too. You lost your mother when you were just ten."

I was stunned into silence.

I had begun processing how Dante knew about the tragedy—my dossier, of course—when in my mind's eye the horrifying scene flashed before me: Mother in the choir loft, her back to me, directing the singers, while several pews over in the church nave below, I sat with my journal, filling its pages with a tall tale lifted from the scene depicted in a nearby stained glass window. Something, perhaps the snap of the railing Mother had been leaning against, caused me to turn and look up. What I saw, no child—*no one*—should ever see. Arms flailing, screaming, she plunged backwards through the void until, with two unforgettable thunderous thwacks, her body cracked against the unforgiving curves and edges of the wooden pews, hemorrhaging and breaking, irreparably.

Pure quiet. Then screams. Sobs. Pounding footsteps.

I took a breath, pushed down the images. "The tear in your heart never mends, does it?"

Dante smiled sadly. "I've been blessed, though, with my stepdad," he said softly. "He's laid down some solid footprints for me to follow. And he's good to Mom."

We were motoring through a commercial section along Gratiot Avenue. Dante's real father, Aldo, the son of Italian immigrants, had been a waiter at a number of neighborhood restaurants in the area and Dante pointed out a few of them. We covered several more blocks of low-rise brick and cement buildings as he continued talking about the past.

At the heart of the account was Aldo's weakness for gambling. He liked to wager his earnings at the track, and the battle over his losses was a constant between Dante's parents. He rubbed the small scar on his eyebrow and confessed that during one heated argument, when Dante had tried to prevent his dad from leaving home, the proceeds of his cashed paycheck on him, his dad had shoved him away. Dante had fallen, his forehead splitting against the radiator.

Besides creating a strain on his family life, Aldo's habit led him to rack up a huge debt with the Purple Gang, the gangsters who had operated in Detroit during Prohibition. Kiki Barclay-Bly and her association with the Purples had been a misstep that changed her life forever. I sensed Aldo had suffered a similar fate and that I was about to hear the high point of the story when Dante swung the Ford down a street lined with towering elms. Tall, two-story frame houses stood behind tidy square lawns set back from the street. Dante's candor was flattering, and I had been listening, enraptured. I was crushed when he pulled over, shut off the engine, and fell into silence.

I regarded the house we had stopped in front of. An amber glow behind shades covering high narrow windows beckoned invitingly.

I turned and met Dante's tender gaze. "Let's go inside," he said, finally.

Chapter Nine

To avoid disturbing his landlady, Dante and I crept up the driveway, eventually reaching the back of the house where an exterior staircase rose to the second floor.

In front, the windows had glowed warmly with interior light, but in back it was completely dark except for one dimly lit shade behind the stairs. The wooden steps, a little rickety, creaked under our feet. A shadow moved behind the shade. Grabbing Dante's arm, I gestured to it. We stared as an elongated pyramid of light slowly revealed itself along one edge.

Mrs. Sarvello did not show herself, but she was there. Like a couple of teens late for curfew, we scurried upstairs and burst through the door at the top.

Dante flipped a switch. "Told you she kept an eye on me." He grinned.

I laughed softly. "The moving shade, the sliver of light…not very subtle, is she?"

We had entered through the kitchen. Dante removed an oblong Pyrex dish from the icebox. "Manicotti," he announced, stripping off the foil cover, setting the dish on the counter. Two rows of ricotta-stuffed pasta, packed tighter than a school of herrings in heat, were wedged inside the dish.

Dante looked at me. "You okay?"

I was, but I wasn't. We were alone in his apartment. He was preparing a late-night meal. We would be spending the next couple of hours eating and talking. I was nervous. I was also excited.

"Um-m, I'm fine. Thanks." I smiled and drifted over to the counter opposite him. Another of Mrs. Sarvello's creations, a layered chocolate-iced cake, beckoned from under a glass cover. There was a note tucked under the cover's edge. *Heard the tapping last night. Thought extra cheer was in order. Fondly, Mrs. S.* "Did you see this?" I asked.

The oven door closed with a clunk. Dante walked over. He patted his stomach. "Dessert, too. When will she stop?" He noticed the note, scanned it, and stuck it behind a toaster fitted with a checkered cover. "C'mon, I'll show you around."

The comfortably cluttered living room reminded me of my Gran Skjold's. An overstuffed, moss-green sofa was pushed against a wall. Side tables, holding fringe-shaded lamps, flanked its sides. An inviting leather club chair with a footstool was angled nearby, a floor lamp with a graceful shade of mauve silk next to it. Light hardwood covered the floor. I was certain the braided rugs and lace curtains were Mrs. Sarvello's even before Dante, a little sheepishly, confided she'd taken over the decorating.

A small wooden dining table with two chairs filled the nook to our right. Dante went to a cabinet and swept out a lace tablecloth. Shaking it once, hard, he let it billow and drop, like a parachute, over the table. Almost before it had touched down, cloth napkins, silver candleholders, and white candles were arranged on top.

"Ooops," he said, crossing the room. "Music."

A wood-grained cabinet housed a Philco floor-radio and a hidden interior phonograph compartment. An adjacent wall unit held Dante's album collection. While he flipped through slim boxes containing the albums, I drifted to a cluster of silver-framed photographs on one of the tables beside the sofa.

A headshot of an attractive woman with dark hair, sparkling eyes, and a beautiful mouth caught my eye first. The woman's mouth, though slightly fuller, was so much like Dante's I assumed she must be his mother. Next, I reached for a framed crayon drawing, lifting it to get a closer look. In the sketch, three stick-figures danced upon a stage. The smallest shape was a girl with a mane of long black curls. She wore a triangular-shaped yellow skirt and danced between two men in straight-legged, purple pants. The men both had dark curls, like the little girl's, but theirs were close-cropped. The drawing was primitive, but from their position and the oversized shoes the threesome appeared to be tap-dancing.

In a sidelong glance, I saw Dante open the tilt-front panel of the cabinet. He placed a 78 on the turntable and gingerly lowered the needle. A haunting melody filled the room. Orchestra sounds quickly faded to background as a sultry woman's voice joined in with lyrics. The music, a sharp change from what we'd heard at the Horseshoe Club, was mellow and romantic.

I looked up at him with a smile. "Who did this?"

"Sophie. My half-sister. She's a teen now. Lives just down the block from here with Mom and her dad, my stepdad, Jimmy Galvin."

Dante took the drawing. Angling it to catch the light, he dabbed a small speck of dust from the glass. "She was just six when she drew this."

My FBI boss was a true family man. And how endearing that he cared so deeply for his little sister. "That's you with her, right? Who's the other figure? Why are you all dancing?"

He smiled. "That's Leo."

"Really?"

"Uh-huh. Leo was a big part of my childhood. He and my father met at Ford Motor Company during one of Dad's many short-lived attempts at making an honest buck. Wasn't long, though, before the two of them were boozing together, gambling together, kissing away a lot of money they didn't have together."

He placed Sophie's sketch on the crowded table and picked up the framed snapshot next to it. "Leo and his bride came all the way from Mississippi to find work in the plants. Housing was scarce. Dad pitched in, helped them build this, shortly after they arrived."

He handed me the photo. The image was faded and cracked, but it was of two men, one Negro, one white. Dante's natural father, Aldo, had wavy dark hair and thick-lashed eyes, like his son. Next to him, I recognized a more youthful Leo. The bond between the two was obvious. They stood before a shed-like shelter resembling a large chicken coop, their arms linked at the elbows, their faces relaxed and smiling. The metal end of a hammer protruded from Leo's pocket; Aldo's free hand held a leveling tool.

"In the car you said your father got mixed up with the Purples. And Leo? Did he get sucked in, too?"

"No. That was the sad thing. Leo didn't know Dad had taken that turn until one night he got word of a party at Kiki Barclay-Bly's apartment. Hearing Dad was there, Leo followed. Saw him talking with a thug. Found out he was a Purple." Dante took the frame from me and returned it to the table. "Actually, the Purple was doing all the talking. Calling in Dad's debt. Next morning, Dad was found floating in the Detroit river. Took a bullet through the head."

"I'm so sorry," I whispered. Goose bumps rose across my shoulders. I hesitated, but had to ask. "And Kiki? You suspect she was criminally involved with the Purples? With your Dad's death?"

His hand was still on the photo of the two men. Sighing softly, he released it. "I didn't know Dad and Leo had been to her place the night of his murder until I pulled Barclay-Bly's file. I cornered Leo. He told me about Dad's connection to the Purples." Dante smoothed his scarred brow with a fingertip. "I was getting stitches, he was bargaining with thugs. Leo also claimed Barclay-Bly didn't know the gangsters were at her party that night. He stuck to the story even after I showed him the file photo of her with the two Purples."

A segment of the jumbled talk between Leo and Dante at the Horseshoe Bar suddenly made sense. "In the bar, Leo referred to the gal havin' the party a few years back. He said she wasn't watching the comings and goings. He meant the Purples crashed her party, uninvited, right?"

Dante shrugged. "He claims he got separated from my dad. He was trying to find him again when he bumped into Kiki. She was concerned, wanted to help. All walks of people had been dropping in all night long. They covered the entire apartment together, questioning guests. Leo says she barely knew anyone by name. Absolutely had no inkling about the Purples."

I read Dante's face. "You think Leo missed something. What?"

"Call it a hunch. Back then she was partying with Purples, and now, more recently, she was caught rubbing elbows with another known criminal, the Countess. Seems incongruous with her current pose as the innocent society matron, doesn't it?"

"Um-m," I said vaguely. "But you've drawn Leo into the case. Why?"

Dante lifted an eyebrow. "What makes you think he's involved?"

"The envelope, the banter at the bar…"

He rubbed the back of his neck. "For now, anything more about Leo's role in all of this is probably best left unsaid."

I looked at Sophie's drawing. "Including the secret of why he's in the picture, dancing with you and your sister?"

Dante laughed. "He teaches tap."

"Leo was a tap-dance teacher?"

"Is. He taught tap in the South before he came to Detroit. Dad's death hit him hard. He lost a best friend. Felt responsible for not keeping closer tabs, especially that last night at Kiki's. Afterwards, he started watching over Mom and me. Eventually they became friends. He got straight because of Dad's death. Started a neighborhood dance studio for kids and teens. Wanted to do some good." Dante chuckled unexpectedly.

"What's so funny?"

"Years later, Mom signed Sophie up for classes. But the distance and the neighborhood posed a problem. She needed someone to go with her."

I smiled at the drawing. "And you got elected. You took lessons, too?"

He found a smudge mark on the table and rubbed it with his finger as if trying to lift it out. "I liked it. Plus, if you could have seen Sophie's face when she saw me dancing, and the fun we all had..." He paused, his expression softening as if he could still picture her delighting in his performance.

His love for his sister was endearing. I touched his hand. A jolt of energy passed between us and a surge of something equally powerful that could burn me.

Dante expelled a deep sigh and the next thing I knew, I was in his arms. A pounding in my ears blocked out all distractions and heightened the sensation of his lips, those beautiful Michelangelo lips, caressing my ear.

A moan, more of a groan, invaded. "Damn!" A timer Dante had set in the kitchen was buzzing loudly. He disappeared into the kitchen. The buzzing stopped. I heard the oven door creak open, then snap closed. A delicious tomato-y scent wafted into the living room.

Dante returned and we settled into plump velvety cushions. He switched off the table lamp, leaving the mauve-shaded floor lamp, near the armchair, to cast the only remaining light in the room. Scuff marks on the floorboards near the dining nook that could only have been made by tap shoes caught the mauve glow. Was that what Mrs. Sarvello had meant about the tapping noise last night?

I felt the weight of his arm as it slipped around my shoulders. "Pucci..." he said, nuzzling close.

A raspy little voice inside my brain, the one that liked to offer an opinion at the most inconvenient of times, piped up. *Careful,* it warned in its grating whisper. *Things are moving fast, maybe too fast. You've only known him for a few days. A few hours, actually...*

The pesky voice was right. I wasn't a good judge of men. Two months ago, in Hollywood, on an unofficial mission, after flinging myself at Mr. Right, who later turned out to be a psychotic killer, definitely Mr. Wrong, I had vowed to be more cautious in the future. I turned, accepting Dante's kiss with my cheek.

A second internal voice, the less conservative one I preferred, chided me. *This man is no maniac like the one you went gaga over in Hollywood,* it said melodiously, its tone sweet and caring. *He's an FBI agent, a good Catholic, a good son, a good big brother, a good neighbor.*

I faced Dante. Our lips touched and I felt a pleasant warmth spread through me. A telephone jangled in the kitchen. Sensing a sigh warm my neck, I was painfully aware that the feathery stream of air had not been intended to stimulate me.

Dante said, "I have to get it."

Moments later, he was back. The caller had been Agent Connelly. Mrs. Blount, the wife of the murder victim, had been found. Alive.

"We've had someone watching her place here in the city," Dante explained, his voice both relieved and excited. "She's been at her sister's farm. Just returned home about an hour ago and Connelly went there. She hadn't heard about her husband's death, so it was up to him to tell her. She fell to pieces."

"She was at her sister's place all this time? Isn't that strange?"

Dante was suddenly keeping a more professional distance. He rearranged himself on the spongy cushions. "Blount was murdered around six a.m. Earlier, around five, a woman telephoned, identifying herself as her sister's neighbor. The sister wanted Mrs. Blount to know that their mother, who lives with the sister, had suffered a stroke. She was needed directly.

"Mrs. Blount tried telephoning her sister to confirm the news, but couldn't get through. So she hopped in the car and raced to the sister's home in the country. To find that her mother was not ill after all. Greatly relieved, she tried to crack the mystery of the misleading call. She drove to the neighbors but they were clueless."

"Of course. It wasn't a neighbor who called. It was someone involved in the spy ring."

"Possibly."

"It's also possible Mrs. Blount fabricated the cry for help."

Dante lifted a shoulder in a half-shrug. "Not likely. She was en route to her sister's at the time of the murder. It was long drive and with the fuel shortages, she decided to prolong the visit, stay all night. Our men are checking her alibi, of course, but it appears solid."

"You said she didn't know her husband was dead. That's a bit odd, isn't it? Why didn't she try calling him before rushing off?"

"She did. But her husband was out on rounds."

"Then why not ring him again, from her sister's? Especially after deciding to stay over?"

"The phones were out, remember?" Dante wedged a finger inside his collar and scratched his neck. "Besides, she'd left him a note."

I shot him a skeptical glance.

"It's true. Connelly found it on the floor, under the stove. Our boys missed it earlier." Dante read the disbelief on my face. "I know it seems incredible. And there's no good excuse. But Mrs. Blount says she left a pen on top of the note. They have a cat. She thinks he may have batted at the pen, knocking it, and the note, to the floor."

I snorted. I couldn't help it. Predictably, Dante smiled.

Then he was serious again. "The theory's as good as any we have so far. Paper had to have slipped beneath there, somehow."

"But why didn't your men trace her to the sister's place right away?"

Dante shifted his weight. "Mrs. Blount's sister is married, has a different last name. By the time we tracked her, Mrs. Blount was already driving back to town."

It was a little unsettling being privy to the inadequacies of the agency guarding our country's internal security. I took a deep breath. "I see. Then what?"

"Connelly brought Mrs. Blount to the morgue to ID the corpse and asked her to examine the, uh, item that had been in her husband's hand. She recognized the monogram. Embroiders it on all of her undergarments, she said."

"And?"

"They were hers. Fortunately the blood was not. It was animal blood."

I frowned. "What about the message, 'bye baby'? What was that all about?"

"We can't be sure, of course, but our working theory is that someone planted the undergarment in his lunch box so he'd know his wife and unborn child were easy prey."

"That's awful. Why would the killer do something like that when he was planning on stabbing him the next instant anyway? Unless…" I squirmed. "Unless the assassin wanted some kind of sick thrill." I shivered, not wanting to believe that what I'd just said might actually be the case.

"We won't know until we have the killer in custody." Dante rubbed the side of his face. "If then."

"So what's next?"

"Renner's spy gig at Willow Run has run its course. We're going to reel him in, put him in the hot seat for a while. Hopefully, get him to talk."

"But what about getting a lead on his handler and any other rogue agents out there?"

"We don't really have a choice. Without Blount, we've lost our ability to predict what they might be plotting next. The message on the lingerie, Mrs. Blount being tricked into going to her sister's—more and more, the signs suggest we're dealing with a loose cannon. They're also reminders that until we catch this bunch, innocent people are at risk. We need to make a move and you can help us."

"How?"

"We're organizing a surreptitious entry. We want to confirm Renner's copy of the confidential plans for the new bombing device is still locked inside his safe."

I struggled to contain my excitement. "Oh?"

"Let's go into the kitchen. I'll brief you in there."

I trailed him into the warm, brightly lit room. At the counter near the stove, he faced me. "I have to go back to the office. Connelly's taken Mrs. Blount there and I need to question her before he escorts her home. How about taking some of this back to the Club?" He lifted the foil cover off the bubbling casserole.

My stomach growled noisily, objecting to another delay. But my feelings were in worse shape. The call from Connelly had interrupted our intimacy, yet Dante did not seem the least bit bothered. I crossed my arms over my midriff, biting back a snarl. "Great."

I watched while he began transferring pasta tubes, oozing with cheese and sauce, to a smaller dish. Shoving thoughts of romance aside, I reminded him of the caper. "You were about to explain my role on the break-in team."

Dante smiled as though amused by the notion. "You won't be taking part in the actual break-in. We need you to gather some intelligence on the layout of Renner's office, especially the location of his safe."

"You don't know where his safe is?"

"It's secret. Part of the overall plant protection system. But if we can pinpoint its location before we go in, it'll save precious seconds once we're inside."

I recalled what he'd said earlier about the company's policy giving managers free rein in designing a security system for their private domain. "But *someone* knows where it is, how to open it, right?"

"Sure. There's a complex arrangement for emergencies, a coded formula that can bypass any of the combinations. But accessing it would require involving executives we'd rather not approach. At least not until we've identified the other insider. Or, insiders."

Basically, I would be doing a site-check in broad daylight during normal business hours. "So what's my modus operandi?" I asked dully, not bothering to hide my disappointment over the powder puff assignment.

"We've made an appointment for you to meet with Renner's secretary, Mrs. Kovacizki. She'll believe you're a journalist there to lay the groundwork for a later interview with a draftswoman in their department."

"That's it?"

"It's a long shot, but while you're there maybe you can convince the secretary to give you the partial combination."

"What do you mean? How?"

"All the executives have an arrangement that allows them to set a partial code which his secretary can complete afterwards. That way, if he leaves some work for her to do in his absence, she's able to access it."

A nasal sound meant to be a laugh escaped. "You must be joking. No secretary worth her salt would give that kind of confidential information to a complete stranger. A journalist at that!"

Dante smiled. "Why not? Overcoming long odds is your specialty, right?"

When he put it that way, I had to smile back. "And this is on for tomorrow?"

Dante snapped a lid on the small container holding my takeout meal. He nodded. "We've got to move fast."

Dante reviewed additional matters important to my meeting with Renner's secretary on the ride back to the Cosmos Club. I was pleased with his choice of interviewees within the tool design department. Her profile was a good match to my journalist cover; even in these times a draftswoman was a rare commodity. Also, my cover would allow me to use the fake press credentials and phony newspaper I'd be using when I interviewed the Countess as the second part of my assignment, later the same day.

At the Club, parked beneath the blue awning, Dante lightly brushed my cheek. "You be careful," he said, his voice a little husky. "And sorry about tonight. Maybe you'll let me make it up to you tomorrow?"

His touch stirred something inside me. The apology may have had an effect as well.

"Don't worry about me," I said with a wobbly grin. "And, yes, tomorrow sounds swell."

He turned to grab the door handle on his side of the car but I was on the sidewalk, waving good-bye before he could get out and do the gentlemanly thing.

Chapter Ten

I stood beneath the Cosmos Club's canopy, pressing the buzzer. Eventually, a craggy-faced string bean in house uniform cracked the door and peered out with a rheumy eye.

"Guest of the VanderKloots," I said.

"A moment," said the doorman.

A multi-tiered crystal chandelier loomed high above in the alcove behind him, casting his face in shadows and accentuating his deeply lined features. He consulted a roster he had carried with him to the door and the expression lines deepened. At last, I was invited in.

He gawked at the container in my hands.

"Dinner," I explained, clutching the dish close, afraid he might confiscate it.

The man had a slight frame and was about my height. He stood in the foyer, the gold-encrusted crest on his burgundy jacket glittering in the chandelier's light. His thin, dark hair was interspersed with broad streaks of white. He turned with an exaggerated sniff, presenting an unkempt mat of streaky hair curling in random wisps in back. "Follow me."

I stalked his slow steps around an antique table graced by an enormous floral arrangement. His shuffling gait was so plodding that when I spied a loose thread dangling from his cuff, I imagined it might also be the remnant of a cobweb he'd untangled himself from before answering my buzz.

The watchman glanced back over his shoulder. "You may not use the elevator. The operator is off-duty and while I am authorized to use it under certain conditions, the noise at this late hour, I fear, would create too great a stir."

I did not say so, but "a stir" was exactly what the place needed. It was like a morgue, the funereal quiet all the more oppressive after a stimulating evening spent at the lively Horseshoe Club, followed by an interlude of romantic music and the promise of seduction at Dante's place.

With a stiff stroke of a gloved hand, the doorman invited me to mount the stairs, letting me know with his silent gesture that the chore of ushering me to my room went beyond his realm of duties.

A staggered display of gold-leaf framed portraits of the Club's past presidents garnished the wall beside the stairs, elegantly attired women with identifying brass name plates beneath. *Mrs. Horace Peabody, Mrs. Charles F. F. Campbell, Mrs. Archibald McKay, Mrs. Charles Horton.* What would happen if Kiki reached her goal and became the Club's newest president, I wondered. Her likeness would be added to the collection, but what about the splinter of brass? *Mrs. Anastase Andreyevich Volodymyr Vivikovsky* could never be squeezed onto it. What would they do? Get a bigger plaque? Etch with smaller lettering? Use her maiden name as Kiki preferred anyhow? I smiled. Each choice broke with the old order and "might cause a stir."

My amusement gave way as I thought of Kiki's aims. For someone who once embraced controversial ideas and radical views and was a flapper who had liked her bathtub gin, becoming a player in the politics of a private women's club seemed dull in comparison.

On the second level, I mounted a narrow, less grand set of stairs, reversing my lofty position and reminding myself that no one had appointed me judge of what was, or was not, meaningful work. Kiki found satisfaction in being a club mucky muck. So what? Hadn't the lieutenant at my OSS indoctrination claimed that socialites made the best women leaders? "Women from the upper strata are accustomed to managing large social gatherings and benefits," he'd said, tagging on another bit of candor. "Women who don't care about money are generally surer of themselves."

At the third floor, I turned left. My room was at the far end. The dish in my hand was still warm. Barely. I beat feet down the dimly lit hall.

The simply furnished VanderKloot suite was a welcome oasis amid the ornate splendor of the Club's vast public rooms. I flicked on the overhead light. Twin beds covered in white chenille spreads were separated by a small table supporting a reading lamp with dual fixtures. Opposite the beds, a writing desk and a tufted club chair with a matching footstool filled a small alcove. A massive armoire was positioned between two narrow windows.

While jotting my name into her appointment book, Liberty had nonchalantly asked, "And how's the lighting in your room?"

I had gawked at her, wondering what she was talking about, then realized she was signaling me to check my suite's ceiling fixture. Hiding messages there was a technique we'd learned in training.

At the room's center, a flat piece of frosted glass, shaped like a seashell, covered four bulbs. I craned my neck, squinting into the pool of light, at last spotting a small gray area in one of the flutes. Dragging a chair over, I climbed onto the seat and reached inside. Gently, I probed the flute, at last grasping a folded piece of paper. It was a note from Liberty. *I'll be in the library at eleven p.m.*, the message said. *Meet me there, if you can.*

Excitement flooded me. *If I can?* Apart from those clumsy moments in the beauty parlor this afternoon, I hadn't seen my friend for nearly a month. I climbed down and checked the bedside clock. Relieved to discover I had time to eat something before I would have to leave, I returned to the desk where I had left my meal and pulled the fork Dante had thoughtfully lent me from my pocket. I took a bite. I wasn't sure if it was Mrs.

Sarvello's superior talent or my ravenous hunger, but I thought I had never tasted anything so heavenly. Forkful after forkful of ricotta-filled pasta went down while I thought about the friendship Liberty and I had developed during training. It was strange to think that when we first met, I would never have believed we would be so close.

In the days before that first encounter, just eight weeks ago, I had been fully engaged in my normal duty, ferrying P38s from left coast to right. Then, August 5th, the unexpected cable: *Report to the OSS Wash.—George C. Marshall, Chief of Staff.*

My spirits had soared, then plummeted. OSS agents gather intelligence and carry out irregular warfare. Nice work if you can get it, but the work goes on behind enemy lines. My duty bound me to the home front. Had someone somewhere missed the obvious, I'd wondered? Still, I had my orders.

Arriving in Washington, I reported to Q building, a rambling, haphazardly designed temporary office complex, headquarters for OSS personnel. In Room 2205, I was met by a shiny-faced lieutenant with big spectacles and pale, plastered-down hair. He handed me a ream of registration forms, grinning as I winced.

I flipped the pages. It was official! I was being elevated to another level of service. I filled in the particulars, checked customary boxes, handed the documents back.

"Congratulations. Glad to have you with us, Lewis," the lieutenant mumbled, giving the paperwork a perfunctory look. "Wondering why you're here?"

I'd been too nervous to ask. "Yes, sir."

"We need a variety of operatives, male and female, at the ready, in different places, at all times. This is where we prepare them. The bulk of our trainees are men, but a small percentage is women. Most of our gals will be sent overseas. Others, like you, will remain here." He described the selection process, including their early reliance on the Social Register as a recruiting source, adding, "The work requires knowledge of a European language and familiarity with the terrain in France where many of them once vacationed."

I squirmed in my seat. "And my qualifications, sir?"

The lieutenant's smile turned benevolent. "Don't worry, Lewis, you have the stuff. You're a WASP. You've got the kind of mobility needed for covering fast-breaking situations, all across the continent. And you understand danger. There's danger in flying planes. There's a different sort of danger attached to this."

"This?"

"You've been identified as a candidate for certain operations, yet to be determined. You're here for an intensive three weeks of training. Normally, we'd keep you for several months. But you have an obligation to the WASP. It's a unique situation and we don't want to pigeonhole you too tightly. So, while you're here, suffice it to say, you'll be part of MO."

"MO?"

"Morale Operations. Black psychological warfare, the art of influencing enemy thinking by means of subtle propaganda. The deliberate use of rumor, lies, and deception to generate confusion and defeatism among the enemy. You know..." The lieutenant let his sentence drift, suggesting he had dished up enough clues already.

But he hadn't. I knew about the overt or "white" propaganda produced by the Office of War Information, but psychological warfare's shadow side was uncharted territory for me.

OWI was the State Department's non-military propaganda arm established to help interpret the war for the average citizenry and make it part of everyday life. Carefully contrived messages distributed to print and broadcast media representatives helped get the job done. OWI also had delegates posted in Hollywood to "coach" movie makers on how best to advance the war effort and keep the public informed on vital issues. It was brainwashing, true, but OWI was committed to a strategy that neither hid sources nor sought to deceive its audiences with false news. Was MO's objective, then, just the opposite?

The lieutenant read my confusion. "Relax, Lewis. You're in the hands of experts. Everything will be revealed soon enough."

The blinds covering the window beside us had been left open. He leaned forward. A beam of sunlight threw its force against the sheen of his skin, coating it like veneer, making his features look suddenly false. "Trust me," he added. "Three weeks from now you'll know everything you need to know about OSS and MO."

I nodded and smiled, but my expression must have looked as chiseled-on as his. Lie? Deliberately deceive someone? Did he know what they were up against? What kind of rigid upbringing they would be trying to break?

I took a breath, crossed my fingers, and prayed for good instructors.

A dreamboat with baby blues and wavy black hair was summoned to escort me to the next phase of induction. He ushered me down long corridors lined with offices identified only by numbers. Through a few open doors I saw rooms decorated with large pink and purple maps of Europe and Asia, marked with pins. On the basement level, my attendant pushed me through a doorway. Clusters of men milled about.

A bruiser of a sergeant with a gourd-shaped face stood behind a scarred wooden counter. The telephone rang. He ignored me and grabbed the receiver. While he muttered something to someone on the other end, I added my name to the roster, found a chair near the door, and sat down, thinking I would reflect a bit. Not that my mind was capable of much calm musing. It raced.

The lieutenant seemed to think I had the right stuff, but what would happen if he knew the truth? That beneath all the bravura lurked a square, small-town Midwesterner. A PK, Pastor's Kid, who congenitally believed in the essential goodness of human nature; who had been raised to believe that if you tell a lie you'll be struck by lightning; and who, as a result, was forevermore doomed to wed deception with electrocution. Which brought up my straight-and-narrow father. His little lamb was about to be baptized into the black arts of lying and subterfuge. Wouldn't he be shocked to know?

I was imagining his expression, feeling a perverse sort of joy, when a bark from the sergeant interrupted. "Come back here!" he hollered to a woman venturing into the hallway.

The corridor splintered off to my left. There was a water fountain halfway down. I assumed that was where the woman, a strawberry blonde with an elfin face, an elegant neck and a trim but curvy figure, had been heading. She never got a chance to explain.

"No one, ab-so-lutely no one, moves around Q without one of two things, an OSS pass or an escort," the sergeant growled. "Now sit down. Wait your turn."

I expected the strawberry-blonde to sink obediently into the nearest vacant chair. I scooted over to give her room near me. But she was no withering violet. The door beside me opened and the dreamboat who only moments ago had squired me down from registration entered. She intercepted him directly.

"You're an escort, right?" The admiring tone in her voice suggested he might also be Eisenhower's younger brother.

"Yes, ma'am."

She slipped a finger into the neckline of her boat-neck blouse and began tracing its curve. "Then how about taking me down the hall for a drink?" she purred, gazing up at him with a smile as silky as her shirt.

Adonis gulped. "W-w-well sure, why not?"

The twosome turned and strolled toward the fountain. Behind the desk, the sergeant, his narrow brow furrowed, his bulbous cheeks shifting side to side, appraised the roster, acting oblivious to having been outmaneuvered. But I knew better. While the strawberry-blonde had been engaging the escort, he nailed her with a glare that had it been a spear would have impaled her.

Our fingerprints would be taken in another room, deeper in the bowels of Q. Adonis began herding our group, twenty men, two women, down another corridor; the strawberry-blonde lost no time in attaching herself to him. I fell in behind the couple.

"This is such a maze," she said in a breathy voice, speaking to our leader. "How do you do it? I mean, find your way around. Is there a map?"

"No, ma'am, it's all up here." Our guide tapped his temple.

"Really?" she gushed. "But the passages all look the same. And it's dark. You must use sensory clues to guide you then. Like that." She cocked her head toward a neighboring door. "That's the Message Center in there, right?" She was referring to the secure area where top secret communiqués were decoded and enciphered.

"Why, yes," our escort marveled. "How did you know?"

What a rube! She *couldn't* know. This was our first foray into these subterranean quarters. She had guessed. What was she up to?

The fingerprinter was a slight man wearing a visor over an otherwise bare scalp. When it was my turn, he took my impressions, nodded, handed me a communal towel.

My name followed the strawberry-blonde's on the roster. "Here," I said, finished with the cloth. "You might want to use this."

She might be all lace and pearls with the fellas, but I put some English on my lob. She caught it with ease of the Girls Professional League's all-star catcher, Bonnie Baker.

A small mirror hung on the wall behind her. She turned and rubbed at the spot. Her discerning eye swept my uniform. I returned the once over. In the past year, I'd grown accustomed to throwing on standard military garb for every occasion. My counterpart, in a knockout blouse and slacks, had put more energy into her appearance.

The fashion plate dropped the soiled rag on the counter and extended her hand. "Hi, I'm Liberty Leach."

"Pucci Lewis." I ignored her hand and eyed her dead-on. "I heard you in the hallway. You deliberately seduced our escort into revealing classified information. What's the big idea?"

She looked startled. Then she laughed. It was a pleasant, tinkling laugh. "I was having a little fun, that's all." She read my expression. "You don't believe me? Look around. What do you see? A bunch of prospective spooks. And why are we here? To learn and practice duplicity. It's the name of the game."

I stared. What had the lieutenant said? Three weeks from now I'd be a pro at using rumors, lies, and deception to gain the advantage? "B-b-but," I began haltingly, "the escort is one of us. What was the point of tricking him into disclosing the location of the Message Center?"

"*Trick* him? Didn't you hear that clacking noise? Teletype machines. And what about that clattering sound, a few paces earlier? A rotary press, you can bet churning out the black pamphlets and leaflets they're so famous—or infamous—for producing here."

Now that she mentioned it, maybe I had heard the sound of a press. I wouldn't have placed it, though, on my own.

I smiled. "Sorry. Guess I got us off on the wrong foot. I have an active imagination. Tends to run amuck at all the wrong times." I glanced around. "Say, what if we've been under surveillance? They'll be on to you—"

"*On to me?* Being sneaky is what it's all about."

"So sneaky you arrived as a student agent, fully trained?"

Another musical laugh. "Now you're trying to flatter me. *Pucci?* Where'd you get a name like that?"

I smothered a sigh and explained.

"Ahhh. Puccini, Pucci," she said. "Got it."

"What about Liberty? That's not exactly a common name either. Sounds patriotic."

Like her outward appearance, Liberty's name evolution was alluring. Her parents had been in China during the last Great War. The conflict had begun winding down when she was born. Consumed with hope for the country's future, the couple decided to name her something symbolic. They chose Liberty, or Liu, a Chinese family name that could also be used as a first name for girls. When she was twelve, her parents decided it was time she experienced life and an education in the States. They moved back to Connecticut where her father still had ties. Soon afterwards, her name was Americanized.

The fingerprinter was at work on yet another pair of hands, giving us the chance to extend our tentative friendship feelers a little farther. Naturally, we both wanted to know what had brought the other to Q. I went first and admitted to being a ferry pilot.

"It's a great job, my dream job," I added, confiding that while no one had actually come right out and said so, I suspected my recruitment had to do with a special stint in Hollywood.

A few months earlier, I had been dispatched there by Miss Cochran to serve as her liaison, overseeing the making of a documentary on our unit. Things became complicated when in the course of my duties I stumbled upon some thieves pilfering military film for Axis propaganda purposes. Certain aspects of the case were still pending and I was prohibited from discussing particulars, but I did let Liberty know that Lieutenant Roy Jarvis had been tracking the ring and he had enlisted my help in capturing them. Jarvis was with G-2, the War Department's Army Intelligence arm. At least I thought he was. In the entire time we worked together, he had not actually confirmed it.

The adventure left me wanting to test my sleuthing skills further, though I never expected anything to come of it. Then, back in Long Beach, the special orders had arrived.

Liberty had received the identical cable. "Marshall doesn't mince words, does he?" she laughed.

Continuing in hushed tones, she quickly retraced her path to OSS, beginning with the fall of 1941 when she joined the highly confidential Oral Intelligence Group at the offices of the Coordinator of Information, the nation's peacetime intelligence agency, in New York. Major General William J. "Wild Bill" Donovan ran COI, and later OSS, building both organizations quickly, from scratch, by recruiting heavily from a close circle of friends and acquaintances. And it was through her father, who knew someone who knew Donovan, that Liberty had managed to secure a coveted desk job at OI.

In June 1942, there was an agency reshuffling. COI was dismantled and, in the aftermath, half of the organization's permanent staff was transferred to the Office of War Information, while the other half joined ranks with the newly formed Office of Strategic Services. As part of the change, Liberty was moved to OWI. She had been perfectly content there, she said, until a major representing OSS approached her with whispered overtures about dark adventure and a "behind the lines" assignment. This had happened just a few days earlier and Liberty was about to explain why it had taken some arm-twisting from the major to get her to make the leap, but the fingerprinter interrupted. Calling us over and pronouncing us "officially recorded," he directed us to security, where our women's indoctrination would continue.

Dreamboat reappeared. Liberty and I trailed him through another labyrinth of underground corridors, at last arriving at a harshly lit sprawling office space where the tone of the secret service organization we were joining was tactfully and tastefully set with posters such as: *A Slip of the Lip Will Sink a Ship*, rendered by a sea of exploding U.S. battle cruisers; and *Someone Talked*, illustrated by the image of fallen, badly injured GIs. Printed messages, peppering desks and walls, were equally subtle: *Are the safes secure? All secret papers put away? All unnecessary lights turned out?*

A droopy-eyed second lieutenant, chewing on a wooden toothpick and seated at a desk in front of a large poster of a pink ear superscribed with *The Enemy Is Listening*, beckoned us with a meaty hand. "All right girls, raise your right hands and solemnly swear…"

The lieutenant spoke rapidly, the bobbing toothpick in his mouth distracting me so completely that I missed most of what we were solemnly swearing to, but the gist was something along the lines that we would never, repeat!, *never* reveal what went on behind the OSS velvet curtain.

We chorused, "I promise." The lieutenant removed his pick.

"OSS is an undercover organization authorized by the Joint Chiefs of Staff," he said, jabbing the air with the wooden sliver as he spoke. "We've got three main divisions. R&A—that's research and analysis—they prepare area surveys and intelligence studies for operational groups. Then there's SI, secret intelligence. Our SI boys infiltrate enemy lines and siphon information back to headquarters. And, SO…" The lieutenant paused to study the splintered chew marks on his pick. "SO is sabotage operations. Men in SO muck about with organized guerrilla bands in enemy territory and engage in irregular warfare.

"We are anonymous," he added, this time lunging the sliver at us. "If people ask you what you do here, you're file clerks. People aren't interested in file clerks, not enough to ask questions. Remember, there are enemy agents in Washington. They're here to listen. One slip and a dozen of our agents could be dust within hours. What branch you girls in?"

"Morale Operations," Liberty and I said jointly. We were in the same unit! We looked at one another and grinned.

A prisoner of my Protestant standards and provincial reserve, I longed to be more urbane. We had just met, but hearing about Liberty's background, seeing the way she handled herself and dressed, I had to believe that in the days ahead, learning the tricks of a new trade with her, some of the sophistication and panache I craved might rub off on me. The good news had hardly sunk in when the security officer drew a deep breath, then exploded.

"Propagandists! Your group was added just a few months ago, but already it has the worst security record of the entire organization."

Then, because he felt so strongly about Morale Operations, the man spent the next half hour—not in the line of duty—telling us how essential it was to take things seriously, in spite of how loosely our branch was run. The lieutenant's tirade was also a welcome first peek into the inner workings of our strange and terrible group. From him we learned that MO operators plied their trade in hundreds of tricky ways. Acting on the assumption that the enemy would more readily believe rumors coming from within its own country and from its own people, MO faked newspapers and clippings supposedly printed in enemy territory; distributed leaflets behind Axis lines supporting underground unrest; and manufactured rumors, or whispering campaigns, suggesting such calamities as the collapse of the German home front or the insanity of its leaders.

The creation of material designed to misinform and create division behind enemy lines called for imagination and knowledge of the region, culture, and language. Also a certain amount of artistic skill. Such a broad array of talents required a diverse band of characters, selected to complement one another, and referred to as "MO Types."

The lieutenant began grousing about the difficulties associated with having every nationality and every sort of occupation on the payroll, and I ventured a glance at Liberty. But she was grinning, obviously tickled pink like me at having been recognized as a good match for the merry pack.

Next up was Psychological Assessment, or S School, a sort of mental clinic run by a team of nationally famous psychologists and psychiatrists who screened OSS candidates using carefully crafted "live" situations designed to uncover the very core of a recruit's personality. The tests were conducted at a colonial mansion, complete with a sweeping verandah, on a 118-acre estate near Fairfax, Virginia. The setting was meant to give the illusion of a country weekend party, with perhaps some skeet shooting thrown in, instead of what it really was: a proving ground where your gray matter was picked apart by a tweedy group who wanted to know what you would do under major pressure, how you made friends, and what situations frightened you.

Liberty and I began by sharing quarters at S and remained roommates in the following weeks. We had already clicked during indoctrination and now we were inseparable, sharing class notes, clothes, confidences, things far beyond the fingerprint towel that first brought us together. At orientation the number one order of business had been the warning not to discuss *anything* with *anyone*. Liberty and I, though, were hard pressed to keep little, if anything, from one another. Especially at night when, before nodding off, we amused ourselves by imagining various scenarios of breaking and entering the men's quarters, two floors above. At S, student agents were required to be incognito. To heighten our entertainment, we compared notes about the male students' real identities, a big no-no as we were supposed to be making our own deductions. The exchanges seemed harmless and were private so no one was ever the wiser. Except us. And it was these small acts of sharing and helping one another drew us closer, although some of the trust between us was built-in. Like mine, Liberty's father had been called by God and sometimes at night we swapped family stories. Not that our experiences were anything alike. My father had been called by a small town parish; global adventure had beckoned hers, a medical missionary. The serendipity—I was a PK, she was a missionary kid, MK—was not lost on us.

Liberty adored her parents, both fun-loving adventurers. Tales of her family's days in China were always the best. My favorite involved an expedition she and her father took to the Great Wall of China. Her descriptions of the people and surroundings, the grandeur of the structure, were exotic, captivating. "This is an actual chip from the Wall," she'd confided on one occasion, pointing to a tiny dark stone set in a dangly earring. She held it up, eyeing it wistfully. "I had pair specially made. But I lost one. Still, I'm glad to have a memento of the trip. Holding it, I always feel close to Dad."

My father had been more distant and while I adored him, I couldn't help envying Liberty's chummy father-daughter relationship. One incident, though, not only underscored his devotion to me, but changed my life. It was just after my mother had died. Wracked with guilt, I refused to talk; barely ate; would not budge from my room. How could I? That fatal evening if I hadn't been so stubborn, if we hadn't fought, she would not have been late for practice. She would still be alive. But we arrived at church. She rushed, out of breath, up the stairs to the loft.

"She wasn't herself"..."Distracted," several of the choir members said after the fall.

Weeks of seclusion and mourning were interrupted when Dad decided to take me on a sightseeing flight along Lake Erie leaving from the Cleveland airport, not far from our home. He had chosen the air tour not because he was a pilot or some sort of thrill seeker. He was a preacher. And by nature he never did anything on a lark. But he was desperate. Anything to lift me from the cistern of depression I'd sunk into. Up and away we went, closer to heaven, and to Mom. The outing sealed my fate. I made peace with her; I also decided one day I would be a pilot. War, and Miss C, had bumped up the flying opportunities. More recently, with Liberty, I had been plunged into a different slice of what would be normally a man's world.

Two days of examination under the "S-scope" later, we emerged: me, properly humbled after my subconscious desires and character weaknesses had begun appearing like a bad case of measles under the strain; and Liberty, who, I had come to discover, was a natural-born actress, none the worse for wear.

Area E, the Spy School, covering the cloak part of a covert agent's job, came next. At E School we learned the fine points of how to search a room, then how to conceal something in the same space; how to tap a phone; how to open letters and reseal them; how to tail someone through hell and high water; how to break into practically anywhere, then get out again, leaving the place looking so untouched even Harry Houdini would be impressed.

The "how-tos" were divulged in classrooms, where we listened to lectures or watched films. But E also had supervised "lab" time. Perhaps it was simply the act of openly indulging in something otherwise forbidden, but while performing such exercises as lock-picking, secret writing, and using ultraviolet light to fluoresce invisible messages, I felt completely at ease. Almost like flying. Practicing interrogation methods was another matter altogether. Trying to trick someone into revealing things unnerved me, and I stuttered and stumbled formulating my questions. An offshoot of my "do unto others as you would have them do unto you" upbringing, I had to suppose.

Liberty, on the other hand, had a repertoire of methods for getting people to open up. At the OI, she had conducted interviews with refugees arriving in New York. The job involved gathering intelligence from them concerning the situation in Europe. The majority of those she questioned were lonely, downtrodden aliens, relieved and grateful to have arrived safely in America. But they were also anxious and wary, and often reluctant to talk. Moreover, a small percentage of them were clever con artists, and part of her job involved screening for enemy agents. Consequently, to be effective, an OI interviewer needed superior interrogation skills and a finely honed instinct. I was lucky Liberty and I were close and I could sponge enough technique from her to pass the course.

Area F, the rough-stuff department, dealing with the dagger part of an agent's education, was my training swan song. At F, techniques on "how to kill" using a small rock, a pencil, even a folded newspaper were demonstrated. Other displays of imaginative tools of the trade exposed us to such innocuous but deadly devices as exploding fountain pens and plastic explosives that looked and felt like chunks of modeling clay until our instructor stuck in a fuse and detonated one.

One day, our instructor, a captain with big protruding ears and a nonstop grin, seemed especially gleeful showing off a new plum, developed "especially for the girls."

"It's a nasty little vial we've nicknamed Who Me?" he announced, holding up a small cobalt-blue bottle. "Inside is a substance with an odor ten times as offensive as a skunk's. All you gotta do is splash it on an enemy official in a crowd. The scent clings to his clothing and person, and he can't appear in public for days." The captain beamed. "Imagine what would happen if someone squirted some of this on Hitler?"

Liberty, who was standing next to me, leaned sideways and whispered, "If I ever got that close to Hitler *I* would use a long knife." Her tone and the twinkle in her eyes made me want to laugh, but I pressed my lips into a line, watching our instructor reach for the next gadget.

"Now here's something in a noisemaker we call the Hedy Lamarr," he said, grinning, holding a round object about the size of a lemon. "Agents use it to distract attention if they're in a tight spot. Or if they just want to create panic in a theater or an office."

The men in our armed forces used images of curvaceous actresses freely. I'd seen my share of them, painted on planes as nose-art. Women's voluptuous attributes were also played upon when it came to naming new devices. This was the second apparatus that I knew of attributed to an actress. The other was an inflatable life vest, "the Mae West." But it never occurred to me that I would learn how the Hedy Lamarr worked while we were still indoors. My eyes widened and I froze in place as the captain announced, "Here, let me demonstrate." He pulled the cap out and tossed the gizmo into a wastebasket. A split second of silence followed, just long enough for me to feel instantly hot and sticky. Suddenly there was the long screech of a falling bomb, a loud explosion, and a flash of yellow flame.

"Just like an air raid, don't you think, girls?" asked the captain as, eardrums ringing, we watched the flame expend itself in the metal wastebasket.

Chapter Eleven

Back in the ultra quiet VanderKloot suite, having polished off every delicious bite of Mrs. Sarvello's manicotti, I dabbed my lips and decided that my silky top and full pants had seen enough activity for one night.

I shuffled through the carefully arranged clothing in the armoire, finally finding the tweed skirt and matching copper twin-sweater set I was after. The pullover felt soft and comfortable as I slid it on, but when a ragged edge of my fingernail caught a thread and ripped away from the skin, I yelped. The torn nail hung by a strand. I yanked it off with my teeth and grimaced. Then I had to chuckle. Glossy Fingers! Leave it to Liberty to come up with such an outlandish name. I stepped into the skirt. And what about those owl eyeglasses and that mousy hair coloring? She would never draw anyone's attention looking so blah.

Precisely what "the art of disguise" course had taught us, I thought, giving the skirt's side zipper a yank and recalling the last time I had seen Liberty. It was on the final day of my three-week condensed OSS course and we were in Area F.

A portion of the F training area included facilities and grounds that before Pearl Harbor were part of the Congressional Country Club. Nostalgically referred to as "The Club," the private facility's once meticulously groomed greens had long since been chewed up by hand grenade practice. Indoors, the formerly elegant ballroom had been transformed into a barn-like classroom littered with folding chairs and blackboards. The vast dining room, previously a place of ornate refinement, now functioned as a singularly unattractive mess hall.

Liberty's goal was to become a full-fledged operative, meaning that she would be staying on for at least another month. After breakfast that day, I left the converted dining hall, planning to roam the corridors in a final sweep of good-byes. A comfy book-lined study had miraculously been left untouched. Peering through a partially open door I saw her slight frame, nearly lost in a giant leather chair, on the far side of the room.

"Liberty, what are you doing in here?" I chirped. "I've been looking all over for you."

Normally, in the company of others, Liberty turned on the charm. Her clear azure eyes lit up, her features came alive, and soon the room was hers. But there she sat, arms crossed over her chest, head pulled down between raised shoulders, her pixie face skewed into a dark scowl. She refused to even look up at me. Wrapped up in my own case of the blues over leaving, I plopped into a chair next to hers. It took some goading, but soon we were commiserating and comparing our woes. In truth, I saw little in Liberty's "problem" to complain about. I was heading back to Long Beach; she had just heard a rumor that orders were in the hopper, assigning her to China.

"I won't go there," she said.

"Why not? Any student agent here would give their false identity to serve in Asia. It's an exotic place. It's dangerous. There's adventure." Besides, I thought, she was born there.

"It's not Italy."

"So? China's a political hot-bed. There's a lot going on."

Liberty grimaced. "Uh-huh, sure. Lots of surveys and studies for operational groups."

War creates strange bedfellows, and our relationship with the Chinese government was multi-faceted. Presently, the Japanese had the Chinese surrounded on all coasts, including the nearby big cities, leaving Western China to the Soviets, Allies, and Chinese-Communists. OSS Research and Analysis had established units in both Chunking and Kunming, and were compiling target studies of Japanese troop movements for the Chinese air forces, led by General Chennault of the famed Flying Tigers.

"Is that what's wrong?" I ventured. "You're worried they'll assign you to R&A and you'll be stuck poring over data in a thatch hut, bamboo shoots springing up all around you?"

Liberty shook her head. "No. My sources tell me I'd be in the field."

"Behind the lines?"

The dull strains of Liberty's voice grated against the thrill in mine. "Sort of."

"What do you mean, sort of?"

"I'd be reporting to Colonel Whitcomb."

I blinked. "*The* Colonel Whitcomb? But he's in charge of all OSS-China Intelligence."

Liberty shrugged. "Uh-hmm."

"But that means you'll be in the thick of things for sure—"

"Pucci, you don't understand," she snapped. "My jump from OWI to OSS…Well, I only agreed to do it after negotiating certain terms."

Liberty's mother, originally from Switzerland, had relatives still living there. During high school, she'd attended a Swiss boarding school and it was there that Liberty had become proficient in languages. General Donovan, our secret service boss, habitually recruited from a close circle of well-heeled friends, the practice earning OSS a reputation as an elitist "Oh-So-Social" organization. She went on to explain that like Donovan, she had scores of reliable contacts and old friends, including boarding school chums who had joined the resistance network in Italy. When the OSS recruiter had approached her at the Office of War Information, she had agreed to make the switch, but only after being assured that she would be sent there.

Her mouth formed a wrinkled pout. "He thought it was a swell idea. 'You'll be an asset,' he said, 'the perfect medium between OSS-MO in Rome and your pals in the Italian underground.' He promised to arrange it."

"Well, that's what you get for being the mistress of languages," I said lightly. "You're the only woman…no, the only *person* I know who speaks Italian, French, German, and Mandarin to boot." It went without saying that Liberty was also the only person I knew who would have the gall to try negotiating with the U.S. Government. And the temerity to be upset at discovering she had been outmaneuvered.

Her voice was another of Liberty's special qualities. It was bubbly and melodic. She also had a lilting laugh. But my attempt at humor fell flat. The lines of her pout deepened.

"Liberty, this isn't like you. You know the way the government works. If you wanted to go to Italy, you should have insisted on duty in China."

She sighed and faced me. "Pucci, assisting Colonel Whitcomb isn't what you think. There's nothing in it for someone with brains or even contacts. It's all about cleavage."

"Cleavage?"

Liberty nodded. "Right. There's a girl shortage there. I'd be cast in the role of party girl, expected to attend all the big official functions."

"And?"

She flapped her hand dismissively. "Soirees, dinner parties, they're great places where a woman, especially a flirtatious one who's conveniently fluent in Mandarin, can pick up lots of valuable information."

I wasn't one for frothy party gowns, but Liberty loved getting dolled up. That day's getup—a banana-yellow shirt, a flowery silk scarf, and pleated linen slacks—spoke volumes.

"Liberty, c'mon," I said, "we need to know how the Chinese think and what they're up to. You'd be doing what we've been trained to do, gather intelligence. And another thing. Since when have you been shy about using your feminine wiles to gain the advantage?"

Liberty's hands were resting on the newspaper she had been reading before I joined her, now folded and forgotten in her lap. Well, one hand was at rest. The other was plucking at the beads on her keepsake silver bracelet. She smiled faintly, but in the next instant she was serious again.

"China is not Italy," she said firmly. "I simply have to find a way to change the orders."

"So, what are you going to do?"

She had been staring at the newspaper. She looked up. Her eyes were narrow catlike slits. "I'm not sure yet. But I'll think of something, wait and see."

The library's pocket doors had been left open. Peering into the semi-dark room, I saw the dim silhouettes of wing-back chairs and hump-back sofas in clustered arrangements resembling tombstones in a graveyard, place marks for the dearly departed.

There she was, tucked into a shadowy corner behind one of the Queen Anne desks. A sconce cast a soft arc of pale light on the tall bookcase behind her. She was reading by flashlight, a book propped in front of her on the desk.

I smiled. Liberty might not be in Italy, but she had won her battle in part. She had not been shipped to China, nor was she in one of the party frocks she had mournfully predicted were *de rigueur* for the assignment. In keeping with her present cover, she wore a pink manicurist's smock, even after hours.

The room was completely still. My footfalls made soft padding sounds against the broad carpet. Liberty's head snapped up, her long neck stretching in a taut line as she squinted into the dark.

"Liber….*Glossy!*" I whooped, nearly blowing her cover.

"Pucci!" my pal burbled gaily, standing.

We hugged and I detected the faint scent of nail lacquer permeating her stiff cotton smock. I dropped to an upholstered chair while Liberty returned the book she'd been reading to a shelf behind her. It was the copy of *Personality Unlimited* I had delivered to her earlier in the day.

She took the seat opposite me, and as we leaned forward conspiratorially the beads on Liberty's bracelet clattered. Her eyes flicked to my wrist; my gaze cut to the tiny cross earring hanging from her earlobe. At school, I'd traded the cross for her bracelet although, back then, the delicate symbol had been part of a necklace my father had given me for confirmation. Momentarily put off that she would alter the piece without asking, I quickly smiled, realizing I should be flattered. She had similarly transformed a pebble taken from the Great Wall of China and, on occasion, liked to wear it like a pirate, or in this instance with the cross, a *religious* marauder, dangling from one ear. The adornment had a deeper value though: its power to remind her of her father.

"I'm dying to know everything," I said, "but, first, please tell me what's so important about that copy of *Personality Unlimited* you just put back on the shelf?"

Liberty was wearing the oversized glasses. Her sharp blue eyes, exaggerated by the thick lenses, blinked.

"Kiki Barclay-Bly, the woman running this year's Book Faire, said you'd requested it. She wanted to bring it here herself, but V-V—that's her husband—wanted to do it instead. So, what's going on? Have you cast one of your *femme fatale* spells on him?"

She laughed the melodious sound so exclusively hers. *This* was the pal I knew and adored.

"What's the significance of the book?" I repeated in a whisper. "And what are you doing here? You wangled your way out of the China duty, obviously, but what about Italy?"

She looked momentarily wistful. "We all have to pay our dues. The book? I didn't ask for it and couldn't say why or even *if* it's important. I didn't find anything special."

I nodded. I'd scanned the book myself on the way to the salon. So why all the fuss? I glanced over my shoulder and leaned forward. "Okay, forget the book. What are you doing here? Why are you under cover?"

When nervous or lost in thought, Liberty chewed the skin inside her cheek, the habit twisting her mouth askew, adding another quirky dimension to her already impish face. She worked her cheek now and I had the sense she was stalling, wanting to answer my questions but afraid of breaching orders. Her cheek went slack.

"Promise not to repeat what I'm about to say to anyone?" I crossed my heart, and she cast a quick glance around the room. She spoke softly. "G-2 sent me. Someone at the Club is passing secret information to the Nazis."

"Wh-what?" I stammered. "I mean, *who*? Who do they suspect?"

"They suspect it has to do with gossip between chairs."

"Gossip between chairs?"

"Right. You know, beauty parlor talk."

"Uh-huh…"

She read my confusion. "There's something about having one's hair done that releases a woman's inhibitions."

"And?"

"The suspect, the wife of a Naval Officer, is one of Clara Renner's clients."

I had a sinking feeling. Had the scenario I feared actually happened? Were G-2 and the FBI working on the same case without the other's knowledge? Had Liberty and I been unwittingly doubled-up?

She looked furtively around the room again. "Personally, I think the woman is just a gossip. Someone insecure who needs to feel important. And what better way to get attention than to let others know discreetly she has access to inside information? You know, drop a hint about what's going on at the base here, something about her husband's activities there, how important her husband is, what his duties are, where he might be going. Pretty soon, everyone's impressed…Classic case of loose lips, if you get my drift."

"But G-2 is responsible for Army intelligence. What brought them into it? And why you?"

"We're cooperating with Naval Intelligence at their request. Naturally, they had her under surveillance first. But then ONI realized they needed a female agent to cover the Club inside.

So they called G-2. The request was shuffled up the line. This was three weeks ago. I was the lucky draw."

"So, this Navy wife, who has she been blabbing secrets to? Do you know?"

Liberty tugged the cross earring. "Actually, she's an admiral's wife and a social linchpin. Has a standing appointment to get her hair combed out by Mrs. Renner every morning. Sometimes I do her nails." She folded her fingers, bringing them to her mouth and blowing on them. "Three weeks of doing manicures and I'm pretty good. I'm also good at being the patsy."

"Huh? She blabbed to you? Why?"

"We needed to see how far she would go. Can't give you the details, but in various ways I let her think I might be a German sympathizer. NAS Grosse Ile is an active facility. Naval air cadets get their primary training there. We're not sure of her motives, or how sophisticated her intentions are, but one thing's sure. She can't be allowed to continue spouting off, especially if she's willing to give information to someone certain to turn it over to the enemy."

"And what happened?"

"She asked me if I wanted a map of the base."

"You're kidding! When?"

"Two days ago."

"Sounds more serious than a mere gossip after attention. Now what?"

Liberty's mouth twisted. She was chewing her cheek again. "I have a meeting set for midnight, tonight. I'll know more then."

I sat back with a sigh. "Liberty, I'm here investigating someone at the club. Well, a couple of people."

"*You are?* Who sent you?"

"FBI." It was Liberty's turn to be rendered speechless. "Amazing, isn't it?" I continued. "Here we are, doubled-up, working for two different agencies and the right hand doesn't know what the left is doing. Who knows how quickly the spies lurking around here could be caught if certain people would work together like they're supposed to."

Liberty remained silent. I raised something else puzzling me. "We could be in my room. Why are we meeting in the library?"

She gestured with her eyes toward the ceiling. "This is better."

She thought the VanderKloots' suite was bugged? My stomach tightened. "Sooo…you suspect other agents are operating here?"

Her eyes shifted. "Perhaps."

We had been assigned to the Club by different agencies, but I wasn't clear why. I couched my next comments carefully. "Kiki and V-V's debate over bringing *Personality Unlimited* to you was odd. Are they suspect?"

"V-V can be ruled out. He's a war hero."

"Really? But he's from Ukraine…"

She laughed. "Uh-huh. They have wars and heroes."

She divulged that V-V had once been a freedom fighter and had participated in an uprising in 1917 after Lenin and his Bolsheviks took over. "He was just fifteen at the time."

I thought of the scores of young men suffering and perishing in the current war and shook my head. "So young."

"In the small countries threatened by megalomaniacs like Lenin and Hitler they're willing to risk everything to preserve their culture and homeland. Satellite countries bordering Russia, like Ukraine, are especially desperate."

I recalled from my history lessons that over centuries of war the borders of most of the smaller nations in Europe had been drawn and redrawn many times. She went on to explain that V-V's underground group was part of the White Russian Army, the faction that eventually booted Lenin out. Afterwards, Ukraine had declared itself independent from Soviet rule but the fighting continued and in the end the Red Russian Army returned to power.

"Anyway, you're right," she concluded. "The experience transformed his life forever. You noticed the fingers on his left hand, didn't you?"

I shook my head, slowly. "No…"

"He was captured. They tortured him. And like I said, he wasn't much more than a kid. But he never broke, never squealed about where his comrades were hiding, even when they chopped the tips of three fingers off, one at a time."

"Holy moley…How do you know all this?"

She shrugged. "It's in his record."

"So, V-V's working with you, is that it?" Her eyes flashed, but she said nothing. Still, I had my answer. "How about others around here? Clara Renner. Any hunches?"

"Clara's been cleared."

Well, not by my agency, I was tempted to retort. I circled back to another woman the FBI had a vested interest in. "What about Kiki?"

Liberty shrugged. "I hope to have a better read after my meeting."

"Who's the meeting with? The admiral's wife?"

"Can't say." Liberty bent to retrieve a paper-wrapped parcel. The parcel, about the size and shape of a shoebox, had been stowed beneath the desk. She saw me staring. "It's for my meeting. Remember, you promised not to say anything about this to anyone. If word gets out to the wrong person, my meeting, everything I've…*we've*…pieced together could fall apart."

I ran the facts through my mental abacus. Two separate cases, two different agencies, two women agents, the right hand operating independent of the left, all of the pieces converging in the same place, the Cosmos Club. The convoluted formula seemed doomed to disaster, but, technically, our assignments did not overlap. G-2 was investigating a Naval Officer's wife who was selling or giving away secrets involving Grosse Ile. I was at the club running down any connections to Otto Renner that would help the FBI build a solid case against *him*. But Liberty hadn't named Renner or his wife Clara as suspects in her case; I hadn't gotten the impression she even knew about him, or that he was under scrutiny by G-2. Neither Blount nor his murder at Willow Run had come up either.

The lines were thin, but a *brief* delay might be defensible.

"You have to wait," Liberty implored before I could share my decision to hold off. "I'm not the only one with big hopes for this meeting tonight. Roy thinks it's our chance to get the names we need…"

"Roy? Roy Jarvis?"

"Uh-huh."

"Roy Jarvis—the lieutenant I solved a case with in Hollywood—is *here*?"

She nodded and the cross earring flipped wildly. "Yes. Okay, your turn. What's the FBI's interest in this place?"

I was still too busy processing Roy's tie to her case to answer. All at once, Liberty frowned. "Merriman, what are you doing here?"

Her voice was normal, but we'd been talking in such low tones it was as if she had shouted. I jerked in my seat and twisted around. The elderly string bean who'd greeted me in the foyer earlier was only a couple of feet from my back. So close, in fact, I could make out the club's motto on the gold crest of his jacket.

No one spoke. Liberty rose from her chair. Keeping my backwards gaze glued to Merriman, I got up, too. Why hadn't I heard him come in? How long had he been there?

Merriman cleared his throat. "Miss Fingers. May I have a word with you please?"

My attention was riveted to his pale, deeply creased face. At a loss over what was going on, I turned back to Liberty. She flashed our visitor a grin.

"Yes, I know, staff is not supposed to be in here after hours. But I was asked to pick up this package from the salon. Miss Lewis couldn't sleep. We bumped into one another in the corridor. She asked if I could recommend a book. We came in here and got to talking. I only just this moment came up with an idea. Would you be a dear, please, and give us a few more seconds to find it?"

Merriman harrumph-ed, but backed away, stationing himself beside one of the camel-backed sofas. Liberty and I went to the bookcase.

"Sorry I let him sneak up on us like that," she said under her breath, "but I was so engrossed, I didn't see him come in." Her eyes, magnified behind the thick lenses, locked onto mine. "Remember your promise."

"Okay," I whispered out of the corner of my mouth. "When I come in for my manicure, you have to let me in on what happened. Deal?"

"Deal."

"What about him?" I nodded over my shoulder. "Think he heard anything important?"

Liberty's finger traced a row of leather bindings. "Nah, I doubt it. He's hard of hearing. But I'll check. Don't worry."

She selected a giant volume, tugging it off the shelf. "Ah, here it is. Just the thing." She handed over the tome, adding *sotto voce*, "Careful who you trust."

I nodded, but in spite of the ominous warning I had to smile at the antidote she had chosen for my insomnia. *Etiquette: In Society, in Business, in Politics and at Home*, by Emily Post. She knew me so well.

"I'll see you tomorrow morning, then, Miss Lewis," she said as I headed for the door.

I peered back over my shoulder. Lifting her parcel, she flashed a confident grin and strutted toward Merriman. I watched her slip her free arm through the string bean's crooked elbow. The situation was under control. In fact, I almost felt sorry for the doorman.

Chapter Twelve

Room service. Such extravagance was not my norm, but the late night serving of Mrs. Sarvello's manicotti had not filled the gully left by the skipped meals and the energy I'd expended the hectic day before. This morning I awoke ravenous. Faced with another hellish agenda, I'd thought advanced fueling would be wise. The gal delivering my breakfast tray had assured me the VanderKloots used the service regularly. So why did I still feel guilty?

My upbringing. I'd cut my teeth under a roof where selfishness was considered a sin, and ostentation of any sort, fancy clothes, glitzy accommodations, exotic travel, was thought to be a sign of moral depravity. Even the parsonage walls had whispered virtuous guideposts. Seated miles and miles away in the VanderKloot suite I could hear their quiet echo: *Respect hard work, suspect pleasure.*

I dropped my newspaper onto the dish strewn tray, intending to deposit it in the hall. *Allied Forces on All Fronts Turning the Tide of Battle.* The paper's bold headline was a beacon of good news amid the jumble of food scraps and dirty dishes. I'd eagerly devoured details from the account while consuming breakfast.

In Russia, the Red Army was fighting back in a major thrust westward. To date more than 500 towns had been wrested from Axis control, liberating about half of the 580,000 square miles of territory the Germans had seized since their initial 1941 invasion. Soviet forces had maneuvered to within 80 miles of Kiev. Kiev, I recalled, was in Ukraine, V-V's homeland. I wondered how the patriots he'd once been aligned with were reacting. While they would be relieved to be rid of the Germans, I expected they would not be happy with their Russian replacements.

In the Pacific theater, U.S. Naval forces were inflicting heavy damage to Japanese island bases. Less than two weeks ago, our Navy and Army planes had attacked Tarawa in the Gilbert Islands. This week, after losing 600 additional men, the Japanese had abandoned the central Solomons altogether.

There was big news in Italy, too. Weeks had passed since our truce with Italy was signed, yet German troops continued to occupy the country, offering fierce resistance. Our forces were slugging it out, moving in a northerly direction, away from the toe of the boot-shaped land. Allied troops had already crushed Hitler's fortress in Salerno; Naples was next to be liberated. Then on to Anzio.

While the banner news lit a small glow of pride in me, I wondered if Liberty was up on the latest. If the heroic push continued, OSS objectives in Italy might be scaled back. Her talents and underground connections would no longer be essential and her dream to go there would be quashed. I smiled. Liberty was driven, but should the winning streak continue I suspected that even she would not begrudge the dashing of her plans.

I shifted my load sideways, resting it on my hip, while I opened the door and slid the tray to the floor. A soft noise and slight motion drew my attention next door. I froze. From my doubled-over position, I observed a pair of black men's shoes crossing the threshold. I gasped. This was a woman's club! What was going on?

Someone from the staff, silly, I told myself, beginning to straighten up. I never made it. The owner of the shoes threw his weight at me. My left elbow hit first, then my hip. Pain, shock, indignation gripped me. I lost focus. At a whooshing noise across the hall, my head swiveled. But it was too late. The door shut, closing off the stairwell and blocking any chance of identifying my attacker. Precious seconds passed while I struggled to pull myself upright.

I dashed into the stairwell. At the railing, I looked down at the twisting flights below then checked the remaining set, rising to the floor above. My assailant had vanished.

Back in my room, I searched the premises, checking behind curtains and beneath the beds. At the armoire, I threw open the doors. My heart hammered. BYE BABY was smeared in bold greasy letters across the interior mirror! I whirled around, afraid of the shadows behind me. Blount's killer knew I was on the case. He knew I was here. *How?*

I shook off my panic. The Club's staff must not see this. I bolted the door, returned to the mirror. The sharp oily scent and slightly gray color suggested the letters had been smeared on with shoe black. I darted into the bathroom, prepared a steaming, soapy washcloth, and scrubbed, my blood roiling. How dare someone invade my room?

I revisited the armoire's innards. Last night, excited and overtired, I hadn't noticed anything strange. Now it was obvious. Someone had snooped through my clothes and left them carelessly wedged to one side.

The FBI's suitcase was on the floor near the back. I hoisted it up onto the bed, aware of a searing tenderness deep in the muscles of my hip and arm.

The FBI lab had come up with a handsome piece of inventive luggage. I found the minuscule slot below the suitcase's latch and jimmied, gently, with a hairpin. The concealed panel gave way with a satisfying click. I sighed, relieved. Gran's derringer and leg holster were safe inside the compartment, in the fitting devised to keep it locked in place.

The rosewood grip felt smooth and cool against my palm while I inspected the small pistol. Convinced it had not been tampered with, I snapped it back into place. My supply of bullets and other items stored beneath the false bottom were in order as well, but the mystery of the smeary threat remained. *When could the thief have entered undetected?* Last night while I'd been in the library with Liberty was the obvious answer. And the logical suspect was the man who had been sneaking out of the room next door and knocked me over. *Who was he?* My scalp tingled. *The old man Merriman?* But what would he be doing in one of the guest rooms? Especially one that was unoccupied. I knew this for a fact because I'd been assured that the suites on either side of mine would be vacant during my stay. Besides, Merriman was ancient. He practically creaked when he walked. He wouldn't have the strength or the agility to broadside me and disappear so quickly. But then, I'd been bent over, an easy target.

My hip ached. I rubbed it. But why would he attempt such a mad escape? He was an employee. My breath caught. What if my assailant was not elderly at all, but someone under cover? Liberty had been working at the club for several weeks. I would ask her if she'd picked up anything, I decided, rushing to get dressed. *After* she spills the lowdown on her midnight meeting.

Clothes Make The Woman. The motto, one that would normally trip from Miss Cochran's lips, occurred to me as I surveyed the suit I'd selected for my disguise as a professional journalist. I did not personally own a suit, but this one, provided by the FBI, was lovely. The nubby aubergine crepe fabric would make the green of my eyes stand out and help diffuse the color of my hair.

My skin tingled as I recalled Liberty had said Roy Jarvis was somewhere nearby. She was lucky to be working for him. Looking back to my assignment with him in Hollywood, it seemed strange that in all the time we'd spent together, I hadn't known which intelligence branch he represented. Now, thanks to Liberty, I knew for certain it was G-2.

I buttoned the jacket and gave it a tug, adjusting the fit. Tailored, with lines that cinched the waist then flared out over the hips, the jacket's peplum-cut style was one I'd always liked on others. The look, I had to admit, catching a glimpse in the wardrobe's mirror, was flattering on me as well.

So Roy was here in Detroit, I mused again, unable to dismiss him from my mind. What a coincidence. And how lovely. Roy was smart and also physically very attractive. He was so handsome that when we first met I mistook him for my movie idol, Joel McCrae. Over time I'd grown accustomed to his stunning outward appearance and begun appreciating what was inside. Ten years my senior and the strong silent type, he had salt-of-the-earth views and a solid temperament that made me feel close to my roots. The jury was still out on whether that was a good or bad thing, romantically speaking. But either way, as a colleague I respected him and considered him a friend.

Still, the Hollywood mission that had brought us together was just two months ago. His memory of me and what I had accomplished there would still be fresh. Why had he picked Liberty to assist him in Detroit, instead of me?

From inside my conscience, the tweezer-tongued harpy reared up. "Your curiosity is petty and irrelevant," she scolded. "Besides, you're immersed in something critical to the future of our country already. You also have a date with the man in charge later tonight."

Me? A two-timing tart? I shook off the harpy, slipped on Liberty's bracelet for luck, and pulled the felt hat that completed my working girl outfit over my short locks. This afternoon I would be getting my hair done and having a chat with Clara Renner. What could I possibly do, or say, to inspire her to speak openly about her husband's whereabouts during the time his associate was being stabbed to death? We had not even formally met.

I did one last check in the mirror. How would I last all day in heels? I never wore them anymore. I sighed, girding myself. It was for the cause.

Executing a graceful pirouette, I realized that I felt more ladylike than I had in a long while. The feeling held firm even as I recalled the threat, now erased, that someone had smudged across the mirror. I tipped my hat at a jaunty angle, vowing to find who had written the message. Zippered pouch beneath one arm, leather gloves clutched in a palm of the other, I strode briskly from the room.

Chapter Thirteen

Dante had promised that the press credentials and other materials necessary to pull off my journalist cover would be waiting for me at the front desk, along with the keys to an FBI-requisitioned car. But first a stop at the beauty parlor.

The salon reeked of rotten eggs. Someone was getting a permanent wave. I breathed through my mouth, letting my nasal passages adapt more slowly. The waiting area with its wicker furnishings and fern print wallpaper was reminiscent of a small lanai and I skirted through the area thinking I might be more suitably attired in a grass skirt and lei.

At the reception desk, I peered into the main part of the salon. A lone patron absorbed in a magazine sat beneath the metal bonnet of a hairdryer attached to one of several orange vinyl-covered chairs along the wall. When no one came out to help me, I went to the folding screen and checked the manicurist's station. The gooseneck lamp had not been turned on and from the tabletop's tidy appearance I guessed Liberty had not yet arrived.

My high heels were fitted with metal cleats to preserve the leather. They tapped sharply as I crossed the linoleum flooring in quick small steps. To my left were the three client chairs where the beauticians applied their magic. In front of the chairs, the wall of mirrors separated the public area from a private annex in back, reserved for staff. At least those were my thoughts as I closed in on the room, attracted by the barely audible sounds of conversation.

The voices were those of a man and a woman. The man's voice sounded familiar. Nonetheless, I was more than a little shocked to see V-V, with his hands on Clara Renner's shoulders.

He twirled around, his handsome features distorted by his surprise. Clara's pink smock clung suggestively to the curves of her hourglass figure and her crown of auburn hair was tousled. Her mascara-laden lashes fluttered as she pressed backwards against the counter near the sinks.

More striking than ever in tall riding boots, jodhpurs, and a tweed jacket, V-V looked as if he'd come straight to the Club from his morning ride. Clara's rapidly blinking eyes fixed me with a dubious stare. They made an odd couple standing next to one another, he looking so tall and proper; she so short and fiery. I hadn't heard what the twosome had been discussing, but having caught them together, I was naturally curious.

V-V wore an ascot beneath his open-necked shirt. He adjusted it slightly. "Miss Lewis," he exclaimed, his accent dramatizing my name, making me smile. "How lovely that you are here." He gave me a slow once over. "And how *lovely* you are turned out."

I blushed beneath my hat. "Thank you. I'm off to an interview."

"How fortunate that you stopped here first." He collected a book from the nearby counter. "I was about to come looking for you. Yesterday you showed an interest in Hoffmann's short stories. I came across the English version of my favorite volume, the one we were discussing. I should like to lend it to you."

"How kind." Remembering what Liberty had said, I ventured a glance at his fingers. Any residual scars had faded with time and the skin was pulled so neatly over the end of the bone that it was not obvious but, yes, the three outer digits were definitely shorter than normal and absent their nails.

She had also alluded to an affiliation with V-V. I wondered if he had been trying to glean information relating to the Naval Officer's wife from Clara before I arrived.

"The story we talked about, 'Mademoiselle de Scudéri,' is included in the collection," he said, handing it over.

"Ah, the haunting mystery. I shall enjoy it very much." My remarks had sounded like a poor attempt at mimicking his formal speaking style. No, more like a cheap imitation of Bela Lugosi. But V-V was not offended.

"You remembered. I am delighted. My darling Kiki wanted to bring it to you herself. But as I was just explaining to Mrs. Renner, she is unable to make it in to the club today."

I had been looking forward to digging into Kiki's relationship with the Countess. "I'm so sorry to hear that. Is she ill?"

V-V shook his head. "Not exactly. She has been on the go too much. She is exhausted."

Dee's concerns about her sister's work habits had been on the money then. I patted the book's cover. "It was doubly kind of you to remember this under the circumstances. I'll read it and report back."

Clara had been standing by quietly. "It's what's expected from Herr General Anastase Andreyevich Volodymyr Vivikovsky." Smiling broadly, she clipped the forehead of her heart-shaped face in a crisp salute.

The remark puzzled me, but V-V looked proud. He squared his shoulders.

Clara and I had not been properly introduced. He did the honors. Clara, who obviously delighted in teasing him, laughed again—a sweet chortle, really—and turned to me. She spoke in a breathy, little voice that coming from someone else might have been irritating.

"I've been behaving like a schoolgirl. I apologize. My comment about the Herr General must have confused you." She grinned. "I call V-V Herr General because he tries to dictate our choice of reading material here in the shop. He disapproves of the movie screen magazines, thinks we should subscribe to more literary stuff. He likes to drop by now and then with what he calls worthwhile publications." She turned to him, eyebrows arched. "Isn't that right, sir?"

"Improve one's looks, improve one's mind?" I contributed, spontaneously.

V-V laughed. "Yes, an excellent slogan for the salon. Mrs. Renner, you should use it."

I smiled. "I was looking for the manicurist. Have you seen her?"

The two exchanged a private look. They seemed worried.

"What? Something wrong?"

Clara glanced at V-V then looked across the small room. Two chairs, engineered to tilt backwards to corresponding sinks, took up most of the space. Shelving above held an array of bottles and jars. Near the shelving was a dark wooden Swiss chalet cuckoo clock.

"Glossy's late," Clara said, her small voice breathier yet. "That's unusual for her. Especially when she has a client booked."

"But I'm early…" I double-checked the clock, this time noticing that the ornamental flowers surrounding the chalet were all hand-painted in pink with rhinestone centers. I turned back to Clara. The pink looked as if it had been custom matched to her smock.

"I was referring to Mrs. Kelly, under the dryer," Clara said. "When Glossy didn't show, I called her boarding house, thinking she might have overslept. It's nearby and the landlady's an old friend." She looked at V-V as if seeking his approval before continuing.

"What is it?" I asked, sounding exasperated, playing up my rights as the inconvenienced client. "If something has happened, I should be told. After all, I have an appointment."

"She wasn't there when I called."

"Wasn't there? Then where is she? Is she coming in to work or not?"

V-V, responding to my growing agitation, rose to Clara's defense. "Mrs. Renner does not know. Neither does the landlady."

I was not supposed to be acquainted with Liberty, aka Glossy. I forced myself to continue sounding indignant and detached. "What? How can that be?"

V-V spoke in measured tones. "When Mrs. Renner telephoned, she spoke to the landlady, who went to call Miss Fingers.

Her door was unlocked. Someone had broken into Miss Fingers' room. All her belongings, clothing, papers, everything, were strewn about."

I shivered. Someone had just invaded my room also. I shivered again.

"Oh my. And Miss Fingers, what about her?"

My concern was genuine, but V-V responded as if he thought I was merely being irksome. "Please, Miss Lewis. Mrs. Renner is already upset. She does not know where Miss Fingers is. It is why I was consoling her when you arrived." His eyes pleaded for a show of sympathy.

Clara was upset? What about me? Liberty was my close friend.

Ah, but if V-V was her partner on the case, he'd be worried too. I tried reading his expression. Something in his look reassured me. I had been holding my breath. I exhaled, telling myself she was fine. Staging a ransacked room could be just part of her cover.

"Of course," I said. "I'm sure she'll turn up soon."

Clara glanced at the wall phone below the clock. "Mrs. Brown planned to call the police, right after we hung up. Said she'd fill me in once they've checked things out."

"I'm supposed to see you this afternoon," I said. "Think Miss Fingers might have a free slot afterwards?"

Clara had begun emptying the amber solution from a clear plastic bottle shaped like a ketchup container into the sink. Tilting her head, she tried stealing a look under my hat. "I'm sure we can make it work."

V-V was ready to leave. "Mrs. Renner, as always, it has been a delight."

Clara's arms were resting at her sides. He took one of her hands and pressed it to his lips. She giggled. "And you, Miss Lewis," he said, turning to me. "Perhaps after you have read 'Mademoiselle de Scudéri' we will have the opportunity to discuss your reactions."

"That would be lovely," I replied, automatically parroting his formal speaking pattern again. "And, please give my best to your wife. Let her know that I still hope to chat with her about the Book Faire, would you?" *And tell Liberty to get in touch,* I added silently, willing him to read my mind.

He snatched my hand, brushing it with a parting kiss. "Indeed, I shall."

Today's clerk was the same woman with the receding chin and horsy figure who'd been on duty at the Club the day before when I'd checked in. She returned with the packet I'd been expecting, giving me a shifty-eyed look as I took it.

I found a private spot along the wall and examined the envelope. No wonder the clerk had seemed wary. The flap was secured with a bold CONFIDENTIAL seal. Just as Dante had promised, the credentials—press pass, driver's license, bogus newspaper—were all inside. I parted the envelope farther, wanting to glimpse my byline below the column head. I smiled. God bless the ghost writers back at headquarters. The subject of my phony interview was Mad Max. They'd chosen well.

Max was a WAC I'd gotten to know on stopovers at Wright Field in Dayton, Ohio. Only nineteen, she was a certified airplane mechanic and engine specialist, and one of the experimental airfield's top mechanics. I crossed the lobby, dropping onto a wing chair tucked into a far corner. Unable to resist reading what I had written about her, I surveyed the room then pulled the newspaper from the envelope. Fabulous! With no effort on my part whatsoever, I'd written a great piece covering Mad Max's war contributions.

I replaced the article, unable to keep from smiling at the author's discretion in deciding to avoid any mention of her tattoos. My pulse quickened at discovering a letter-sized envelope, addressed to me, containing a personal memo from Dante.

"Sorry, we need to postpone our plans again. Something unexpected has come up. Meet us at headquarters this afternoon, after your appointment with Mrs. Renner. We'll brief you then."

Something unexpected? Daring to dream that it involved Liberty, perhaps Roy, maybe even the two agencies at last coming together on the same page, I was already feeling excited when I read the memo's last lines and felt a bigger kick yet. "Not sure how you'll finesse it, but remember *don't let Mrs. Renner change a thing.* You're already perfect, just the way you are."

Chapter Fourteen

A stop at Plant Protection Headquarters was mandatory for anyone calling at Willow Run. A beefy beet-faced guard with an undershot jaw manned the visitors' lobby from behind a curved counter. His hooded eyes followed me as I snaked between a couple of tall, leafy plants in ceramic pots then skirted a row of uninviting chairs on my approach to the counter.

The guard's royal blue jacket was worn open over a gray shirt and black tie, the coat's front panels partially concealing a bowl-shaped paunch. On the drive in, I'd passed the Orange Lantern, the roadhouse near the plant's perimeter where Renner and Blount met for their final session before Blount was murdered. The joint did a brisk business with employees who liked to drop by after work. Judging by the number of cars parked there this morning, the men coming off the graveyard shift were no exception. Venturing toward the guard, observing his florid skin and morose expression, I could picture him hunched over the tavern's bar, nursing a beer, venting his gripes.

At the counter I glimpsed the man's badge. Officer Flynn. "What's your business?" The gruff greeting matched his bulldog face.

I stated the nature of my visit and Flynn asked me to open my pouch. He dumped the contents. The back of his hand, thick with tufts of dark hair, crawled through my belongings, a tarantula after prey. The creeping hand stopped. I resisted the urge to turn and run, watching the stubby fingers seize my powder compact, then my lipstick tube. He clasped them by the fingertips as though wary of contracting an exotic disease, as he inspected them. The cosmetics, elements of my undercover girl kit, were set aside. I began humming softly to myself, trying to appear outwardly cool while a few more items suffered his groping attention. At last, seeming satisfied, he tagged the pouch and returned it, leaving me to stuff my possessions back inside while he registered my name in a log.

A visitor's number was jotted on a temporary badge indicating my destination. Badge pinned in place, bag tagged and coded, I turned and was ambling toward the door when a "Halt!" from Flynn stopped me. My heart raced. I spun around to face him. "Wwwh-at?"

"Not so fast," his voice boomed through the deserted lobby. "You'll need an escort. Searls," he called over his shoulder, "get out here."

A pimply, tow-headed guard emerged through a partially open door behind the counter. He followed at my elbow, eventually climbing into the passenger side of the FBI Ford I'd left parked in the lot outside. Luckily, this model had no two-way radio or other identifiable equipment.

The Plant Protection building stood between the main inbound and outbound gates. I nosed out of the building's lot, curving along the plant's interior byways, following Searls' direction. He knew a lot of people and as he waved to them, I became conscious of the platoons of protection men, on foot or motorized scooters, patrolling the roads and parking lots.

Searls directed me to park in a spot only yards away from where two days earlier I'd met with Miss C. Renner's office was in the foot-portion of the L-shaped plant. We got out, passing the detached Administration Building on our way to the entrance.

A guard posted inside checked my pass and we started down a corridor long enough to land a Lib. I let my tow-headed guide lead the way while I lagged behind, reading the etched lettering on the glazed glass doors on either side of us. We were passing through Research and Development, I realized, aware that the secret plans for the night-bombing device Renner had somehow pilfered and copied had been produced behind one of the doors. Which one, I wondered?

The endless hall spilled into a centralized secretarial pit before continuing on through a doorway on the opposite side. The hub contained several rows of desks occupied by women typing. The flow of people streaming in and out of the area was constant, and when we arrived the preoccupied secretaries did not even bother looking up. A balding man in a brown suit entered through a set of double doors off to the side. A loud burst of machinery and truck noises came in with him, momentarily cutting off the continual clack-clacking of typewriter keys. I turned, catching a glimpse of a loading dock before the doors closed.

Searls left after introducing me to Beth, an attractive, bubbly brunette. Beth wore a navy pleated skirt woven with white hash marks and a white open-neck blouse. A tiny blue sapphire on a delicate gold chain rested in the crook of the neckline's V.

Accompanying her down another vast corridor, I stared at more closed doors. Behind them, Renner's Tool Design team worked on the jigs, fixtures, casts, and molds needed for the new or modified parts developed by the engineers in the R&D wing. Dante suspected that Renner took secret plans out of the plant by hiding them inside his brace. Having just experienced some of the plant's security measures firsthand I wondered again, how was it possible?

I said, "Research and Design usually work hand in hand, especially during the development phase. But your teams work in separate wings. How do they coordinate what they're doing?"

Beth frowned then smiled. "Only a reporter would ask something like that." *Not necessarily,* I thought, returning Beth's smile as she elaborated.

"The Research and Design groups operate under an umbrella department called Development Engineering. The department has conference rooms where they get together on the second floor. Oh, and engineers from both groups regularly visit the Loft."

"The Loft?"

"Uh-huh. All of the masters, or original drawings, are kept up there." Beth looked over. "You ought to see the place, if you can. It's a huge room with lots of windows to catch the light. Drafting tables are everywhere, but there are never enough. All engineering changes have to be done there and with the recent increased demand for bombers and our stepped-up production, the changes are constant. The engineers spread out, work on the floor, if they have to."

She was echoing Twombley's words. I nodded.

I knew a little something about the arbitrary policies associated with design work from my previous job in an aircraft plant. "What about cabinets with flat files for storing thc originals? Are they in the Loft, too?"

Beth took my insights for granted. "Uh-huh, they fill the entire center of the room."

It went without saying the drawers would always remain locked. "Are there special circumstances under which an engineer can check out a master?"

She laughed. "No, it's not a lending library. The originals are kept under guard and can never leave the Loft. That's why it's so congested."

How then had Renner removed the plans to borrow them overnight?

"What about managers? Are they governed by the same rules?"

"Of course. But managers supervise the modifications. They don't actually do the drawing." Beth came to a halt. She nodded to the door in front of us. "Except for Mr. Renner. He's old school. Insists on doing the department's high-level drawings himself."

Goose bumps skated across my shoulders. "Aaah..."

She opened the door and we stepped smartly into a small anteroom. Mrs. Kovacizki stood in an open doorway on our left.

"Why, Beth," she said. "Good morning."

Mrs. Kovacizki was a short dumpling of a woman, with a rounded face, delicate nose, and rosy circles blooming on full cheeks. Her light hair, threaded with silver, was pulled off her face, then braided and secured in a coiled crown atop her head. She wore a brown cotton sack dress with a leaf motif in muted fall tones. The frock made her look motherly, rather than professional, as she folded her hands over her rounded middle.

"I was about to get some dictation Mr. Renner left for me last night in the say-ay..." Her eyes darted and she hesitated.

My heart sank. She had been about to say *safe*.

"But what a nice surprise," she continued. "And who did you bring with you?"

Beth grinned. "Pucci Lewis, the reporter who's going to write about Wanda." She was referring to Wanda Sands, the subject of my purported interview.

Proper introductions followed with Mrs. Kovacizki insisting that I call her "Mrs. K," like everyone else. "Oh, but this is wonderful," she beamed. "Otto's, er, Mr. Renner's report will have to wait." With a swoosh of her hand, she dismissed her boss, her assignment, and the location of the safe.

"No, please. Get that dictation tape you were after first. I don't want to interrupt."

The ends of Mrs. K's desk and typewriter stand had been pushed together to form an L, with the typewriter stand abutting the door to Renner's office. Circling her desk and dropping into her secretarial chair, she acted as though she hadn't heard me.

"It's a zoo out there," Beth said. "I have to get back to my station." On her way out, she reminded me I would need an escort when I wanted to leave. "Call me when you're ready."

Mrs. K gestured to a pair of wooden chairs across the desk from her. "Have a seat."

A window in the wall behind her stretched from waist to ceiling. Venetian blinds, which could be shut for privacy, had been pulled up. I selected the chair affording a panoramic view inside her boss' office.

I squared my satchel on my lap. Mrs. K's eyes were a vivid blue, nearly the same hue as Beth's sapphire, and if I read the twinkling in them correctly, she was bursting to share something with me.

"Beth's like a daughter to me," she said. "This may be a big place, but with some it's like we're family."

She was being coy. "Uh-huh." I smiled, inviting her to continue.

"Well, we are family. What I mean is Beth is my daughter's best friend. *One* of my daughters, that is. The one you've come to interview."

My spine straightened. "Your daughter is Wanda Sands?"

"Yes," Mrs. K chortled, clapping her hands.

A sinking feeling had begun settling over me. Mrs. K was *in favor of* my writing the article. Was it possible the interview would actually be arranged? Dante had been so sure of Renner's opposition that we hadn't bothered discussing such a scenario. Now the possibility loomed before me. And I had done nothing to prepare.

"You might want to read an article I brought along to assess my writing style first," I said, unzipping my pouch, fumbling for the article about Mad Max.

Mrs. K dismissed the idea with a limp-wristed wave, claiming someone from "upstairs" had already sent along one of my stories for review. "It was a fine piece. You're an excellent writer."

"Uh-huh," I mumbled modestly, although I remembered being impressed by the true author's talent as well. "What about Mr. Renner? He needs to bless the interview before I can actually start, right?"

"Well, of course. But that's merely a formality. Otto will agree."

"How do you know?" I swallowed. "I mean that's wonderful, but how can you be so sure?"

"Women deserve more recognition for the way we've stepped up to the line." She giggled. "Assembly line, that is. Otto is always saying so himself. And Wanda is an inspiring example. She quit working once she married, but when Ted was shipped overseas, she needed a distraction. She applied here. In our family we try to sidestep unpleasantries by keeping busy rather than dwelling on them," she explained. "Especially when it comes to matters over which you have no control. Like war. Once Wanda got over the shock of working full-time again, well, she wanted to give it her very best. So she enrolled in a factory course."

"At the airplane school?" Searls, my pimply-faced escort, had pointed the facility out to me. Built adjacent to the plant, it was nearly as large as the Administration Building. The school's tuition-free curriculum, developed for the factory's mechanics and other technicians to help them keep up to speed, was also open to any other interested employees.

She nodded eagerly. "Yes. The sessions are staggered to accommodate all shifts. Wanda took every engineering drawing class offered. She was only a draftsman when she started but after nearly two years of specialized courses—" Mrs. K paused, practically shivering with pride, "she was one of only two women selected for Tool Design. Now she's designing long drill jigs for parts of our B-24s' wings and hulls."

"She's accomplished a lot. Think she'll stick with it once her husband comes home?"

"It's the education that's valuable. After all, there's no way of knowing what will be in store when her Teddy comes home." She slumped a little in her chair. "If he does." Silence followed.

"You said you have another daughter, Mrs. K?" I asked, filling the awkward gap.

Her bosom swelled. "Yes. Gisela is an assembly-line inspector."

"Here at Willow Run?"

"Yes. At first she thought of being a riveter but, ugh, that's noisy, dirty work. And Gisela is small, like me." She smoothed the front of her dress, pulling the leaf-print fabric taut over her globe belly, and laughed. "But not so round. It was Otto, in fact, who encouraged her to try for the position."

"Hmmm." While Mrs. K rattled off the preparatory courses Gisela had taken, mathematics, precision instruments, rivet theory, care and use of various metals and so on, I began committing the layout of Renner's office to memory.

Mounted on the wall straight ahead was an oversized blueprint of the plant floor, color-coded to identify production and non-production areas, including offices. Nearby, a large drafting table faced two tall exterior windows. To the left, I could see an edge of his desk. The rest of it, as well as the rest of the room, was blocked by the section of wall housing the office doorway.

Mrs. K had paused as if awaiting my response. I had only been half-listening.

"So, Gisela has a unique job as well," I said. "What does she inspect, exactly?"

"Because she's small and can get into places other inspectors can't—to put a testing gauge on a part, for example—she's usually on the wing sections."

"With the dwarfs?"

Mrs. K blinked. "Why, yes. Their size makes them invaluable for working inside the main wing on the final assembly phase. Gisela spot checks their work."

I nodded. "I saw one of them on my way here. Blond, bowl cut…"

"Chaplin," Mrs. K said. "He works with Gisela. Actually, for her." Mrs. K smiled. "Drops by here now and then. Surprised me more than once. I'm small, he's smaller." She hesitated. "Say…maybe you could interview Gisela, too. Write a story highlighting sisters who are employed in unique but different positions in the same plant."

The angle had potential. I was back to stalling. "Hmm…"

Mrs. K's thumbs began to twiddle. "Such visibility would help distinguish my girls from the other women employed here."

So that was it. Willow Run offered plenty of opportunities for women, but competition was stiff. A factory stage-mother of sorts, Mrs. K wanted to give her girls a leg up.

"Willow Run is a big place, but we're family. I've known Otto since the day he arrived in Detroit."

The stakes for molding her daughters' futures had doubled. Her will to convince me of the good rapport she had with her boss doubled with them. The history of their relationship spilled out in a rush.

It turned out Mrs. K and her daughters lived next door to the Renners. Clara's father had passed away some time ago and to help make ends meet, her mother began taking in boarders. Otto Renner had moved in two years ago, when he took the job at Willow Run, intending to stay only temporarily. But then romance began to blossom between him and Clara. They married and, sadly, Clara's mother died unexpectedly shortly afterwards.

"Oh, my goodness, look at the time!" Mrs. K exclaimed, springing from her seat. "Otto will be here soon. I need to type his report. We don't want him in a bad mood when we present your request, now do we?"

"Bad mood?" I observed, teasing. "Judging from your description, Mr. Renner will be canonized one day."

Mrs. K smiled, but something in her expression wasn't right. She began fingering the chunky string of amber beads resting on her ample breasts. "Otto has not been himself lately." She was very solemn.

I thought of the stress he must be under, spying. "Too much pressure from the job?"

"Something with his stomach, he says."

"Ulcers?"

She frowned. "He won't say. And that's what worries me." She strode to the threshold of Renner's office, hesitating before going in. "Perhaps you'd like to sit over there while I get the dictation tape." She nodded in the general vicinity of where she expected me to go.

I didn't need to turn around to know there was a waiting area with two chairs and a small table, holding a fan of magazines, behind me. The chairs were strategically positioned so their occupants could not peer into Renner's office. I'd noted the arrangement, and its shortcoming, when I'd arrived. "I'm comfortable where I am, thank you."

Mrs. K raised her pencil-thin eyebrows and I shifted deeper into my seat. I removed my compact from the zippered pouch and, opening it, lifted the case to my face. My nose was shiny, I noted, studying its mirror. I lifted the velvety pad and swabbed on some powder. In the corner of my eye, I could see Mrs. K still immobilized by indecision. I knew what would get her moving.

A fine line of sweat had gathered above my upper lip. "Need to look my best," I said, tackling it with a few quick pats. "Especially if I expect to convince Mr. Renner to let me do *two* interviews."

Mrs. K let go of whatever it was she had been wrestling with. She sashayed into Renner's office, and I thought I heard her humming. Keeping the open compact in front of my face, I watched her pause in front of the plant blueprint on the wall across from me.

She looked over her shoulder. I had removed the cap from my lipstick tube and was holding the stick to my mouth. I began coating the imitation cherry-red gloss over my lips. The greasy product was revolting. Really! With all their expertise couldn't the lab boys come up with something better for our spy kits? But then why would they? They didn't have to wear it, I thought, fighting to keep the slick stick from skidding from my lips. Or maybe, I speculated more generously, the skimping left extra funds for inventing sophisticated weaponry and gadgets. Like the twist-off lower portion of the tube, for instance. Inside was a tiny ampule of "Who Me?" the potent smelly substance introduced in F school training for emergencies. Then there was the miniature camera-compact I held in the palm of my hand…

My concentration shifted from applying cosmetics to peeping through the compact's mirrored lid. The camera's zoom lens, built into the lid of the thin powder case, was so powerful that it brought everything on the far side of Renner's office close up. Dante and Connelly had been skeptical when I'd suggested bringing a secret camera along. I persisted, only to learn the FBI, having no women agents, had no female-friendly devices. At my suggestion, we contacted OSS and requisitioned a specially tailored kit from them.

Mrs. K, her back to me, appeared to be studying the schematic drawing. Keeping the mirror close to my face, I stared through the tiny lens at its center, my heart pounding in my ears as she slipped her fingers under the drawing. The blueprint was tacked onto cork board and had been cut vertically. She pulled and the floor plan parted, the two halves coming away from the wall like cupboard doors. I held my breath and pushed one of the microscopic buttons along the edge of the compact's lid. The lens zoomed, bringing the large dial, formerly hidden by the blueprint, into closer view.

The dial was set into a corrugated metal door. Mrs. K spun it a few times then stopped. My finger found another tiny button. I pushed. There was no click, but I heard the hushed whir of the shutter inside. Even looking through the lens, the arrow and numbers were not perfectly distinct and I could not be sure I had captured the number where the dial's arrow had been pointed. The film would need to be developed and the image blown up back at FBI headquarters before we would know for certain what, if anything, I had recorded.

Mrs. K spun the dial quickly two more times. With each pause, I fired the camera's button. Her hand left the dial and my finger left the button. I pulled the compact away from my face. I sensed her furtive backwards glance as I continued primping and staring, now from a normal distance, into the mirror.

Presumably convinced that I was totally narcissistic, she turned back to the wall. Gripping a handle, she yanked upwards and the section of corrugated metal, operating like a dumbwaiter door, pleated as it vanished into the wall. A safe with a fireproof metal door had been installed into the drywall behind the covering. Beneath it were two broad, shallow drawers, set in a metal facing. The drawers were Renner's private flat files, used for storing blueprints and drawings, I surmised, snapping a couple of quick shots.

My nose remained buried in my compact as she gripped the safe's sturdy handle. Poised to capture what was hidden behind the door, I held my breath.

"Mrs. Kovacizki, what are you doing?" a strong male voice barked behind me.

Adrenaline coursed through me and I felt its hot path. Otto Renner!

Mrs. K whipped around and I clamped the compact shut, nearly taking off the tip of my nose and sending a tiny cloud of powder floating through the air.

My visit to Willow Run had been set to coincide with a time when Renner would be outside the office at a meeting. Yet here he was. And I'd been so preoccupied with keeping Mrs. K focused in the camera's lens, I hadn't heard him enter. Had he seen what was in my hand? Could he guess what I'd been doing? Without turning to look at him I palmed the thin powder case, slowly lowering it to my lap. I slipped it into my pouch, aware that my hand was trembling.

Renner's question had been polite, but the anger in his voice was obvious. In his office, on the other side of the window, his secretary appeared unruffled. "Otto," she said, her folded hands held demurely over her tummy. "You're early."

This time Renner spoke in a stern tone, like a parent addressing a truant child. "I repeat, Mrs. Kovacizki. What are you doing?"

I'd been watching him out of the corner of my eye. He continued to ignore me and my breathing came a little easier. I turned slightly to get a better look.

I half-expected an aging engineer, one who'd spent his entire career working in a factory, to have gray hair and a doughy physique. Perhaps even a paunch. But Renner's hair was completely brown and he was thin, in fact quite slender. He wore a dark suit and dark tie. The suit fit loosely and his white shirt gaped at the neckline in back. For a moment I thought maybe Mrs. K was right to worry, that he had suffered a sudden weight loss. Then I noticed the suit's fabric. It had a slight shine and looked cheap. His stance was sturdy, his pallor normal, and ultimately I concluded the coat's slouchy fit had more to do with what he paid for it than any problems with his health.

Again, Mrs. K ignored her boss' interest in her activities. She lifted her eyebrows and gestured toward me. "We have company. Did you notice?"

"The raised blinds suggest *you* are the one who did not notice," he retorted.

Acknowledging me with a slight nod, he breezed into his office. He moved so quickly there wasn't time to detect any sign of a leg brace. I barely noticed a limp. On the other side of the window he tugged at a cord and the horizontal slats clattered noisily, diving to the sill.

My mission was technically over. Anxious to leave and deliver the film in my compact to the lab, I considered calling out an excuse and bolting. But an abrupt departure might raise Renner's suspicions. Besides, I needed an escort.

The office door was partially open and I could hear the duo speaking behind the drawn blinds.

"You know better than to expose the safe to a stranger's eyes," Renner said, his voice low and tight.

Mrs. K was uncowed. "It could not be avoided." A sudden silence was followed by an unaccountable change in her deportment. Her voice choked, then shook, as though she were on the verge of tears. "I am only one person. One secretary juggling too many balls. You won't allow me to have an assistant. I do it *all* on my own." She sniffled, then her nose honked loudly.

"Forget it, Edith," Renner said, his voice gentle now. "We'll take this up again later."

"But the dictation recording is still inside the safe."

"Leave it. The transcription is not critical at the moment."

There was a soft rustling sound from a far corner of the office. I thought it might be Renner, shuffling paperwork on his desk.

"Good. I see you have typed up the engineering briefs," he added. "I need them for the conference. You may go now, Edith. I should like to review them beforehand."

For the first time, the starch in his diction registered. I wasn't sure, but I thought I also detected a slight accent. Or was it affectation?

I slid to the edge of my seat, expecting the wondrous manipulator to emerge. She didn't.

"Otto..."

A cushion squeaked and I pictured Renner collapsing into the chair behind his desk. "Yes?"

"The young lady waiting at my desk is here to see you about the Women in War Work interview. I read the sample..."

Her voice dropped to a near whisper and it was impossible to catch what she said next. But it wasn't necessary. I knew whatever she was telling him was favorable.

"No, no," Renner said, vehemently, the sudden harsh words careening through the semi-open door, causing me to flinch. "I am too busy now."

She began snuffling again. There was a significant pause.

"All right, all right," he snapped at last. "But tell her we need to make it quick."

Mrs. K, eyes glistening, poked her head around the door. "Come in, Miss Lewis. Mr. Renner will see you now."

On wobbly knees, I rose from my chair. "Thanks," I said, brushing past her.

Renner sat behind a desk composed of dark wood and simple lines. He had been carrying a leather attaché case when he arrived. Propped open on the desk, it rested between neat paper piles, arranged with military precision. He was studying a document as I entered. "Miss Lewis," he said, looking up.

The man was evil to the core and I should have been frightened. Instead I found myself staring back, fascinated. There was a worried look in his deep-set eyes, but then, a German spy operating out of a U.S. war plant would have plenty of concerns—even without Blount's murder.

Renner launched out of his high-backed chair. We shook hands and he motioned to a chair facing him.

Across the desk, he studied me inquiringly. The probing stare was exaggerated by the jaw muscle he reflexively knotted and unknotted. Neither Renner, nor Mrs. K, had bothered turning on the overhead fixture. We sat in natural light created by sun streaming through the partially covered windows. His thin, straight hair shone in the light and my stomach curdled as I registered the color of his eyes. They were green, like mine. Caught in the golden glow, they telegraphed a keen mind. A quick hello-good-bye was my objective, but a token attempt at securing the interviews would be required first.

"I understand Mrs. Sands is your secretary's daughter, and that her sister works here also, as an inspector. From what Mrs. K has told me, a story about the sisters seems a good fit for my series. It has that human interest hook that my readers, my *many* readers, love."

Renner had been drumming his fingers on the arms of his chair. He stopped. "I am sorry, but it will not be possible. As you have gathered by now, Mrs. Kovacizki is not only a loyal, excellent secretary, she is also a friend. I should like to make her, as well as her daughters, happy. This, however, is a particularly difficult time for me, er, *us*. The department is under a great deal of pressure. We, that is, Wanda, cannot spare the time."

Mrs. K had left the office door open upon returning to her desk and, in truth, I'd only heard a few typing pecks since I'd sat down. Now I would have sworn I heard the soft rattle of amber beads.

"You'll have some disappointed ladies on your hands," I warned, trying to sound ominous.

"If I am not permitted to get back to the business at hand, they shall have to face something more devastating than not having their success stories featured in a newspaper."

"What do you mean?"

Renner's thick lips spread into an uneven smile. The look was either smarmy or remorseful, it was impossible to tell which. "What do I mean? I mean that an interview with Mrs. Sands is out of the question. My department's work is more important to the war effort than your story. Perhaps another time. I am sorry."

I leapt from my seat. Renner stood, as well. He extended his hand across his desk. I reached to shake it. A book case covered almost the entire wall behind him. Over his shoulder, a glamorous headshot of Clara stared back at me. It occurred to me that Renner might discover I had spoken with his wife before we met. Perhaps I was thinking too deeply, but if that were to happen and I had not mentioned meeting her, he might become suspicious.

"That's a striking photo," I said. "Your wife?"

He smiled. "Yes."

"What a coincidence. I spoke with her this morning. At the Club with Mr. Vivikovsky."

Renner's eyes shifted. "You saw Clara this morning at the Club?" he asked, repeating what I'd already said. "With V-V?"

"Uh-huh, I'm staying there. Female factory workers make up only one of the segments I'm covering in my columns. Ladies who perform volunteer work in women's clubs are another. I stopped by the salon and Mr. Vivikovsky was there, canceling a hair appointment for his wife." I drew an involuntary breath as a vision of the couple in the salon's back room flashed to mind. V-V's hand had been on Clara's shoulder when I'd barged in. The gesture had seemed intimate and I still wasn't certain what had been going on between the two. But I hadn't intended waving any flag in front of her husband, either.

My cheeks felt hot as I looked into the keen eyes of the enemy spy who was presently trying to read something in my face. Or in my mind. "Do you know Mr. Vivikovsky?" I inquired hastily.

Renner's reply was quick as well. "No. No I do not. I am due at a critical meeting shortly. I have papers to review beforehand." He rounded his desk and began escorting me to the door. "Mrs. Kovacizki has the number for the Club. She will call you when the time is right to come back for the interview. *Interviews*," he said, correcting himself loudly so she was sure to hear.

The telephone rang, preventing her from grilling me when I re-entered the anteroom. At the same time, Beth popped in. "Ready for your escort?" she asked.

Waving to Mrs. K, I whispered my thanks. "See you soon," I added, scooting out the door following Beth.

Chapter Fifteen

I left one sticky situation for another. After dropping off the film of Renner's office and asking the boys to begin the developing process right away, I went to the County Jail.

On the sixth floor, I was met by the stout, sour-faced guard with the bad teeth who had been on duty when Dante, posing as a lawyer for the *Detroit Free Press*, had appeared with my release papers. Ordinarily, a caller would be deposited in the visitor's area with the prisoner sequestered in an adjacent room and communication taking place through a small window set in a barrier wall. Agent Dante, believing the Countess would feel less constrained talking in her private digs, had fixed it so that I could meet with her there. If the matron was curious about my return and the unique circumstances surrounding it, she did not let on. She turned and began leading me to my encore performance.

From the catwalk outside the common area, I glimpsed the Countess seated at one of the tables embroidering a ruffly white cloth. Near her a mound of threads, small skeins in assorted colors, covered the tabletop. The matron turned the key and tugged a lever. The barred door shot across the threshold. The Countess looked up with an expectant expression. Her eyes, alive with the anticipation of who might have come to visit, flashed with anger. Stabbing the threaded needle into the fabric, she leapt up and flung it to the table.

"You," she snarled. "The phony jewel thief. Why have you come? Who sent you?"

"Hold your horses," I said in a low voice. "I'll explain, soon as we're alone."

She followed my gaze to the matron, who, correctly reading her signal to leave, made a show of jangling her keys. "I'll be just outside." She nodded to the catwalk door. "Holler when you're ready."

The door closed with a ratcheting clank. I turned to the Countess. "You're right. I'm not a thief, I'm a reporter. The inmate thing, it was a ruse to get a story."

She lifted her eyebrows in mock surprise. "In-deed. Well, well, well."

She circled the table so it stood between us. She sat down, sidesaddle, on the bench. Uncertain how long—or if—I would be welcome, I remained standing.

A pack of Camels was buried in the crush of colored threads. Sweeping the mound aside, she picked it up. Her dead-eye gaze remained on me as she plunged a cigarette into her holder and lit up. "Ah-nd so-o, you are a reporter. A *gutsy* reporter," she said, smoke escaping from the sides of her mouth. "And just what sort of gossip would bring a poorly disguised inmate—now a decked-out snoop—back to a god-forsaken place like this?"

My palms, even my fingers, felt damp with perspiration as I dug into the manila envelope I'd brought with me. Pulling out my faux Women in War Work article about Mad Max, I dropped it in front of her. "I'm not after gossip, I'm after true stories. Here, take a look."

She scanned the piece, looking more than a little wary.

"I'm staying at the Cosmos Club, where you lectured," I added. "There's still a lot of buzz about you and about your, er, arrest, circulating among the members."

The Countess arched an eyebrow. "Buzz?"

"They're curious about why you became a spy and, to be frank, how you managed to carry on with a fiancé and your German associates by day, then, by night, dish the dirt to the Feds."

"*You* managed to lie to me," she retorted sharply. "I freely admit to doing what was necessary to survive and to having the ice in my veins necessary for carrying out such tasks. This is what happens when you have no one to fall back on. And what, pray tell, is the rationale behind your deception?"

"I'm an investigative reporter on assignment," I said, grasping for the right mix of innocence and gall. "I got the idea for an interview with you, a female spy and counter agent. I imagined the lead. *The Dark Side of Women in War Work: The Account of a Reluctant Spy*. Now there's a provocative story."

"One that would boost the sales of your newspapers," she observed slyly.

A small smile played at the corners of her mouth. "Ah-nnd who should be credited for the *brilliant* notion of sending you in here as a jewel thief?"

It was tempting to give credit where credit was due, but exposing Agent Connelly was not an option. "Uh, me," I said. "But that's why I've come back. It occurred to me if I disclosed my true motive you would recognize the advantage and help me with my story."

"Advantage?"

"Yes. I'm giving you a chance to tell your side of things. You said the FBI lied to you. Why be misunderstood? Why let others exploit you? Tell me the truth, so we can tell the world."

She flicked a lengthy cap of ashes into a sardine-can ashtray. "You make it sound simple."

"It is." I snatched the *Free Press* article from the manila envelope. I shoved the paper across the table. "It's painful to admit, but it's gotten so competitive that some reporters will sensationalize an account or make short shrift of checking for accuracy before running an item. This piece, for example."

She gave the article a fleeting glance. "Hmpff."

Her blasé response was the flip side of what I had expected. Headlined *As a Spy the "Countess" Did All Right for Herself*, the story was nothing more than a glorified account of the clothing, jewelry, and other personal items the Countess had accumulated during her spy heyday.

In the outer-wear category, the reporter claimed, besides the mink coat she'd brought to jail, she owned a sable cape, three mink stoles, a silver fox jacket, two Persian lamb coats, a Persian lamb muff, and four mink hats. In the evening wear department, her hoard included twenty-nine dresses and two genuine lace mantillas. For daytime, seven suits in fabrics ranging from tweed to velvet. To match the varied ensembles, an assortment of handbags and gloves.

The inventory journalist had even deemed the two-way stretch girdles owned by the Countess newsworthy. He felt "compelled," he said, to mention the "unmentionables" because foundation garments "have been practically unobtainable for several years now."

The writer concluded with the observation that the Countess was in for a long prison term, making this contention when she had not yet, in fact, admitted any culpability in the indictment brought against her.

I had been counting on the shoddy excuse for journalism to stir her passions, get her dander up. I was disappointed. "When I was here before, you said you wanted to tell your side of things. What better way to do it than by giving your adversaries a taste of their own medicine? You know, fight back in the press. It would be ironic, don't you think?"

The FBI's ex-counterspy lifted a neatly folded pillowcase with an embroidery design stamped across its hem. The square of cotton had been hiding a stash of news clippings.

"That is nothing. Hoover's agents, who have purposefully stayed away for three days now, had a matron deliver these items just this morning." She selected a society column from the top of the stack. "Look."

I skimmed the breezy opening.

> Dripping real and fake jewelry, the vivacious and smartly gowned Countess endeared herself to Detroit's upper crust as lecturer and hostess. (She served sherry with a dash of British accent on the side!)

"And this," the former charm consultant said, thrusting a second item my way.

> Rather haughty was Grace Buchanan-Dineen, bogus countess, when she was arraigned in Federal Court under charges of being head of a German spy ring. Her regal bearing and affected mannerisms of European culture made her a hit with Detroit club women while she allegedly garnered secrets of local war plants for the German Gestapo.

A photograph accompanied the column. The clip trembled in her hand. "They have placed a shot of me next to that harlot spy, Mata Hari."

The Countess was featured in a conservative dress, tastefully detailed at the neck and sleeves with piping. Beside her, her body seductively arched in a belly-dancer's pose, the Great War's Mata Hari was scantily clad in harem clothes. I shook my head sympathetically.

She swiveled her head, dragged on her cigarette, and eyed me harshly. "I am being victimized by a hostile press. Tell me, why should I believe that you will not do the same?"

I was feeling more than a little victimized myself. My eyes flicked to the ceiling, hoping to find an electronic bug to glare at. The Bureau had already isolated my mark and made her desperate for a confidant. That had been help enough. Why had they overplayed their hand? What was the point of agitating her with the malicious articles?

"Those articles are not my handiwork," I said, pulling my gaze back to her. "Why do you think they're giving you such trash?"

The possibilities unfurled in a single breath. "They want me to know the public has no sympathy for me. That the American people do not perceive me as an agent of the FBI, but as an enemy spy and a ringleader. They want to make it clear that, until I capitulate, they will ignore my demands while encouraging the press to fan the fire of the public's hysteria."

She tapped the inventory article. "One of the matrons, not the sour bitch who was just here, but a cheery one who wants me to think she is my friend, confided that it was my fiancé who provided the press with this list."

I gasped. "Butler betrayed you?"

She shook her head. "No, never. The matron was lying, trying to trick me."

"But why would she do that?"

The Countess looked at me in disbelief. "So that I would fall deeper into despair. So that I would feel entirely alone, completely vulnerable."

"But how can you be sure? If Mr. Butler didn't give the press the list, who did?"

"Who do you think?" she sneered. "The very same government representatives who provided me with all those newsworthy items in the first place. The same high-minded officials who directed me to 'dress nattily' and pose as a *trés continental* refugee so that I might mesmerize audiences as the self-styled lady of charm."

"The *Abwehr*?"

The Countess raised her eyes to the ceiling. "No. Whatever money my comrades managed to send was confiscated. I was working for the FBI, remember? They doled out the funds."

The Bureau must have a big budget, I thought. Besides the furs, clothing, and unmentionables already described, the Countess had accumulated an extensive jewelry collection, including scores of earrings, rings, bracelets, watches, pendants, lockets, and pins. Liberty had once been close to acquiring a similar arsenal of special spy "weaponry" for her assignment in China. The errant thought left my brain as quickly as it had entered.

"Why would the FBI give a list like that to the press?"

"You mean, besides making me an object of ridicule?" She stood up. Arms crossed over her chest, she began to pace. "They want me to know that besides being omnipotent, they are deadly serious." She rubbed her forearms with her hands as though warding off a sudden chill. "Espionage carries a maximum sentence of death. The other day, a column arrived letting me know that the ultimate penalty is being considered in my case."

I shifted uncomfortably. The U.S. District Attorney had announced that he would *not* seek the death penalty, admitting that they simply didn't have the evidence warranting it. Dante had shown me a clip on the decision when I'd first arrived. Tempted to put her mind at ease, I resisted. Dante and his team were purposely feeding her the misinformation. I had to trust that they knew what they were doing.

"Ah, but what does it matter?" She slid back onto the bench opposite me. "I do not have the will left to survive long-term confinement. If I escape the hangman but am sent to prison, my death will be certain regardless."

Her face was so forlorn I reached across the table and placed my hand over hers. "You'll make it. You're strong. You've survived more than most people could already. I'll tell you what else." I waited until she was looking at me. "If you give me the scoop about the FBI's promise to let you off scot-free, I'll write it up and the world will read about their duplicity in my paper."

She yanked her hand out from under mine. "Do you think I'm so desperate as to believe such a thing could happen? Your editor would never print something negative about the Justice Department." She shook her head. "No, it is no good. I am up against the wizards of propaganda. Even if by some miracle your paper would agree to do it, the authorities would simply use their power to stir up more publicity meant to destroy me and my fiancé. You and your editor might make the headlines as well."

I nodded. "Lousy idea, you're right. We don't want to antagonize the FBI unnecessarily. But there's another way to present your side. The personal profile. Tell me, so I can tell our readers, why you became a spy."

Her shoulders heaved. "Ahh, more sensationalism to help you sell more copies."

"No. It's called winning the sympathy vote. Making publicity work *for* you instead of against you."

She took a long moment to think. Standing, she picked up the overflowing ashtray and began walking to her cell. "It seems there is no other choice. You are my only link to the outside."

"Hold on, I'll need to take notes." I removed a stenographer's pad and retractable lead pencil from the envelope. Pencil poised, I suggested, "Why not start at the beginning. When and why did you decide to become a spy?"

"It wasn't a professional decision," she retorted. "The turn of events goes back to my family—how I was raised, the death of my Papa..." Bringing the ashtray with her, she resumed her seat across from me, continuing to talk while lighting up.

The Countess was born in Toronto. Her great-great-grandfather, whose title she used, was the last Count de Neen of Brittany in France. After convent school, and following in the tradition of her European peers, she traveled extensively, taking in various cultures throughout the Continent, acquiring an appreciation for art, jewels, and fashion. Learning to be an engaging conversationalist, discussing current events and world news at fashionable dinner parties, was central to her studies as well.

The first hiccup in her idyllic existence occurred when her parents separated in the early 1930s. Her father moved first to London, then Paris, before settling in Budapest, his daughter with him as his hostess and travel companion.

"And what a magical time it was," she said, her tone becoming nostalgic, as if she were slipping back to Europe in the early '30s. "So many invitations, such fascinating people, and, ah, what stimulating discussions. It was at a dinner gathering in London, actually, that I became interested in the pro-fascist Mosley group. Nearly everyone in our crowd was involved..." She sighed and her expression turned dreamy over the political debates that went on during the gatherings in their Budapest apartment overlooking the Danube.

Another time I would have rolled my eyes or had trouble trying not to gag while listening to such a pretentious, irksome account. But I was too busy jotting notes to look up even when the enchanted tone in her voice became sad as she described the next turn in her life. In 1938, their charmed existence was interrupted when her father became ill with a heart condition. Holed up in Budapest, they hoped for the best, but his health continued to decline.

"There were many who lent their support during this difficult time." A billowing stream of smoke escaped with her sigh. "Especially Sari."

"Sari?"

"Sari deHajek. A former friend. I had lost track of her after she left to attend Vassar College in the States."

I frowned, trying to place the name. Then I remembered. Dante had told me about Sari deHajek during my first briefing. In 1939 and 1940, while an exchange student at Vassar, deHajek crisscrossed America making presentations on Hungarian folklore and gathering information on U.S. war preparations. Under the tour's auspices, she also made contact with possible fascist sympathizers, eventually compiling over 200 names in a small green and black address book. Later on, deHajek recruited the Countess. And it was her address book that the Countess brought with her to America a year later.

By early 1941, the Countess' money had run low. As a resident of a country that technically had become part of the Axis, her funds had been impounded by the Canadian government. She had to face her predicament. "How was I going to get along?"

I could not resist the obvious. "What about getting a job?"

"Pursuing the development of my personality was hardly practical training. Wealth, position, glamour—what else did I know?"

She lifted an eyebrow and her nose went up.

"Then," she said. "Fortune showed me the way." "Fortune" was a sudden memory of her achievements as a gifted orator in school. "I shall follow Sari's path and become a lecturer, I concluded. And so I went to her for advice." A puzzled look crossed her face. "Or, did Sari come to me?" She shook her head. "I forget. Sari knew I supported fascism and asked if I would help promote the cause in America. Things were getting rough in Europe. Anyone who could get out, especially to the States, was considered fortunate. I accepted." She held her left hand out, admiring her glittering ring. "Ahh, but all of that is in the past. My future rests with Mr. Butler and his seed money now. He is saving so that when this is over we will be able to build a new life together, wherever fate may take us."

My pencil stopped. Her expression had noticeably brightened, yet I did not see that she had much to offer Butler in return. "Your fiancé's loyalty is admirable. You're lucky. Is he, uhm, disappointed you're in jail, charged with espionage?"

She braved a small smile. "No one since my Papa has been so kind to me. I kept my arrangement with the FBI secret at first even though I knew my apartment was wired and moving pictures were being taken of everyone who came and went, including him. How could I tell him? But then I was put in protective custody and the FBI forced my hand. When he learned the truth, I learned the true strength of his commitment. We have been engaged for nearly eight months and he has never wavered, even when our evening visits were reduced to two hours spent with an agent present. Can you imagine such humiliation?" Her chest heaved. "Or such love?"

"Incredible."

As quickly as her mood had buoyed, it collapsed. Her eyes welled up and she turned away. While the Countess searched her pocket for a handkerchief, I crossed the painted cement floor, pausing inside her cell to observe Butler's photo stuck into a crack between the wall and her metal-plate mirror along with a sepia-toned photo, presumably of her father. Butler's neatly combed white hair and tweed jacket made him look dapper, I thought, my gaze lingering on his kind face, lively eyes and gentle smile.

Above, a protruding folded-over corner on her father's picture drew my eye. In European fashion, the photo had a rough-cut scalloped border. I suspected the corner had been jammed into the slit around the metal mirror at one time, causing it to bend. The paper had yellowed with age. I started to flip the edge up with my thumb and noticed the letter T, written in pencil, on it. I looked closer. On the glossy, photo side of the paper, scratch marks made by the pressure of a pencil suggested more writing on the back.

The Countess was stuffing the handkerchief into the pocket of her jumpsuit. Curious, I gave the photo a little tug, freeing it so that it slipped to the floor.

"This fell," I said, turning the portrait over as I picked it up.

What I read looked important. That is, any name and address written on something belonging to the Countess could have far-reaching consequences.

"There's a name on the back, Tazio Abbado, followed by a Detroit post office box. Did you know it was there?" I set the print on the table before her. "Is this your father's writing?"

The Countess squinted. "Nooo—Sari wrote that."

The blood seemed to stand still in my veins. I had been holding something that a notorious enemy operative had once held. I was at once thrilled and repulsed. I did my best to keep my voice casual, inquiring, "Oh? And who's Tazio Abbado? Why did she give you his address?"

"Mr. Abbado is a fence."

"A fence? Why would you need a fence?"

She lowered her voice. "A few precious stones were included in the spy supplies dispatched by the German naval attaché in Lisbon. If and when I needed more funds, I was to contact Abbado. Give him the goods. I never had the chance. Fate intervened and I was conscripted by a certain two-faced government agency." She projected the last sentence bitterly toward the cellblock door.

She stood and began to pace. "My strength—Mr. Butler's strength—had always been rooted in the belief that I would never be thrown in jail. But we were deceived. *It is only for a few days*, they said. *It is for your own protection*, they said. Ha! All along their plans were to keep me for weeks, months, *years* of mental torture."

Dante had covered the particulars of her arrival and capture in New York. What he had not clarified, though, was why she had been brought up on the same charges as the others. Even I perceived a certain injustice when it was through her efforts the ring had been caught.

Halting beside the newspaper articles on the table, she sneered at them. The inventory article was on top. She ripped it from the stack, crumpling it between her hands. "Now they have hit rock bottom. They want to destroy my relationship with Mr. Butler, the only thing I have left."

She winged the newspaper ball across the cellblock. It landed on the skeins of colored thread, piled on the table. The tangled heap reminded me of the former charm consultant's tendency to embroider the truth, especially when her personal well-being was at stake.

"Listen, Countess, you're in jail. You're accused of espionage. And while you'd like to believe otherwise, you have no leverage to make demands. My advice to you is this. Cooperate. Offer to testify against Thomas. Plead guilty if they insist. That's what will get you out of this jam. That's your ticket to a lifetime of happiness with Mr. Butler."

She pounded the table with her fist. The rumpled nest of threads bounced. "I will cooperate only when I have their assurance that I will not be sent to prison. That I will be exonerated." Her piercing gaze blazed with defiance.

My head was spinning. I had done my best to help her resolve her problem. I drew a long breath. Enough about her needs. On to mine.

Leaning forward, in my best stage whisper, I said, "A source tells me that a new unit of German spies has infiltrated Detroit. My contact had names. Walter Blount. Otto Renner. Heard of 'em?"

"Blount. No, he is not familiar." She frowned. "But Renner, hmmm. I know the name somehow…"

The creases in her forehead multiplied and deepened. She snapped her fingers. "Yes, that's it. There was a beautician at the

Cosmos Club. *Her* name was Renner. Mrs. Clara Renner, yes?" She looked expectant. Or was it shrewd?

"Yes, Clara Renner," I repeated. "The beautician. Do you know her husband?"

She seemed genuinely bewildered. Then her face lit up.

"Ah, yes! Of course. I did meet him once when I had an appointment with his wife. He dropped by with a bouquet of flowers. She gave him a book. *And* a loving peck." She smiled wistfully. "He looked at her in the way Mr. Butler looks at me. It was sweet, I tell you."

She lit a cigarette and squinted, her eyes narrowing against the smoke. "So the beautician's husband is an espionage suspect. But why are you asking me about him? The FBI never did."

I shrugged. "Wish I had an inside track to what the FBI knows or doesn't know. It's just what I heard. But about Mrs. Renner, how well did you know her?"

"She styled my hair on just one occasion. When I tried getting a second appointment, she was always booked."

"And Kiki Barclay-Bly, the woman who brought you into the Club to speak? How did that come about? Were you two friends?"

"Miss Barclay-Bly has been a loyal supporter. Is that why she is under suspicion?"

"I didn't say she was under suspi—"

"Miss Barclay-Bly is not a spy," the Countess cut in. "She is a dear woman, very kind. Maybe too kind. And her sister is a gem, as well. She introduced me to my Mr. Butler—"

I sensed something had clicked. Or unclicked. She paused abruptly and dragged on her cigarette, staring off into space.

In the distance a cell door clamored loudly. She stirred and whispered, "I have told you what I know about the FBI's plot to come between my fiancé and myself. I am determined to counter their efforts. Your editor managed to get you in here twice. See if he will use his pull to arrange a visit from Mr. Butler. When it is set, I will reveal what I know about the Barclay-Blys."

Chapter Sixteen

At the door to the salon I ground to a halt. A large piece of thick cardboard had been jerry-rigged over the lower half of the door to replace a missing section of glass.

"Yoo-hoo. Anyone here?"

On the reception desk, a spiral-bound appointment book lay open over a blotter, the exposed pages marked off in hourly blocks. All afternoon appointments had been lined out. In the manicure section, my morning appointment was scratched through but I had not yet been penciled-in in the afternoon. Kiki's name had been struck out as well. I flipped backwards, noting she had been in nearly every day over the last two weeks.

I checked the manicurist station. Dead. Where was everyone? And what had happened to the door?

The sound of running water pulled me toward the back room, where a faucet had just been turned on. The rushing noise stopped and I heard a series of sharp cracks, like someone rapping a plastic container against a countertop. I arrived at the room's entrance as Clara, studying a vinyl-coated chart, was coming out. We stopped short of bumping into one another. Still, she gasped.

Raising a finger to her lips, she motioned over her shoulder. Dee Barclay-Bly was seated in one of the chairs fronting the sinks along the wall. Her chin-length black hair was matted and wet. I knew it was Dee from the thick eyebrows and pearl earrings.

An open magazine lay neglected in her lap. Her eyes shut, her chin tucked against her chest, she appeared to be dozing.

Clara led me toward the main part of the salon. "Sorry, but I don't want to disturb her," she said, her voice sweet and breathy. "She could use a few winks."

"Where is everyone?"

Clara twisted a tiny medallion attached to her smock above her heart. It was a gold pin forged into a soldier's profile. A private, he wore a tent-cap. An exaggerated lock of hair, extending from beneath the cap's peak, formed a swooping curl above his brow. She noticed me staring.

"Beauticians Behind Our Boys. On the third Thursday of every month, members of B-BOB contribute their tips for that day." Her glance flicked to the appointment desk then to the patched door. "Our tips went down the drain today with our cancelled afternoon appointments."

"What's happened?"

"The day has been awful from the get-go. First, there was the upsetting call with Mrs. Brown, Glossy's landlady. Then a police investigator stopped by, asking lots of questions."

"Oh…So Glossy never showed up?" I asked in genuine alarm. "No word?"

"No. And the inspector said everything in her room was ripped apart. Even the lining of an armchair had been hacked to shreds with a knife." Clara's mascara-laden lashes fluttered. She looked anxious. "Pucci, are you all right? Let's go sit down."

We crossed the salon to the cozy lanai area and chose love seats opposite one another. We settled onto lumpy cushions. The beads on Liberty's bracelet fluttered, tickling my forearm, and I tried resurrecting my earlier optimism concerning my pal's whereabouts. Dante's memo, asking me to an unexpected meeting, left me hopeful that her disappearance, as well as her ransacked room, would be explained then. Ideally, Liberty, and Roy Jarvis, would be present with Dante at headquarters.

Clara leaned toward me. "You sure you're okay?"

I smiled. Her voice was so sweet and she seemed so caring, it was difficult to imagine her being involved in anything that would harm our country or aid its enemy. Yet she was married to a known spy. I needed to learn on which side of the fence her patriotic loyalties were grounded.

"I'm all right, thanks." I began sliding my over-taxed dogs out of the high heels I had been tramping around in all day. "You said the investigator asked a lot of questions. What did he want?"

"He wanted to know about Glossy. *And* her clientele. He knew names. Asked about some of them, directly." Clara removed her shoes: white leather with a chunky heel, personalized with pink laces to match her smock. She swung her legs up onto the couch, folding them beneath her.

"How about the Countess? Did he ask about her?" She stared at me blankly. "You know, the woman accused of spying for the Germans. Her story is in all the papers. She lectured here."

Clara fell back against the sofa. She grimaced then laughed. "You mean Grace Buchanan-Dineen! Yes, I did her hair. *Once.* But don't remind me! She put me through the wringer so good that when she finally sashayed out of here, I told the girls that if she ever tried to schedule another appointment, tell her that I'm booked through next year."

The Countess had told the truth, then, about their relationship.

"The investigator must have inquired about her though."

"Why? She was arrested before Glossy was hired." Clara twisted her B-BOB pin. "He took Glossy's manicurist's license. It has her photo. Said they planned to use it for an All Points Bulletin they're sending out." Her cupid-bow mouth, shiny with a fresh coat of coral lipstick, curled into a coquettish smile. "Hope it's legit."

"What do you mean?"

She was smiling broadly now. "Glossy was new to manicuring. Claimed she'd had two jobs in salons before applying here. I went along with her, but I knew she was fibbing."

My stomach fluttered. "Really? How'd you know?"

"Have you seen one of her manicures? The brush rarely stays on the nail so there's always polish coating the skin alongside. And the way she shapes nails—" A burbling sound escaped her throat. "The lopsided look is a specialty."

"Why do you let her stay on?"

"I like her. She needed a start. She also agreed to work for tips only until she could establish a following. The clientele here is mostly elderly. They don't seem to mind, or notice, her mistakes. They come in to socialize. Glossy has traveled to nearly every country in Europe and can tell yarns about every single one of them. China even." She grinned. "Besides, who could resist hiring a manicurist with the name of Glossy Fingers?" We laughed.

Clara wore a white uniform under her pink smock. The skirt had crawled up her thighs and the metal clasp of a garter hook, snapped through the wide band at the top of her rayon stocking, was exposed. She tugged the hem down over it. On the sofa across from her, I recalled Kiki's numerous appointments in the scheduling book and shifted positions as well.

"You said the investigator asked about Glossy's clients. Did she ever do Kiki Barclay-Bly's nails?"

"Why, yes. Many times."

"And while she's here, do you do her hair?"

"No, I've only given her one cut. About three or four weeks ago, I think."

"But her husband was canceling an appointment just this morning."

"Uh-huh, her bangs need a trim."

"What about her color? It must need regular touching up. Who does it?" I was pressing my luck asking so many questions, but it was imperative that I establish how well Clara and Kiki knew one another. I could only hope, as I'd heard was the case with many hair dressers, she took pleasure in dishing a little dirt.

Clara went along. "It's a rinse. She does it herself."

The telephone on the appointment desk jangled loudly. She sprang from her seat. "Who's there? Who's there, please?" The receiver slipped from her ear. She lowered it to its cradle and stared into space, obviously troubled. Suddenly, her face screwed into a look of frustration. "Men. Men!" she repeated in a trembling voice.

The declaration was broad brush, but I had already narrowed the possibilities of who she might be angry with down to one individual. "Was that your husband calling?"

Her chin trembled, but she jutted it out defiantly. "Ww-we've had our first fight. He's made ten calls like that since he left. He's jealous. Thinks I'm cheating on him. Wants to be sure I'm here, I guess."

"The broken glass? The canceled appointments? Is he responsible?"

Her lips pressed into a shiny coral line. "He's never done anything like this before. It's stress." With a sigh, she explained that the stepped-up production at Willow Run was forcing him to put in long hours and leaving little time for rest.

"Sleep deprivation is known to make people go wacky," I said, speaking as someone who'd had the cautionary note drummed into her in flight school over and over.

I'd struck a chord. She nodded, grateful for my understanding. "It's true. Last night he flew off the handle for no good reason. And today, well…this." She gestured to the door. "After storming in here and in front of everyone—" her voice wobbled—"accusing me of being disloyal, he demanded that I stay away from the traitor who seduced me."

"Traitor? Seduced you? Who?"

"I don't know. He just barreled out and slammed the door so hard it shattered."

Poor Clara. Their clients must have been agog. No wonder she and the other beauticians had decided to call it a day.

"I'd like to get my hands on whoever is spreading the rumor," she added, the timbre in her voice growing.

"Rumor?"

"Yes. Someone told Otto they saw me in a man's arms. Here, in the salon. What gall! If I had a lover and wanted to carry on, why would I do it in public? In my place of business?" She shuddered. "If I ever get my hands on the lunk head floozy behind the rumor, I'll give her a free haircut."

My eyes darted to the fern wallpaper. *I* was the lunk head floozy! I had told Renner about Clara talking privately with V-V, although I didn't recall saying they'd been in an embrace.

"Don't worry, he'll realize his mistake," I said. "Besides, if you've been together for an entire year and this is your first spat, that's actually pretty good, isn't it?"

Her generous mouth formed a lopsided smile. "I guess that's right. Especially as I'm an O'Hara, through and through. Otto has been my calming force. And, up until now, a true romantic. Flowers, candy, love notes." The smile grew. "On Monday we celebrated our anniversary with a candlelight dinner. He surprised me with this locket." She tugged at a fine gold chain around her neck.

While she fished for his token of love, I did some quick calculations. Blount was killed Tuesday morning, around six. In other words, the morning following Clara and Otto's romantic celebration.

Clara at last freed the treasure from beneath her smock. Heart-shaped, like her face, it had a small diamond in its center. I cooed, admiring the locket, but even to my untrained eyes, it looked cheap. Like Renner's suit. It made me think that the Nazis weren't paying him much for his traitorous deeds. Or that his earnings were being siphoned elsewhere. To a getaway fund, perhaps.

Clara wedged her thumbnails into the crack separating the heart's halves, attempting to flip it open. "He put our pictures inside."

"Hmmm, nice. So, Monday night you had dinner together. How about afterwards? What'd you do?"

She frowned. "What are you getting at?"

"You said he's been under pressure, working late hours and all that. I was just wondering if he went back to the factory."

She forgot about the locket. "Otto was in no shape to go back to work. That's what's so strange about all this. We had an incredible evening. Made love *all night long*."

I felt the blood rush to my cheeks. Clara giggled and blushed as well. "You asked for it." She turned wistful. "It used to be like that every night, but now thanks to Ford and the war, it's work, work, work. Even at home. Otto doesn't know it, but a few times, late at night, I've seen him drawing at the kitchen table."

I made an involuntary choking sound. It went unnoticed. "That's it!" she exclaimed. "Why didn't I think of it earlier?"

"What?"

"The reason he's been acting so peculiar. At dinner, after we relaxed, had a little wine, he confided that he's been having trouble keeping up with his boss' demands. 'I might be forced to retire sooner than expected,' he said. I completely missed my cue. He's worried about our security!" She paused, then positively glowed. "It's ironic, but I think I have another piece of the puzzle, too."

"Oh?"

"My mother left me some money. I've been exploring investments. One involves a business expansion. I've been speaking with a financial counselor on the sly, sorting things out, before I present the idea to Otto. I bet the lover he thinks I'm involved with is him!"

"Hmmm." I wasn't sure how to respond, but it didn't matter. Clara shifted gears.

"Say, you have an appointment scheduled with me, don't you?" She tipped her head, trying to see under the slouch-brimmed hat. "What do you have in mind?"

I'd been wearing the hat all day. I removed it. "You tell me. I'm open to suggestions."

A perplexed look crossed her face. Then she remembered the chart on the sofa next to her. "A new color might be nice."

She gave me the vinyl-coated card. I scanned the swatches of hair adhered to it, intrigued as much by the range of colors as by their names: Sable Brown, Ice Blonde, Toasted Almond, Moroccan Spice.

She nodded toward the back room. "I've got Navajo Black setting on Dee."

I found the blue-black tint among the samples. "Same color as her sister's?"

"Uh-huh." She turned to consult a wall clock behind her.

Someone in the salon had a thing for cuckoo clocks. This one, a more elaborate version of the Swiss chalet clock in the back room, featured an expansive deck and colorful, hand-painted figures of a grandfather, a blond dog, a girl and a boy, a pine tree—even sheep. Flowers in bright yellows, blues, and reds, many with glittery centers, were strewn in clusters around the deck. Boxes of the colorful flowers festooned the shuttered windows and the railing of a narrow deck. A silent cuckoo, looking at once startled and embarrassed, stood exposed in an open doorway over the balcony.

Clara caught me staring and laughed. "Cute, isn't it? Too bad it's broken…I always forget. Do you have the time?"

I consulted my watch. "Two-fifteen."

"I'll need to shampoo Dee in a few minutes."

"But the salon's closed. Why are you doing her hair?"

"She'd heard her sister cancelled and called, begging for the slot."

It wasn't that simple, I could tell. I waited. After a hesitant start, Clara gave up the rest of the story.

When Dee had arrived, Flo explained that they were closing. Dee started to leave, but then stumbled and fell. Clara was nearby on the telephone. She rushed to help her. But Dee was so disoriented Clara and Flo had trouble getting her back on her feet. At first, Clara worried Dee had been hurt. Then, after smelling liquor on her breath, she concluded Dee needed time to sober up before leaving.

I clucked sympathetically. "A year ago she was jilted, left at the altar. Did you know?"

She leaned forward and spoke softly. "Well, mind you, it's only gossip between chairs, but several of my clients have suggested it was her sister's fault. Philip, Dee's fiancé, had a wandering eye. Rumor is, one day it landed on her sister. They had a fling but managed to keep it from Dee. Until now."

My shoulders heaved. "Dee's fiancé and her very own sister." I straightened up. "Wait a minute. The ladies around here like to stir up trouble, especially when it comes to Kiki. They'd hang anything and everything they could on her. Who told you this? Do you remember?"

"Well, several clients did. And, yes, it's hard to know if it's true, but it's what I heard." She grabbed her pink-laced shoes. "Speaking of Dee, I gotta go."

"I've got to run, too," I said. "But, uh, one final question."

"Yes…"

"Where'd you get all these clocks?"

"Why, from Glossy…Curious, the one in the manicure area—it didn't work either—it's gone."

Acting on a wild hunch, I climbed up onto the couch and unhooked the elaborate chalet. The pinecone-shaped weights, dangling below, flopped madly. I steadied them, holding them gently in my free hand, and stepped down. Clara's eyes were enormous.

"Don't worry. I know someone who can fix this. He's an expert, owes me a favor. I'll have it back here before you know it. Promise."

"I—I'm not sure…"

"I'm a guest, you can trust me. Say, Clara…" I cradled the clock. "I'm thinking about including Navy wives in my piece about Women in War Work. There's a base near here called Grosse Ile. Do any of the wives come to this salon?"

Clara, already dumbfounded by what to do about my nipping the clock, looked even more unsure of herself. "I have a client whose husband is an admiral. A regular, been coming to me for years. But she's very private. I'm certain she'd never agree to speak with a reporter."

Liberty had painted an altogether different image of the Navy wife, saying she was a dangerous blabbermouth, spewing confidential information to anyone who would listen. Had Clara turned a deaf ear to her client's loose lips? Or was it just the opposite? She recognized a perfect source and wanted to protect her?

"Not even if you made a personal request?" I pressed.

She fixed me with a harsh look. "I won't ask. Like I said, there's no point. She would never agree to talk with you."

I had crossed a line. I shrugged and smiled brightly. "Okay, no problem. I'll think of something else."

Chapter Seventeen

The cleats on my heels clicked rhythmically as I crossed the headquarters' garage on my way to the lobby. I kept my eyes peeled, finally identifying Dante's car from the charms hanging from the chain on the rearview mirror. Funny how the mind works: the percussion of my cleats, together with the sight of the mementos, triggered a vision of the stick-figure drawing of Dante dancing with his sister and Leo. I'd seen the rendering at his flat, and the momentary passion we'd shared there came back to me as well. I recalled the warmth of his breath on my ear, and my shoulders tingled with the pleasant shiver skating across them.

Waiting for the elevator, I scanned the lobby. An elderly gentleman wearing a long coat and newsboy cap stood at one of the barred windows, talking with a postal clerk. The flyaway strands of his white hair and his stooped posture reminded me of Merriman, the Club's string bean doorman, and the gnawing unease I felt about him returned.

Before leaving the Club, I'd dashed to my room with the cuckoo clock. Driven by a throbbing certainty that the clock held a clue to Liberty's disappearance, I'd removed the small screws and lifted off the thin metal plate in back. There didn't appear to be anything unusual about the inner mechanism, but I'd noted a series of numbers below the movement as well as the name *G. Becker*, above the word *Freiburg*, written in brown ink on the wooden housing. Placing a quick call to my Uncle Chance, I passed along the information. At his direction, I had also located a customs sticker pasted discreetly on the side. I'd assumed that Liberty brought the clock into the States while she'd been attending Swiss boarding school. But the sticker was dated just four months ago.

Uncle Chance promised to do some checking, and we agreed to talk again in the morning. By then, it was possible I would already have all the answers I wanted, directly from the source.

On the sixth floor, I was met by Dante's secretary, who told me her name, Miss Tempest, and invited me to accompany her to a conference room where she said the men were waiting.

"This is bold of me," she said, as we strolled an interior hallway, "and I hope you won't mind. But the other gals and I have been talking."

The secretary stopped beside one of the closed doors and faced me. Behind the bottle-bottom glasses, her eyes darted. She was younger than I'd thought, probably just nineteen. She was also prettier than at first glance.

"We, the other gals and I, want you to know that we're behind you. We think what you're doing as a pilot, and now as an operative, is, well, *inspiring*."

"Why th-thank you," I stammered. "It's nothing, really."

The secretary held my gaze. A certain sweetness in her expression made me think of Clara Renner. "Yes, it *is* something. You're proving yourself against incredible odds."

I thought I must be blushing. Anxious to turn the tables, I recalled my well-equipped luggage. "Are you the person I should thank for the phantasmagoric undercover wear?"

"It was a joint effort." She made a grand sweeping gesture, acknowledging her cohorts stationed behind the doors along the deserted hall. "We all contributed ideas and everyone pitched in with the shopping." Her expression grew solemn. "Um-m, we want you to know something else."

"What?"

"Have you had one of Mrs. Sarvello's home-cooked meals yet?"

I blinked. "Why, yes."

"How about the soft shoe routine? Has Dante, uh, Agent Dante, told you about his sister? Let you know he tap dances?" Pounding footsteps, racing down the hall, froze the secretary's expression. The hammering footsteps stopped.

"Thank you, Miss Tempest, I'll take over."

I knew the voice. Turning, I faced the agent whose prominent lantern jaw bore an uncanny resemblance to Dick Tracy's. "Hullo, Special Agent Connelly." I forced a smile.

He returned my greeting with a stiff nod. Then his piercing gaze drilled Miss Tempest. "Lucky I caught up with you. We're in the room three doors down. The reassignment was posted this morning. Didn't you *see* it?"

Miss Tempest's glasses had slipped down the bridge of her nose. She shoved the heavy frames back into position. Behind the thick lenses, her tawny eyes blinked furiously. "My vision is fine, thank you."

Her voice was taut and her mouth twitched as if she wanted to add something else. Instead, she gave him a cool nod.

She turned to me. Maybe it was my imagination or a refraction of light hitting her Coke-bottle lenses, but I had the distinct impression she was trying telepathically to warn me about something. The attempt was too vague. Her allusions to Dante's "seduction package" had been plain enough, though. She and the other secretaries wanted me to know that, true to his namesake, Dante had a devilish side.

Connelly's complexion was beet red, the ruddy tone all the more flagrant against his stiff blond hair. He clasped my elbow and steered me to the appropriate room. Squaring his shoulders, he opened the door, all but pushing me inside.

An immense walnut table filled the center of a windowless room. The leather chairs around it looked comfortable, as if selected with tedious discussions in mind. Presently, all of the seats were abandoned, their occupants having left tablets, pens, and pencils as placeholders. Along one wall, a credenza held a telephone and a water pitcher with a ring of glasses. A wooden plaque emblazoned with the FBI seal hung above the low cabinet while life-sized photographs of the Director and our President dominated the wall directly ahead. My earlier rapidly swelling spirits deflated. Neither Liberty nor Roy was in the room.

Agent Dante stood at the far end of the table, conferring with a Navy officer. He broke away and ambled toward me. I drank in his cuddly physique, his thick, sleepy lashes, and was about to zero in on his scrumptious mouth when the quiet echo of Miss Tempest's warning interceded. A sudden chill, like an icy splash of water, hurtled me back to reality.

Dante flicked a glance over my ensemble. At the spark in his expression, I smiled, anticipating the compliment I felt certain would follow. He arched an eyebrow, but otherwise let the moment pass.

He extended his hand and I took it. Bully for him! He might be able to pull off a professional façade, but at the familiar touch of his palm I felt a rush of warmth and knew I was pink-faced.

He smiled. "Miss Lewis, I'd like you to meet Lieutenant Grey Simmons. He's here for the weekly gathering of Army, Navy, and the Bureau. It's our chance to discuss matters relating to domestic intelligence and coordinate our cases, jointly."

Coordinate their activities? Work together *jointly?* Just who did he think he was trying to snooker? Liberty and I had already crossed paths.

I strained to keep the sarcasm out of my voice. "Anything out of the ordinary on this week's agenda?" Dante's palm felt suddenly clammy. Or was the clamminess mine?

"It's why you're here." He released his grip.

I shook hands with the lieutenant, a slender man with large protruding ears, a wide mouth, and a bland smile. I surveyed the table. "But if this is a joint meeting, where's G-2?"

The lieutenant and Dante exchanged a private look. "My Army counterpart was tied up, wrestling with something else," Simmons replied. "He asked me to act on his behalf today."

"Might be nice if he let us in on the particulars," Connelly muttered, sauntering over to a stack of documents at one end of the table.

I wasn't sure what was going on, but the tension between the men in the room was palpable. Meantime, my curiosity was at the boiling point. Had they heard anything about Liberty?

I turned to Dante. "You mentioned a special agenda item concerning me?"

He adjusted the knot of his loosened tie. "Simmons has informed us that a Navy officer's wife, who is also a member of the Cosmos Club and frequents the beauty shop there, has filed a report claiming that Clara Renner asked her for a map of the Grosse Ile Naval Base."

I felt my eyes bulge. Dante had it wrong. It was Liberty, not Clara, who had done the soliciting. But if Dante and ONI had it backwards, Liberty and G-2 wanted it that way. My thoughts cut back to my meeting with her and the promise I had made. Why didn't she want Dante to know about her mission? And why wasn't G-2 here today?

My focus returned to Dante as he explained that two days had elapsed since Clara approached the woman, actually an admiral's wife. She had delayed reporting the incident because of her longtime relationship with Clara and because she did not want to believe the worst. Also, her husband was out of town and due back the next day. She'd cooled her heels, filling him in on the situation the moment he returned. The admiral notified intelligence directly.

"I was brought into the case just last evening," Simmons said, "and we decided to place someone inside the Cosmos Club, undercover. I raised the idea in our opening session this morning, only to discover the Bureau was already a step ahead." Simmons' wide mouth resumed its insipid smile.

Dante cleared his throat. "That's right. We had already positioned you there, Miss Lewis, but our resources were concentrated on her husband. It's ironic, actually. Connelly and I had planned on discussing our case with the group. Then the surprise news from ONI jumbled everything. We've spent the last couple of hours sorting out who knows what and fitting together the pieces."

And smoothing Simmons' ruffled feathers, I thought.

"On the bright side, now that all agencies involved are pooling information, we have a wider web in place, which means we can close in on Renner, and possibly his cohorts, that much sooner." A cigarette was tucked behind Dante's ear. He adjusted it. "Connelly?"

Connelly looked up from the documents he had been perusing. "Way I see it, ONI and G-2 are riding our coattails on this one. Willow Run is a civilian operation. Military should keep out of it."

I frowned. Was he kidding?

A muscle along Simmons' jaw flexed. "Ford has a private contract. The facility is government owned. You were obliged to share the information immediately."

Connelly *had* been kidding. He smirked. Too late Simmons caught the expression and realized his mistake.

Dante shot me a questioning glance. I arched my eyebrows, conveying that I understood what was behind the interchange. Plant Protection had correctly followed regs by calling in the Bureau after discovering Blount's body. But then, because the corpse was found on government-owned property, military intelligence should have been notified immediately afterward. They weren't. Instead, the FBI, with Plant Security in tow, had forged ahead independently.

Simmons went on, this time addressing Dante. "A lot of manure got piled up in the barn because someone on your watch forgot to slide the door open when they should have. You boys have some heavy shoveling to do if you don't want the brass to get a whiff of this load of crap. It's up to you."

Dante and Connelly exchanged uneasy glances while my gaze flitted from one agency representative to the other. It was as though I were an umpire caught between two teams squabbling over whether a player's foot had touched the base or not. But this was no game. As voiceless teammates drafted by opposing camps, Liberty and I had been placed in competition ourselves. Possibly my friend's room had been ransacked and she had vanished because of it.

I looked from Dante to the lieutenant again. Should I level with my boss? What about Simmons? Shouldn't he be told the truth, that the bad seed was actually the admiral's wife, and not Clara?

I had walked into a hornet's nest of interagency rivalry. I didn't fully understand the nuances of the sport. Moreover, it was still possible that G-2 and Roy had private knowledge of Liberty's whereabouts, and that there was a legitimate reason for keeping their involvement in the case confidential. I took a breath. I had made a commitment to Liberty, my friend. I would keep my promise to her at least until I could verify why G-2 had been absent from the meeting today. But I was still jittery.

Simmons seemed to read my mood. "Let's table our protocol dispute and get to the other matter involving Miss Lewis now, shall we?" He motioned for us to take seats then nodded, indicating Dante should begin.

He pulled the unlit cigarette from behind his ear and tapped it against the table's edge. "The new information implicating Mrs. Renner concerns us. It's one more loose end. We've decided to bring Renner in following the black bag job at Willow Run tonight."

My stomach fluttered. "Tonight?"

Dante nodded and related that they had been doing everything possible to keep the investigation into Blount's murder discreet, but a source close to Renner indicated he was showing signs of unraveling. Before my arrival they and the other strategists, who were now temporarily out of the room, had concluded that the risk of Renner moving or destroying the evidence in his safe, possibly slipping out of the country, was getting too great. Their intent was to confirm that the plans for the night-bombing device Blount had said were in Renner's safe were indeed there. Afterwards, what they found would be used to help convince Renner to finger his handler and any other rogue spies.

"The photos you took at Renner's office will be a great help," Dante added. "Excellent eye. Congratulations."

I wanted to jump up on the big table and dance. "They turned out then? Great."

He removed a set of photographs, fanning them. What a camera! Every shot, including the ones of the sequential numbers on the safe's dial, had been captured. The lab had blown them up and all three numbers were readable.

We reviewed the pictures more thoroughly while I described the office layout, including the safe's location. As I talked, I also made a sketch. Finally, since no one had volunteered who had been selected for the team, I asked. The men batted glances back and forth, and I felt the familiar fluttering in my chest. Had Dante changed his mind? Had I made the cut?

My hopes were dashed. Without meeting my eye, he revealed that six men, two each from the three intelligence arms, had been selected. He rattled off their range of expertise, from safes and locks to cameras and radios. I made a small croaking sound when flaps and seals rolled off his tongue.

Dante would head the team. I was already aware that he held a law degree; now I was surprised to learn he was also proficient in German. His language skills meant that he would perform the role of team evaluator, appraising all documents found in Renner's safe, deciding what should be photographed.

For a moment I thought Connelly had been left on the bench with me. But before Dante finished, he indicated Connelly had the important responsibilities of building a strategy for Renner's interrogation, as well as overseeing certain logistical aspects vital to the break-in.

An awkward silence followed. I had not been asked to join the team or even participate in off-site support. I was crushed.

We had not yet covered my interviews at Willow Run. Determined to maintain a professional demeanor in spite of the rejection, I began reviewing what I had learned from Renner's secretary, Mrs. K. My observation that she seemed to have a great deal of influence over Renner, so much so that he bent over backwards to please her and to help her daughters, interested the men. They were equally intrigued by the tale of my unexpected encounter with Renner at Willow Run. His mood was cool but on edge, I informed them, before going on to describe the dark side of his personality that had emerged later during his confrontation with his wife at the Club.

Dante and Simmons were impressed with my handling of the unforeseen meeting, citing his abnormal behavior as further evidence that the time was ripe to reel him in. On the opposing end of the pole, Connelly thought I should have found an excuse to leave the moment Renner arrived, suggesting I had needlessly exposed my cover. I shrugged off his comments. Then I brought them up to speed about my meeting with Clara, indicating she had confirmed her husband's alibi for the night of Blount's murder and had not revealed any discrepancies suggesting her story differed from his. Her contact with Grace Buchanan-Dineen was limited to only one hair-cutting session, I elaborated, pointing out that the singular event had soured any future relationship between the women, permanently.

I hesitated, then summed up. "I must, in good conscience, add that I'm not entirely convinced Mrs. Renner is part of the ring."

Connelly countered, "But the admiral's wife said…"

"I know what the admiral's wife said. She claims Clara asked her for a map of the base. But how do you know she's telling the truth? What if she made the story up?"

Connelly asked incredulously, "Why would an admiral's wife lie?"

"To get attention. To reinforce a need to feel important. To get back at her husband for something he did—or *didn't*—do." Good reasons raised in my conversation with Liberty.

"The admiral's wife didn't lie," Simmons said flatly. "She's solid. We've checked."

I was a sucker for the underdog. What other reason could I have for stubbornly plowing on as Clara's advocate? "Okay, so Mrs. Renner asked her for a map. How do you know she was getting it for her husband? How does that prove she's part of his ring?"

Connelly made a choking noise. "You put two and two together."

My tone was measured. "I have nothing solid, but my gut tells me she's not involved. I feel compelled to let you know that."

Connelly snickered. "*Your gut*? What are you saying? A bit of girl talk in a beauty parlor and, presto, with a wave of a hand, she's absolved? How about some facts?"

I glared at him. The stiff waves in his hair still held the lines drawn by the teeth of his comb. The styling was so perfect he might have been wearing a hand-sewn wig. An *ill-chosen* wig.

I ripped my gaze from him and focused on Romeo. In private, Dante had repeatedly praised my instincts. Now would be a good time for him to put Connelly in his place. Occupied with flipping his unlit cigarette on the table, he passed on the chance.

I cleared my throat and continued, first assuring them that Clara's connection to the Barclay-Bly sisters was also strictly business, saving the "chair gossip" involving Kiki and Philip for last.

"So Kiki had an affair with her sister's fiancé," Dante muttered under his breath. "Well what do you know."

Simmons had been following our tripartite exchange without comment. He tugged a large ear thoughtfully. "So, if Renner didn't do it, who's your murderer?"

"The lieutenant who sent Blount out on the training maneuvers that cost him his hand was dishonorably discharged. Could be him." Dante frowned. "Or, most likely, Renner's handler…"

"With help from someone on the inside," Connelly said. "Someone who knew the layout and was familiar with Blount's routine. We know Renner was in cahoots with an employee able to help him pass faulty castings through assembly safeguards. Maybe this employee, likely an inspector, discovered Blount was squealing. This inspector would be desperate to save his neck, right?"

I drew a shaky breath. Until this moment I'd dismissed Connelly's theories as bunk.

"You might have something there," I began, slowly. "Mrs. K's daughter, not Wanda, the one I was supposedly assigned to interview, but the other one, Gisela, is an inspector. Works inside the main wings, on the final assembly phase. According to Mrs. K, it was Renner who pushed Gisela in that direction. Could he have drawn her into his web somehow?"

"Has anyone checked out this daughter?" Simmons asked.

Dante and Connelly exchanged glances.

"Uh, no," Dante said. "Blount swore that before their night out at the Orange Lantern, Renner had never breathed a word about other insiders. And when he finally spilled the beans, he didn't volunteer any names."

"It's possible that Renner himself didn't know who the mole on the assembly line was," Connelly added. "His handler may have deliberately set it up that way so the identities of his spies remained secret from one another. That way if he lost a man to the other side, the defector wouldn't be able to give anyone else away."

"The setup would also give the spy master leeway to assign one ring member to spy on another, incognito," Dante said. "To be sure everyone remains loyal."

"Hey..." I searched first Dante's face, then Connelly's, as a fuzzy thought took shape. "Didn't one of you say Renner was born in the States?"

Connelly nodded. "Yeah, why?"

"He's got an accent. It's hardly noticeable, but it's there."

Simmons had been jotting something into a small notebook. He looked up, zeroing in on Dante, but Connelly spoke first.

"We ran a check..."

"Then ONI will run another," the lieutenant snapped, cutting him short.

We were back to the interagency grudge match. My stomach tightened.

At the head of the table, Dante had been bouncing the pink eraser on his pencil against the table's waxed surface. The noise stopped. "We haven't covered your jail visit yet," he said.

"What's to cover?" I asked. "You were listening, right?"

"We've been *here* for the better part of the day." Connelly cast a dark glance at Simmons, suggesting the fault rested with him.

Dante whacked the eraser against the table. Connelly settled back into his seat, methodically cracking his knuckles while his partner continued.

"We had a man positioned at the jail, yes. But you had the advantage of watching the woman's expressions and body language. What's your take? Is she being straight about not knowing Renner and Blount?"

I gawked at him. Did he understand the irony in what he was asking? He hadn't spoken up for me earlier when Connelly had ridiculed me for defending Clara, based on my gut. Now he wanted "my take" on what the Countess had said?

I waited a few beats longer. "Yes, I believe she is leveling with me. With good reason. She had hoped to be exonerated by now. But beyond that, she'd like to get on with her life. Thinks I can help by clearing the way for a visit from her fiancé."

Connelly snickered. "The fiancé. We've got that ground covered. Heard he's considering breaking off the engagement."

"What are you talking about? He's devoted to her."

He didn't reply, but the sneer on his face said it all.

"Go on," Dante said, addressing me.

I did, concluding with the terms the Countess had laid out.

Dante's pencil tapped the table, loudly. "We can't ignore her. We need to know if the sisters are involved."

"What about Leo's progress?" Connelly asked. "Anything?"

"Not yet," Dante replied.

I pulled my steno pad out of my satchel and flipped pages. "You might want to check out this name and address I found in her cell," I said, repeating the information on the fence, Tazio Abbado, that I'd found behind the photograph of the Countess' father.

"I've decided I want Pucci on the break-in team," Dante announced, abruptly. "She's a pro on flaps and seals. The man we lined up is too green."

Connelly's jaw dropped and my heart was jack hammering so loudly I thought everyone in the room could surely hear it.

I smiled at Dante. I glowed. I tingled. I felt so good it was like I was flying.

Connelly's face was beet red. "What? Take a woman on a clandestine mission? What if there's trouble and she crumbles? She could compromise the mission. And what if she can't keep a secret afterwards?"

Dante's voice was smooth and sure. "Lewis is in. She's trained, she's been inside the office premises. I'm confident in her abilities."

No additional objections followed. Dante was the mission leader. He raised a final item of business. Still convinced that the Barclay-Bly sisters were somehow linked to our case, he asked if I would return to jail for a third session with the Countess. It was a grim task made worse, as I would have to begin the meeting by informing her that her wish to see Mr. Butler had been denied.

Across from me, Connelly's thin mouth had twisted into one of his schoolboy smirks. His arrogance made Dante's latest challenge suddenly irresistible. I accepted. My reward, Connelly's incredulous look, was instantaneous.

Chapter Eighteen

I left the conference room with Dante, who told Simmons and Connelly he wanted to discuss the break-in with me, in private. When we were alone, he suggested we continue our discussion outdoors. Given the FBI's propensity for eavesdropping, and sensing that there was a second sub rosa layer yet to be disclosed, I scuttled two steps ahead of him to the elevator.

Downstairs in the main lobby, uniformed guards stood beside the bank of doors at the main entrance. They each gave Dante a discreet nod as we passed.

Outside, I grabbed his arm. "I got a tip Roy Jarvis is in town. He's G-2. Was he the rep who was supposed to be in the meeting but cancelled?"

Dante stared at me. "I've been in contact with Jarvis several times in the last twenty-four hours, but let's find someplace more private first. Over here."

We strolled to the far end of the portico, pausing beside a limestone column in the corner. I searched Dante's face. "What's going on? Do you know something about Liberty?"

"She's disappeared."

"I know. We were together just before it happened. Last night, shortly before midnight."

Dante looked surprised. "You saw her last night?"

I nodded, hurriedly filling him in on my surprise encounter with her at the Club. I described her changed appearance, stifling a grin as I repeated the *nom de guerre* she'd selected for her wartime role as a manicurist. The light moment ebbed as I reported her disturbing absence from work that morning.

"Her disappearance, is it connected to the sting? Is she all right?"

Dante stared over my head, looking perplexed.

"It's okay," I assured him. "Liberty told me she was working for G-2."

He came back to earth. "She what?"

I should have known he'd be upset with us for confiding in one another. I rushed on. "She had to. We were both at the same club, undercover. We suspected there'd been a mix-up and that we'd been assigned to the same case. We figured we needed to come clean with one another or risk botching things up altogether."

Dante remained eerily still.

"We didn't go into detail," I added. "She revealed just a little about her—uh, G-2's—side of the case, and I barely had the chance to admit I'd been sent by the FBI."

"Which case?"

I squinted up at him. "The case that placed Liberty in the Cosmos Club, posing as a fascist sympathizer, testing the admiral's wife to see if she could get her to steal a map," I replied impatiently.

I watched a school of pigeons pecking the cement on the steps below. I shook my head. "I can't believe that an admiral's wife would want to sell out her own country. Why is she doing it, do you know? Has a loose screw? Needs money? Husband do something unforgivable?"

Dante had no ready answers and my list of troubling issues still held an important straggler. "Simmons…ONI…they have it all backwards. Why does G-2, and now you, the FBI, want them to think Clara Renner is the *femme fatale*? Why aren't all agencies leveling with one another, like you're supposed to?" Out of breath and out of questions, I paused.

"We *are* leveling with each other."

"No you're not." The words echoed hollowly in the surrounding silence.

"We are. Clara Renner asked the admiral's wife for a map of Grosse Ile Naval Station."

"But that's not what Liberty said. Where is she? What's happened to her? And why wasn't Roy at the meeting?"

Dante's gaze caught mine and held. "Roy Jarvis is in Washington D.C. juggling a host of unsolved national security matters, recently upgraded to top priority. Liberty—by the way, I never heard of her before Jarvis brought me in on the matter—went out on a field test in the Washington area a month ago. Never returned. The incident hit his desk yesterday."

"But I just saw her—" I paused, letting what Dante had said sink in. "*A month ago?* But that's when *I* completed training."

He nodded. "Right. But you were enrolled in an accelerated course. She had weeks of instruction remaining."

A tiny spasm pulsed in front of Dante's ear. There was more. "What?" I asked, cautiously.

"The Countess and her ring of spies were arrested a month ago. Liberty vanished the day after."

My stomach dropped. "What are you saying? You think she's an enemy agent? Not possible. She's a good person, the daughter of missionaries. She was recruited by OI. She passed OSS security checks—"

Dante placed a hand on my arm. "Liberty's your friend, you have a bond. But think a minute. She was working undercover as a manicurist at the Cosmos Club. She told you G-2 placed her there. That Jarvis was running her assignment. They didn't. He wasn't. What do *you* suppose is going on?"

I sighed. "She lied to me. Why?"

"Not sure. What I do know is, after she went AWOL, an investigation launched by her trainers led them nowhere. G-2 was contacted and asked to cover matters domestically. Jarvis took the reins yesterday. He contacted the parents and they pointed him here. He also checked her records, saw you listed as her former roommate. He followed up with Miss Cochran, hoping to contact you for some insights."

"She told him I was in Detroit and he contacted you…"

Dante slipped a finger under his shirt collar, tugging it away from his neck. "Let's walk." He bounded down the stairs. His long strides and my fitted skirt made it impossible for me to keep up. He waited on the sidewalk.

Tall commercial buildings formed a canyon around us. Earlier, when I'd entered the Federal building, the air had seemed oppressive. Now it positively brimmed with the exhaust and grime spewing from passing automobiles. I unfastened my jacket; Dante loosened his tie and undid the button under its knot. We started down the block.

I looked over. "You mentioned Liberty's parents. Do they know she's missing?"

Dante nodded. "Uh-huh."

"They must be worried sick."

"They don't have much contact with her."

"That's strange. Liberty and her parents have always been very close."

Dante shook his head. "Not according to the Leaches. They told Jarvis they've hardly spoken to one another in years."

"Years?"

"Uh-huh." He paused and looked over. "Pucci, did you know Liberty was adopted?"

"Adopted? Nooo…"

A malaise moved through me and my bones felt weak while bit by bit he revealed her background.

When she was only hours old, Liberty had been left in a box on the Leaches' doorstep. The couple, both medical professionals, she a nurse, he a doctor, had no children of their own. After a futile search for the baby's mother, they decided to adopt.

The pivotal moment came when Liberty was fourteen. A typical teen, more willful and mischievous than most, she had already pushed her parents' tolerance to the brink. On one particularly trying day, in a fit of frustration and anger, Mrs. Leach lashed out at her husband, saying, "She's a wicked little brat! Maybe we shouldn't have adopted her after all!"

She regretted her words the instant they left her mouth. A million times more once they learned Liberty had overheard them. Shocked by the discovery of her adoption, she pummeled them with vengeful outbursts that went on for days. Once she had calmed down enough to listen to reason, Mrs. Leach tried to make amends. But by then something in Liberty had changed. She told her mother she had never felt connected to them, had no desire to be like them, and now, having at last learned the truth, she felt a new sense of inner peace and freedom. According to Dr. Leach, after that her behavior regressed even further. She became surly, sullen, and completely antisocial.

My mind reeled. How could my friend have told me something so different? Why?

I tried to make sense of it. "And so, unable to think of anything better, they sent her off to boarding school in Europe..." I hesitated. "Her mother's sister is in Switzerland. Liberty lived with her aunt and uncle, learned all those languages there. That part of her past is true, right?"

"Yes, but putting an ocean between them did little to mend the familial relationship. Communication remained next to nil even when she returned home on breaks."

"But she was adopted, never knew her real mother, had never been told...the trauma—"

I was feeling a little shell-shocked myself, the sensation suddenly magnified by the haunting image of *my* mother, her blank green eyes bulging with the terror of her free-fall from the church loft. The sick despair I'd felt afterwards, kissing her unresponsive cheek, came flooding back. "I'm sorry," I'd whispered, my tears flooding the planes of her immobile face, running to catch in the crook of her twisted neck. *Sorry* for saying I didn't want to go to practice with her that afternoon; *sorry* for refusing to leave the house until she gave in and let me wear my patent leather Sunday shoes, not the high-top brown oxfords prescribed to correct my pigeon-toed feet; *sorry* for making her angry, making her late, making her rush so that she was distracted when she got up in front of the choir, turned her back to the railing... *Sorry, sorry, sorry.*

Dante must have sensed the anguish churning within me. He clasped my elbow, drawing me close. "The Leaches might not have been perfect parents, but they loved their daughter. They made a mistake and did their best to mend it. They gave her opportunities—Swiss boarding school, summers abroad until the war started. Later, when she wanted to attend Vassar, they helped arrange it."

I nodded, but my brain whirled and I felt slightly nauseous. We walked in silence.

"Liberty's parents directed Roy to Detroit," I said after a while. "Why was that?"

"They thought she might be visiting a young man who was part of the crowd she ran with in Europe." He glanced back over his shoulder. "A group of young radicals, according to the Leaches. Supposedly, this chum immigrated here in the fall of '41."

"Fall of '41? That's when the Countess arrived. Immigration control would have a record."

"Right. He registered as an alien—Tazio Abbado—and we've followed the trail to his last known address. No sign of him, though. Or Liberty. But we're still digging."

It wasn't getting any better. "*Tazio Abbado*?"

"Uh-huh. The same guy the Countess told you is a known fence."

He didn't say it, but we both knew Liberty's pre-war job at the Oral Intelligence Group involved interviewing refugees and screening for *agents provocateurs.* She was at the organization in 1941, when both the Countess and Abbado would have passed through.

"Was he put on the Watch List?" Dante shook his head. I swallowed. "Has Liberty been identified as the OI agent who cleared him through?"

"No. But our office has been on the case for only a day."

We hovered near the curb of an intersection, waiting for the light to change. "I know things don't look good for her," I began softly, "but I'm wondering. If she's crossed the line, why was her room ransacked? Who would have done it? It wouldn't have been Liberty. Who then? Could it have been someone involved with Renner?" I waited while a car with a faulty muffler rattled past. "She had a midnight meeting to go to. What if the appointment was a ruse? Maybe she was lured somewhere, shanghaied by someone from Renner's group. It's possible, right?"

I had been watching Dante's expression closely. "You're not completely convinced she's with the enemy either, are you? Is that why you didn't mention her disappearance to Simmons? You wanted to shield her?"

He lifted his shoulder in a half-shrug. "Let's just say I'm not prepared to throw one of ours to the lions before it's clear what's going on."

A snarl of pedestrians had formed around us. I pressed closer to him and felt the thick muscle of his upper arm tighten. I glanced up. Our eyes met and I recognized the tenderness that made my heart go zing. I squeezed his forearm.

The light turned green and we were swept into the crosswalk. We strolled, and I raised a different aspect of the case that was nagging me. "Do you know the investigator who visited Liberty's landlady at the boarding house?"

Dante bobbed his head. "Yes."

"Are you aware that he went to the Cosmos Club and questioned Clara Renner?"

He nodded again.

"And supposedly by then she had already asked the admiral's wife for a map of the base, correct?"

"Pucci, there's no *supposedly*. Mrs. Renner asked for, and was given, the map." He read my startled expression. "Not an accurate map," he explained, softly. "Things the enemy would be looking for—runways, storage tanks, barracks, and the like—they'd all been redrawn."

False map or not, Clara Renner was in the soup. Right up to her mascara-laden lashes. And I had thought she was innocent. What had happened to my ability to read people?

I viewed the crowd around us with an Impressionist's eye, melding the forms into a blur of soft shapes and colors, and quietly groaned again. First Liberty had duped me, now guileless Clara appeared to be aligned with the enemy. Imagine! After telling me she loved her beauty parlor work and that she wanted to grow her business so that her husband could retire.

I clenched Dante's arm. "I don't want to think the worst," I began, haltingly. "And I can't believe I could be so wrong about her—"

"Who?"

"Clara. She confided that she had some money secretly squirreled away. Said someone—not her husband—was advising her, helping her make private investments."

"And…"

I lowered my voice. "Could it be by *investments* she meant gathering U.S. secrets and maps? Selling them to *you-know-who*?"

Dante stared at me like he thought I had finally come to my senses. "Sounds like you've struck gold, now you need to mine it." He thought for a second. "She trusts you. In the morning, we'll arrange it so she's left for work before we pull Renner in. That way, you'll have another chance to talk to her, find out what you can about this adviser before she hears we've got her husband."

It was my turn to stare incredulously. But I didn't object.

We hadn't yet discussed the black-bag job. We'd been keeping an eye out for a decent place to have a bite to eat and talk. The clang of an approaching streetcar inspired a different venue entirely. Our eyes met and we moved quickly, dodging through two lanes of stalled traffic. I had placed one foot on the bottom step, propelling my body forward as I lunged to leap aboard. Dante grabbed my arm, yanked, and pulled me back.

I stumbled and he righted me, apologizing and explaining that he was in the habit of conducting periodic checks for tails.

Such evasive maneuvers had been covered in my training, but his sudden execution of one had caught me off guard. Which was the whole idea.

Another streetcar approached from our left. A blur of red and ivory, its polished glass and brass trim winked in the fading light. Behind us, the lanes of traffic cleared. A small group had been huddled curbside, waiting to cross. Now they scurried toward us.

We climbed aboard. The first bench beyond the rear doors offered the privacy we were after. We wouldn't have anyone in front of us and there were only three rows, including a long bench spanning the width of the car, in back.

"Do you know Merriman?" I asked, as the trolley lumbered off.

"Who?"

"Merriman," I repeated. "The night doorman at the Cosmos Club."

I quickly described the theft of Liberty's note, getting knocked to the floor, and finding the warning on the mirror. I concluded with my suspicions about Merriman being the intruder, and indicated that he was probably the last person to talk to Liberty before her secret meeting.

Dante was in the dark about the man. If G-2 or ONI had assigned someone masquerading as Merriman to work inside the club, he had not been informed. He assured me that he would look into the matter once we were back at headquarters. At the mention of headquarters, I at last remembered to thank him for including me on the break-in team.

"No thanks necessary. You deserve the chance, you earned it." His dark eyes glimmered. "Besides, a woman who can hold her own with Connelly deserves every privilege she can get."

The next few moments passed in silence. The rod riding the cables above clacked periodically and I envisioned the sparks flying from them while I contemplated what it would be like visiting Renner's domain for a second time. I imagined myself treading through a minefield of possible traps. Of course, Dante would be there, leading the way. Strong, wily, courageous, handsome…

An explosion—actually a spark arcing down from the wires—suddenly obliterated Dante from my vision. Now *I* led a team. All women. We stole into Renner's office. I crept to the safe…

Dante leaned forward to glance out the window. "Let's hop off next stop, grab another trolley back downtown. You'll need to stop by the requisition room, pick up the clothing and equipment you'll need for tonight. I'll bring you up to speed about the mission along the way."

Chapter Nineteen

Back at the Cosmos Club, with nearly four hours to kill, I longed to do what every other red-blooded woman dreamed of doing after an exhausting day on her feet. Take a bath. But other than breakfast, I'd consumed only one Hershey bar throughout my entire crazy day. I was famished!

I emerged from the Club's elegant dining hall following a superb meal of Dover sole smothered in a lemony white sauce. The chocolate mousse dessert had been tempting, but I resisted, downing two cups of thick black java instead.

My room was one flight below. Feeling recharged, I started down the corridor, heading for the interior stairwell. A familiar figure approached from the opposite direction. Newly coifed and all dolled up, the woman didn't register until after she had passed. It was Dee. She had introduced the Countess to her fiancé, Nelson Butler, and the breadth of her relationship with the former spy remained open-ended. I made a snap decision. I would rest later. If not before the break-in, then after.

"Hi, Dee," I said.

Dee whirled around. "Pucci Lewis," she called loudly. Her satin spike-heels wobbled slightly, carrying her toward me.

Dee wore a white satin tunic over flowing black trousers, the ensemble a bold change from the conservative silk dress she'd worn when we'd first met at the afternoon tea. The chic outfit, while flattering, was more along the lines of what her sister Kiki might wear. The apparel wasn't the only copycat item, I noted, as she drew closer. A day earlier, her hair had been pulled back into a tight chignon. Now it was worn loose, in a chin-length bob, and the circle of white at her temple had been banished by a blue-black dye.

Dee had been looking me over as well. "Why, you look positively beat. Bad day?"

I smiled. "Not a bad day but a *full* day, including several interviews and some leg work researching my stories."

Unlike her sister's bob with its fringe of thick bangs, Dee's new cut was all one length and worn parted on the side. She tucked a section of dark tresses behind her ear, the curve of inky hair a graceful frame for her pearl-studded earlobe. She was eyeing my FBI-issued bag. Made of sturdy black canvas, trimmed with leather, the satchel was surprisingly light considering it contained the tools of trade I would need for the evening's surreptitious entry.

"Research material," I improvised. "I was on my way to the lounge. Join me for a sherry?"

Did babies cry? She hooked her arm through mine. "Lovely. A nightcap would be just the thing."

I knew from the way she leaned on me that Dee had had enough to drink already. But in one of my less noble moments, turning a blind eye to her problem, I ordered a carafe of sherry from a passing member of the staff.

In the lounge, a vacant pair of club chairs beckoned from near the fireplace. It wasn't obvious, but the clasp on Dee's handbag was undone. We took our seats and a piece of paper—actually, an endorsed bank check—sailed out. I caught it before it could touch the floor. The name and address of a law office was printed in the upper corner; the Barclay-Bly sisters were the joint payees on the line at the document's center.

I handed over the draft; she hadn't even realized she'd dropped it. At the same moment, a waitress arrived with a decanter and glasses.

Sherry was light, my day had been hard. With a delicate clink, Dee and I toasted to good health, good friends, and a quick end to the war. I took a tiny swallow, savoring the mellow hazelnut flavor plus the soft burn of alcohol going down. It was possible the taste was all the more pleasant knowing that when I raised my glass again, I would only pretend to take a sip. A long night lay ahead and my mind needed to be absolutely sharp.

"So glad I didn't lose this," Dee said, returning the check to her handbag, securing the clasp. "Promised Kiki I'd deliver it tomorrow."

"I was in the salon earlier. Heard she wasn't feeling well. Nothing serious, I hope?"

"Last night, she had a splitting headache. Took a sleeping pill. This morning when I called, the effects hadn't worn off. She was groggy, still not up to par, that's all."

Her glass chinked softly as she set it on the butler table between us. I poured her a fresh shot. "Kiki agreed to an interview for my piece on the Cosmos Club. When do you think she'll be back?"

"V-V's convinced her to take another day or two off."

"With those viperous women conspiring to squelch her election campaign and the Book Faire coming right up? Doesn't that seem odd?"

"When V-V sets a course, there's no use trying to change it." Dee caught my look. "It's true. Personally, I think she gives in to his need to run things too readily. This time, though, he's brewed up something even I can't resist." She smiled. "Tomorrow Cook is packing a picnic for us and we're taking the electric launch out for a cruise down the river. It's something we used to do monthly when I'd bring her check." She became animated, describing the boat and the pleasures of meandering along the river, eating and enjoying one another's company and nature. "Last few times, though, she's been too busy."

"You bring them a monthly check?"

"Not *them*. Kiki. It's her allowance."

I must have looked puzzled.

"In their will," she explained, "our parents tapped me as their executor."

"I see. But Kiki's older, isn't she?"

"Yes. My sister was pretty irresponsible once upon a time, and our parents never got over it."

"Your parents put you in a rough spot. But why do you have to deliver it? Why not let your lawyer do it, or just mail her the check?"

Dee sighed. "The will stipulates I have to do the deed in person."

Growing up, I was taught never to discuss money openly. The subject was too personal; it simply was not polite. Yet I could not shake the sense that the senior Barclay-Blys had been concerned about more than youthful missteps in structuring their will. I tiptoed further down the delicate line.

"But it's been years since Kiki has done anything wild, right? Did they have reason to think she was up to some new sort of mischief?"

Dee looked irritated. "I don't know what my parents were thinking. But it wasn't that Kiki had somehow regressed. It doesn't matter anyway. Once I hand the money over, she's free to do whatever she wants."

I pushed on. "Was it V-V? Were they afraid he would take over her funds?"

"Our parents trusted V-V," she said a little too quickly. "They gave them the Rouge River property and enough money to build their dream house as a wedding present."

"That's not the same as willing them half of the estate," I countered.

She shrugged and looked suddenly morose. "It was their money, their will. Let's leave it at that, shall we?"

I wanted to say: No, let's not. Your parents wanted to control Kiki's life, even from the grave. They must have had a reason. *Tell me about it.* But it was her family and I knew to back off. I let her finish her drink in peace.

Her eyes were teary when she set down her glass.

"It might help to talk about it," I said softly.

"Well, it's just, well..." She faltered, then her thoughts escaped in a rush. "Sometimes I worry that she loves him too much. A woman should never surrender herself to a man so completely. It can only mean heartache in the end."

I restrained a noisy sigh. Instead of a dark family secret, she was alluding to her private experience with the cad who'd left her at the altar.

"Talk about devotion," I said in a bright voice, shifting to the other liaison I had in mind. "What do you think of the newspaper accounts describing Nelson Butler's relationship with the Countess?"

Seeming stumped by the abrupt transition, Dee knitted her eyebrows into a dark line.

I continued. "She led a secret life apart from him, first as an enemy agent, then as a counteragent for the FBI. Today she's in jail, yet Butler swears he still loves her. Now *that's* devotion, don't you agree?"

She glanced around the room. "I introduced them," she whispered.

"What was she like?"

"She was all right, but now that we know she's a spy…" She hesitated. "I included her in a small pre-wedding dinner party I was hosting. Everyone liked her back then. She and Nelson had so much in common, I sat them together."

I put my glass to my lips, pretending to take a sip while she drained the dregs of hers. "Tell me more about the party. Who else was there? Anyone zany or notorious besides the Countess?" *Any additional German secret agents?*

Beneath her thick eyebrows, Dee's eyes glittered. "You truly are one die-hard reporter, always digging for that scoop, aren't you?"

With a shrug, I raised an eyebrow suggesting that, yes, I was.

She gave a resigned smile. "The party was fourteen months ago. No one of any notoriety attended, nor do I recall anyone doing anything scandalous or saying something newsworthy."

Dee's ease and confidence in talking about her and Kiki's relationship with the Countess made me think she was telling the truth. Why then did I still feel uneasy?

Dee rubbed the vivid blue paint blotch staining her index finger with her thumb, as if trying to erase it.

"While you were in the salon, getting your makeover, did you happen to notice, has the manicurist returned?"

The thumb paused. She held her paint-stained hand aloft, fingers splayed, and laughed. "Kiki is the one obsessed with getting manicures." She knit her eyebrows. "But what do you mean 'returned'?"

"Haven't you heard? Miss Fingers didn't show up for work this morning. No one's heard from her. She vanished without a trace sometime in the night."

"I *hadn't* heard, how awful!"

I nodded, Dee's reaction barely registering. Her comment about her sister's nail-grooming habits had reminded me of the skirmish between Kiki and V-V over *Personality Unlimited* when I'd first seen them in the library. They had both wanted to deliver it to Glossy, but Kiki eventually won, saying she was going there anyway to schedule a manicure appointment. Manicures were not free and her hands had been perfectly groomed already.

Adrenaline coursed through me like a drug. I wanted to bop myself on the head. Why hadn't I pieced it together earlier?

An urge to get to the Club's library overwhelmed me. I checked my watch and sprang to my feet. "Sorry, have to go. Expecting an important call. I'm late. Please forgive me."

Chapter Twenty

The library was deserted. At the corner desk where Liberty and I had met the night before, a pair of shaded sconces had been left on, casting the room in dim pockets of shadow and light. The evening before, the lamp on the desk had been turned off and Liberty was reading by pen light. At the time I figured she had just wanted to be discreet.

The light was a miniature TL-122. I'd seen her slip it into the pocket of her smock. The remarkable part of what I'd observed, then quickly stored away, was that the tiny torch had been throwing off a violet-blue glow. This meant Liberty had used an ultraviolet filter to convert the torch. Made of black glass with both a smooth face and a diffusing one, the filter eliminated most of the visible light in the beam. The remaining rays emitted were ultraviolet. Simply put, last night she had been scanning the text for a secret message. Guarded with each other, she hadn't explained and I hadn't asked.

I pulled the desk lamp's chain. Soft emerald light washed the shelves. The book's familiar dark blue spine was where Liberty had left it. I removed the thin volume.

I sat on the brocade-covered chair occupied by Kiki a day earlier when we'd first met. She had locked the center drawer before we left. In my FBI bag, I assessed the array of tools. This was a simple job. I selected the proper pick from a slotted pocket.

The drawer pulled open with a rattle. The bottle of nail polish Kiki had considered taking, then left behind, was on its side. In righting the bottle, I checked the contents, noting that the clear polish inside was nearly depleted.

The bowels of the drawer were dark. I retrieved my miniature flashlight—not a TL-122, but another model suited for the job—and ran the beam over the drawer's interior, the palm of my hand patting from one item to the next. The finds, such as they were, amounted to papers and receipts relating to the Book Faire. In a final patting sweep, my fingers met the rough cow-grain surface of a letter-sized accordion file lodged in back. I propped the torch on the desk so that the beam shone on the file.

The first item was a dog-eared, pocket-sized softcover book. I flipped it open. The fine hairs along the back of my neck stood on end. An illustrated explosives manual in German! Questions ping-ponged inside my brain. Who did it belong to? Kiki? It could also be Grace Buchanan-Dineen's. Kiki had invited her to the Club. Maybe the speaker-spy had asked her hostess to hold onto it for her. I checked the inside cover for an inscription, then thumbed the pages. Whoever it belonged to, it was a strange thing to find locked inside the desk of the Club's Enrichment Program committee chair. Bewildered and somewhat numb with shock, I set the manual down.

My next discovery, two cancelled checks signed by Kiki, stapled together and made out to Philip Chambers, Dee's ex-fiancé, was equally perplexing. Dated a week apart, they had been written a year ago, in July, the month of the couple's intended wedding ceremony.

Dipping back into the file, I unearthed a note attached to a faded postcard of the Eiffel tower, announcing Kiki and V-V's marriage. Addressed to his attorney and signed by the senior Mr. Barclay-Bly, it read, *Check him out carefully*—Ah. Proof Kiki's father had been concerned about his son-in-law's character. And quite possibly the impetus for structuring his estate in a way that would protect his daughter.

Next was a memo. The gist was that an investigator, hired by Barclay-Bly, had discovered that the Parisian friend who introduced Kiki to her chauffer had lied. V-V was not a descendant of bluebloods like she had claimed. His name had the proper pedigree, that much was true, but he was not a bona fide Vivikovsky family member. A records check in Ukraine that might have uncovered his true roots had proved difficult and, in the end, was abandoned.

So her father had believed Kiki married a fraud. *But was he?* Before escaping to Paris, V-V had been a freedom fighter striving to save his country from Stalin. What if in trying to erase his past he was forced to take an assumed name? In wartime, switching one's identity was commonplace and in many instances the only option for survival. And another thing, Liberty had vouched for V-V…

Uncertainty gripped my soul. How much weight did Liberty's word actually carry? It appeared she had not told the truth about Roy or about G-2. Had she also lied about finding nothing of interest in the charm book?

I shoved the disquieting thoughts aside and returned to the memo.

Y-Y LV IDOVH

The letters hand printed in the upper right hand corner in pencil were so faint I hadn't noticed them earlier. Obviously a coded message. We had studied plenty of sophisticated cipher substitution codes at Spy School, but my immediate instinct was that this was an elementary example, requiring nothing more than Cipher 101 basics. Y-Y unscrambled was surely "V-V," and applying to the balance of the message the substitution logic of falling back three letters, I came up with V-V IS FALSE. Underscoring the memo's point.

The last item in the pouch was a wedding invitation. At least that was what I deduced, examining the heavy ivory-colored envelope. I was wrong. Inside was a thick piece of card stock. On it was a hand-written poem.

The love of my life came not
As love unto others is cast,
For mine was a secret wound—
But the wound grew a pearl, at last.

I got to the salutation and my breath caught:

Kiki, my love—A gift in your favorite palette, pink.
May they be seeds of pleasure, as you are the love pearl
of my heart. Yours with deepest devotion, P

I blinked a couple of times, trying to decipher the meaning in the message. The sender claimed Kiki's favorite color was pink and the poem referred to pearls. I stared at the correspondent's initial, P. So were the rumors true? Had Philip given "Kiki, my love" pink pearls? If so, why was Dee wearing them?

What had Renner's secretary, Mrs. K, said? "We do our best to sidestep unpleasantries by keeping busy rather than dwelling on them. Especially in those matters over which we have no control." Who could understand the powers of love? Or lust? An ember in the fireplace snapped. Hurriedly stowing the items, I relocked the drawer.

At the door to my suite, I studied the seam above the handle. In the morning, I'd trapped the doorframe with a strand of hair. The fine strand, hardly long enough, barely dark enough, remained suspended across the crack, lightly glued in place with saliva.

Secure that no one had invaded my room in my absence, I went in and set the book on the desk. Dropping my bag to the floor, I did a quick but thorough check of the room and armoire.

I removed Gran's derringer from the suitcase, placed it on the desk, keeping the grip within reach and the snub-nose angled toward the door, and picked up the copy of *Personality Unlimited.* The uniform off-white paper made finding telltale signs of an invisible message all the more difficult, but I scrutinized a large sampling of pages before turning to the table of contents and skimming the headings: *Make-up, Dress, Manners, Character Improvement…*

Liberty had said her meeting was at *midnight.* I randomly flipped to page twelve, part of the Make-up section. The irony was incredible: secret ink was *invisible;* page twelve described the transformational powers of *vanishing* cream!

I drew a shaky breath then scanned for coded transmissions that might be hidden in the typewritten text. Next, I did a word search, hunting for obvious marks or evidence of distorted lettering. Finally, I tried to analyze the subject matter covered on the page, hoping to uncover a coded missive.

We recommend using a good quality vanishing cream. Less oily than cold cream, it will not merely puff up the skin and smooth out its texture, ridding it of lines, but may also be used as a foundation for face powder. The cream makes the powder cling evenly so you have a smooth finish…

A few more lines and my eyes began to cross. I fell back in my seat. An instant later, I bolted upright. I moved the book close to the desk lamp. Keeping page twelve separate, I held it up to the light. There! The surface along the paper's top margin was marred by several colorless scratches.

I placed the open book on the desk and brushed the marks with my finger. The rough edges of the nearly invisible lines resembled the samples we'd examined in training suggesting someone had used a stainless steel nib of a fountain pen, or another sharp writing implement, to create a message written in phantom ink.

A colorless fluid, phantom ink was invisible until a black light was shone over it. My hand trembled as I wrenched the portable dark light, requisitioned for the evening's break-in, from the bag on the floor next to me, and switched it on. A jerky scrawling note appeared. The communiqué, fluoresced now in a brilliant blue, said: BEAUTY SHOP. MIDNIGHT. HELP ME. MUST NOT RETURN TO OKPLATE.

The primitive writing and the incomplete phrase were the earmarks of an amateur. I moved the light around the page again, but could not find any additional writing. There were certain techniques critical to writing with secret ink. Number one, using a firm surface. It also takes practice. If the writer ran out of ink, the problem might go unnoticed. A common blunder when your ink is invisible.

I concentrated, reexamining the message in its entirety. The first part was clear: meet the recipient in the beauty salon at midnight. Liberty's tryst had been scheduled for the same time, leading me to conclude the correspondence had to be for her. The message was not from Liberty, we had practiced using our ink sets together and I knew her handwriting, and that meant the message had been written by whomever she was supposed to meet. The last part, unfortunately, still made no sense. MUST NOT RETURN TO *where?* And OKPLATE*?* What was that? Code? Part of the name of the rendezvous spot?

I scanned the adjacent page, then hurriedly whipped through the entire book, giving each page a quick ultraviolet sweep. Nada. Zippo.

I needed to approach the problem from a different angle. Prior to Liberty, Kiki had been the last person in possession of the book. She had fought to keep it from her husband. She had wanted Liberty, and no one else, to receive it. Was that it? She knew it contained a message?

My brow furrowed. But if Kiki had written it, how had she obtained secret ink? Phantom ink was not something the average Joe or Jane could get his or her hands on. OSS agents were trained to write with it, and recognize it, but even they rarely used the stuff. Mainly the ink was utilized by Germans or, in a broader sense, Europeans. My theory didn't make sense unless one or both of the women were enemy agents.

It was also possible the writer was a covert enemy agent and that Kiki had merely been the agent's courier, acting to help entrap Liberty and lure her somewhere private. But why the beauty shop? If the sender had intended to harm Liberty, or kidnap her, why not choose someplace more discreet? I swallowed. Why had Liberty said the book held no clues?

I slapped the book closed. With my elbows propped on the desk, I ran my hands over my face, rubbing the skin until it hurt. Too many questions and I had no answers.

Kiki Barclay-Bly would have some. Dee had referred to the estate's location. I would be passing right by it on my way to the Orange Lantern tavern, the appointed meeting place for the break-in team.

LaVue Rouge was a short hop off Michigan Avenue, the main road from Detroit to Ypsilanti. I knew the route well, having taken it on my previous trips to and from Willow Run.

The couple's home was off the main road, but I'd found a map in the Ford's glove box showing the back roads. Passing through Dearborn, I left Michigan Avenue and took a spur that eventually dumped me onto a narrow country road that followed a westerly course, parallel to Michigan. Silhouettes of maples and elms, as well as a few sparse pines, lined the thinly forested properties on either side. I knew from studying the map that the Rouge River ran along the strip of land off the driver's side. I'd also noted that the stretch of river closest to the road was just short of where Dee had indicated the gate would be. My window was open and I had the Ford in low gear so that I could listen for river sounds.

The croaking sounds of a bullfrog concerto grew in volume. I lifted my foot from the gas and listened more carefully. At last, a gurgling noise. I braked.

High above, gossamer clouds whisked a full moon in waves of varying intensity. A sudden burst of moonlight illuminated a massive gate anchored on either side by stone pillars, the flourishes of curlicues and ornate tulips in the door's grillwork exactly what Dee had described.

I followed a blackened drive, the course roughly paralleling the river, off to my left. A rutted lane intersected, also from the left. I slowed, trying to see where it went, but after a few yards the lane disappeared into an inky, moon-spotted landscape. A horse whinnied in the distance and a second horse neighed back, and I decided the lane must lead to the estate's stables or barn.

A short distance later, I rounded a bend. Directly ahead, a monstrous home built in the style of an English castle dominated a clearing. Slits of golden light blazed from tall rectangular windows, three tiers high, forming an uneven pattern along the breadth of the structure's elongated stone façade. High above, the moon was still veiled by fast-moving, vaporous clouds. The light changed and the silhouette of the mansion's crenellated roof suddenly resembled a jack-o-lantern's squared-off widespread teeth, gnawing at the sky. A string of fireplace chimneys created a second staggered row of teeth, while an angular turret at the tip of the southwesterly wing resembled the rook from a giant's chess set.

My first impression of the house was so consuming that I didn't hear the engine sounds of the approaching automobile until it was just ahead of me. The car's headlamps were dark. They abruptly snapped on. The sudden bright light nearly blinded me. I had a terrible vision of returning my FBI loaner with its side bashed in. Imagining Connelly's smug grin, I recovered, tugging the wheel and veering onto the lane's narrow shoulder.

My headlamps momentarily flooded the passing car's interior and I saw two men in the front seat. The driver was bald and had a thin, gaunt face; the passenger's round features and wild thatch of white hair were a distinct contrast. I caught a flash of the passenger's white lab coat and then they were gone.

The dust from the speeding car had not yet settled as I pulled into the horseshoe-shaped gravel driveway fronting the mansion, my nerves rattled by the close encounter. It was around eight o'clock, and I suspected I might also be jittery about calling on Kiki unannounced. The English translation of the E.T.A. Hoffmann book V-V had lent me was on the front seat, part of the excuse I had invented for my impromptu visit. Grabbing it, I exited the Ford, observing another automobile, a gray Studebaker, parked a short distance away in the driveway's shadows.

I peered through a narrow pane of clear beveled glass bordering the arched wooden doors at the entrance. At the mouth of the foyer, tasseled sashes held drawn velvet drapes. Beyond the parted drapes, a pair of dim sconces created a murky hallway.

I pulled the turtleneck of the heavy black sweater required for the evening's mission higher up my neck and crossed my arms, rubbing them against the cool night air. It was good to be in casual clothes again, but my lingering survey of the elegant entryway made me wonder how my relaxed appearance would be received. Indeed, whether I would be received at all. Was the doorbell working? I poked the pearl button again.

At last, a tall, thin maid wearing a black dress with a white collar and cuffs appeared in the hallway. She smoothed her ruffled white apron and flicked on the light, then pressed her nose to the glass and looked out. I recognized the fuzzy bouffant and small round scars riddling her skin. The maid staring out at me was Irina Popov, my former cellblock mate from Wayne County Jail.

"Irina," I said squeezing inside the vast vestibule, stomach churning wildly. "What are you doing here?"

Irina's hazel eyes were wide with surprise. "Praise the Lord, it is our jewel thief," she said, clasping her hands together.

I praised the Lord, grateful that Irina's hallelujahs had been reasonably restrained.

"Shh," I admonished, glancing about for lagging greeters who might be curious about a nighttime caller. "What are you doing here?" I repeated.

"Agency sent me. Special assignment."

Did she mean one of the intelligence arms? "Which agency?"

"I am eyes and ears for—" She paused. Her normally open expression grew suddenly hard. She straightened her back. "I been Merry Maids free agent for many years." Her eyes narrowed. "And what it is you are doing here, Miss Pucci?"

Her recovery was smooth. Smoother than I would have expected from the recent immigrant and Holy Roller I'd met in jail. But give me a hundred to one odds Dante was the Merry employer who had planted her in the mansion and I'd take it.

"I'm a journalist," I explained, then openly admitted to having been in jail in hopes of getting a scoop on the Countess. In confessing to the ruse, I hoped to strike a balance between being honest enough to win Irina's trust, possibly as an undercover girl-mate, and shady enough to play off our bond as former cellmates. I also let her know that I'd come to LaVue Rouge to interview Kiki and return a book.

"Your turn," I said.

Her rapid-fire English tested my interpreting skills now and again, but I got the lowdown on what had brought her to the estate and what she'd been doing since her arrival.

This morning the couple's maid had called in sick. Irina served lunch to "Mr. V"—as she referred to V-V—and to his friends, then cleaned up afterwards. "The Mrs." had not left her room all day, but following V-V's direction, Irina had ministered to her needs the entire day, too. Finally, about fifteen minutes ago, having delivered a tray to the master suite, she had collapsed into a chair. Then I'd rung the bell.

She held her apron by its scalloped ruffles, rubbing them like rosary beads between her thumbs and fingers. "I do not think The Mrs., she is able to talk with you," she added tentatively.

I opened my mouth to ask why. A loud crash resounded above us. Startled, we glanced at one another. If I'd had to venture a guess, I would have said a chair, maybe a small table, had fallen over in one of the rooms upstairs.

I eyed the staircase. A carved oak railing climbed one side, ending at a landing with a bank of tall casement windows inset with stained glass. Above the landing, another flight of steps rose to the second floor where an open balcony looked down over the entrance hall.

I stepped deeper into the foyer and gazed skyward to a vast open space that vaulted past a third floor and stopped at a beamed ceiling from which an ornate chandelier dangled.

The hall was completely quiet again. I turned to Irina and shrugged. There was another crash, followed by a scream.

I bolted for the stairs. My flat shoes and casual clothing were emancipating. I took the steps two at a time. On the landing, the knob at the railing's top acted like a fulcrum, catapulting me around the sharp turn and flinging me up the next flight.

I heard Irina on my heels. Pulled by another crashing noise, we raced for a room down a hallway to our right. We hesitated at the door.

"It is the master suite," Irina said, her voice trembling with fear or exertion, or both.

I placed my ear against the door. I heard a whimper. With syncopated precision, I knocked, turned the handle, shot open the door.

◇◇◇

The couple stood near the fireplace across the room. Kiki, clad in peach satin pajamas, moaned. Eyes closed, she fell into V-V's open arms like a rag doll, one of her feather-poufed high-heeled slippers flying off backwards.

V-V's startled gaze flicked to Irina, then back to me. He wore a paisley smoking jacket, and dark slacks, and was slipper-clad as well. Kiki's limp body shifted and his slippered feet parted as he braced himself to support her.

"What happened?" I asked.

V-V rearranged Kiki and shrugged. "She was eating dinner, got up to stoke the fire. I was at my desk, working—" He nodded to a large desk against the wall. "I heard a crash…"

The fireplace tools had toppled over. Behind him, angry flames leapt from logs stacked on andirons, sending embers up the flue. Two delicate chairs were positioned near the hearth, but a small table had been knocked over. Nearby, spatters of red wine and meal remnants sprinkled a section of the white pile carpet. Shattered china and brass fireplace tools were strewn helter-skelter. The poker had landed slightly apart from the main disaster.

Grunting as he picked up Kiki, he demanded, "Why are you here?"

"We heard a scream."

"You heard a groan," he replied emphatically.

I held my tongue. I hadn't come to argue.

Kiki's head lolled against V-V's arm as he carried her to a monstrous bed set on a platform that dominated the room. He stepped up onto the dais, his broad shoulders straining against the fine silk of his paisley jacket. "Don't worry," he said, addressing us over his shoulder. "It is just one of her spells. She will be fine after a little rest."

Observing Kiki cradled in his arms, it was hard to imagine she would be anything but fine.

Irina mounted the platform and drew back the covers, exposing sheets of gold satin. Behind the bed, an extended flounce of pleated gold draped the wall.

V-V placed his wife on the sumptuous sheet. He turned and his chestnut eyes, sharp like a hawk's, and caught mine.

"You were explaining why you are here?"

I nodded. "Your wife and I agreed to meet at the Club today to compare ideas and discuss innovations for raising money for the war effort. This afternoon my editor called. Wants me go to Chicago tomorrow to cover a new development. I wanted to be sure you got your Hoffmann book back. I thought I might also try working in the interview. Obviously, I've come at a terrible time. Sorry."

He focused on my empty hands. His eyebrow lifted inquisitively.

I managed a smile. "The book is at the bottom of the stairs. I dropped it when your maid and I heard the crash. We ran up here to help." I strolled to the elevated bed to get a better look at Kiki. "What kind of spell is she having exactly?"

V-V shrugged. "The doctor does not yet have the precise medical term for the disorder. There should be tests, of course, but she is always too busy. Meanwhile, he—we—refer to the condition simply as 'spells.'"

Dee had been concerned that Kiki was working too hard, but she had not mentioned spells. "What does the doctor think is causing them?"

V-V's broad shoulders sagged. "It is always the same. She works hard at the Club, she frets about her sister, she gets tired, a little melancholy, then gets a headache and she faints. Like this." He reached for the satin covers, carefully arranging them around her still form.

I regarded Kiki's face. Her normally porcelain skin was a ghastly gray and the thick fringe of bangs had flopped sideways, exposing the strawberry birthmark. In a final comforting gesture V-V brushed the hair back into place and bent to kiss her.

He straightened up. Irina had left the dais to begin cleaning up the mess at the hearth. The sounds of silverware and glass shards hitting the tray drew his attention, but then Kiki moaned and he turned back to her. While he hunched over her, soothing her with his words, like a crab on sand I inched quickly backwards until I was at a small writing desk I'd observed when I rushed in. I kept him in the corner of my eye as I panned the area surrounding a ream of engraved paper, hoping to find a sample of Kiki's handwriting.

The sheet on top contained several lines of feminine handwriting, but it was too large to slip into my pocket without folding it first. Too much rustling, too much motion. My fingers twitched. Several sheets had been wadded up and left beside the stack. I chose the closest one, stuffing it into my pocket.

"She all right?" I asked, edging away from the desk.

V-V nodded and stepped off the platform. "Fine. She is sleeping now."

At the fireplace, Irina's forehead was deeply furrowed. She had seen me swipe the wad of paper, I guessed, sending her a pleading glance.

V-V addressed her. "Remain here and keep an eye on Mrs. V while I escort Miss Lewis to the front door."

I faced Irina. "I'll be back," I mouthed, before turning to follow him.

As we descended the stairs, V-V asked, speaking distinctly and quite loudly, "So you'll be returning directly to the Cosmos Club?"

I couldn't fess up to my real destination. "Uh-huh, that's my plan." The Hoffmann book was right where I'd dropped it. "There it is," I said, springing down the final steps, scooping up the volume. "Excellent—*creepy*—mystery, by the way. Thanks." I spun around to hand it to him. It was only a shadow of movement, but in the corner of my eye as I reeled I saw one of the heavy velvet drapes near the door stir.

"It was very kind of you to drive all the way out here to return my Hoffmann," V-V said, loping down the final steps. "And how timely…"

He lowered his voice. His eyes burned into mine. "I have been asked to convey a message. A certain friend wants you to know she is well. She has left the country. You know her destination. That is all."

My pulse raced. "G-gee…" I stammered. "Great news. Thanks."

V-V looked uneasy, as if he'd had misgivings about sharing the private communiqué. His gaze bored into mine again. "It is a pity my wife could not give you an interview, as you would have liked. But in coming here you have risked exposing a story upon which the very security of Detroit, the Midwest, possibly the entire nation, rests. Your friend begs you, keep her secret to yourself a while longer."

"But…" I could not think of what else to say, nor could I move. Even as he opened the arched wooden door, signaling me to leave, saying he must get back to his wife.

Chapter Twenty-one

Turning the car out of the estate onto the deserted back road, I pondered Liberty's request to maintain her secret a while longer. Too late. The cat was already out of the bag. And I did not intend keeping her affiliation with V-V or his disclosure that she'd left the country private either.

The reflection of lights in my rearview mirror tore me from my musings. The headlamps had materialized so abruptly that the automobile must have pulled out from a driveway or side lane. I sped up. So did the other car. Michigan Avenue was only another mile, and when I reached it I eased into the flow of light nighttime traffic. A glance in the mirror confirmed that my tail was still with me, keeping a discreet distance. I was unable to see the driver, but the vehicle was recognizable: the gray Studebaker I'd seen parked in the estate's horseshoe driveway upon my arrival.

Coming up on the block before the Orange Lantern, I swung onto a side street, cranking the wheel in a sharp U-turn and dousing the lights. Precious seconds passed, but no gray vehicle. I emerged from the side road, checking my mirror repeatedly to be sure the driver had not doubled back.

The parking lot adjacent to the tavern was about a third full, but it was nearly eleven, the hour when the afternoon shift ended. Soon the next wave of plant workers would begin arriving. I needed to be inside the FBI truck beforehand or I risked blowing our cover. With no time left for puzzling over the Studebaker, I wove among the abandoned cars, hunting for Dante and the team.

The panel truck was in a deserted back lot reserved for overflow parking. I parked and beat feet toward it. Painted black and backed into a far corner, it had a billowy white cloud as the backdrop of a logo stenciled on its side. An airborne Liberator had been painted above the cloud. BUGS AWAY, the name of the phony pest control company under whose auspices we would be entering Renner's office, was emblazoned on the plane's nose. Beneath the fuselage, a giant cockroach, a bomb strapped to its belly, had just been released from the Lib's bomb bay and was plunging downward.

At the truck's rear doors, I knocked. *Two raps, pause; one rap, pause; two rapid raps, stop*. The square windows near the top of the doors had been blacked out. A few seconds passed during which I assumed someone was peering out of a minuscule peephole checking my identity. Finally, the chrome handle flipped downward. A hand reached out. I grabbed it.

"Glad you made it," Dante said, heaving me up inside.

A mesh-protected bulb, like the ones mechanics use to illuminate the tight spaces in which they work, was suspended from the interior ceiling. Four men in dark clothing were huddled around canisters and other equipment.

"Sorry I cut it so close," I said. "Had to pay what I thought would be a quick visit to a sick friend."

"Our mutual friend?"

He was referring to Liberty. "Sorry, no. But leaving the friend's home, I picked up a tail." I described the gray Studebaker and the evasive maneuver I'd used to ditch it. Dante's brow was furrowed. "Don't worry," I added, "I used extra caution pulling into the lot."

He still looked concerned. "Positive you lost him?"

"Absolutely."

He nodded.

My associates looked as if they had all stepped off the same Midwestern farm. Clean-cut, nice looking and with uniformly muscular physiques, they all had pale eyes, fair complexions, and blond flat-tops. On a team mission, such wholesome fungible looks were an asset as they could easily blend into a crowd should a fast getaway be necessary.

Dante did the introductions. Each man had been assigned a code name having to do with his area of responsibility. The safe cracker, who was also our lock expert, was called Fingers; the camera expert, recording any suspicious documents, Eyes; the radio man who would be on the inside with us keeping communications open with the lookout posted outdoors, Lips. From slots concealed in the sides of the truck, and through a minuscule peephole I'd correctly guessed was in the back door, his counterpart, Ears, would be covering the area around the building's entrance, scouting for late-night visitors. A cooperating supervisor, who knew only so much as to be able to help pave the way inside, had put Development Engineering on notice about our fumigation project. A schedule indicating the times their section of the building would be off-limits had also been posted.

As agent-in-charge, Dante was code-named Doc. Finally, as the flaps and seals specialist assisting Doc in checking questionable documents for codes, ciphers, and secret ink, I was Nurse. We took a moment to review the sketches and photos of the office layout. Next, we ran through communications procedures and discussed various scenarios of what we would do once inside. Dante admonished us, "Keep in mind, this search of Renner's office is illegal. If we're caught we blow our chance of nailing Renner, plus the government will disclaim all responsibility for our actions."

Everyone, including Doc, had already slipped on coveralls. Made of black cotton twill, the jumpsuits zipped up the front. A logo patch with the company bomber and bomb-strapped bug was stitched over the breast pocket; a larger version of the emblem had been stenciled onto the back. Mine slid comfortably over my slacks and turtleneck. I tugged the zipper and it made a soft buzz fleeing upwards. Doc flipped a billed cap onto my head, suggesting I keep the pliable rubber hood that was also part of my disguise at the ready. Wartime or not, a woman who would take a job stomping out bugs and rodents would be considered eccentric, and we could not afford to draw any unnecessary attention.

Our weapons were minimal. Dante would be carrying a revolver and blackjack while the rest of us had been issued gas guns. As a final precaution, we checked them.

The facilitating supervisor had cleared our admittance through Gate 10, the inbound entrance for all trucks arriving at Willow Run. We would follow normal security procedures, subjecting our truck and gear to the requisite inspection. A search raised the stakes, but Dante had been discouraged from trying to win an exemption, as special requests always raised a red flag and could ultimately backfire, drawing closer scrutiny once we were inside. To that end, all canisters, spraying devices, and traps that might be related to an extermination business had been left in sight; all equipment that might appear suspect was hidden in compartments beneath the truck's elevated floor.

Dante and I climbed into the panel truck's cab, leaving the rest of the team seated on the two benches bolted to the interior walls in back. He started the engine and pulled the knob for the lights. "You okay?" he asked, looking over.

We were about to break into a locked office of a government-owned factory. The idea of getting caught and returning to jail terrified me; the expression I pictured on my father's face horrified me even more. Yet I was also keenly aware of embarking on an adventure few would know about much less have the privilege of experiencing. That was as heady as it got.

"I'm doing swell," I replied, smiling back across the cab at him.

Telling Dante the news about Liberty, as well as V-V's ominous send-off, needed to wait until after the break-in. His briefing could not have made it clearer: our focus needed to be one hundred percent on the job at hand.

I recognized the unbuttoned jacket and protruding paunch of the guard at the Gate 10 checkpoint immediately. My skin crawled. It was Officer Flynn, the chunky, florid-faced guard who had been manning the lobby desk when I'd visited Willow Run earlier in the day.

"The guard knows me," I whispered, slipping the loose rubber hood over my head.

Flynn reviewed the copy of our contract then leaned in to scrutinize the cab's interior. My eyes were riveted to the windshield but I sensed his gaze pause on me. I did not breathe.

"Need to check the back." Flynn pushed away from the door with a grunt.

"Fine," said Dante, hopping out while I expelled an audible sigh.

Muted voices and the sound of equipment being shifted across the floor penetrated the small sliding door at my back. Then silence. Resisting the urge to fling open the trap door and have a look, I discovered a hangnail and nibbled at it until at last Dante returned.

Flynn's gruff voice penetrated the cab as Dante climbed in. "Everyone on-site's required to wear a badge. You'll need six." He handed the identification to Dante, charging him with returning the badges once we had finished.

A lanky youth with shiny, pock-marked skin and a pencil-line mustache sauntered outdoors and coolly surveyed our truck.

Flynn hitched up his pants. "Outsiders have to be escorted. The Kid here will take you over."

The Kid stepped astride a nearby factory scooter. We chased the scooter's taillights along a spottily lit lane that serviced the back of the L-shaped factory. I regarded the windowless concrete walls and metal doors. *Hadn't I left County Jail?*

Dante cracked the small trap door behind our seats. "We're here," he said, projecting his voice softly through the narrow opening. "You men ready?"

Several hushed voices chorused back. "Yeah." "You bet." "Let's go, Doc."

The Kid had dismounted his scooter. "This is the section where you'll be working," he called, indicating we could begin unloading.

I stood amid the equipment we'd piled near the truck's rear door. Hoisting a canister onto my back, I lifted my black bag. Fingers, Eyes, and Lips had already loaded up. Dante slammed the door, leaving Ears inside, and we marched toward the door as a unit.

A lamp suspended from a curved metal rod illuminated the entrance as our escort tugged open the door. He motioned us inside. After checking to be sure Dante had his directions straight, and reminding us that he would remain nearby until we finished, he began closing the door.

"The offices with the infestation problem were left unlocked," he said just before the door clicked shut.

We followed the corridor to Renner's office. Beyond the frosted-glass door the room was completely dark.

Dante surveyed our group with a sweeping glance. "Ready?"

Inside the anteroom, we pulled on fitted leather gloves. Dante tried the door to Renner's private office, but it wouldn't budge. "Blast. Son of a gun installed a special device of some sort. Fingers..."

Fingers slipped a small metal pick into the lock. Dante turned the handle, cracked the door, and paused. "Eyes, the washroom is right down the hall. How about getting set up in there, we'll get started in here."

Once we were inside, our objective would be to uncover Renner's drawings of the night-bombing device. We would also be on the hunt for evidence pertaining to other espionage activities, such as letters or records containing names or leads to other spies, drop-site addresses, strategic enemy plans or drawings of secret devices, and any data that could be used to mislead the enemy. Eyes would use the darkroom he was setting up in the restroom to photograph the items, then process the film to be sure we had the shots we wanted. Back at headquarters, the prints would be developed in the lab. Later, after Renner was brought in, the photographs would be used to inspire his cooperation.

Beneath his coveralls, Eyes' thick neck and broad shoulders bulged as he lifted his black bag and collected a second valise containing his photo equipment, including cameras, collapsible tripod, film, special lights, and chemicals for developing.

Dante entered Renner's office and closed the blinds before turning on the light. Signaling me to wait by the door, he motioned to my counterparts. The men each took a section of the room. Light fixtures, sills, and furnishings were examined for traps. I studied the stacks of paperwork, thinking they looked nearly as high as they had twelve hours earlier.

Something on the floor behind the desk caught Dante's eye. He got down on one knee to take a look. Fingers, having completed his search of a potted fern, started toward Doc, gesturing for me to follow. A leather case had been shoved into the corner behind another plant. Sensing Fingers and me behind him, Doc motioned to a nearly invisible wire which ran to an electrical outlet in the wall. He disconnected the plug and opened the case: It contained a sound recording device. I had seen the exact model demonstrated in training. The beauty of the recorder was an extremely sensitive switch that could be rigged to be thrown automatically whenever someone spoke. It was creepy to think that Renner might have my voice preserved for his private purposes on a recording somewhere.

No one had made a peep since we'd entered. Dante found another wire connected to a port in the side of the briefcase. Holding it between his fingers, he followed it to the bookcase behind Renner's desk, where he found a microphone attached to the photograph of Clara. On the opposite side of the room, Fingers discovered yet another wire taped discreetly along the baseboard. It led him to a second microphone attached to the underside of the drawing table across the room.

Lips, turning up nothing unusual in his area, took a seat at a table near the door. He donned earphones connected to a radio inside the open case positioned in front of him. Satisfied we had uncovered and exterminated all existing electronic bugs, Dante asked Lips to contact Ears inside the truck. Ears had nothing to report other than that The Kid was guarding the door, whiling away the time smoking cigarettes.

Eyes returned, having set up his equipment in the washroom. Lips remained at the table, tuned to the radio, keeping an eye on the anteroom beyond. The rest of us went to the color-coded blueprint near the drafting table. The giant drawing was affixed to cork board. After carefully examining the board's edges for a trip wire, Fingers slipped his hands beneath the center of the rendering. My mouth felt dry, watching him pull the twin panels apart to reveal the pleated dumbwaiter door.

Fingers leaned into the wall, placing an ear near the large dial at the door's center. I held my breath, my gaze riveted to his thumb and index finger as he deftly spun the knob. He tugged the corrugated metal inset and it gave way, sliding noiselessly toward the ceiling and exposing the wall safe. He gripped the safe's handle. This morning when Mrs. K was similarly poised to open the safe, Renner had made a surprise appearance. Fingers pulled the handle, the door opened, and when nothing unexpected happened, I gave the men a thumbs-up.

I took my position at the table we planned to use for the sorting process while Dante began examining the inside of the safe. He handed over several legal-sized manila envelopes and I arranged them on the table.

At the safe, Fingers gave a low whistle. Curious, I edged up behind Dante. He had discovered a false bottom. He opened the trap door and was reaching for a long tin box inside when Fingers signaled Dante to freeze. A barely visible string had been placed in a zigzag pattern across the top. Inspecting the container more closely, Fingers also called our attention to a fine white dust coating the lid.

A few quiet seconds passed while Fingers sketched the pattern of the string's layout so that he would be able to reaffix it in precisely the same manner. Next, using the beam of a small flashlight and a hand-held implement resembling a dental tool with a tiny mirror, he checked the safe's interior for other booby traps. Finally, the box was cleared for removal and Dante slid it out, positioning it between the piles of manila envelopes on the table.

The elongated lid lifted easily. He flipped it backwards, resting it on the table. The box contained a large envelope. As Dante carefully extracted it, something long, thin, and weighty slipped to the side.

Fingers pointed to some reddish-brown streaks on the envelope's exterior. "Blood?" he whispered.

"Could be," said Dante. He unfastened the flap's wing-clasp and looked in. "Eureka."

Carefully, using only the tips of his gloved fingers, he withdrew the prize. A push dagger. I knew the weapon from training. Made by the Brits, the specialty dagger combined a round, ice pick-like blade with a three-fingered grip that added power to the thrust. Designed to be used in close combat, it was particularly effective in a surprise attack when approaching a victim from behind. The blade readily penetrated clothing, flesh, and tissue, and was favored by female agents because of the extra supportive grip.

A flaky, rust-colored matter clung to the tip and to parts of the weapon's spiked gray metal blade. Looping a finger through the grip, Dante dangled the dagger, rotating it, giving us all a chance to examine the weapon, before he returned it to the envelope.

"Hold on. What's this?" He removed a newspaper clipping that had also been inside. It was yellow with age and we stared over his shoulder, trying to read it.

"Is it German?" I asked.

"Uh-huh," he replied, absorbed in the article.

"What's it say?" Fingers whispered.

"Something about a merchant seaman. Age twenty-three… Named Wilhelm Oskar Mehnert…Jumped ship in Galveston, Texas. Uh, was on shore leave, got into a scrape, broke an ankle. A doctor…*someone* treated him. Wasn't there when the ship set sail, next morning. The desertion raised a lot of questions...Mehnert had been a corporal in the Kaiser's Army during the last war.... Served in a machine gun outfit, earned several medals...It surmises the young seaman didn't want to return to Germany because of post-war economic conditions." Dante flipped the paper over. "Ah, dated September 12, 1922. It fits. There was a terrible depression in Germany then."

He placed the clipping beside the envelope. "Eyes, be sure to get a shot of this. I'll want to study it more thoroughly later."

Numerous other manila packets awaited our inspection. He shoved the metal box aside and, following a prearranged system for sorting, spread the papers out on the table, culling out any suspicious documents, handing them over to me. While the two of us evaluated papers, Fingers went to Renner's desk and examined ledgers and reports, occasionally showing Dante an item of potential interest.

Within minutes, a small stack of material had accumulated, including a roster of names and addresses that looked interesting, as well as carbon copies of instructions describing how to use invisible ink and how to apply various make-ups for disguise. Once he had enough to get started, Eyes left the room.

His search of the desk completed, Fingers turned to the adjacent three-drawer file cabinet and flipped through folders. Meanwhile, the portable dark lamp was getting plenty of use. I ran it over every document Dante turned over to me, testing for hidden messages. He had also given me two sealed envelopes. I opened them using my special razor device. One envelope contained a business letter inscribed with an awkward personal note near the end.

"Mother arriving Billy Boy's seventh," Dante said, reading the line out loud when I showed it to him. He frowned. "Hmm, 'Mother' might be code for a convoy. What do you think?"

I shrugged. "It's possible. And Billie Boy...?"

Dante studied the letter again. "A secret landing spot, maybe. Bilbao's a port in the north of Spain, near France." He handed the document back, asking me to try ultraviolet light, then reagent, if necessary.

Eyes reappeared with the sheaf of papers he'd finished documenting. He left with a new collection, and Dante and Fingers returned to their individual searches while I examined the letter under the purple glow of my lamp.

Certain secret inks do not show up under black light, but sometimes the same stubborn ink will respond when swabbed with reagent. When no writing appeared, I dipped a swab in a small jar of the chemical included in my kit. I "stripped" the paper by running the swab diagonally across the page. My neck was tense. I rubbed it and scrutinized the damp lines. Reagents were both good and bad. If the letter contained a secret ink message, the special compound would cause it to develop and appear as brown ink and we would have something incriminating against Renner. But then the bad part. The developed ink would remain visible and we would not be able to return the stained letter to the box. Bad or not, I wished for something tangible to appear. To no avail.

I dipped another swab, executing a second pattern, and studied the fresh application. I sighed. "No hidden message," I reported. I placed the paper beside the proper envelope to dry.

"Put it in that final stack for Eyes," Dante said. "Headquarters will want to know about anything even vaguely referencing Bilbao."

I pushed out of my chair. "Want me to check the drawers?"

Doc had already turned to another document. He looked up. "Huh?"

"The drawers built into the wall," I said. "Shall I check them?"

He glimpsed his watch. "Yeah, sure." He turned to Fingers, who was closing a cabinet drawer. "Nearly finished?"

Fingers' shoulders heaved. "Looks like it."

"Good. We need to vamoose. Take what's left to Eyes. Once he's snapped them, help him pack up."

Fingers left the room with the small pile of documents. I hesitated, my hand on the upper drawer's pull. "We haven't come across the plans for the secret night-bombing device Renner supposedly copied and stashed in here. You don't seem concerned."

Dante was assembling documents, arranging them in a prescribed order. He frowned. "Maybe with the hubbub surrounding the murder, he decided to move them or stash them at home. We'll know tomorrow after we interrogate him." He lifted an envelope, preparing to place a batch of papers inside. "Besides, Eyes has shot a booty of stuff we can use."

"Enough evidence for probable cause, maybe. But now with Blount dead, without an outright confession, you don't have the solid link I thought you needed before going up against Renner..."

"Pucci, he has a dagger in his safe."

"But is it the actual dagger used to kill Blount? If it is, I'll bet it's been wiped clean of prints." Dante's eyes narrowed and I knew he didn't appreciate the direction I was taking. But I couldn't stop. "Possession of a knife doesn't prove he's been pilfering Ford's secrets for the *Abwehr*. Or that he's the assassin. Plus, if he is the assassin, why would he save the dagger?"

Dante shrugged. "Panic. Nervous about passing it through security. Fear of where to stash it, or dump it, so it wouldn't be found."

"Still, it doesn't make sense. He'd only be inviting trouble keeping it. What if Mrs. K saw it..."

Dante returned to shuffling papers. "Lewis, our mission is accomplished. We came here to mine enough material so that Renner knows that *we* know what he's up to. We've done that. In fact, once we let on we've found the dagger he'll be champing at the bit, wanting to help us. Now we've got to skedaddle."

I nodded. He was right. I opened the drawer. About four inches deep and three feet wide, it was indeed designed to hold flat files. But it was empty. I shoved it closed and pulled out the drawer below. I paused. Inside, directly behind the pull, stuck in a crack, was an orange card that looked like a badge.

Maneuvering the card with my finger and my letter opener, I removed it. I felt a fluttering in my chest. It was a factory badge and it wasn't Renner's!

"Someone could have planted the dagger, though, right?" I asked, excitedly.

Dante's head was bent over a document. He knitted his dark eyebrows together and looked up. "Sure. And if that's the case, Renner would be equally anxious to squeal on whoever he suspected put it there." His gaze flicked to the orange card in my hand. "Why do you ask?"

I handed over the card, turning it so he could see the picture on the back. It was Chaplin. The dwarf.

"Bingo! Looks like we've nailed the unidentified insider." He set the badge on the table. "I should say *you* nailed him. Good work. We'll get Eyes to snap a shot of it."

I pulled the drawer open wider. Dante checked the time. "Two minutes."

Three plastic sleeves inhabited the drawer. Two were empty, but one of them held a large parchment envelope. Its flap was sealed. I flicked on my pen light. Holding the envelope aloft, I ran the fluorescent beam over the contents and recognized the dark lines of a drawing.

Fingers and Eyes reentered the room. "Eyes," I said, setting the envelope on the drafting table and using my fine-bladed opener to unseal it. "Get a camera."

"Pucci," Dante interjected, "there's no time."

I probed the flap, lifting it gently. "We make time, or this goes with me."

He turned to Eyes. "Your gear all packed?" Eyes' valise was at his side. He nodded.

"Take out the bare minimum. Get a few shots of what she's got, but make it quick. We need to document that card, too." He gestured to Chaplin's badge then turned to Fingers. "Fingers, reactivate Renner's listening device while I finish returning these documents. You'll need to replace the string and re-dust the box when I'm through. Lips, start packing up your gear. By the way, what's going on in the lot?"

While Dante was giving directions, I began unfolding the large, transparent sheet of tracing paper I'd removed from the parchment envelope. I smoothed the delicate paper, flattening it against the table. Next to me, Eyes held a small, sophisticated camera.

"Zowee," he said, clicking away at an illustration that was actually a hand-drawn map.

A three-page, typewritten document was also part of the discovery. On the outside chance the pictures did not turn out, I skimmed the pages, attempting to memorize every possible detail. The hurried perusal was doubly challenging as I had to leave the pages on the drawing table so that Eyes could photograph them, and I had to prevent myself from yelping over what I was reading.

The final minutes were devoted to cleanup. Once everything had been carefully replaced and the dial on the safe reset to its original reading, Dante doused the lights and opened the blinds.

Fingers took out a small whisk broom. The last of the group to leave, he walked backwards, sweeping our footprints from the carpet as if we had never been inside.

Chapter Twenty-two

Our gear had been reloaded, the men were in the back, and Dante and I were once more settled inside the cab. Outdoors, the temperature had tumbled and air rising from the fan on the dash had fogged the windshield. It would take a few moments to clear, but we weren't leaving right away anyway. The Kid had ordered us to stay put while he gave the section of the building we'd sprayed an all clear. Fortunately, anticipating this sort of scrutiny, we had squirted the baseboards with faux extermination chemicals, actually a harmless deodorizer.

Dante looked over. "I caught a glimpse of the map. Looked like an air raid plan. What about the attachment? Did it explain?"

I nodded. "I read it quickly, but the gist is that some nut wants to send a string of German bombers from Norway over the Great Circle Route to Canada. The map, hand drawn by the way, identifies the bombers' eventual targets with yellow flames. All major Midwestern cities, Minneapolis-St. Paul, Milwaukee, Chicago, Cleveland, have one."

Dante raked his fingers through his hair and sighed. "We've known the *Abwehr* has a master strategy for launching sabotage plots stateside in the U.S. Looks like we, no *you,* stumbled onto one of them. What else?"

Turning slightly in my seat to face him, I shared my hurried take on the rest of the document. The author wanted Hermann Goering, commander of the *Luftwaffe*, Hitler's national Air Force, to send a fleet of transports with a crew of engineers and enough men and supplies to build a bomber base in an uninhabited section of Canadian wilderness called the Keewatin District.

The memorandum claimed that a landing field could be cleared within a few days. After the base was established another fleet, this time Heinkel bombers, would arrive. The bombers would be tuned up, refueled, and loaded with destruction ordnance before taking off for their targets along the Great Lakes, all of them sitting just over the horizon, like ducks on big ponds.

"Detroit is the scheme's initial target," I told him.

Dante's expression was grave. "So it's true. Someone is gunning to finish off what Operation Pastorius started." He was referring to the Nazi saboteurs, dropped off by U-boats along the Atlantic seaboard, just over a year ago.

The fan had begun blowing warm air. He cranked up the defroster. The windshield cleared and we saw The Kid leave the factory and hop on his scooter. Dante shifted into first, the engine whining with the strain of its load as we took off after our escort.

I chuckled softly. "Some scheme. An air raid over Detroit. Can't wait to hear what Renner tells you about the dimwit who dreamed it up."

Dante's eyebrow arched. "Hey, don't knock it. The idea's actually brilliant."

"Brilliant? Har har," I said, mockingly. "You're joking."

I looked at Dante. He wasn't.

"It's ludicrous!" I huffed. "A Nazi bomber could never get near Detroit. He'd have to get through a wall of spotters, Canadian fighter planes, American interceptors, and anti-aircraft guns. Not to mention all the logistical problems. How can you say it's brilliant? It's impossible!"

He might think the plot was brilliant, but he was none too happy about it. His face was grim as he peeled his gaze from the road and met mine. "It's not impossible. Berlin's probably the most heavily guarded city in the world right now, yet with all its defenses, the Germans can't keep the R.A.F. from bombing it regularly. And think of Pearl Harbor. A raid like the one you just described would have the similar supreme advantage of surprise."

He faced the windshield again. "Hitler knows an attack on Detroit that destroys a few military and industrial targets won't bring us to our knees. But he also knows it would crush American spirit and boost German morale. Think of Doolittle's raid over Tokyo. The attack did only minimal damage to military and industrial sites, but it brought the war home to the Japanese for the first time. It was a daring low-level daylight raid, it forced the enemy to take costly defensive measures. It was great for our country's morale after the blow of Pearl Harbor. The invasion described in the memo could have the same impact."

A heavy feeling shrouded me as I grasped his logic. "Point taken."

We had left the factory. The country road we were following was dark and deserted. He eased the truck onto the shoulder and killed the engine. "I promised Connelly we'd radio in once we were clear of the factory. I can ask him to collar Chaplin. I'm also expecting an update from Jarvis. His team's been scouring records and he was planning on interviewing Liberty's parents a second time. Maybe there's been word."

He cracked the sliding window and instructed Ears to remove the two-way radio from its hiding place, then slipped outdoors to join the men in back. He left the trap door slightly ajar and I was able to catch muffled bits of conversation as he conversed on the radio.

We were on the road again a short while later. Dante announced he would be returning to headquarters immediately after dropping me off. My teammates would go with him and deliver the push dagger to the lab for testing, plus take the film to the photo lab for developing. Meanwhile, Connelly had assigned a team to Chaplin.

"What about Merriman?" I asked.

"Your instincts about someone being in disguise were right."

Connelly had been to the Club. After questioning Merriman and the staff, he had searched the room next to mine. A uniform, identical to Merriman's, was hidden in the closet. In a wastebasket, he found an empty bottle of shoe white, a nearly empty bottle of shoe black, and the stub of a Max Factor No. 6 blue-gray liner.

I tugged my ear, listening intently. I'd been taught to use the exact items as part of the tricks we were taught for appearing older. The blue-gray pencil was effective for accentuating facial lines and deepening eye-sockets or coloring in dark circles beneath the eyes; shoe-white, grayed down with a bit of shoe-black and applied to the hair, added years to a person's looks.

I recalled meeting Merriman for the first time. His features were so deeply lined they'd seemed unnatural. His streaky, flyaway hair was also unusual, and I remembered thinking at one point he might be wearing a wig. Had I even been observing the real Merriman? I frowned as somcthing in my memory bank rippled to the surface, then submerged again before I could grasp it. Finally, I shook my head slowly. "So there are two Merrimans, one of them in disguise. And if the real Merriman is not part of Renner's ring, the other one is. Whoever he is," I added, "there were any number of other less chancy ways he could have tried scaring me off than entering my room. Which leads me to believe he was at the Club for another purpose."

"This Merriman-clone, whoever he is, cavalierly tossed the tools of his trade into a trash can where anyone could find them. As though he's sending a message: he has no fear of getting caught. Conceit," Dante added a moment later, "let's hope it continues. We'll nab 'em that much sooner."

"You haven't said anything about Liberty," I ventured. "Any news?"

"There's a paper trail leading clear back to Switzerland. Which means that part of the investigation will take more time. But Mrs. Leach has developed her own theory of what's happened to her daughter."

"Really? What?"

"Her sister in Switzerland heard through the grapevine that Liberty's boyfriend was sent to serve in Italy. Mrs. Leach thinks Liberty found a way to join him." His tone was cynical.

"Liberty had a boyfriend?" I was amazed.

Dante looked equally surprised. "You didn't know?" He shook his head. "No, you couldn't have known. You would have recognized the name, Tazio Abbado. She met him in boarding school."

The world as I knew it had taken another 180-degree turn. I sat in stunned silence. Abbado. An enemy operative with a direct connection to the Countess and who, it would appear, was the inspiration behind Liberty's goal to be assigned to MO in Rome.

"Mrs. Leach's theory might sound weak," I began slowly, "but she may be right."

I disclosed my discovery of the secret message inside the copy of *Personality Unlimited.* I also provided a rundown of my stop at LaVue Rouge, including my shock at seeing Irina there. I sent Dante a significant glance but did not press him to explain. It could wait until later. By the time I got to my parting conversation with V-V, I had a sinking feeling in my stomach.

"Whatever Liberty is up to…" I began haltingly, "wherever she is, V-V is tangled up with her."

His eyes flashed with something. Shock? Fear? Anger? "What are you saying?"

Reluctantly, I revealed Liberty's plea that I continue to delay telling anyone about our meeting, about her mission, about her leaving the country. "V-V said that he'd been asked to convey the message and that the very security of Detroit, the Midwest, possibly the entire nation, rested on my keeping the secret."

Dante's expression was locked up, rock hard. We turned onto Michigan Avenue. Only minutes remained before we would be back at the Orange Lantern.

He might not want to talk, but I did. "We've assumed Tazio is an enemy agent because his name was on a picture in the Countess' possession. Besides, pegging him as a bad guy fits with your agency's assumption, based on her parents' information, that he was a liberal radical of some sort. But the Countess claims she never made contact with him. And Liberty has never tried to hide the fact that she has friends in the Italian Underground. What if he's part of a faction assisting the Allies?"

Dante didn't scoff, but he didn't look convinced either. "Hmm, interesting. But if she was planning on leaving the country, why was she at the Club undercover as a manicurist?"

I shrugged. "It's what we've got to find out. Besides, finding a way to sneak off to be with her lover in Italy is the only bright scenario I can possibly envision right now for what might have happened to her."

Dante smiled sympathetically. The smile faded. "Look, Pucci, right now I can't say for sure what's going on. But I plan on getting to the bottom of things soon as I'm back at headquarters."

We had arrived at the tavern. He turned in to the front lot. It was late, but a smattering of cars still occupied the lot, and from the porch the orange globe above the door glowed softly. We entered the darkened area in back. Pulling up beside my Ford, Dante left the engine running.

He looked over at me. "I want you to promise me you'll go directly back to the Club, lock your door, get some sleep. Stop fretting about your friend, about V-V, about what might be going on at that estate. We have the murder weapon, our boys are watching Renner. Trust me—everything is covered."

I smiled. "Okay, fine."

His smile was guarded. "In the morning, after you've questioned Clara, bring that book with the phantom ink message to headquarters. If what you found is a part of the puzzle, by the time you arrive we should have most of the picture laid out."

"Can't wait to see where it fits," I said, climbing out. "But don't forget I'm meeting with the Countess tomorrow, too. Won't take long though, I expect, given I have no leverage to work with." I pulled a face. Dante did not smile as I expected.

"Lewis, even this late in the game, whatever dirt she might have on the sisters could still make a huge difference. And remember, keep your guard up with that woman. She's a certified pathological schemer."

Chapter Twenty-three

At the door to my room, I squinted. Someone had replaced the strand of hair I'd glued across the seam with a dark brown strand. A second invasion! How dare him!

I still had the tear-gas pen in my pocket, left over from the break-in. I presumed the intruder had already come and gone, leaving a strand of hair behind to taunt me or fool me, I wasn't sure which, but I took out the weapon, shoved open the door, and flipped on the lights.

Whoever had entered my room had nabbed the cuckoo clock I'd foolishly left on the desk. I moaned, "You dirty rat." Had the dirty rat also stolen the copy of *Personality Unlimited?* I raced into the bathroom, where earlier in the evening, before going out, I'd moved it. Eyeing the book, safely taped to the back of the porcelain tank on the commode, I savored a small ping of glory.

My thumb on the pen's trigger, I searched the rest of the suite, checking curtains, dark corners, and the underbellies of the beds. Satisfied I was alone, I double-locked the door, then peeled off my clothes, leaving them where they dropped. Gas-pen in hand, derringer beneath my pillow, I wearily crawled into bed. One eye refused to shut, but a few vigilant minutes later it surrendered as I gave in to something resembling sleep.

Soft gray light filtered through a crack at the center of the heavy drapes. Beside me, the clock ticked loudly from the table. I yawned lazily, blinking several times, before rolling over to read the time. Six a.m.! Recalling the day ahead, I hurtled from my bed.

A quick, cool shower later, I began throwing on clothes, recycling the dark slacks and saddle shoes from the night before, but drawing the line at the black turtleneck, still reeking of faux extermination chemicals and lying as if it were dead on the floor. A gray sweater-set would do fine, I thought, consulting the mirror before plopping down at the desk.

My grip on the telephone receiver tightened in increments corresponding to the seconds ticking by while I waited for the operator to connect me with my Uncle Chance.

"Hullo. Is that you, my little Miss Puccini?" he asked at last.

I chuckled. "Yes, it's me. And I'm short on time, sorry. Was your colleague able to dig up anything on the Swiss clock?"

It was my uncle's turn to chuckle. "It's not Swiss."

"What?"

"The Swiss are known for clock-making and watch-making, and because so many of the cuckoo clocks use the Heidi Haus design, they're also credited with inventing them. It's a misconception. Cuckoos originated in the Black Forest area of southwest Germany."

My uncle loved history and he loved antiques and he loved sharing what he knew on the subjects. Fortunately, my uncle also loved me. Remembering I was in a rush and needed only the icing, not the cake, he got down to business.

"Now about your clock. The name inside the housing, G. Becker, refers to the clockmaker Gustav Becker. You said Freiburg was imprinted below G. Becker. Of course I can't say for sure unless I see it, but my colleague found an engraved plate from an 1852 exhibition there featuring his work with a whimsical design similar to what you described."

"In other words," I speculated, "it's likely my clock is a genuine Becker. And my assumption about its origins was wrong." Was my belief that the clock held a clue to Liberty's disappearance off the beam then as well?

"What's unusual is that it has a serial number. At the time your clock would have been made, serial numbers were generally found only on clocks of better quality. And if you're wondering if the registration can be traced," he added, reading my thoughts, "forget it. German records are not accessible. And even if they were, that clock could be eighty, ninety years old. Lots of ledgers to sift through. *If* they still existed."

Uncle Chance asked me to describe the clock's design again. I had to do it from memory, of course. I mentioned the chalet clock in the staff room as well.

"Flowers with rhinestone centers. *That's* unique. Makes them sound dreadfully kitschy. Even for cuckoo novelty clocks. Very un-Becker-like..."

My scalp tingled. *Rhinestones.* Was that the connection?

We said our good-byes and I rushed to the door, more anxious than ever to get to the salon. My hand was on the knob when I remembered the crumpled piece of stationery in my pants pocket. My FBI costumer had thoughtfully selected slacks with roomy pockets for storage. Digging deep, I removed the balled-up paper. *What had she been writing?* I peeled open the ball, gently ironing it with the palms of my hands.

The page contained only two lines of writing. My breath caught reading them. *Dee, I know how deeply you loved Philip. Can you ever forgive me for hurting you—*

It was an apology, maybe the beginning of a confession! Were the rumors true then? Kiki had had an affair with her sister's fiancé?

I thought for a second. Even if true, what had made Kiki decide to admit it now? My heart grew heavy thinking about what the disclosure would do to Dee. Her psyche was so delicate and tortured already.

I sighed, folding the crinkled paper, and slipped it into the pocket where *Personality Unlimited* was now stashed. I'd taken the notepaper hoping to compare Kiki's handwriting with the phantom message inside the book. The test would have to wait until later.

◇◇◇

A small lamp on the appointment desk lit my path as I skirted the counter, my destination the room in back where light glowing from the open doorway suggested Clara had already arrived.

Unlike the pumps I'd worn the day before, my saddle shoes did not have cleats and my footsteps were nearly soundless. I crossed the heart of the salon, the shadowy forms of empty client chairs and hairdryers in the near distance off to my left.

In the back room Clara stood at one of the sinks, head bent, her hands clutching the porcelain edges, sobbing. Was I too late? Had the FBI notified her about her husband?

I rapped the door frame with a few light taps.

Clara's hands flew to her face. She spun around. "Whaa… Whooo…" she sputtered, peering through splayed fingers. "Oh, it's you…"

"Are you all right?" I asked, easing into the room.

"I'm okay," she said, unsteadily. "Give me a sec, will you?"

My gaze cut to an empty spot on the wall where the cuckoo clock strewn with rhinestone flowers had once hung. Clara blew her nose, ran some water, and splashed her face.

"Better," she said, her voice muffled by a washcloth she dabbed over her skin.

"What happened?"

She took a gulp of air. "Otto went off the edge again. This time he said he was going t-t-to leave me."

Knowing the FBI was picking him up, maybe at this very moment, I almost said he didn't really have a choice in the matter. Instead I asked, "Why? I thought last night you were going to straighten things out. Come clean about your investment adviser."

"I did. I told him there was no affair. That V-V was merely helping me leverage my money. But that riled him up more. I don't understand. He and V-V are old friends."

I blinked. V-V was Clara's investment adviser? V-V and Renner were friends? In his office, Renner had denied knowing V-V. Why?

Before I could formulate any sort of response, Clara asked, "What brings you here so early?"

For this, I had a canned answer. "Finished breakfast, had a few minutes to spare before shoving off on another round of interviews. Thought I'd drop by, reschedule my appointment."

"Oh, right. Yesterday, we had to cancel. The book's out front."

I placed a firm hand on her arm. "We don't have to do it now. The other operators will be arriving soon. Maybe it would be better to take a moment to compose yourself, maybe splash on a little more cool water?"

"Thanks, probably not a bad idea. Plus I do need to get things put away before the day gets too crazy." Her gaze flicked to the two bundles of laundry wrapped in stiff green paper on the counter. The package Liberty had with her in the library had been wrapped in similar paper.

"How long have your husband and V-V known one another?" I asked, watching her open a drawer and remove a pair of scissors.

"Oh, they go way back to Otto's bachelor days. After Otto and I first became a couple, they drifted apart for a while. Now they manage to get together about once a week, have a beer, swap stories about the old country." She cut the string on one of the tightly bound packages.

"Oh? Your husband was originally from Ukraine, too?"

Clara's eyes skipped away then skipped back. "Well, no. Otto's German. Came here as a young man. But he doesn't like to bring it up. Everyone is so wary of immigrants these days."

"Uh-huh…"

She raised her chin. "It's nothing to hide. Otto is a U.S. citizen."

My smile was strained and I hoped my knowledge of what her husband *did* have to hide was not plastered all over my face. "Of course."

The hair on my arms prickled. What had she said? *They swap stories?*

The Countess had described an occasion when she'd seen Otto Renner visit his wife at the salon. He'd given her flowers and she'd given him a book. V-V had also lent me an English translation of the E.T.A. Hoffmann book Kiki had mistakenly brought to the Club for her Faire. Then, there was the volume of *Personality Unlimited* which I had hand-delivered to Liberty, aka Glossy, that harbored a secret message and was currently nestled deep inside my pants pocket. The way books were being whisked around the Club at such a dizzying pace seemed overly coincidental.

"V-V has a thing for fine literature," I said. "How about your husband? Besides exchanging tales about the old country, do they also exchange books?"

She looked at me. The heavy mascara normally caking her lashes had all but washed away. Without it, her face appeared more childlike and innocent than ever. "V-V brings in books for Otto all the time. So does Kiki. I take them home, bring them back."

She pulled paper away from a stack of snowy towels. Lifting up on her tiptoes, she tried pressing the heap onto a shelf, just above her reach.

"Here, let me, I'm taller." I laid my hands over hers and gave a shove.

She wiped her hands down the front of her smock. "Thanks." Her fingers caught the corner of what looked like a brochure in her pocket. She removed it, folded it in half, and returned it.

My eyes widened, registering what the brochure actually was. "You said V-V was helping you build a little nest egg. I'm not too smart with money myself. Mind if I ask what you're investing in?"

Clara smiled, her swollen eyes closing as her features softened into a look of ecstasy. "An island resort."

"A *what*?"

Her eyes flew open. "Well, not really a *resort*. More of a health spa and casino. You see, there's a Navy base on an island in the Detroit River…"

"NAS Grosse Ile," I whispered.

Her half smile made her look sly. "Why, yes, that's right."

My glance fell to her smock. "Yesterday, you said you had a client who's the wife of a Navy officer. Did V-V ask you to get a map of the base from her? Is that what's in your pocket?"

She glanced down. "Uh-huh, the architect needed it for the sketches."

"Sketches? Sketches of what?"

"I just told you. Our project. It's only a vision now. We need more funding, so we're soliciting additional investors. But we need a professional rendering first. A must, according to V-V, if we expect anyone to actually consider putting money up."

Were we on the same page? How did a map of Grosse Ile Naval Air Station relate to a spa project? "Wow," I said, thinking I suddenly got it. "Is your group planning to build a recreation area on Grosse Ile? Something like Belle Isle Park?"

NAS Grosse Ile and Belle Isle were both islands situated about a half-mile offshore in the Detroit River. Separated by several miles, Grosse Ile was on Federal land, while the smaller property of Belle Isle, to its north, was city-owned. Belle Isle was packed with things to do. Walking paths, athletic fields, bridle paths, canoeing in the summer, skating in the winter, a symphony shell, a conservatory, an aquarium, a zoo—the features went on and on. Mobs of people frequented the park, especially in the summer when Detroiters desperate to escape the downtown heat sought an oasis.

"No, not like Belle Isle," Clara huffed. "We're not after families. We aim to be a private facility, a getaway, for adults." Green paper rattled noisily as she opened a second package, containing neatly folded client kimonos. "A golf course, fencing club, and casino…" Her voice trailed off. She waved her hand. "Well, you get the idea. Like I said, I can't tell you everything. We're in the early stages."

"And *your* role?"

Her face lit up. "I'll be in charge of the spa." Clara's voice grew progressively more excited as she described the facility's three-tiered design, conceived to accommodate the customized spa indulgences she and her staff would offer. In addition to the more traditional beauty treatments such as facials, massage, and hair styling and coloring, instruction in nutrition and diet, as well as classes in gymnastics and exercise, was also part of the vision.

She cleared her throat and tried toning things down. Not altogether successfully.

"The base has landing strips and hangars," she whispered. "V-V has proposed starting an air shuttle service to accommodate guests from outside the Detroit area. We're borrowing ideas from famous spas in Europe, but who knows? Europeans may soon be looking to us for inspiration!" She raised her hands and flipped them outwards, palms up. "Why not?"

"Indeed, why not?" I said, doing my best to sound convincing. "So you, er, V-V thinks the military will vacate the island, then?"

She nodded. "He's confident it will happen. One of the investors he's lined up, a big wheel, has big time connections."

I wondered whether V-V and their potential fellow investors knew about the plot to bomb Detroit. *That* would be a way to effectively evacuate the island, I thought wryly.

Clara sighed and looked suddenly morose. "I'd like to think it will all work out. Otto should retire…" She patted the puffy flesh around her eyes, lightly. "Soon."

We were quiet for a moment as she opened a cabinet beneath the counter and began stuffing it with the clean gowns. Could she truly not know what her husband had been up to at their kitchen table in the middle of the night? I wanted to think so. I also thought her dreams for the spa and her husband's retirement, while naively preposterous, might be considered a reasonable explanation for approaching the admiral's wife.

"What did you tell your husband about the project?"

Behind her swollen lids, Clara's eyes blazed. "Otto didn't give a hoot about my passion for the spa. Said it would never happen.

What capped things off was his demand that I stop seeing V-V immediately. He even gave me an ultimatum. Imagine!"

I shook my head sympathetically. "What happened next?"

"He left. I heard the car peel out of the driveway. Went off to confront V-V, I guess."

"And you haven't seen him since?"

"No. I went next door. Spent the night at Mrs. K's." Clara sighed and stared glumly at the clump of paper in her hands. "How could he be jealous of someone like V-V?"

"Looks, charm, money, snappy dresser?" Clara actually chortled and I pressed on with a few more questions. "Your husbands are friends, but you and Kiki aren't. Why's that?"

She shrugged. "We're from different worlds." Her eyes shifted as if recalling something unpleasant.

"You mentioned you cut her hair—"

"About three weeks ago. She stopped in without an appointment. Asked me to cut bangs to help hide the burn."

I thought of Kiki's birthmark. "The strawberry mark on her forehead? That's a burn?"

Clara's look suggested we shared a secret. "You noticed. She claimed she tripped near the fireplace. Met up with the hot end of a poker when she landed." Clara's raised eyebrows suggested the explanation had not been very convincing.

"What do you suppose really happened?"

"It's the mark of a fireplace poker, all right. But I wonder if someone branded her with it."

"Who? *V-V?*"

Clara nodded, but suddenly seemed less sure of herself.

"Wait. Are you saying you think it's possible V-V could actually do such a thing?" My stomach curdled as I recalled the spilled poker on the floor in Kiki's bedroom last night.

She touched her face. "Men do strange things when they're jealous. Maybe he heard about the affair she had with Dee's fiancé."

"Yesterday you said the story was chair gossip," I reminded her gently, while inside my pants pocket Kiki's crumpled note felt like it was on fire. "And V-V says she's suffering from exhaustion. Maybe she actually did fall and hit her head. It's possible, isn't it?" I wasn't trying to counter Clara's theory, but if she was describing the real V-V, I wanted some meat with the accusation.

Clara sighed and rubbed her forehead, as if willing her brain to clear. "I don't know what's true and what's not anymore. Someone brought up the affair again, recently. Whoever it was seemed positive it was true."

A voice called from the front of the salon. "Yoo-hoo, Clara, you here?"

Our time was up. It was one of the other beauticians arriving.

My gaze careened to the blank spot on the wall. "Where's the clock?"

Clara looked up. She seemed genuinely startled. "Why…I don't know."

Chapter Twenty-four

The matron directed me to the visitor's area, a small room with wooden chairs positioned in front of a long, narrow shelf. In front of each chair, above the shelf, was a small mesh-covered window. I folded myself into a seat while the jailer went for the Countess.

I had been able to come up with only one strategy for my third meeting with the former spy. At its core was my resolve to be straightforward and honest. Thinking I might feel more at ease without the FBI monitoring our conversation, I had taken my honesty-is-the-best-policy decision one step further and rejected the chance to meet with her in the cellblock, opting to converse under normal inmate conditions. Now, staring at the barrier wall, observing the stark setting, I wondered about the wisdom of my decision.

A jangling of keys was followed by the groan of a heavy door opening then closing again. I propped my forearms on the shallow platform and peered through the tightly woven screen. On the other side was a barren room, its walls shiny with a fresh coat of gray paint. I heard the scraping of a wooden chair. A navy blue jumpsuit flashed across the mesh.

"So-ooo, it is *you*," the Countess said, settling into her chair, making eye contact through the screen.

The window framed her head and shoulders. She sat forward, her elbows resting on the ledge opposite mine. Our faces were very close. Though softened by the mesh, her appearance was ghastly. She had not looked all that well before, but now dark circles ringed her eyes and her unhealthy pallor had taken yet another ashen turn. Her singular attempt at grooming, a haphazardly applied coat of flagrant red lipstick, looked cheap against her gray-white skin. On my last visit, her hairdo, although flattened, had retained some semblance of the upsweep style Billie had fashioned. This morning, the swept-up arrangement had been reduced to a crushed honeycomb of tangled locks, several oily tendrils drooping against the sides of her face.

"My idea for featuring you in my Women in War Work series was squelched," I said directly. "I'm sorry."

Her monotone reply was so low and heavy that the words ran together like one long groan. "Then there will be no visit from my fiancé…I am lost…no one can help me now."

"I tried. I'm truly sorry."

Seconds of silence passed. She sighed. "Sorry? No, you have been right all along. I should have listened to you sooner."

"Why's that?"

"I wanted revenge. I wanted my name exonerated. I wanted my freedom. You suggested I see things realistically. I am a foreigner, accused of espionage. I am incarcerated, I have no influence. 'Cooperate. Plead guilty, if they insist. Do these things and you will be with your fiancé sooner,' you advised."

I shifted against my unforgiving chair. I hadn't expected her mood to be so submissive. I also did not recall being so expansive in counseling her. Nor so wise.

"You're reconciled to serving time then?"

She turned and lit a cigarette. The diamond solitaire on her earlobe glimmered with the movement. "Miracles are possible, but I am better off not to count on them I think."

The FBI's ex-counteragent no longer sounded bitter. Resigned, was more like it.

"Last time I was here we talked about Kiki Barclay-Bly, the woman who invited you to speak at the Cosmos Club. You said you had information about her and her sister, Dee."

She dragged on her cigarette, letting the smoke drain lazily from her mouth. "*Ahh*-nd why pray tell are you so interested in the Barclay-Bly sisters? More specifically, how will what I know about them help my pitiful situation?"

"Well…I'm still going forward with the series and have plans to cover the Book Faire. If there was an interesting angle about them, say having to do with politics or loyalties…" I let my words trail off.

The Countess held her cigarette holder, staring at the smoldering reed of tobacco on its end, acting completely bored. "Yesterday I knew from your curiosity that any information I might have about them could be a useful bargaining chip."

"You mean as a get-out-of-jail card?"

"But of course."

"And now?"

"Now nothing. I am resigned to serving a prison sentence. What possible advantage could there be for sharing?"

I thought fast. "A goodwill offering. My boss' contact, the one that got me into your private cellblock twice, will take it as a sign that you're willing to cooperate. In return, they may be willing to leave Mr. Butler and his good name alone."

She took a slow drag off the cigarette and exhaled with a long sigh. "All right. But my proviso is this. What I will tell you is off the record. It is not for your newspaper, but for the ears of the Special Agent in charge of my case exclusively. Will you agree?"

I nodded. "Yes. And you've made a wise choice."

Her eyes narrowed. "My choices are limited. My true love has promised a little nest will be waiting for me to fly home to, once I am free. But what funds would he have should the men of the FBI decide to play rough with him?"

I restrained a smile. Of course! Why had I been worried? She had her own good reason for wanting to be open with me. "I think you've zeroed in on what's truly important."

"I am afraid I missed what was truly important when it was right in front of my nose."

"Oh?"

"Yes. It was only after you asked the questions about the sisters, that the possibility occurred to me."

My heart pounded. "What possibility?"

On the other side of the barrier wall, she stubbed out her cigarette. An acrid stream of tobacco-infused air seeped through the mesh opening. "In thinking about the sisters, I remembered the night of Dee and Philip's engagement party. There was a brief period when Anastase tried to monopolize me. I rejected what I thought were his advances, especially when he began confiding details about his relationship with Kiki. I assumed he was trying to win my sympathy. Such an *o-o-ld* ploy that one."

"What do you mean?"

"You know—" She placed a hand over her heart and raised her eyes to the ceiling. "Poor me. My wife has been unfaithful. I have worked hard to provide for her so that she might have everything she wants. Yet, how does she show her appreciation? By being unfaithful! Then, according to the over worn scenario—" she patted her heart in a speeded up rhythm, imitating a quickened heartbeat—"he expects you, the beguiled woman, the one to whom he is telling his sob story, the one he hopes to win as his mistress, to fawn all over him with the love and affection he so *rightly* deserves."

Her lips stretched into a tight smile. "What is the man thinking, I have always wondered. Does he truly believe a wife who has whatever she needs and wants would then rush into another man's arms? Does he not realize that he may have played some small part in the woman's dissatisfaction?"

The former charm consultant's understanding of the ways of men ran miles beyond mine. "You're saying V-V, er, Anastase, made a pass at you?"

"Yes...I mean no. I *thought* that was his intention. Now I have come to understand he was trying to signal me. Let me know who he was."

I scooted my chair closer, its wooden legs scraping the cement floor noisily. "Who?"

"My contact."

I gasped softly. "And he was trying to tell you this by flirting with you?"

"No," she replied impatiently. "By telling me his wealthy wife was having an affair."

There it was. Confirmation. Kiki and Philip.

Her theory, the Countess continued, was that in engaging her in the brief conversation about his wife, her wealth, her cheating heart, V-V was somehow testing her, seeing if she would pick up on his intent.

"Intent?"

"Yes." She squared her shoulders and thrust her chin out in a show of dignity. "If I had been paying closer attention, it would have been obvious, what he was saying. He was planning to use the situation to convince her to divert funds to the fascist cause."

I gripped the narrow ledge. "You're saying he intended to use the affair with Philip as a means for blackmailing his wife?"

She shrugged. "Why not?"

"Blackmail." I sank back in my chair. "But why would Kiki go along?"

The Countess lifted an eyebrow. "She loves him. She loves her sister. She's afraid of him."

I thought of Kiki's crescent-shaped burn and nodded. "Dee was already emotionally overwrought. If she discovered her sister's betrayal, she'd go right off the deep end. But how could he do it? Pit one sister against another?"

The Countess scoffed. "*How?* Unwavering devotion to the cause are prerequisites for those of us privileged to be selected for secret service. In Anastase's case, the characteristics were imprinted early on."

She talked about V-V's formative years, repeating what I'd already gleaned from Liberty concerning the impact of being born into a nation troubled by ethnic strife and political repression. She also served up something new. V-V had experienced severe trauma as a child. When he was very young, his mother died under mysterious circumstances. His father, a mean drunk, was rarely around afterwards, leaving V-V and his two older brothers to fend for themselves.

"How do you know all this?"

"Sari told me."

Botheration! Sari deHajek again. Sari was the woman who had befriended the Countess in Hungary and helped care for her father in his final days. It was also Sari who later recruited the Countess, even escorting her to Berlin for espionage training.

She continued. "When I was still in Hungary, and Sari was grooming me for my U.S. lecture tour, she alerted me to a former freedom fighter turned devout Nazi who was to be my main contact after I arrived here." Her shoulders heaved. "It was only after my conversation with you yesterday that I realized Sari had been referring to Anastase Andreyevich Volodymyr Vivikovsky."

I whistled. First, because I was impressed with her smooth delivery of the difficult name; second, because I was still more than a little bit flabbergasted by the news. What about his alliance with Liberty? And, equally vital, whose side were they actually on?

"What about the book of names Sari gave you? Why wasn't his name in there?"

"He was a mole too important and buried too deep to be logged in a book." She lit a cigarette and exhaled noisily. "Besides, an agent of his renown goes through identities as often and as effortlessly as a chameleon changes colors. Even Sari was uninformed about the name the contact currently calling himself Anastase would be using."

Behind the mesh, the Countess grew visibly melancholic. "To think, while Anastase was feeding me bait about his unfaithful wife, her sister and their wealth, my head was in the clouds. If only I had been alert, if only I had followed what I learned in training, how different things might have been. If only..." Tears welled up in her eyes.

The poor Countess, her chance to help the fascist cause had sailed right by her. But I hardly felt sorry for her. I was thrilled. I had extracted valuable intelligence, and I could hardly wait to share it.

Chapter Twenty-five

The bark at the base of the giant pine penetrated both layers of the sleeve of my sweater-set, prickling my skin. It was as if the tree with its rough texture was urging me away from the safety of its cover. Instead, I huddled closer. I was on stakeout, directly across the road from the massive wrought-iron gate, and needed to stay put until help could arrive.

Following my session with the Countess, I had tried to telephone Dante before leaving the jail, only to learn that one of the women arrested with the Countess had agreed to enter her plea. Dante and Connelly were in court, involved in the proceedings.

"Renner's skipped," their secretary, Miss Tempest, told me. "Sometime this morning he gave the agents tailing him the slip."

"Not possible!" I was aghast and unable to hide it. I took a deep breath. "Now what?"

"There's an intensive search on for him."

A shiver danced across my shoulders. Hadn't Clara said that when her husband stormed out of their house he might be heading for a showdown with V-V? Was he holed up inside V-V's estate with him? The Countess had said V-V was a sleeper spy. If true, who knew what might be going on there.

My breath caught. For an instant the blood stood still in my veins. Had V-V duped Liberty? Placed her in jeopardy in some kind of triple cross? Gotten her kidnapped—I swallowed—or *killed*, to keep her quiet?

"Let Agent Dante know that I'll be going to LaVue Rouge," I said. "Tell him it's urgent that he meet me there. I'll be waiting for him. He should look for my Ford. It'll be parked near the front gate. But tell him to look carefully. I'll be hiding it."

I had left the jail and returned to the Club, stopping just long enough to check messages and to strap on Gran Skjold's derringer. *Personality Unlimited* begged for a final perusal. Something about the volume was different from the one the Countess had lent me. Yes, it contained secret writing, but something else.

I flipped it like a pancake, examining the leather cover's front and back. That's it! The copy in my hand had been personalized.

I turned to the inside front cover and stared at the gold-embossed rectangular-shaped bookplate depicting a detailed Renaissance scene of a scholar writing at a desk beside an open window.

...OKPLATE! The missing piece in the phantom ink message: *BOOKPLATE!* Perhaps: *SEE BOOKPLATE?*

My razor-tool made quick work of the paste applied in tiny dabs to the rectangle's corners. On the plate's front, an inscription below the Renaissance scene read *To Kiki, From Your Loving Mother*. On the back side, lines of small, neat handwriting, applied with a fine-tipped fountain pen, covered the surface. I'd seen a fountain pen on Kiki's desk in the master bedroom at LaVue Rouge, its tall peach-colored feather curving majestically up and away from a white marble base. The balled-up note paper I'd snatched from that very desk was now neatly folded and squirreled away in my pocket. I dug it out. But matching the script on the stationery to the printing on the bookplate was not helpful. Complicating things further, the four-paragraph message was in code. The first letters, Y-Y, suggested it was same elementary cipher substitution code I'd come across earlier, on the memo hidden inside Kiki's desk drawer.

I found a scrap of paper and went to work on the opening paragraph.

KHOS! Y-Y'V KDWUHG IRU VWDOLQ GULYHV KLP. KRUURUV! PB PRQHB JRHV WR QDCL FDXVH. EODFNPDLO. NQRZV EULEHG SKLOOLS OHDYH WRZQ

deciphered became:

Help! V-V completely mad. Hatred for Stalin drives him. Horrors! My money goes to aid the Nazi cause. Blackmail. Knows bribed Philip leave town.

This definitely was from Kiki! Heart racing, I unraveled the remaining three cryptic paragraphs.

Coerced Renner. Conducts terrorist training here. Plans sabotage. Have evidence!

Fear for my life. My sister. Truth must come out. D must know I acted out of love; did not betray her.

P=Don Juan. Everyone knew, but D. Tried seducing me, *his lowest betrayal. Repulsed; P more determined. Sent gift: pink pearl earrings & necklace! Enraged. With V-V, confront P. Cad demands deposit to consider options. Timed his exit to reap the best sum.*

The cancelled checks in Kiki's drawer, I thought, squinting to read the final incomplete line. *Morning of the wedding…*

She didn't explain, but somehow the pearl jewelry had found its way to Dee. And V-V, perhaps using the love poem written by Philip, had found a way to leverage the situation into a means for gouging money from his wife.

Reading the note had heightened my apprehension about what might be going on at LaVue Rouge. I left the Club, raced to the estate, and settled into my current stakeout spot beneath the mammoth pine. Unsure of when Dante might arrive, I was biding my time, keeping an eye out for the G-men he'd assured me were covering the place. They wouldn't be conspicuous, I knew; and it was more likely they'd be watching the mansion instead of covering the estate's perimeter. Still, I needed something to keep me calm, while awaiting reinforcements.

Beyond the gate, a funnel of dust swirled down the lane, coming toward me from the house. I pressed my back deeper into the prickly bark and waited until the noise of the engine grew loud enough for me to be reasonably certain the vehicle had reached the gate. Leaning forward, I glimpsed a champagne-colored sedan slowing to round the stone pillar. Tires bit asphalt, and the driver, a tough-looking thug with buzz-cut hair and the neck and shoulders of a weightlifter, peeled off in the direction of downtown Detroit.

The property line was enclosed by a spiked ornamental fence extending from the curlicued gate. I scooted across the narrow lane, aware that I would have a better view of the occupants of any additional cars barreling in or out of the estate if I were inside the cove of shrubs bordering the fence.

Moments later, a man appeared, walking a horse in the woods beyond. The horse had a white coat stained with large blotches of chocolate, an Appaloosa. The Appaloosa was not saddled and one of its legs was swathed in white tape. I guessed the horse had injured its leg and the man leading him was a trainer, exercising the animal as part of the healing proccss. The trainer, a Negro, wore denim overalls and a white collarless shirt, his sleeves rolled up. A newsboy cap partially covered his fuzzy salt-and-pepper hair.

The man and horse were following a bridle path coming from the Rouge River that defined the property to my left. Leafy fall-colored trees, muted by a gloomy sky, formed a backdrop. When they were about fifty yards away from me, the trainer stopped and glanced around. He vaulted onto the horse's back, and I recognized the wide nose and white stubble along the man's chin. The trainer was no trainer. It was Leo! My pulse quickened as I remembered that Leo sometimes assisted the Bureau. Could he be part of the team surveilling the estate?

I wanted to call out but before I could, he kicked the Appaloosa's flanks. The horse clearly was not injured; he galloped off with Leo riding bareback.

When I had driven through the grounds the night before I'd thought the horse stable was located near where Leo appeared to be racing. I checked my watch. One or both of the men in the house, V-V and Renner, knew something about Liberty's whereabouts, I felt sure of it. And while I waited for backup, she as well as Kiki and Irina could be in grave danger.

Seeing Leo on the grounds infused me with confidence and bolstered my resolve. Back across the road at the Ford I left a note on the dash, amending my earlier instructions to Dante. *I've seen Leo. I'm following him to the stable. I'll wait for you there.*

The gate had been left open. Sprinting a zig-zag course through the sparsely forested grounds, I reached the cover of a broad-based tree near the stable and paused to catch my breath.

The stable was part of a cluster of three buildings that together formed a U. I was near the left leg, an outbuilding made of weathered wood. The stable, another low-lying wooden structure fronted by horse stalls, was off to my right. A stone shelter I thought might be a bunk house spanned the two legs; a vacant dirt yard filled the U's center.

No Leo. In fact, the place was so eerily quiet that a clump of tumbleweed somersaulting across the yard would have seemed natural. Finally, a horse in one of the stalls whinnied.

I stared through the large gaps in the slatted wall, assessing the interior of the outbuilding before me. No sign of horses or other animals, but I did observe a horse cart, suggesting the building was used as storage space. The space would offer protection as well as a good perspective of the surroundings.

I entered cautiously. The light was dim and the air was thick with the musty-sweet smell of hay and manure. It took a moment, but my eyes adjusted and I could get a fix on not only the cart but the tack dangling from big hooks along the wall. Peering through another slatted wall, I observed that the adjacent stall was also vacant.

I went to the front and looked out on the dirt courtyard. Opposite me, the upper halves of the Dutch doors enclosing the stalls were open, the long faces of chestnut, palomino, and black stallions protruding through them. I heard male voices somewhere out back. I turned and listened. Two men were approaching from the central bunk house, their voices and the clip-clop of horses' hooves growing louder.

The entourage halted near a back corner. The men continued their conversation as I crept over, listening and hoping one of them was Leo. The fit of the boards at the rear of the building was tighter than anywhere else and it was impossible to see outdoors. Finally, dropping to my knees, I found a suitable gap.

"After you have seen to our guest's horse, go back and check on Dr. Shevchenko. Make sure he does everything necessary to make our latest visitor comfortable."

The clipped tone of the rider's voice sounded familiar. I also recognized the boots and jodhpurs. It was V-V! My vantage point gave me a uniquely limited perspective of his steed's lower half. The hooves were perfectly manicured, and his gray and white coat had been brushed to a dull shine. The other man, clad in olive green fatigues and Army boots, stood beside the dapple gray, holding the reins of a second horse.

"Yah sure, Cap-i-tan," the fatigue-clad man replied.

My blood froze. The second horse was an Appaloosa with a bandaged leg. I tilted my head every which way, trying to see above me. Where was Leo? A platoon of shivers charged my spine. Was he the guest V-V had been referring to?

"I must go to the boat house," he said. "But Zerov, after you have looked in on our guests, be sure Dr. Shevchenko has the merchandise in order. Then, find Yakutovych. Let him know the truck that will pick up the good Doctor's shipment is due here shortly. Yakutovych and his men are to help load it. Tomorrow is spaghetti night at the base. That means the staff will begin preparing the sauce tonight. The goods must reach the kitchen well beforehand."

"Yah, Cap-i-tan. What a 'moving' experience the chef and his staff will have with Dr. Shevchenko's special ingredient." The twosome chortled loudly over the comment.

"Hand up the picnic basket, Zerov. I must go to my wife. She will be feeling anxious."

From my crouched position, I saw a wicker basket pass from Zerov's thick fist to V-V's black-gloved grip.

"Ah, you are making joke, Cap-i-tan, yes? She cannot be feeling anything but relaxed, thanks to our good Doctor."

The men were engaged in double-speak that did not sound good for Kiki.

The dapple-gray snorted, protesting the extra weight of the basket. V-V's gloved hand reached for the rein, drawing it up and forming a loop against the horse's neck.

"Today you will also get the green light from Berlin, yah?" Zerov asked.

"Berlin," V-V scoffed. "Yes, today is the latest in a string of promised dates. Why they are having such difficulty making contact, I do not understand. By now I had hoped to have the actual document in the *Abwehr's* hands in order to coordinate the ground and air attacks. It is a travesty. Our men are trained and at the ready, but they must hang back, hovering at the start line, while *I* await the checkered flag from Berlin."

Zerov grunted. "I am sure they will make contact soon."

"Soon may be too late. But thanks to Cardillac we have an alternate funding source."

They were discussing the air raid plot! And V-V had formed an underground army!

Cardillac? *Who was Cardillac?*

The villain in V-V's favorite Hoffmann story, Mademoiselle de Scudéri, was called Cardillac. A Jekyll-Hyde sort of character, that Cardillac was by day a renowned genius-jeweler, by night a robber and tormented dagger-wielding serial killer.

V-V's mount's hooves danced, raising a tiny cloud of dust. Zerov grabbed the steed's bridle, patting the horse and calming him.

My throat had felt parched even before dust-strewn air reached it. Now I swallowed a few times to moisten it.

"See you at the bunker then." V-V pressed his boot into his horse's flank.

Bunker? I squinted after him. Had he meant boathouse?

V-V headed toward the river. I watched until he was out of sight, then turned my attention back to Zerov. He was gone. I assumed he was following V-V's order, leading Leo's Appaloosa to the barn. Sidestepping rapidly past the sulky, I went to the front and peered out again. *What had happened to Leo? And where was Dante?*

A burning sensation seared my gut. I couldn't return to my car. The note I had left for Dante said that I would be at the stable. If he had already arrived and was on his way to meet me, either plowing up the driveway or dodging through the forest, I would miss him.

I checked my watch. I couldn't remain inside this shed either. Kiki was a helpless pawn in the plot V-V and his associate, Cardillac, were brewing. But without a sense of how many other disciples V-V had in reserve, it seemed foolhardy to dash after him.

Dr. Shevchenko was in charge of some guests. Leo likely was one of them. He would know what was going on. And if I could find him, maybe we could team up, intercept V-V before it was too late.

I shoved open the door. A hedge of bushes edged the bunkhouse exterior. I did a quick visual check and dashed for their shelter.

The bunkhouse was built of the same craggy stone as the mansion. Three windows along its back wall suggested two, perhaps three, small rooms inside. I crept along the back, pausing at the first window to listen. Hearing only the chirping of a distant bird, I cautiously rose and peered in. The double-hung window was smudged, but I could make out a heavy wooden work-table strewn with lumps of coal and a timing mechanism. Electric cable, an array of fuses, and more timing devices littered the floor near the wall. A tall shelf held large commercial-sized containers labeled *Baked Beans, Fruit Salad, Olives.*

Next, I panned the labels on a stack of boxes. I shivered and a fresh crop of goose bumps surfaced along my shoulders. *Tomatoes.* The shipment I'd overheard Zerov and V-V discussing earlier! A hand truck was parked alongside.

With my spine pressed against the craggy wall, I slithered sideways to the adjacent window. It was open. I crouched beneath the sill, then slowly inched upwards. The room was nearly twice as large as the first. Painted white and containing several metal tables, it was clearly a laboratory of some sort. On one table, clear liquid in a glass flask boiled above a Bunsen burner. Near the flask, an oversized syringe with a thick needle lay discarded near an assortment of potatoes, beets, and turnips.

A blur of white moved in a corner on the opposite side of the room. Dr. Shevchenko! Bushy, dark eyebrows were a curious contrast to his wild thatch of white hair. He wore a monocle and, in a second glimpse, I recognized him as the man I'd seen on the passenger side of the car fleeing the estate last night. At the time, I'd assumed he was a medical doctor; now I thought he might be the lab's distinguished scientist.

The doctor stood up. On the floor, near his feet, two figures were partially blocked by one of the metal tables. I leaned sideways to get a better look. Otto Renner and Leo! Propped into semi-seated positions, their backs wedged against low stacks of stuffed burlap bags, they were out cold. Above the men, Shevchenko held a syringe with a long needle.

My forehead, damp with sweat, felt suddenly icy as the door opened and a man in fatigues swept in.

Shevchenko turned. "Zerov."

My heart quickened. Up to now, I had only seen V-V's assistant from the waist down. I stared. A thin man with a gaunt face and small eyes, he had a jagged scar along the length of one cheek and his hair was buzzed off so that he looked completely bald.

His boots clumped noisily as he crossed the room to join Shevchenko. I ducked down, my heart thumping madly inside my chest. It was imperative that I find out what they were up to. I took a deep breath and released it slowly, willing the hammering in my ears to stop.

"Ah, Dr. Shevchenko, is that one of your new incendiary pencils on the table? I tossed one yesterday, for practice. *Whoosh. Bang!* Marvelous! But tell me, how does it work?"

"Spontaneous combustion," the scientist replied. "A narrow chamber inside is filled with a special compound. Once oxygen enters the chamber, the pencil—BOOM!—it explodes. Making it more wondrous yet, all trace of the device disintegrates with the explosion."

"And this gimmick you are inventing with these vegetables. It is based on the same principle?"

"Yes. Only in these—" Shevchenko paused and I pictured him squeezing a potato or one of the other vegetables on the table. "—I *inject* the chemicals directly."

"So then to set it off you slice open the vegetable and toss it?"

There was a long sigh. I imagined the scientist scratching his head.

"At this early stage, I am not certain the vegetable can be thrown without a finger or a hand being blown off. And the Cap-i-tan is not willing to risk one of his troops, or any more of *his* fingers, to try it."

A restrained laugh was quickly stifled by a suggestion from Zerov. "What about his wife? Perhaps she will have a moment to toss a little garden salad before the sisters shove off on their river excursion."

A chortle followed, then the doctor's voice turned somewhat nostalgic. "Ah, the wife. If she had not burst in here we would all be feeling less pressure…"

"Forget it, Shevchenko. It is not your fault. With all the preparations that have been going on these past few months, it is astounding that she did not discover the truth long ago. And the Cap-i-tan does not hold this against you. He has wanted to step up the action for some time, and now he feels the initiative to move forward, strike an initial hit on the Naval Base. It is even possible that he will set things in motion on the bigger plan today." There was a sly chuckle. "Say…maybe in considering the fate of our special guests, he will authorize a vegetable toss by one of them. What is their status?"

At Zerov's appearance in the lab, Shevchenko had set the syringe on the metal table. He picked it up. "Renner has just received another injection. He will not move for at least another two hours. The dark-skinned new arrival I will shoot up soon, but for now he is still out cold from the blow you administered to his head. See for yourself."

Zerov's boots clumped off to where Leo and Renner lay in a heap. A burning sensation, worse than the one I'd felt earlier, seared my stomach. I had met the man they were calling the "Cap-i-tan." I had shaken hands with him. He'd *kissed* my hand for godsakes! He'd lent me a book. I'd swooned over his continental charm. Tittered at his lofty jokes. But this wasn't funny. These men were the Pastorius replacements. And V-V was their leader.

I drew a shaky breath. Disaster was brewing and I had no one to help me stop it. Enlisting Leo's aid was out, and Dante's arrival was a vexing unknown. Until I could devise a miracle for turning back the speeding train, I had to get every scrap of information I could. I tuned back in as Zerov spoke.

"Those labels you have designed for the canned goods are perfect reproductions."

Shevchenko's voice was buoyant. "We have done our best to duplicate the tomato brand the Navy base chef purchases exclusively."

The bastards. Their plan was to hijack the real delivery truck, bring it here to the estate, load it up with crates of tomato-can bombs, and then deliver them to NAS Grosse Ile. That was why they'd wanted the map from the admiral's wife.

"And the special feature?"

"All it takes is a puncture. Air seeps in, the can explodes."

"Then let us hope it takes a full kitchen crew to make spaghetti!" The pair belly-laughed.

The twosome could be a couple of characters out of a bad B-movie. Unfortunately, these bad actors had serious fire power at their disposal.

Dante had suspected Kiki might be part of Renner's gang. She clearly was not. She was, however, in serious trouble. I had to get help.

I felt the stick beneath my foot an instant before it snapped. Fortunately, another round of uproarious laughter erupted and I did not think the men had heard. But I also did not see myself waiting around to discover whether I was right.

Shrouded in the evergreen thicket, I fought to calm my bounding pulses. Absent Dante, it was up to me to try to rescue Kiki. But how? V-V was with her.

I knew what Gran Skjold would say. "You won't know what's possible until you dirty your hands trying."

First, I needed a clear sense of what was going on. The goons in the lab had been an excellent source. I slipped my Gran's derringer out from its holster.

The bunk house door creaked open. Zerov squinted in the grey afternoon light then turned to speak over his shoulder. "I am going to the front gate now, to await Yakutovych."

He disappeared around the side of the building. I waited until I could no longer hear the heavy clumping of his boots crossing the hard dirt then pitched through the doorway and into the lab.

Shevchenko was standing beside the metal table. His monocle popped from his eye socket and his hand floundered as he reached to grasp the bubbling flask, the Bunsen burner, a vegetable bomb—any weapon. To no avail. He caught the glint of my gun and froze.

"Put your hands at your sides. Keep them there. I've no time to waste. I know there are soldiers here on the grounds. How many and where are they? Are they with the Captain? Where'd he go?"

The aggressive tone in my voice sounded impressive, even to my ears. Shevchenko's Einstein-like shock of white hair trembled visibly.

"Don't hurt me. The plan is underway. You cannot stop it."

I waved my gun. "Talk."

He clamped his mouth shut.

I hadn't risked the confrontation for nothing. "Tell me about the plan. Details..."

"Bombs, sabotage, murder, that be the plan, you know, you know what I mean?"

The voice was weak but I would have recognized it anywhere. Leo!

I turned my head. Out of the corner of my eye, I saw the doctor's gaze veer right and left. "Don't try it," I warned. "Got you covered."

Keeping the nose of my derringer trained on him, I backed toward Leo and Renner.

I looked down. My stomach flip-flopped. A swollen open gash on Leo's forehead looked nasty. "Your head...Are you all right?"

The wound was caked with dried matter but was no longer bleeding and the surrounding area, while puffy and undoubtedly sore, looked clean.

"Uh-huh. Got caught. Got a knock to the noggin, is all, you know."

Leo and Renner had been tied up, their hands behind their backs, with thick, coarse rope. Leo shifted and tried maneuvering upward against the stack of stuffed burlap bags supporting him. He groaned. "Ouch."

"Wait. I'll find more rope, tie up the good doctor here, and help you."

"No. No time, know what I mean? There's trouble goin' down here. Girl, ya gotta go get Dante. His men."

"Don't worry, they're on the way. But what's going on here? Do you know?"

He spoke fast, and I strained to keep up with his patter, but Leo, under the guise of a stable hand working for the estate next door, had been observing the activities taking place on the LaVue Rouge grounds. A short while ago, he'd trailed a truck loaded with men to the outskirts of the estate.

"Them cats had a motor, I had a horse." He lost them. "Came back here, heard this bad actor"—Leo nodded sideways in the direction of Renner—"behind the stable, arguing with the cat they call Capt'n. This here cat is all crazy-like." Again, he was referring to Renner. "Says the Capt'n's been movin' in on his lady. Wants to snuff the Capt'n.

"Capt'n, he has other plans. 'You made a second drawin' of the air raid plot,' he says all mean and fierce-like, talkin' to this here cat, Renner. 'Whatcha plannin' on doin' with it? Goin' to the feds?'"

So Zerov twisted Renner's arm until Renner confessed, Yes, that was his intent. It was the only way he could think of to get out of "the game" for good. He'd planned to do it anonymously. Then, with V-V out of the picture, he would be free to return to his normal life. And to his wife, whom he loved dearly.

The strategy might have worked, too, but when V-V began pulling Clara into his scheme, Renner lost his cool.

"Comin' here was the cat's undoin', know what I mean, you know?"

I shook my head. "I, that is *we*, Dante and I, know about the drawing. Uncovered it in Renner's safe. But that's a new spin on what it was doing in there."

"The cats planted a knife too. Did ya see it? See an old news article?"

"Uh-huh." I'd been keeping one eye glued to Shevchenko. Now, in a quick sidelong glance, I mentally tried to calculate how I might free Leo from the criss-crossed rope configuration. The trussing looked so masterful I feared that even with my hands free I would not be able to undo it. *Where* was my backup?

"But how'd you get into this jam? What gave you away?"

"Had to make a move, you know, you know what I mean? Cat in the military threads had a stick, like a big toothpick. Shoved it under this cat's fingernail wantin' to lift it off."

I winced. And winced again as Leo described how, while trying to stop Zerov, he'd gotten knocked to the ground, then conked on the head. He'd come to before Renner was given his second injection. Fearing he was about to die, Renner wanted Leo to know that he wasn't a Nazi. He was the sailor in the article who'd jumped ship in Galveston, twenty-one years ago. He'd taken an assumed name, hoping the secret police in Germany wouldn't find him. But nine months ago they'd caught up to him in the form of their sleeper spy, V-V. Renner's position at the factory was ideal for procuring secrets for the Fuehrer and V-V had used threats against Renner's family back in Germany to force him to go along. Renner told Leo all this in the hope that the explanation would somehow reach his wife.

"He had names. Cat called Cardillac the brains. Had the idea to plant the knife, let this cat here, Renner, take the rap for killin' some other cat called Blount. *He's gonna disappear anyways,* I heard the Capt'n sayin,' referrin' to Renner. Somethin' about a poison the doctor's cooked up. Makes a body decompose from the inside out. Has some crack-brained scheme brewin' for Kiki, too. And her sister…" Leo's voice had gotten weak and his normally rich mahogany skin looked ashen. He tried moving again. Another groan.

My gaze remained locked on Shevchenko. He wasn't wearing his monocle so perhaps he couldn't see me observing him. That might explain it. Or maybe he thought I was too chicken to use my gun. But the entire time Leo was recounting what Renner had said, the doctor's hand had been inching toward a nearby cauliflower.

"Halt," I barked. His hand jerked and whipped to his side. I gestured to the hypodermic syringe and vial at the end of the table. "Move."

I hated shots, but I forced my hands to remain steady as, keeping Gran's derringer pointed at his heart, I instructed him to prepare an injection. He sought my permission to replace his monocle, which had hung loosely by its strap since my surprise entry, then reluctantly did my bidding.

"Sleep well," I murmured, watching his bony frame ease to the floor and fold into a lump. "Leo." I kneeled at his side, gently shaking him. But he was out also. I checked his pulse then brushed his cheek with my hand. "I'll be back."

Chapter Twenty-six

Back at the stand of pines, I discovered a bridle path that curled through the woods. The path twisted and I veered with it until I heard the rushing sounds of the river. A downwards sloping trail met a line of willows at the water's edge. I took the track, darting through a curtain of lacy tendrils at the bottom.

The soil was soggy. My saddle shoes made light, sucking sounds as I crept between the mushroom-shaped trees, keeping the veil of foliage on my right. Through it, I saw the broad expanse of lawn climbing upwards toward the mansion. At the top, the rear of the house was completely exposed, and tall windows looked out over the river.

I followed the bank, at last arriving at an incline up to the house. I was below the mansion's north wing. My gaze skated upwards along the lush slope to a rose garden bordering the angular turret at the wing's end. No entrance was obvious. No human activity either.

I emerged from the willows to charge the gradual rise, at last coming upon a border of rough limestone inset with a recessed entry. The door was ajar but the depths beyond were completely black. My bravado waned.

Somewhere beyond the dark crevice, Kiki was facing disaster. On the floor in Shevchenko's lab, Leo was out cold. I was the only one who could help.

I dove my hands into my pockets. The rosewood handle of my derringer felt solid and smooth against one palm; in the other, the thick oxidized cylinder of the gas-pen felt dense and cool. Imploring the Woman Upstairs to watch over me, I drew out the weapons and slid through the crack.

I planted my back against the nearest wall. The chill and smell of mold slipped like a damp overcoat around me as seconds of pure silence followed. Gradually, my eyes adjusted to the darkness and I became aware of muted streams of light feeding through fissures in and around the giant double doors, blocking the river entrance. I was in the launch area, a space about the size of a single-car garage. Above me, a low ceiling was supported by wooden beams; around me, stone-faced walls were reinforced with timber posts.

Water lapped the edge of a boat berth directly in front of me and I assumed that the small pleasure boat, tied to posts and bobbing in the water, was Kiki's. A droning male voice disturbed the water's peaceful lapping. Then quiet again.

I stood on a plank of the walkway. The voice had come from somewhere off in the near distance to my right where the walkway widened before disappearing into what appeared to be a deep storage space. Warily, I studied the blackened area, alert for additional sounds. An anguished "*Ai-eyy*," from a second voice I thought was Kiki's, resonated through the dark.

"What is wrong, my darling? Are you not comfortable?" It was V-V. His questions, steeped with malevolence, ran together like a snarl. Some soft shuffling noise followed. Kiki did not respond and I listened for other voices, afraid of who else might be nearby, relieved to hear nothing.

I stared into the cavernous black space, this time noticing a dim circle of flaxen light flickering like a firefly from a lantern resting on the ground. Another moan from Kiki and everything in me tightened. I could not stand by without doing something. But what? My weapons were only effective if I could get to close range.

I needed a free hand to guide me through the dark. The derringer, although more lethal, was the more volatile instrument in my arsenal. I tucked it away, then ran my thumb along the pen's cap. It did not actually come off but had a tiny ball bearing on its end. Pressing it released a chamber of tear gas, shooting it out through the pen's point. My thumb found the raised bump and stopped.

"*There,* is that better?" V-V's voice purred. "If not, do not let it concern you. Your sister is due to arrive soon. Then, party time! Drinks for the house! Soon to be *my* house."

The laugh that had once charmed me now sounded like the creepy announcer on one of my favorite radio shows, *The Shadow*.

V-V continued talking and I quietly sidled along the wall, my right hand probing the rocky surface ahead, leading me toward the pale, twinkling light.

Kiki's voice sounded strained and it wavered, but I was close enough now to hear what she was saying.

"Wh-what are you planning? Torture?"

"Torture? Oh no, my precious. Do not worry." V-V's voice had practically hummed with malice. Now it oozed with feigned compassion. "No, my sweet. In a concession to my chief assistant who likes to think she comes from a lineage far more refined than mine, you and your beloved Dee will have champagne, laced with a dose of Schevchenko invention, before any shots are actually fired. Just enough so she will indulge me. Write a note revealing that her sister's betrayal, on top of Philip's, is more than she can bear. Confess that although her sister has already ingested a poisoned drink, she craves the added satisfaction of firing a bullet through her sister's head, after which she intends taking her own life in similar fashion. Our Dee finds alcohol, with or without pharmaceuticals, impossible to resist, right, my darling?"

Lush moss, its texture like thick velvet, tickled my fingers, then I felt rough stone again.

Sweat filmed my face and soaked through my sweater.

"Ah, double confession notes. Such convoluted poetic justice. More brilliant, perhaps, than even Hoffmann might have conjured up, don't you agree, my love?"

"Don't do it—" Kiki gasped. "I'm your *wife*. Help me, I'll help you…"

"*Help*, you say?" V-V yelped, giving me a fix on where he stood. "You want help? No, my darling, I have no sympathy for you."

I had made it to the next post. V-V stood beside another beam about fifteen feet away. The sputtering lantern was on the floor beside him. It threw off enough light for me to pick out a heavy wooden door set into the rock wall between myself and the couple. Kiki, still clad in silk pajamas, her back braced against the pillar, was on the floor next to V-V, chin tucked against her chest. A curtain of hair covered her face. Her arms, thrust backwards, were behind the post. I assumed they were bound. A coil of rope was on the floor against the wall just behind V-V; next to the rope, a picnic basket and a neat stack of clothing.

V-V extracted something from the basket. A syringe. Dropping onto one knee, he pressed his face close to his wife's. Her head jerked and she squirmed, trying to pull away.

"Why would I feel sorry for you?" he snarled. "The money, the privilege, have been yours, always. Even after we married, your parents arranged things so their darling daughter would remain responsible for doling out the household payments: a pittance to the gardener, a shekel to the maids, an installment to the decorator, an allotment to this charity, to that club, a few coins to her charming but useless husband…No, I cannot feel sorry for you. If you had not discovered Shevchenko's laboratory, then tried to go behind our backs, even after you had supposedly renewed your loyalty to me and to the Fuehrer, you would not be in this pickle. But here you are…"

Kiki struggled to speak. Her voice was a mere whisper. "You can stay. I'll go. Just untie me…"

V-V's head snapped back. He gaped, wild-eyed. "Untie you? Why? Where would you go? To that scrawny female agent pretending to be a journalist?"

Deep in the shadows, the scrawny female agent pretending to be a journalist stealthily switched her weapon of choice.

"No, sorry, I will not let you desert me, not like that spineless snake, Renner. I wanted to believe he would come around. Especially now that his wife has joined us." V-V paused and grinned. "Not that she *knows* she is with us yet. Any more than she is aware that her beloved Otto will soon become just another ingredient in one of Dr. Shevchenko's recipes."

He had been holding the syringe near Kiki's temple. Now, grabbing her by the hair, he tugged her sideways, positioning the tip of the needle against her neck. Kiki's eyes bulged in terror. "No, this way is best"—he pressed the needle in—"I will no longer need to grovel—"

With my derringer poised in front of me, I pounded across the plank floor. V-V sprang up, his hand groping the wall. My grip tightened on the trigger. A light bulb snapped on, caught me in its yellow glow. I blinked, hesitated. A slight kick. The report combined with a ping as the derringer's bullet hit stone wall. V-V grabbed my wrist and threw me against the wall. My breath left; my gun went flying. A raspy gurgle pulled air into my lungs, something sharp bit my neck.

The syringe V-V had been holding to Kiki's throat was now pressed into mine. My left wrist remained trapped in his vise-grip against the wall. The needle scratched my skin. An intense sensation, like a bee sting, trailed in its wake. I flinched and tried to pull my head back, but it was lodged against hard stone.

Beneath the circle of light, V-V's face suddenly tightened with pain. I glanced down. He was wearing the same riding habit he'd worn when I'd walked in on Clara and him in the back room of the salon. Only now the arm of his tweed jacket had a frayed tear just below the shoulder seam. My eyes had adjusted and I could see a dark red stain seeping into the tight weave of the surrounding fabric. I'd winged him!

V-V's features smoothed, then turned hard and sinister. He narrowed his eyes, leaning so close his aquiline nose nearly touched mine. "Ahh, our lovely journalist. What are you doing here? Who sent you? Speak!"

Light glistened in the tiny beads of sweat rimming V-V's forehead. He drew the needle across my neck again. My body tensed.

There was a sound behind the heavy wooden door. He turned his head. The gas-gun leapt from my pocket. I depressed the trigger. Startled, his hand with the syringe fell away. I ducked, whipping my head sideways to avoid the fumes. I glimpsed my mark. His eyes were shut, his face puckered against the sting of the tear gas. He coughed. Too late, he covered his face, trying to protect it. The syringe dropped from his hand. He doubled over, collapsed.

My lungs burning from the gas, my vision blurred, I panned the floor, searching for the syringe. My attention whisked back to V-V at the same moment he managed, miraculously, to flip over onto his back. I flinched, expecting him to leap up. But V-V would not be standing anytime soon. The syringe had lodged itself deep in his thigh. I made no effort to help him as he lifted his torso ever so slightly, his arm flailing in an agonizing attempt to remove the needle. But the pain was too great. Or maybe it was the drug taking effect. He slumped backwards.

I searched the floor again, desperate to recover my weapons. I dropped to my hands and knees. The heavy door was opening. Too late, I tried to stand.

"What's taking you so long, Anastase? Berlin is on the radio. They have a drop site for you, but their radioman is insisting that you give the required code personally."

Even before the figure emerged, I knew who it was. I gulped. "Liberty..."

Chapter Twenty-seven

Liberty had a stiletto up her sleeve. Sniffing the air, she drew the knife and kicked. A pain like molten lava seared my gut. I buckled forward, grasping my midriff. The ridge of Liberty's hand whacked the back of my neck with a solid chop.

I was flat on my stomach. She stood over me. I struggled to catch my breath. "S-so you *are* one of them."

"I have *always* been one of them."

Liberty was wearing Army boots and green fatigues, like those worn by Zerov. I sensed the movement of her foot then felt an almost unbearable crush of weight press against the small of my back. I gasped.

She gestured with the stiletto. Its ice-pick blade flashed dully. "All right, stand up. Don't try anything funny. You're no match for me and you know it."

The point of her blade found the sweet spot between my ribs, near my heart, and she backed me up against the wall. There was a rushing in my ears, but I needed to keep her talking until help could arrive. Or until I could make a grab for my gun.

"So you're V-V's assistant—"

"*Assistant?*" On the ground, near the wall, about ten feet away, V-V was perfectly still. She flung him a sidelong glance and smiled a little. "Looks like I've been promoted to running the operation now, haven't I?"

"But you won't kill Kiki and Dee—"

"The idea was mine in the first place."

"*No...*"

"Poor, stupid Pucci," she said, and smiled.

"Y-You joined OSS," I said, mining familiar territory, trying to understand how a close friend could have morphed into an assassin pressing a knife to my heart. "Why?"

"To infiltrate the organization. To uncover its methods, pass them on to Berlin, why else?" She smiled mockingly. "And how else do you suppose I could have tricked you without first knowing about G-2? And Roy? Besides, I needed to keep involved in something useful until I could be activated."

Her blunt assessment and the notion of what her maneuverings meant to the security of our country frightened and emboldened me.

"The feds are on to you. They know about the phantom ink message inside *Personality Unlimited*. They know it was Kiki who wrote it, that it was meant to reach you..."

Her dead-eyed gaze shot ice water through my veins.

Badgering Liberty, I realized belatedly, would only hasten her intent of sending me to an early grave.

But she smiled. "Your threats mean nothing. I will never be captured."

The Countess' charm bible had a Golden Rule covering the art of socializing. *On those occasions when you would like to impress your partner, or put your partner at ease, remember that everyone likes to feel as if they are the most intelligent, special human being on the planet.* While I didn't care about charming my foe, I did need fresh ammo to keep her chatting.

"Well, that ploy involving the secret ink message certainly had me fooled," I admitted.

"You're all fools." Liberty eyed me warily then smiled. "You were always good at getting to me with that Midwest PK sweetness-and-light, slather-on-the-guilt crap. Stuff it. You want to know something, ask. There's no reason for me to hold back anything any longer. You're going to die anyway, just as soon as"—she chortled softly—"as soon as Dee arrives for her sisterly outing. Someone's gone to pick her up, did you know?"

A sharp pressure at my midriff forced my answer. I glared at her. "Uh-huh."

"That's better. You want to know about the phantom message?" She leaned closer. The warmth from her body and the smell of her sweat brought bile to my throat. She sent Kiki a fleeting sidelong look. Whatever V-V had shot her with had taken effect. I had interrupted him before he could administer the full dose from the syringe, but she was eerily still.

"Initially, Anastase was able to control our golden goose over there by threatening to tell Dee about the supposed tryst with Philip. But then our little goose tried to outmaneuver us." Liberty's lips twisted crookedly. "Anastase and I differ when it comes to using force. I prefer brains; he prefers brawn."

Kiki's obsession with the Book Faire at last made sense. "A tactical weakness," I said. "In order for your murder-suicide scheme to succeed, the women at the Club needed time to absorb the misinformation you were sowing about Kiki. And Kiki needed to remain in circulation while the rumors took hold. Possible only if she showed no signs of physical violence, and only as long as the Club's manicurist was nearby, keeping watch."

Liberty permitted herself a quick, smug smile. "Picking up news of war preparations from clients was a rewarding side benefit."

Liberty tilted her head as if she'd heard something. I turned my ear, listening as well. Water rippled against the dock and V-V whimpered softly from the floor. The lantern made a spitting noise.

The quiet unnerved me. *Flatter her, keep her talking...*

"So, the entire operation hinged on your ability to finesse things at the Club..."

Her eyes danced. "You could say that. Especially these past few days when Kiki's agitation was at its peak. Her every departure from the estate, even under the influence of threats and Shevchenko's drugs, was a huge risk."

The nail polish bottle in Kiki's desk drawer...invisible ink. "To keep her from spilling the beans to a sympathetic stranger, you befriended her, told her you were with G-2 and that you were there to rescue her. You even gave her phantom ink, devised a code, to use in an emergency."

"Bingo!" Liberty ran the tip of her tongue around the edge of her mouth. "Now just what sort of clever method do you think I should devise to get rid of you, Miss Smarty Pants? How about this? Let Dee have the honors. Yes, I can see the headline. Agent shot while trying to break up scuffle between estranged sisters!" She cocked an eye at me. "Maybe your FBI admirer will run it in his *faux* newspaper." There was a sharp prick at my midriff. "But first, march."

In one smooth move, she gripped me by the elbow, turning me and shoving me in the direction of V-V. The piercing pressure that had threatened my abdomen now jabbed a sensitive spot near my spine.

Over my shoulder she said to me, "Kiki became quite hopeful, actually. Her trust was her undoing. But you were right earlier. It was a test. In writing the secret message, she signaled her intent to betray us. Her time on the outside was up."

There was no mention of the secret bookplate message written in regular ink. Maybe *Cardillac* wasn't so smart.

Beneath my sweater, a bead of perspiration dribbled down my side. "The night watchman clothing in the room next door to mine. Another disguise?"

"Ha!" Her laugh ricocheted against the stone walls, echoing loudly. "Bent over, picking up a newspaper, *the perfect target.* You didn't know what—or should I say, *who*—hit you, did you? It was me. Halt."

V-V was out cold on the floor beside us. Behind me, I sensed Liberty crouch and scoop up the rope.

She prodded me with the knife, directing me toward the post. Kiki was slouched against the thick wooden beam on the opposite side. Again, before I could react she threw down the rope and with a push, spun me around. My back slammed wood. At my feet, I felt the press of Kiki's tightly bound fists against my ankles, but she did not react.

Liberty shifted her stance and the platinum cross she'd converted to an earring swayed with the movement. Her irreverence in dangling a religious symbol from her ear suddenly repulsed me and I stared at the cross, struck by how a universal symbol of hope could look so foreboding.

I forced an upbeat tone. "So the uniform let you move around freely on the nights when Kiki stayed late or spent the night at the Club."

"Yes, but you're talking about the past, when it was important for her and Dee to remain alive. Now you've snuck in here, a witness to their demise." Liberty shook her head twice, slowly. "Bad timing."

My skin crawled and a wave of revulsion washed over me as I rued my naïveté again. How had I missed this side of her?

I felt pressure beneath my rib. Doing my best to ignore it, I concentrated on the ruby chip at the hub of the cross earring, remembering how I'd thought the necklace was too conventional, too religious for me. I recalled the thrill I'd felt exchanging it for an exotic Chinese bracelet. Pools of tears blurred my vision. Was this my due, then, for being ungrateful? For turning my back on family? On religion?

I gulped. "But why are you so bent on killing her? *Them*?" I refused to add "us."

"All their money goes to Anastase." V-V stirred. "Don't worry, Anastase," she said, projecting her voice in his direction. "I'll take care of everything. Just like I took care of that one-armed squealer at Willow Run."

"You killed Blount?"

"You're surprised? Why? Don't you think I'm capable?"

I nodded. "Sure…"

"Hands behind your back."

Slowly, I raised my arms, bending them backwards. Liberty wanted to tie me to the post. But, first, she needed rope. It was on the floor, just out of reach. A possible diversion.

The knife point was really beginning to hurt. I groped for something positive. "But your mother said you have a boyfriend.

That he's serving in Italy. Ever since we met, you've wanted to go there."

Liberty laughed. Then her eyes shifted. "You talked to my mother...What else did she say?"

The strange look in Liberty's eyes frightened me. I began stammering. "Sh-she didn't say where, or with what unit, if that's what you're worried about."

"Idiot! She wouldn't know *which* unit. Tazio is not with a *U.S.* branch of service. He's with the *Abwehr*. He's with me."

Liberty's eyes were blue dots in white saucers. I held my breath. On the floor, V-V groaned softly. The possessed look vanished. I expelled a ragged sigh. "Where did you meet Tazio?"

She smiled. "Tazio? He was a friend of Sari's. We met in Europe."

I cursed inwardly. Sari deHajek, the *Abwehr*'s top recruiter, rears her ugly head once again.

"You love Tazio," I said. "I can see it in your face. Is that why you turned your back on your country, on everything you always believed in? For him? For a man?"

At the center of my midriff, I felt serious pressure, then a flash of heat. I squirmed, trying to push away. A warm, wet sensation followed. Clenching my lower lip between my teeth, I froze and bit down hard.

"You don't get it, do you? Mother Leach couldn't bring herself to tell them, could she? I *hate* America," she said gutturally. "I *hate* my father. I *hate* his snobbish righteous friends. I *hate* all things religious. I *hate* God. I hate *her*."

I hated the sight of blood, especially my own. The stiletto had pierced my skin and I was definitely bleeding. I assured myself the puncture was nothing more than a flesh wound, so far, and refused to look down.

Hands lightly cradling the post at my back, I slid slowly downward, assuming a squatting position as I went. "Tell me about how China fits in," I said more desperately than I would have liked. "You weren't born there, so when did you go?"

Liberty's once lilting voice erupted with a high-pitched, "*China?* I was never in China."

I felt newly numb. "What? But you grew up there. Your parents were missionaries, you went to the Great Wall…the bracelet…your name is…"

She seemed to choke. Her eyes blazed. A dull flash, then pinpoint pressure at the center of my forehead.

Feet spread, she stood above me, squinting down the stiletto's long, needle-thin blade, its sharp tip perched lightly against my flesh. "Sooo…how does it feel to one day, out of the blue, discover everything you knew was just an illusion? To have everything you believe in turn out to be a pack of lies?"

I gaped at her from my crouched position. "B-but you speak Chinese, otherwise you wouldn't have been able to—" *To dupe all of the government people who hired you,* I finished silently. I blinked, wanting to take back my words. She had already proved the impossible was possible.

She lifted her chin and affected a haughty pose, not unlike the Countess. "I'm multilingual, that much is true. Unlike stupid Americans, the Swiss take pride in knowing several languages."

Swiss. Clocks. Flowers. Rhinestones.

"The cuckoo clocks. Piggy banks to finance boom and bang schemes?"

She appeared stunned. The pinpoint pressure eased.

"I know about the clocks," I told her. "You used them to smuggle in diamonds. My Uncle Chance helped me figure it out." *Big deal. What was I going to do about it?* The uniform. "You broke in, took the clock from my room, didn't you?"

She did not gloat as I expected. "Get it through your head, Lewis," she growled. "I believe in Hitler. I believe in what he believes. We're the chosen race. We'll rule the world." She leered at me. "Right after we get rid of the inferiors, that is, including you."

I stared cross-eyed at the pick-like blade with the blood—*my* blood—on its tip, my desperation mounting. My gaze flicked sideways to the open door. "What about that message a minute ago? Wasn't something important coming through on the radio?"

Liberty smiled. She placed her index finger against her temple. "The information we need is all in here—" The gesture was precisely the opportunity I had wanted.

Shoving her, I dropped to the ground, diving for my gun, rolling then leaping upright. Liberty recovered. Her arm swinging like a pendulum, she lunged, the stiletto carving arcs in the air. I stumbled, collapsing onto one knee. The stiletto rushed toward me. Squaring my arm in a position of defense, I aimed the derringer. A clamoring noise near the boathouse entrance erupted. Men's voices on the other side of the cave shouted. The light went out. I reached into the dark. My fingers hooked the tiny earring. I yanked; she yowled. A burning pain scored the inner flesh of my arm. I got off a shot. It rang through the boathouse, echoing off the walls.

I felt suddenly dizzy. There was a pitiful moan. Me? Someone close to me?

Willing myself to stand, I snapped on the light. It had been V-V's groan, not mine. The stiletto protruded from his chest.

"Pucci!" Dante called, rushing toward me, bracing me as I collapsed.

The clamor of his unit running up behind him revived me. I straightened up. "Liberty?" I asked, tentatively. "What happened? Did you see? Did I hit her?"

Dante's hair was damp with perspiration. A bead of sweat dribbled down his forehead, catching the light. He checked me over. "You're hurt!"

"I'm okay…Liberty?" I repeated.

"Can't say. We're chasing her."

"But V-V was a sleeper spy. So's Liberty. She's also an assassin. She killed Blount, now she's stabbed V-V."

He nodded. "We know about Blount. Chaplin told us, back at headquarters."

"Good, you got him…" I licked my lips. They were parched and cracked. I teetered.

"Medic, quick."

A G-2 medic appeared at the same time two ONI men rushed over to check on Kiki. V-V was hidden in a shadow.

"V-V needs help first," I said, gesturing in his direction. The medic swept a practiced eye over me, then went to check on him.

"Your hand," Dante said softly, "You're bleeding."

He was staring at my clenched fist. The tip of my thumb was blood-caked. I opened my palm. "Her earring." My hand trembled. Dante took the converted cross. He nodded to the crimson stain on my sleeve. "What about that?"

The gash along my arm was not all that deep, but I'd lost a fair amount of blood. Gingerly placing a hand over the stain, I applied pressure to quiet the throbbing ache beneath. Dante cupped my chin with his hand, lifting it. His lips clamped into a line as he studied the scratches on my neck and along my jaw. My forehead bore a slight wound also, I realized, watching his fretful gaze pause to assess the damage.

My cheek burned with pain. I raised my hand to cover it. "It's nothing. But I'm in no shape to help with the search," I admitted reluctantly. "But you should go…"

A rivulet of blood stained my sweater below my sternum. He took it in, smiled faintly and released my chin. "Don't worry about the chase. My men are on it. I'll catch up. Soon as we get these wounds tended." He turned back to the medic. "How is he?"

The medic had been kneeling beside V-V. He shook his head and stood. "He's gone."

The medic, who wore an armband, with a cross parted the rip in my sweater and studied my arm. Dante looked away while he examined the wound beneath my sweater. Next, he scrutinized my neck. "Got everything I need to dress these in my kit," he announced.

"Good," Dante said. "Let's go into the bunker, find a place where she can sit down."

The ONI men were still with Kiki. They had untied her, but she was too out of it to stand. I wanted to go to her, but Dante insisted I get off my feet. He directed the medic to evaluate Kiki, adding that we would wait for him inside.

We passed through the doorway Dante's men had sprinted through moments before, into a bunker, a tunnel-like space dug into the deepest part of the knoll. An extension of the boathouse, it had the same low, curved ceiling and stone walls, reinforced with timber. Bare bulbs, strung along the ceiling's center, washed the narrow room with stark light.

A quasi bomb shelter and communications planning center, the musty space was stockpiled with weaponry, including an assortment of rifles, machine guns, grenades, and timing devices propped against the sloping walls. Machine guns aimed in the direction of the house were mounted on tripods, their muzzles protruding through three small openings, paralleling the grassy slope outdoors.

A turret had been carved into the arched ceiling on the dugout's far end. At its center was a column with a machine gun on a swivel base. A chair for a gunner had also been installed. Built on a principle similar to that used in a bomber's turret, the chair and its occupant could swivel with the arc of the weapon's firing range.

"Zounds," I said, staring with a mix of shock and awe.

Dante also looked awed. "A person could mount a small war out of this room," he marveled.

"Precisely what V-V had in mind. *Cardillac...*" I added under my breath.

Dante had been steering me to a long table in the center of the room. "What did you say?"

My former friend had confessed to killing Blount; now with V-V's death she had become a multiple assassin. An *exceptional* multiple assassin. In a matter of seconds, in a blackened cave, she had found V-V and dispatched him, then vanished.

Suddenly weak from stem to stern, too wrung out to respond, I slumped into the nearest chair. Dante perched on the edge of the table next to me. I looked up at him.

"Liberty killed V-V. Why'd she do it?" I whispered uncomprehendingly. "They were on the same side."

"He was injured, unable to escape," he said matter-of-factly. "Maybe she thought he'd crack under questioning, reveal some plans we aren't aware of yet."

I placed my hand over the circle of blood on my sleeve and shook my head. "I always knew Liberty was a good actress. But this level of pretense—how did I miss it?"

Dante touched my shoulder. "Look at me." I looked up. "There's nothing you could have said or done to change things," he said, softly. "The *Abwehr* got to Liberty long before the two of you ever met."

"I know." A deep sorrow closed over me while I debriefed myself of everything Liberty had revealed to me.

Afterward, Dante nodded knowingly. "It all fits." He ticked off points on his fingers. "At a difficult age, her relationship with the Leaches turns upside down when she finds out she's adopted. She's dispatched to a foreign country. A war is brewing. She's troubled, vulnerable. She feels alone, she's looking for a palliative. Any shrewd *Abwehr* case officer would recognize the susceptibility and prey on her instantly."

"Yeah, Sari deHajek, for example," I said bitterly, informing him that besides spending time together in Europe, the two women had attended Vassar in the same year.

I thought of my boss, Miss Cochran. She too had grown up in an adoptive home, on Tobacco Road, in the South, with a similarly difficult childhood. "Bleak, bitter, and harsh," was how she had once described it. But unlike V-V and Liberty, whose early hardships had led them to evil, she'd transformed her difficulties into a positive, had turned herself into a striver. What was at the core of such opposite outcomes?

"Now what?" I asked. "V-V's been training saboteurs. And they're not here anymore. They're holed up somewhere with Tazio. Maybe she went to join them—" My words caught. "Or lead them."

Dante was staring at a dark corner where a large patch of moss climbed the wall. Squinting, I saw a slight protrusion on one side and realized the blanket of fuzzy greenery was actually a camouflaged doorway. Blame it on trauma, maybe loss of blood, but I'd momentarily forgotten about Dante's men. They must have dashed through the secret door.

I looked at him. "Would you *please* go join your team? I'm fine."

Lines fanned out from Dante's eyes as he smiled. "I know you are. But like I said, my men are handling things."

The hairs at the back of my neck bristled. I turned to Dante. "There's a lab on the property. They're sending a shipment of explosives, disguised in cans of tomatoes to NAS—"

Dante interrupted. "Shhh…it's okay. We're on it. Chaplin broke under questioning. Told us everything. Including about the band of Ukrainian desperadoes based on the grounds. We came prepared."

Dante's unit had arrived at the estate first and intercepted Zerov, Yakutovych, Dr. Shevchenko, and a few others loading the hijacked truck intended for NAS Grosse Ile. Then his men fanned out over the grounds.

"Leo is with Renner. Did you find them at the lab? Is Leo all right?"

The medic had entered the bunker and it was he who replied, "Renner is heavily sedated and Leo has a world-class headache. But they'll both be okay. Same with the lady we moved from here. She was drugged, but she'll be fine."

I removed *Personality Unlimited* from my pants pocket, placed it on the table.

"There's a bookplate inside that explains Kiki's role in what's been going here and how V-V managed to get the upper hand. She's got some patching up to do with her sister, but once you read it, I think you'll agree Kiki was a genuine victim."

Dante did not look completely convinced, but he took the book, slipping it inside his breast pocket.

"You were at the house," I said to the medic. "Irina? Is she okay?" He nodded. I turned to Dante. "Your 'eyes and ears'?" His eyebrow shot up. He looked away. "What about Dee?" I remembered in a panic. "One of V-V's acolytes went to fetch her."

"Don't worry," Dante re-emphasized with a smile. "Lieutenant Simmons is on that. She's at the house."

He continued, "The lab has a secret passage. We split up. Some of us went underground. Everyone else fanned out topside. Our trail led us to the river and eventually here."

"And you arrived in the nick of time. I'm safe," I said pointedly.

We were rocked by an explosion. Dante raced to the hidden door and vanished through it.

I sat with my bad arm resting on the table. I watched, willing myself not to be squeamish, while the medic lopped off my sleeve.

"It's the latest wartime style," he joked, "saves on fabric. You look great in it."

He dabbed the scratches at my neck and on my face with alcohol, then checked the laceration beneath my sweater. "It's only a minor puncture wound," he assured me, deftly dressing it.

Using a flat stick resembling a wooden spoon used for eating ice cream, he scooped out a dollop of dark amber cream. Steadying my injured arm with one hand, he swabbed the incision with the stick. Too late, I realized he was applying creamed iodine. The gash, hardly noticeable until now, was on fire.

My eyes popped, but I refused to scream. Gritting my teeth, I smiled—probably made more of a grimace—forcing my arm to relax while the medic slathered my wound, buttering it like it was a slice of dried toast and not raw flesh.

I surveyed the maps above his head, desperate for a distraction.

On the map of Europe, V-V had poked pin-mounted swastikas into England and France as well as a host of smaller countries Hitler's legions had either conquered or were currently in position to take over. On a separate map of America, swastika pins dotted the East Coast and Great Lakes region. I began tallying them, but the Rising Sun symbols, peppering the West Coast, intervened. I was curious. Was it possible, as part of his grandiose scheme, that V-V was willing to cede California, Oregon, and Washington to the Empire of Japan?

The third map was a blown-up duplicate of the map we'd found in Renner's safe. I tracked the string of Heinkels, following the Great Circle Route out of Norway to Northern Canada. Near the border, pins in assorted colors marked the bombers' final targets: the industrial cities of the Midwest.

The air inside the bunker smelled damp and earthy like a newly excavated grave. I drew a long breath, turning away from the disturbing depiction, opting to watch the medic apply a thin strip of gauze to my throbbing arm.

Dante stepped through the doorway.

I immediately asked, "What was the explosion?"

"It was on the outskirts of the estate. We haven't pinpointed the exact location. Connelly is due here any minute. He'll have more information." He looked down at my arm and his eyebrows pinched together. "Hurt much?"

"Nah," I scoffed.

Ears, our teammate from yesterday's job at Renner's office, followed Dante through the entrance. He nodded briefly to me, an expression of sympathy and admiration on his face. He and Dante examined the radio gear on a console pushed against the bunker's stone wall, including a short-wave transmitter, a receiver, and a backup generator. They began exchanging ideas about what to do in the event transmission came through. Attracted by a flurry of noises in the boathouse, I leaned sideways, straining to see who was out there.

Chapter Twenty-eight

Connelly breezed into the bunker. He frowned. "What happened?" he asked, catching my gaze. He actually looked concerned.

"Long story, but I'm fine. What about Liberty? Any sign of her?"

Connelly's once black suit was caked with dust, his shirt stained and sweaty. His tie, stuffed into his jacket's breast pocket, protruded haphazardly. "None. Two separate passages, heading off in different directions, both showing signs she'd taken them. Obviously, she couldn't have. It was a setup, meant to trip us up. Which it did. I took some men one way, Simmons went the other. He hasn't reported in yet."

"How about the rest of V-V's gang?" Dante asked.

Connelly brushed an unyielding blond wave. "Nothing yet."

I turned to Dante. "The Countess isn't connected to V-V's ring, by the way. Hadn't a clue about what he was doing. She missed her chance." I briefed Dante and Connelly on my final meeting with her. "She's ready to cooperate. Even testify if there's a trial."

The men exchanged a private look and thanked me.

"So what will happen to Renner? V-V confessed he used coercion to draw him into his ring. And Renner copied the bombing raid drawing so he could turn it over to you. At least that's what he told Leo."

"Coerced or not, he aided the enemy," Dante said firmly. "Think about the truck with defective parts. Think about what would have happened if Blount hadn't come to us, if we hadn't intercepted delivery. He may have been reluctant, but we'll definitely do our all to see that he's tried as a traitor."

My upper arm had begun to seriously throb. I dug my fingers into the muscle surrounding the wound. "And after you intervened, halted the delivery," I said, glumly, "V-V had Blount, the squealer, silenced. Cardillac confessed."

"*Who?*" Connelly asked.

Somehow associating Liberty's alter-ego with the crime made the reality of who she had become easier. I brought him up to date on the rechristening.

I sighed. "Chaplin let her into the factory. Why'd he get involved, anyway? He had a good job. He's an American..."

"He went nuts at being passed over." Dante caught my glance. "I don't mean because of his size. For the inspector's job that went to Gisela—Mrs. K's daughter. They turned him by offering him big money to bribe the guards."

Red-faced and out of breath, Simmons paused just inside the door, panting. "We've lost her."

I gasped. Connelly kicked a vacant chair. Dante, unable to mask the strain in his voice, blurted, "What the hell happened?"

"The tunnel led to the adjoining estate. We didn't know it was the path she'd taken until we reached the end." Simmons was sweating. He pulled out a dirt-smudged handkerchief from his jacket and dabbed his face. "Lucky we weren't any closer. She tossed explosives down the hatch. The mound of dirt and rocks was so thick, we couldn't push through. We had to backtrack." The handkerchief paused on one of his huge ears. Simmons took a breath. "She's gone, left no trace. The search continues, but—" He shook his head.

Dante punched the fist of one hand into the palm of the other.

My hand rested over the dressing on my arm. The deep pain beneath had evolved into a dull ache. I sighed. "That's it then."

Dante turned on me. "The search for Liberty or Cardillac or whatever she's calling herself these days doesn't end here.

You know her better than any of us. I want you to stay on this case."

I felt an excited fluttering in my chest. I did not think I would succumb again to an invitation to a private Mrs. Sarvello meal in his apartment. But the chance to continue in this line of work—to keep Liberty on my radar screen…

I came back down to earth. I was committed to the WASP. "Sorry. My ferrying duties come first."

Dante's dark eyes met mine. "You'll do both."

My decision was easy. And instantaneous. "You understand I'll need to clear this with Miss Cochran."

He nodded. "Flying will be part of your cover."

Long ago, Liberty and I had made a vow to keep in touch. One way or another, our paths would intersect—I knew it in my bones. I still had the Chinese bracelet she'd given me. And now I had the cross earring I'd given her in friendship, the cross earring I'd ripped from the ear of a sworn enemy of my country.

I reached for it. A sharp pain rippled down my arm.

Of course I would find her.

Of course this would not be the last chapter.

Afterword

This book is a work of fiction inspired by two sets of WWII heroines—the Women Airforce Service Pilots (WASP) and the women in intelligence—and by an actual home front spy case involving a countess-counteragent.

Ten years ago, in casual conversation with a friend, I learned that her mother-in-law had been a pilot during WWII, transporting fighter planes along the East Coast for the military. "She was a WASP," my friend said.

WWII was a time of tremendous opportunity for women. I knew that. But I had never heard of this elite unit. "That was over fifty years ago," I said incredulously, doing the math. "She would have just turned twenty-one."

My friend hauled out her mother-in-law's scrapbook. We pored over old photos and articles. I learned that 1,074 women were admitted to the WASP; 38 of them lost their lives. Their duties included towing targets for gunner training, conducting test flights, and ferrying every variety of military aircraft, including the biggest bombers and the fastest fighters, all across the continental U.S. The objective was to free up male pilots for combat missions in war zones.

The women delivered a total of 12,650 planes of 77 different types. Problems with machinery, fuel, and weather were routine, and ferry pilots were issued guns to protect the valuable planes they flew in the event of enemy contact. Still, acceptance into military aviation ranks did not come easily. The women endured everything from patronizing raised eyebrows and outright resentment to sabotage attempts. Yet their sense of duty and unwavering passion for flying catapulted the women "above and beyond" it all; of course, it didn't hurt to have the wind at their tail, provided by the founder and leader, test pilot Jackie Cochran. She won the necessary political battles to keep the program up and running, even expanding WASP flying opportunities along the way.

A thirst to learn more about these women drove me to one of my favorite places, the library. And when I raised the subject with others, I found the WASP to be a well-kept secret. Fine, I thought, I'll write about these women and their heroics. *I'll* spread the word about them. My story's protagonist would be a composite of members of the WASP. Jackie Cochran, the real-life leader, would also play a role. Heady stuff.

I saw writing a story about these women of courage and action as an escape away from my own conventional life. But escape often means venturing far away, only to discover you've never left home. I began wrestling down a plot and it was brimming with espionage, a DNA quirk that runs in my blood.

My parents were Hungarian refugees who arrived in the States in 1947 following eight years of missionary service, and the birth of my four siblings, in war-torn central China. Born in Ohio, the family's "Miss America," I was weaned on my parents' tales of isolation and survival, and their arduous exodus to the U.S. Like Tarzan and Jane, popular icons then, they'd lived in the jungle and had their share of heart-pounding adventures: navigating the family in sampans through storms and floods, dealing with coiled cobras and malaria, and encountering Japanese fighting units.

My parents had expected to return one day to China and also to their homeland, but Mao in China, Stalin in Hungary, closed the door. Their dreams adrift with the shifting political winds, we settled into a series of parsonages at outposts in northern Michigan and Minnesota, eventually landing in Illinois.

In 1956, correspondence arriving from family in Budapest prompted hushed discussions. I was a wisp of a child, so I drew little attention anyway. Perched on the stairwell just off the living room, I was an invisible recorder, absorbing my parents' anguished conversations about the evils of communism, the revolution, freedoms lost, their fears for family—strife, torture, imprisonment, death. It was a time when magazines, such as *LIFE*, printed graphic black-and-white photographs of insurgents, caught and hung by their feet from trees in Budapest's main square; streets were spattered with bodies and littered with rubble left by tanks. I sponged up the images. And I would never forget the line of teletype that had skittered across the foot of our television screen one grisly day, weeks earlier. "*Civilized people of the world, in the name of liberty and solidarity, we are asking you to help. Our ship is sinking. Start moving. Extend to us brotherly hands. People of the world, save us. S-O-S.*" The plea, from Hungarian freedom fighters believing the U.S. and United Nations had promised to come to their aid, went unanswered.

Waves of Hungarian refugees sought sanctuary in Chicago, a few of them passing through our home. The arrival of a young man, a former freedom fighter in the '56 uprising, was particularly memorable. Rough-edged porcelain stubs protruded from his gums where his front teeth should have been, and the tips of his fingers on both hands were disfigured. I was at once repulsed and curious. We went for a walk. We strolled and he described the horrors of living under communism, explaining the disfigurement was part of the torture inflicted on him for trying to escape.

So it was that when I began plotting *Lipstick and Lies*, I couldn't help transmitting what I had absorbed from my parents' stories and the personal experiences passed on by the freedom fighters into the book's events and characters.

The investigative process took me to local libraries where I scrolled through reels of microfilm and microfiche, perused WWII magazines and newspapers, and browsed through what few point-on books I could find. A *Look* magazine piece, "How

Hitler Can Bomb the Midwest—A Nazi Raid on Detroit Is Not Only Possible but Probable," showed promise. I copied it.

I devoured biographies and histories of the period, one day stumbling upon a true tale of home front espionage involving female enemy spies. One of them, a countess trained at Ast X, the Harvard of spy schools in Berlin, infiltrated our country in 1941, posing as a lecturer and charm consultant. My definition of women of action and accomplishment had suddenly broadened!

My vision of the book grew and I stepped up my sleuthing. The archives at the Hoover Institute at Stanford were next, and a visit to the Textual Division of the National Archives in Washington, D.C., followed. There, pawing through research stacks, I uncovered a line buried in an FBI letter that gave me goose bumps. The countess-operative, besides heading up a ring of Nazi spies, was "*a known espionage agent who is also working for us.*"

A countess-counteragent! I had found the backbone of my story.

The enticing kernel inspired a letter-writing campaign. I penned requests to the Bureau of Prisons, then the FBI. Soon reams of correspondence and newspaper clippings pertaining to my historical event of choice (many with lines and words blacked out) overflowed boxes stuffed into a crammed office closet. I found magic in the clutter. I frequently sat sifting the pages, delighting in the archaic gems preserved in the old-school style of writing. The treasure trove was also where I prospected for answers to niggling questions about the countess' *modus operandi*. How could she live such a baldfaced lie? And double lie? How could she carry it off for so long, nearly two years?

It was at this stage in the process that I came to know another group of unsung WWII heroines, the women in intelligence. I had already conducted numerous interviews with Peggy McNamara Slaymaker, a former WASP. Then John Taylor, senior archivist at the National Archives in Washington, introduced me to Elizabeth MacDonald McIntosh, a former female operative with the Office of Strategic Services—precursor to today's CIA. Here was another government branch where groundbreaking wartime opportunities for women had unfolded.

Franklin Delano Roosevelt was the first president to realize that America's greatest hidden source of manpower was womanpower. Major General William J. Donovan, Wartime Director of OSS, explained the impact of women in his agency in this way:

> *The great majority of women who worked for America's first organized and integrated intelligence agency, spent their war years behind desks and filing cases in Washington, invisible apron strings of an organization which touched every theater of war. They were the ones at home who patiently filed secret reports, encoded and decoded messages, answered telephones, mailed pay checks and kept the records. But these were necessary tasks without the faithful performance of which an organization of 26,000 people, with civil and military personnel, could not be maintained.*
>
> *There were some, however, who had important administrative positions and others with regional and linguistic knowledge of great value in research, whose special skills were employed in exact and painstaking work such as map making, cryptography and research.*
>
> *Only a small percentage of the women in OSS ever went overseas, and a still smaller percentage was assigned to actual operational jobs behind enemy lines.* *

As the intelligence agency grew in size and scope, a morale operations (MO) branch developed. MO dealt with "black" psychological warfare, or the art of influencing enemy thinking by means of "subtle" propaganda, ostensibly coming from within the enemy's own ranks. Mrs. McIntosh served with the MO branch and was one of the select few to serve behind enemy lines.

A trip to Detroit, the scene of the crime involving the true-life countess-counterspy, was another must in the discovery process. There, I viewed archives at the Henry Ford Museum in Dearborn and visited a maximum security jail where the titled enemy operative and her cohorts were held for seven months before they were sentenced and transferred to federal prison.

Back home, my personal archives, thick with articles and documents, continued to be my inspiration, while snippets of my family history dogged me, insistent on somehow being recycled. It would take seven years before I could successfully weave the true tales into a work of fiction highlighting these women's stories—both dark and light—as I had set out to do. What remains a mystery are the final chapters of the countess' life. Correspondence and news articles culled from my archives that bear on this point are included on my web site, www.margitliesche.com. You are invited to review the materials and form your own conclusions. I would enjoy hearing your speculations.

*From Donovan's introduction to *Undercover Girl,* a memoir by Elizabeth MacDonald McIntosh, published in 1947. A more recent book, *Sisterhood of Spies,* also written by Mrs. McIntosh, was published by the Naval Institute Press in 1998.

To receive a free catalog of Poisoned Pen Press titles, please contact us in one of the following ways:

Phone: 1-800-421-3976
Facsimile: 1-480-949-1707
Email: info@poisonedpenpress.com
Website: www.poisonedpenpress.com

Poisoned Pen Press
6962 E. First Ave. Ste. 103
Scottsdale, AZ 85251